Destiny Soria spent her childhood playing with sticks in the woods and exploring such distinguished careers as Forest Bandit, Wayward Orphan, and Fairy Queen. In later years, she ran away to New Zealand for seven months, where she backpacked across the wilderlands, petted fluffy sheep, and gave tours of a haunted prison. After nearly a decade of cubicle life, she made her escape to pursue her dream career of being a full-time author. Nowadays she lives in Birmingham, Alabama with her cat, where she writes books featuring magic, mystery, and an excess of witty banter.

FIRE WITH FIRE

DESTINY SORIA

HODDER

First published in Great Britain in 2021 by Hodder & Stoughton
An Hachette UK company

This paperback edition published in 2022

1

A CIP catalogue record for this title is available from the British Library

Hardback ISBN 978 1 529 36972 4
Trade Paperback ISBN 978 1 529 36973 1
Paperback ISBN 978 1 529 36976 2
eBook ISBN 978 1 529 36974 8

Typeset in Adobe Garamond Pro

Printed and bound in Great Britain by Clays Ltd, Elcograf S.p.A.

Hodder & Stoughton policy is to use papers that are natural,
renewable and recyclable products and made from wood grown in sustainable
forests. The logging and manufacturing processes are expected to conform
to the environmental regulations of the country of origin.

Hodder & Stoughton Ltd
Carmelite House
50 Victoria Embankment
London EC4Y 0DZ

www.hodder.co.uk

FOR CHLOE GRACE,

MY FAVORITE ELDEST NIECE

ONE

If she were a litigious sort of person, Dani was reasonably certain she could've had her best friend charged with attempted murder. Tomás drove like he was trying to kill them both, with one hand on the wheel and the other stuck out the open window like an invitation for a wayward motorist to amputate. His sensible 2004 Toyota Corolla, which had been passed down through multiple older siblings before reaching him, did not seem likely to survive for his kid sister to inherit, judging from the groaning deep in the engine every time he accelerated. Or braked. Or turned. Or thought about turning.

"Is it supposed to be making that noise?" Dani asked, raising her voice over the blaring indie rock that Tomás favored in the afternoons.

"What?" He made no move to turn down the music.

"Is it—" Dani hit the power button on the center console, cutting off a hipster mid-croon. "Is your car supposed to be making that noise?"

Tomás squinted into the sunlight—he could never keep up with his sunglasses—and listened as the Corolla groaned (normal), squeaked (normal), and then began clicking (not normal).

"Huh," he said. "That's new." He reached to turn the music back on. Dani let him, but compromised by turning down the volume to a tolerable level.

"If this car explodes, I want you to know that I'm not crawling through the wreckage to drag your mangled body away from the flames," she said mildly.

"Cars don't just explode." He paused, scratching at a thin patch of stubble on his neck that he'd missed shaving that morning. "I mean, *probably*."

"I'm going to have them carve 'Gone but Never Forgotten . . . Probably' on your gravestone." She reached over and flipped down the visor for him. The sliding panel over the mirror had broken off years ago, and she caught a glimpse of his brown eyes in the fingerprint-smudged glass. He grinned at her.

"I like it." He had a face made for grinning—all dimples and white teeth and smooth brown skin. There had been pimples there last year too, but they had obligingly vanished along with the last of his middle school awkwardness. He'd gotten his braces off, his growth spurt, and two girlfriends (not at the same time) over the course of the previous summer, and he'd arrived at junior year a bona fide heartthrob, and single—much to the joy of at least half the girls in their class.

"That reminds me," said Dani, plucking the ponytail holder off her wrist to pull back her hair. Tomás took a curve too fast, and she grabbed the handle over the door to brace herself. Outside the pollen-streaked window, through breaks in the trees, she caught glimpses of the green and golden valley rolling into the foot of the mountains. "Jenna McKinney asked me for your number today."

"That's weird."

"Weird that she asked, or weird that she asked me?"

"Weird that we're talking about my grave and you brought up Jenna McKinney. But also, weird that she asked you. Did you give it to her?"

"No. She pronounces your name wrong. It annoys me." For the most part, Dani didn't care about Tomás's dating life, but she wasn't above the occasional tiny abuse of power when it came to cute girls who spent three weeks flirting promisingly with her via late-night text before revealing their actual agenda on the last day of school. Not that Tomás needed to know all that.

"Oh," he said noncommittally. "Maybe I'll see her tonight."

"Maybe."

Dani and Tomás had been friends since seventh grade, when he'd been the new kid in school and she'd been recently bereft of a best friend. Their origin story was a bit of a legend around the middle school and had followed them to William Blount High. Darryl Lewis, the class ass-clown, had yanked Tomás's Saint Christopher medal right off his neck, and when he saw how much it upset Tomás, had initiated a very mature game of keep-away. Dani, who had never been a fan of the game—or of Darryl Lewis, for that matter—had ended it with equal maturity by punching Darryl in the nose. She'd earned herself a two-day suspension, and found Tomás on her doorstep the next afternoon with her homework and a giant bag of Skittles. Some friendships were meant to be.

And yet, five years and many bags of Skittles later, he still missed her driveway every time he drove her home.

"Turn," Dani said, and Tomás slammed the brakes and wrenched the wheel to the left. "Jesus Christ!" Dani banged into the car door, then steadied herself with both hands on the glove compartment as the car bumped down the rutted gravel driveway, which led downhill through a copse of pine trees.

"Language," Tomás warned, with more habit than conviction. He was ostensibly Catholic; which was to say, he attended Sunday mass with his family every week and always wore his medal, but otherwise had never expressed much interest in religion. Too much distraction in school, friends, and everything else his abuela termed "secular." Dani couldn't blame him. She knew a thing or two about distractions.

"I wouldn't have to ask for divine intervention if you would stop driving like a deranged orangutan."

Tomás's only reply was to sail over a dip in the driveway without slowing. Dani bounced high enough in her seat that her head smacked into the roof of the car. At this rate, the Corolla wasn't going to survive another day, much less another owner. The driveway to Dani's house was like its own road, winding through the trees and undergrowth a quarter mile before the property opened up to their front lawn. Thanks to a wet season, the grass was bright green, with neat flower beds encircling the handful of oaks that had survived her grandparents' landscaping fifty years ago when they built the house. The nearest neighbor was twenty acres away through a young forest and overgrown fields, so to Dani, home always felt like its own private world.

The afternoon sun filtered through the trees and cast dappled shadows across the gabled roof, which featured a prominent widow's watch; it had always seemed an incongruous detail for a farmhouse built in the middle of the Smoky Mountains. The whitewashed front porch, with its handmade rocking chairs from the local Cracker Barrel and a wind chime that Dani's older sister Eden had crafted in the second grade from broken glass bottles, conjured *Southern Living* visions of hot summer nights sipping sweet tea and watching fireflies. Neither of which her family had ever done.

"Thanks for dropping me off." Dani unbuckled her seatbelt as the car rolled to a stop and hefted up her bag from the floorboard between her feet.

"You need a ride tonight?"

"No, Eden got roped into dinner with some family friends, so the Jeep is all mine."

"Cool, cool." Tomás tapped an absent rhythm on the steering

wheel as he peered through the streaky windshield at the house. All the curtains were drawn, which wasn't unusual, even in the middle of the day. "Need help with your bag?"

"Do I need help with the backpack that I've carried every day by myself for years?"

Tomás shot her a glare, and she laughed as she pushed open the door and slid out. Her shoes crunched on the new gravel that her parents had trucked in last week. The gravel supposedly was part of the normal upkeep of the old family estate, but Dani and her sister both knew it was to impress these "family friends" her parents were so excited—and tight-lipped—about. Eden had apparently met them a long time ago, so she joined in their parents' smug intrigue, which meant that Dani very emphatically didn't give a shit about it. On principle.

"Don't worry," Dani said, leaning down to meet his eyes. "Eden will be around all summer. I promise I'll help you stalk her later." Tomás had been crushing on her older sister ever since he'd first laid eyes on her, which Dani didn't understand but also didn't mind facilitating; it kept Tomás happy, and Eden would never so much as give him a second glance anyway.

"You're a true friend."

"See you at the bonfire." Dani shut the door and waved him off. She took the front steps two at a time, her backpack slung over one shoulder. She found her mother in the living room, balanced on the back of the couch with a duster in one hand and a half-full glass of what looked like her favorite rum and Coke in the other.

"You're late." Her mother didn't glance down. She was laser-focused on whatever dust bunny she was chasing along the top of the bookshelf. She rose up on her toes, one leg extended behind her like a ballerina, and stretched gracefully to swipe the duster across the farthest corner. Then she straightened and dropped to the ground, her bare feet almost silent on the woven rug. She hadn't spilled so much as a drop.

"That was impressive," Dani said, hoping to distract her.

Her mom took a sip, eyeing her over the rim of the glass. Her shoulder-length brown hair was pulled into a messy ponytail. She was wearing black yoga pants and one of Dad's old Emory University T-shirts.

"Thank you," she said. "You're still late."

"It's the last day of school."

Her mom made an uninterested sound and started dusting again. Analisa Rivera was not the kind of mom who snapped photos of her kids on their first day of school, stuck A+ tests on the refrigerator, or planned end-of-year barbecues. When Eden graduated high school, there were no announcements mailed or CONGRATULATIONS! banners hung. The Rivera family celebrated different kinds of milestones.

"Where's Eden?" Dani asked, shifting her backpack to the other shoulder.

"She's already at the barn."

"She couldn't wait for me?"

"I'm sure she would have," her mom said sweetly, "if you had been on time."

Dani groaned and raced up the stairs to her bedroom. She knew from experience that the later she was to practice, the longer Eden would keep her there. Her older sister was stricter than a drill sergeant when it came to training.

In less than five minutes she'd changed from her school clothes into compression pants, a teal cropped tank top, and running shoes. She sprinted downstairs and through the house to the back door, shouting a hello to her father as she passed his office. Since Eden had taken the ATV, Dani had to wrestle her bicycle down from the wall of the mudroom and pedal like mad across the back forty —which, on top of being muddy and mostly uphill, was in desperate need of being mowed.

By the time she reached the barn, she was dripping sweat and panting. It was a barn in outer appearance and name only; there had never been any livestock in residence. Half the floor was speckled black rubber like the high school's weight-lifting room, and the other half was one massive blue training mat. One wall was lined with exercise balls, dumbbells, punching bags, and weight benches. That was where the resemblance to high school gym class ended.

The opposite wall was like a visual history of warfare, mounted with weapons from various time periods and countries of origin. They were mostly for display purposes only, though not always.

Dani stood in the doorway for a few seconds, watching Eden's back as she scaled the climbing wall installed on the far side. She was almost at the top, about twenty feet up, just at the juncture of the sixty-degree overhang. She was wearing her helmet and climbing harness with a chalk bag clipped on a belt. There was an auto belay device installed at the ceiling, but the line was retracted and the carabiner empty. Eden had stopped using the belay when she was fifteen, Dani even earlier. Milestones.

"Don't let me interrupt," Dani called out. She dug through a bin on the shelf by the door and grabbed two hand wraps.

Eden was silent for a while, contemplating her next move.

"You're late," she said finally. Then she leapt for a hold, catching it with her fingertips. For a couple heart-pounding seconds, she dangled freely with only the narrow crimp keeping her from plummeting to the ground; then she managed to hook her toes around a foothold.

Dani realized she was holding her breath and forced herself to focus on wrapping her hands. It took Eden less than thirty seconds to finish the climb. She pulled down the carabiner from the auto belay, clipped it to the loop on her harness, and released her hold. She swung back and descended to the floor, her posture precise and her landing light.

By the time Dani had finished wrapping, Eden had stripped off her climbing gear and was chugging from a water bottle. Dani retrieved another pair of wrappings from the bin.

"Great dyno at the end there," she said. It was an actual compliment this time, not just a distraction tactic.

"Thanks. I beat my best time." Eden swiped her arm across her mouth and took the wrappings. Dani and Eden both took after their mother, with light brown skin that rarely burned in the summer and dark brown hair and eyes. But where Dani was short and compact, Eden was almost as tall as their father and lean like a ballet dancer. She was wearing a loose gray tank top over a neon pink sports bra and black leggings with a matching pink stripe down the sides. Dani had no doubt she'd coordinated the workout attire the night before. Eden would probably spend all day in the barn if their parents would let her.

"You need a warmup?" Eden asked as they both slipped off their shoes and socks and began pulling on their boxing gloves. There was headgear and various other protective equipment on the shelf, but that gear had gone the way of the belay.

"Thanks to an impatient sister of mine, I biked all the way here," Dani said. "I'm plenty warm."

"Fine. Muay Thai rules?" Dani nodded, and they moved to the center of the floor. "Did you work on your footing like we practiced?"

"Yes," Dani lied, raising her gloved fists to mirror Eden's. The truth was, she rarely came to the barn outside of their normal training sessions. It was annoying enough to be bossed around by her older sister two hours a day, five days a week, without cutting into her precious free time to do *more*. Dani went along with the training and conditioning, her father's lessons on tracking and wilderness survival, and her mother's lectures on lore and ancient weaponry, because that's what it meant to be a Rivera. But she wasn't about to abandon her friends, her hobbies, her *life* like Eden had, for the sake of the family legacy and some distant, mostly theoretical threat.

They tapped gloves and shifted into their stances, each making a few preliminary jabs to test the other's reflexes.

"Raise your guard higher," Eden said, "and square your hips. This isn't boxing." To demonstrate her point, she threw a right side kick. Dani raised her left knee in an attempt to check the blow, but her leg was at the wrong angle and Eden's kick caught her hard on the hip. Reluctantly, she fixed her stance and raised her hands higher to protect her head. It always felt unnatural to her to leave her torso unguarded, like she was inviting a swift kick to the ribs, and Eden had never been able to give her a good explanation other than "That's the proper technique." Finally, Mom had explained to her that the invitation was the whole point. Lure your opponent into a strike, and then use it against them.

They both got in a few good hits, gradually quickening the pace until their bodies were a flurry of motion. Hands, feet, elbows, knees—each put to brutal purpose, bone connecting with soft tissue. It was Dani's favorite part of sparring, when Eden was too focused on her own technique to critique Dani's and it was all about primal reflexes and rapid-fire strategy. Eden's own guard was starting to lower with fatigue. Dani took the opportunity to fake a low kick, and as Eden raised her knee to check it, Dani changed the angle to a high kick, slamming into the side of Eden's head.

Her sister retreated a few steps, blinking rapidly, but Dani advanced without giving her a chance to recover. She threw a left cross into Eden's stomach. Eden crunched down to block, and Dani pushed down on her shoulders while drilling her right knee upward into her sister's ribs. It was a solid blow, and much to Dani's satisfaction, she heard a curse from Eden as she disengaged.

They kept sparring, but all the landing blows were Dani's now, with Eden struggling to maintain her precious technique as she checked and blocked. Dani wasn't paying much attention to her own form, focused instead on hammering strikes into every opening she could find.

"You're too sloppy," Eden snapped, her voice equal parts exhaustion and annoyance. "Wasting energy on fancy moves isn't how you win a fight."

On the last word, she launched into a roundhouse kick, but Dani was ready for her. She kept her right arm up against her body to block the kick, then hooked her left arm under Eden's ankle. She spun around to the outside of the leg so that she was standing at Eden's left side, then swept a kick into Eden's other leg while pushing into her chest. With a terrible *whump*, Eden hit the floor in a tangle of limbs.

She struggled to right herself but finally collapsed onto her back, gasping up at the ceiling. Panting, Dani stood over her. Her own limbs were quivering with fatigue, but she couldn't help a grin.

"Fancy moves like that?"

"Where the hell did you pick that up?" Eden demanded.

"YouTube."

Eden made a strangled noise somewhere between a groan and a sigh.

"All that flash is meaningless without good technique."

Dani rolled her eyes and walked away. She ripped away the

Velcro strap on her right glove with her teeth and yanked it off. Even with the padding, her hand bones were aching.

"For some reason, your sermons on technique are less convincing from the floor," she called over her shoulder.

"This isn't a joke, Dani." Her sister rolled to her feet, wincing. "Why can't you take any of this seriously? You know what we're up against."

Actually, I don't, Dani thought. *And neither do you. Not really.*

"What makes you think I'm not taking this seriously?" she asked instead, ripping off her other glove and whirling to face Eden. "It doesn't matter if it's Muay Thai or boxing or fencing or freaking stick-fighting, more than half our sparring matches end with you on the ground. I hit every target. I beat every record you set. What more do you want from me, Eden?"

Eden's breath had steadied, and she stood motionless with her gloved hands loose at her sides. Her expression was stony, which somehow made Dani feel worse than if she'd looked hurt.

"I want you to stop acting like any of this is for our own edification." Eden had their mother's habit of over-enunciating words when she was angry. "It's not our egos at stake here. It's the fate of the goddamn world."

"Oh, here we go," Dani muttered, turning back around and flinging her gloves onto the shelf.

"What's that supposed to mean?"

"If it's all the same to you, I'd rather skip the 'fate of the world' lecture today. I have plans tonight. Normal teenager plans."

A pause. She heard the sounds of Eden removing her own gloves.

"I'm sorry if our family's responsibility gets in the way of your summer fun," Eden said, her voice quieter now but no less angry.

She came up beside Dani and set her gloves neatly back in their place. "Let me ask you something, though. Do you ever wonder why Mom and Dad hung that on the wall in here?"

She gestured toward the top of the door frame. Dani glanced up, even though she already knew what she would find. It was a bleached white skull, long and lizard-like, but the size of a Volkswagen Beetle. A pair of spiny ridges ran along the center of the head, flaring into two slightly curved horns. Double rows of teeth like a shark's filled the grinning mouth. It was the pride and joy of the Rivera family. The constant sentinel over their training. The ever-present reminder of that distant enemy.

A dragon skull.

"Because mounting it over the fireplace might raise some suspicions when we have house guests?" Dani asked innocently.

"Because it could have just as easily been Mom's or Dad's skull rotting in that dragon's cave somewhere, if they hadn't taken their responsibilities seriously. If you come face to face with one of those in the flesh, your stupid YouTube stars aren't going to be any help."

"And you think any of this will be?" Dani gave a short, incredulous laugh as she cast a glance around the barn. "You think a dragon is going to wait for you to find a weapon and take up the proper stance? You think that a perfect right hook is going to be any use against those teeth? For Christ's sake, Eden, all the technique in the world isn't going to save you if a dragon decides to barbecue you for dinner."

"And your devil-may-care, anything-goes attitude is?"

"I'm not like you," Dani said. "I fight to win."

"So do I!"

"No, you fight to be perfect. It's not the same."

Eden set her jaw and squared off to face her. For a second,

Dani thought she might throw a punch, but then she shook her head.

"Fine. Let's put your little theory to the test and see which of us would survive the longest."

"You got a dragon chained up in your closet that I don't know about?"

"No, but we have the next best thing." Eden looked toward the opposite corner of the barn, where a tarp covered something large and lumpy.

Dani followed her gaze and smiled.

"Okay, but we have to do it for real. No safeguards."

Eden hesitated, then nodded.

"Okay."

El Toro, which was an affectionate nickname bestowed by Analisa, was a home-built, custom-engineered contraption that most closely resembled a mechanical bull. Instead of a saddle and fake horns, it was equipped with retracting spikes the length of baseball bats, electrified whips meant to mimic the swinging of a dragon's tail, rubber pellets the size of paintballs that shot much faster and hurt much worse, and of course, the constantly rotating nozzles that breathed fire at random intervals.

El Toro was a death trap that could only be shut down by a small red button on its underbelly—or, in case of emergency and utter failure, a kill switch on the wall. It was one of the only training tools in the barn that required strict parental supervision. Dani had only faced it once, Eden twice—every time on the easiest setting, and every time with the safeguards in place. Spraying water instead of fire, the spikes blunted with rubber tips, the lashes' electric current shut off, and the pellets moving at a quarter-speed. Even then Dani hadn't come close to besting it, and Eden had only managed it earlier that year, by the skin of her teeth.

But Dani had been fourteen the last time she tried it. She knew things would be different this time.

Together they dragged the contraption to the center of the barn. It took Eden nearly ten minutes of fiddling to get everything set up properly.

"I'm first," Dani said when it was finally ready.

"Fine by me." Eden sauntered over to the kill switch and snatched the stopwatch from where it hung on a peg. "Do you need a safe word?"

"Screw you."

"Haven't heard that one before."

Dani took a second to collect herself, staring down the two giant bolts that served as El Toro's eyes. Then she hit the green button on its head. The light blinked slowly, giving Dani ten seconds to back up and take her position before the machine roared to life. And "roar" was the first thing El Toro did, bellowing out a stream of flame in a complete 360-degree spin. Dani felt the heat of it on her chest as she leapt back. She used her momentum to drop into a backwards somersault, then rolled up into a crouch, ready for her next move.

She watched the ever-changing configuration of spikes and lashing whips, instinctively searching for a pattern, though she knew there wasn't one.

"You know, waiting for the battery to run down doesn't count as winning," Eden shouted from her safe distance.

Dani shot her a dirty look, which was a mistake. In her split second of distraction, she missed the red pellet shooting from El Toro. It caught her in the collarbone. She swore, spotted an opening in the spikes, and bolted forward. Whips danced around her like demented jump ropes, and she ducked, skipped, and twisted to avoid them. She could have sworn she felt the buzz of electricity raise the hairs on her skin. Three more pellets shot out in quick succession. Two were wide, and the third she sidestepped. A spike shot out, lancing into the gap between her elbow and side. Dani stared down at it while her heart skipped a beat, then she had to lunge to miss another whip.

There was a faint wheezing sound, and Dani realized what it was just in time to hit the deck. Another jet of fire spewed above her. Dani blinked and saw a whip sailing toward her face. There was no time for swearing or even thinking now. She'd devolved into a creature of pure instinct. She reached up—only a split second after the fire had abated, judging by the sizzle of heat over her hands—and grabbed the spike above her. She swung her feet forward and off the ground like a gymnast mounting a high bar. She didn't quite have the momentum to swing into a handstand on the spike, but she managed to climb atop it. Then she planted one foot between El Toro's eyes and jumped across its back. She hit the ground in a crouch.

The mechanisms on El Toro were randomized, but their general placement was determined by the proximity sensors inset all over its body. When Dani landed on the opposite side, she took advantage of the brief delay as El Toro recalibrated to her sudden change in position and rolled underneath it. She jabbed upward, slamming her palm into the red button.

A loud whirring, and then silence. She closed her eyes, panting for breath, and grinned to herself. She rolled back out and climbed to her feet, dropping a theatrical bow. Eden clapped dutifully, though she looked less than impressed.

"Two minutes and six seconds," she said. "Not bad."

"Your turn," Dani said, taking the stopwatch from her. "Safe word?"

"'Screw you' does have a nice ring to it." She made her way to

El Toro, giving it a companionable pat on the head before hitting the green button and moving back into position.

Dani couldn't quash a swell of excitement in her chest. She liked to compete, and she loved to win, but more than anything —and this was a secret she intended to take to her grave—she loved to watch her sister kick ass. She had ever since she'd been seven years old, spying through a crack in the barn doors while nine-year-old Eden moved through fencing drills with the grace of a dancer, scaled the climbing wall with hardly any missteps, and hit eight out of ten targets with a Sig Sauer P238, all with the cool confidence of a cop in a crime drama. Those were the days when dragons were barely a fairy-tale concept to Dani, and training was a thrilling promise instead of a daily chore.

Her sister's obsession with technique was a pain, but the truth was that Eden was good at what she did. Better than any of the other scattered dragon hunters Dani had met in her life. Probably even better than their parents. Dani couldn't help but feel a certain sense of sisterly pride at that, even though she would never admit it out loud.

El Toro quaked to life with less panache than it had for Dani, but soon enough the whips and pellets were flying. True to form, Eden ducked, rolled, jumped, and dodged with elegant, military precision. Within the first thirty seconds, she had already gotten close enough to the machine to touch it twice, but was stymied both times before she could get underneath.

As the stopwatch ticked ever closer to two minutes and Dani was beginning to think she might actually best her sister on this one, a whip lashed Eden across the stomach. She yelped. Dani ran forward a couple steps without thinking, but forced herself to stop. The only thing Eden would hate more than losing was interference.

In the next moment El Toro bellowed out a column of flame.

Eden was distracted by another whip flying toward her, and side-stepped—right into the line of fire. She cried out, a sickening sound of pain that reverberated through Dani's own body. She took another involuntary step forward.

Eden twisted free from the flame—it looked like it had just gotten her shoulder—and stopped with her back to the machine, gasping loudly.

Then, mid-rage, El Toro died, its whips falling limp and spikes freezing in place. Dani blinked, wondering how Eden could have possibly reached the red button from where she stood.

"What the hell do you two think you're doing?"

Dani spun around at the voice and found her father standing behind her, his hand lowering from the kill switch. He eyed Dani for a few seconds, and when she didn't reply, turned his glare to Eden, who hadn't moved. A muscle in his jaw twitched. Dani looked and saw, with a sinking feeling in her stomach, what he had seen: the tip of a spike, which had obviously been in the process of extending when he hit the switch. It was a couple inches from the back of Eden's neck.

TWO

Ever since she was little, when her parents had first explained to her that the medieval myths of Tempus Dracones weren't just fanciful cultural metaphors, as was widely accepted by modern scholars, Eden had felt like there was a shadow lurking at her back. A shadow that was somehow both ephemeral and weighty, both terrifying and comforting. She wasn't sure if she believed in fate or chance or divine calling, but *something* had put her on earth in this time and place, the daughter of a legendary family of dragon slayers.

That shadow was her constant companion. A sense of dread. A reminder that she was one of the few bastions protecting humanity from dragonkind. A promise that every bruise and burn, every drop of sweat and blood, was leading her closer to her destiny.

And that was why on days like this, when nothing went right and her little sister was driving her up a wall, Eden wouldn't let herself lose perspective. So what if Dani effortlessly achieved every benchmark that Eden had to fight tooth and nail for? So what if Dani could casually dismantle the importance of all their training? So what if Dani could waltz in at seventeen and conquer El Toro like it was no more dangerous than a toaster?

So what.

Eden straightened up and walked toward her father, determinedly maintaining her strict posture despite the agony in her shoulder and the sting where the whip had caught her across her abdomen. James Rivera was a Scottish expat who had married into the Rivera family (and, as per tradition, taken the name) when he was barely a year out of university. Though he looked more like an absent-minded professor with his messy blond hair, tortoise-shell eyeglasses, and perpetual ink stains, he'd proven a good match for Analisa, who had already distinguished herself in the limited dragon slayer circles by the time she was a teenager. While his fighting skills were middling at best, there was no one who could track a dragon faster and pinpoint its location more accurately than James Rivera. Not that there were very many dragons left to hunt these days.

Her father looked her over, his arms crossed, his brows furrowed. She knew that look, though it was usually directed at Dani, not her. That nebulous line between anger and worry.

"It was my idea," she said, not bothering with excuses. "I told Dani it was okay." She was going to be in trouble anyway, and there was no reason for Dani to miss her big bonfire. She hadn't shut up about it for weeks.

Her sister shot her a surprised look, which Eden ignored. James watched her steadily, and she could practically see the gears turning in his head while he decided how to respond. Where her mother lived on impulse and instinct, her father was a thinker, weighing every decision with care. The balance was one of the reasons they worked so well together, both in dragon-hunting and in marriage.

"Dani, go back to the house," he said finally. "Your mother wants you to do some chores before you leave for the party. Eden and I will clean up here."

Dani looked like she wanted to argue, but Eden shot her a harsh look, and she shut her mouth. She scooped up her socks and shoes and headed for the door without even putting them on. When she reached the threshold James called after her, and she turned back.

"Did you go first?" he asked. Dani nodded warily. "What was your time?"

"Two minutes, six seconds." She was smart enough not to sound smug about it.

He waved her off, and she left. Eden caught a glimpse of a suppressed smile as her dad turned back. She pushed down the hard knot that had formed in her chest and craned her neck to examine her shoulder for the first time. The skin was red and blistered but there wasn't any muscle visible, and it hurt like hell so the nerves hadn't been damaged.

"What were you thinking?" her father asked, after a long, uncomfortable silence. He grabbed her mostly full water bottle from the floor and wetted a clean gym towel.

"Is that a rhetorical question?" She caught the towel when he tossed it to her. Biting her lip against the pain, she draped it carefully over her shoulder to start cooling the burn.

"I suppose it is." He still had a faint Scottish brogue, which became more pronounced when he was upset. He went to the cabinet where the first aid supplies were stored and pulled out a bottle of antibiotic ointment and a roll of gauze. He came back to her side and gently peeled back the corner of the towel to survey the damage. Eden bit her lip harder. This wasn't her worst training injury, but it was definitely in the top five.

"I'm sorry," she said when the continued silence became too hard to bear. "I know it was stupid."

More silence. She clenched her hands into fists to stop them from fidgeting. Finally, her dad sighed.

"Your mother and I will be discussing supervision during training from now on," he said, though not harshly. "And I have half a mind not to let you join us for dinner tonight."

Her heart dropped. This dinner was too important. She'd been looking forward to it for months.

"Dad—"

"But you're not a kid anymore," he went on. "I just hope you understand that in the real world, consequences are usually more severe—and permanent—than bed without supper." He looked meaningfully down at her shoulder, and she nodded.

"I understand."

"Good. Now sit down and rest while I put away El Toro." He handed her the ointment and gauze. "Tomorrow we'll decide if you need an appointment with Dr. Bellamy." Just like that, he was all business. Sometimes she imagined his mind as a constant running checklist of tasks, each one crossed off in succession, never deviating or doubling back.

Once the barn was straightened up and all the gear put away, her dad applied the antibiotic ointment to the burn and wrapped her shoulder neatly in the gauze. Neither of them spoke. Some people might have found his brisk, efficient manner cold, but for Eden it was much more comforting than a melodramatic show of parental concern. Her dad drove them back to the house on the ATV. It was a warm afternoon, but the humidity wasn't bad, and the air was crisp with sunlight. The fields they traversed had been farmland a long time ago, but once the Riveras had taken up residence, the land had been left mostly untouched. Eden had always liked the look of it, a vague memory of cultivation overrun by time and nature.

In the backyard, they parked the ATV in the shed that also housed the riding lawnmower and various other lawn implements. Eden's dad gave her a kiss on the temple and told her to get ready for dinner. She climbed the back steps. A tinge of pain told her that she'd pulled her left hamstring at some point. Just great. Inside, the vacuum cleaner was running, and she could hear strains of The Killers, which was her mom's music of choice for household chores. Everyone in the family pitched in to keep the house reasonably clean, although none of them were neat freaks unless you counted James's obsession with disinfected kitchen countertops. Analisa, her current cleaning frenzy aside, was probably the least concerned with an orderly house—another thing she and Dani had in common. She traveled a lot, doing freelance journalism for various publications—mostly stories about cave diving in Nepal, swimming with sharks in Haiti, and other fantastical adventures for rich millennials to aspire to.

Eden didn't mind keeping up with the day-to-day chores, usually while listening to an audiobook of required reading for one of her college courses. She found it relaxing. But tonight's guests had prompted an upgrade from clean to immaculate, and it was all hands on deck.

She sneaked through the back hallway and darted up the stairs while her mom's back was turned. She didn't feel like explaining the bandage on her shoulder right now. Once she locked herself in the bathroom that she and Dani shared, she was able to pull off her shirt and get a good look in the mirror at the wound from El Toro's lashing. The only remnant of the whip's impact and the brief electric shock that had seized her body was a thin red welt. For some reason, that made it even more humiliating. After all these years of training—two more than Dani, and with ten times more dedication—El Toro should have been a cinch for her. Instead, she'd hobbled away with a welt and a burn while Dani remained, as always, untouchable.

Her vision blurred, and she wiped her eyes ferociously. Involuntary tears from the burn or the sting of the whip, she told herself.

That's all. She closed her eyes and took a deep breath. The moment of pause she allowed herself turned out to be a mistake, because as soon as her focus slackened, her brain immediately switched gears. Releasing a hiss of pain through her teeth, she tugged at the edge of the gauze to examine the burn again, convinced that she'd missed something, that it was really a third-degree burn, that she was going to find peeling skin and charred muscle, that an infection would spread through the rest of her, rotting her from the inside out, that this was how she would die—not from a heroic stand against a dragon, but from a training accident that she was too slow, too *weak* to beat.

She couldn't see anything but blurred pink and white through her tears, and she realized the ache in her chest was because she was starting to hyperventilate. An instinct honed from a childhood full of panic attacks made her turn on the cold faucet full blast and plug the sink. Her psychologist's voice spoke soothingly in her head, barely decipherable through the roar of her own spiraling thoughts. *Focus on your five senses. What can you touch? What can you see? Hear? Smell? Taste?*

While she waited for the sink to fill, she counted her way through. One, the faux marble countertop was cool and smooth under her fingers. Two, there were flecks of dried toothpaste on the mirror. Three, the whooshing of the water and the dull rumble of the vacuum cleaner downstairs. Four, the sharp chemical scent of her deodorant. Five, the salt of the tears leaking onto her lips.

The sink had filled, and she plunged her face into it. The mammalian diving reflex, her psychologist called it. Eden didn't care so much about the science behind the technique, only that it worked. She kept her face submerged as her lungs ceased their spasming and her heartbeat slowed. It was like all the focus she had lost boomeranged back to her.

The burn wasn't life-threatening. She wasn't dying. She was okay. She was safe.

When she couldn't hold her breath anymore, she lifted her head, staring into the rippling basin as water drained from her face in rivulets. Slowly, she unplugged the sink, then started to undress, purposefully keeping her mind blank and numb. It was easier that way to stay in control.

So as not to irritate her wounds, she gave herself a quick sponge bath and washed her hair with the shower's detachable spray nozzle. By the time she'd finished, Dani was banging on the door for entry, declaring that she was going to be late for the bonfire. Eden, bundled in her robe with her hair in a towel, checked the mirror to make sure that her eyes weren't red and unlocked the door.

"Hey," Dani said with a startled look, as if she were somehow surprised to find Eden in the doorway. "Mom asked if you could find the wineglasses in the china hutch and wipe them down."

Eden didn't know if it was a sister thing or a Rivera thing to pretend like everything was normal, but she wasn't going to complain. The only thing worse than smug Dani was guilty, apologetic Dani.

"Okay," she said, slipping past Dani and down the hall toward her bedroom. "Have fun tonight."

A hesitant pause.

"You too."

Eden shut herself in her room and grabbed her phone from the nightstand where it was charging. It was almost five o'clock, and dinner was supposed to start at six. A nervous flutter in her stomach. It had been over a decade since she'd last seen Calla Thorn and Alder De Lange. Sorcerers were even fewer in number than dragon slayers, and twice as reclusive. The fact that the high sorcerer herself and her lieutenant were coming to dinner at the Rivera house was tantamount to a White House invitation.

Actually, Eden was pretty sure the president would have garnered less fuss.

The reason for Calla and Alder's visit tonight was still a mystery. When the high sorcerer invited herself to your house, you didn't ask questions. Eden had overheard her parents discussing it more than once — not that she was purposefully eavesdropping, of course. Apparently, when Calla had invited them to Stonecrest all those years ago, the reason for the visit had been equally obscure. Analisa maintained that the high sorcerer wanting to make the acquaintance of the region's top slayers was only to be expected. After all, they shared a common enemy, even if historically sorcerers and slayers had kept to their own kind. James, on the other hand, had his doubts that social or professional niceties played any role in Calla Thorn's private agenda.

Sometimes it occurred to her, usually during mundane moments like this as she flicked on the bedroom light and sat down at her vanity with her makeup bag, that her life seemed rather like a fairy tale — or at least it would to an outside observer. Dragons and sorcerers. Clandestine meetings and ancient weaponry. Old blood and older magic.

In reality, it was just a lot of days like today. Training until her body nearly gave out, only to learn she still wasn't up to snuff. Nursing wounds. Enduring lectures. Weathering panic attacks. Wondering if the day would ever come when it would be her turn to face off against her family's age-old enemy, and if on that day she would even be ready.

She told Siri to play some Halsey, whose drawling, subtle rage never failed to psych her up, and by the time she'd dried her hair and gotten dressed, Eden had begun to feel more like herself. The blue sundress she'd picked out for tonight had bare shoulders, which wasn't ideal. She raided her mom's closet and stole a white cardigan. The edge of the bandage was still visible, but it was well camouflaged.

As she made her way downstairs, she heard the Jeep start up in the driveway. Dani probably could have wheedled her way into joining them for dinner if she'd wanted to, but in typical Dani fashion, she had only a passing interest in Calla and Alder. "I'm sure they'll come around again," she'd said to Eden with a shrug. As if a high school party replete with drunk teenagers and cheap hot dogs offered the same social currency as an evening with the two most elite sorcerers of all time.

Eden hadn't even attended her own high school graduation. It had seemed like a pointless ceremony, when they were mailing her the real diploma anyway. She'd spent the day perfecting her knife-throwing form.

The vacuum cleaner had been put away, and her mother was artfully rearranging some books on the coffee table. Her hair was frizzy with exertion, her cheeks pink with stress. The Killers still blared from an unseen speaker, wailing about burning down the highway skyline. For Christmas last year, Eden had presented her mother with two of their more recent albums, and Analisa had blinked in genuine consternation at the idea of anything existing beyond *Sam's Town*. She'd offered a very convincing show of gratitude and listened to each album once, out of motherly politeness. Neither had made an appearance again.

"It's five thirty," Eden told her.

"Shit." Analisa straightened up. "Can you—"

"I'll get the wineglasses."

"And the—"

"Cheese board?"

"What would I do without you?" Her mother made like she was going to touch her cheek affectionately, but was distracted by some other concern mid-motion and darted past Eden toward the stairs. "I'll be down in a few minutes!"

There was some more muffled cursing, then The Killers cut off abruptly and the bedroom door slammed. A smile tugged at Eden's lips as she set about organizing the final touches of the evening. Wineglasses were polished and lined up on the sideboard in the dining room, which was usually the home of hastily dispatched junk mail and the occasional dirty dish that, for whatever reason, hadn't made it all the way to the kitchen. She set out the two red wines and a white that her father had bought especially for the occasion, all featuring elegant cream-colored labels with embossed French script. After a second thought and a quick Google search on her phone, she dug out an ice bucket to put the bottle of white in. The Riveras didn't usually go in for wine and charming family dinners.

At fifteen till, she set out the cheese plate on the coffee table. Her mother had picked it up at a specialty store in town, which apparently catered exclusively to people who wanted to impress important guests. According to the label on the plastic covering she ripped away, it was actually called a charcuterie board. Eden read it out loud to herself, right as her father wandered into the living room.

"Char-*coot*-ury," he said, correcting her pronunciation. At some point he'd managed to shave and slick back his hair in a way that made him look like a suave lawyer from a TV show, albeit a lawyer in a tweed jacket with elbow patches and a truly hideous olive-green tie. "Smells good in here."

"That's Mom's homemade dinner," Eden said, eliciting his

warm, rumbling laugh. The menu tonight consisted of garlic bread bruschetta, penne alla vodka, and vanilla panna cotta, all of which had been ordered ahead and delivered by a catering company that afternoon. Eden wasn't sure if her mother was planning on actually telling their guests that it was homemade, but she'd made sure to surreptitiously stash all the incriminating bags and logo-stamped boxes in the garbage can outside. Just in case.

"Was that the doorbell?" Analisa called, half-dressed and leaning so far over the balcony that Eden was afraid she'd lurch headlong to the hardwood floor.

"No," she and her father said together.

Analisa disappeared again.

"I don't know why she's so worried," James said with fond amusement. "Knowing Thorn and De Lange, they'll make a point of arriving fashionably late."

True to his prediction, it wasn't until fifteen after that the doorbell rang. At that point her mother was downstairs again, pacing from room to room, double-checking that everything was in its place. Her father had picked up on her nervous energy and was in the process of re-knotting his tie for the third time. When her mother didn't immediately appear, Eden stood up and smoothed out her dress. Her stomach was fluttering again, but it was mostly excitement now. She went to the door and opened it before the bell rang again.

"Hello," she said, trying to project an air of confidence and casual grace. An equal, greeting equals. Though truthfully, she felt nine years old again, picking uncertainly at a grubby Band-Aid on her finger while bearing the weight of the high sorcerer's undivided scrutiny for the first time.

"Hello, darling," said Calla, breezing inside with a *whoosh* of silk and the faint scent of roses. "Alder is just taking a call. He'll be along shortly. Analisa, what a *vision* you are! You haven't changed a bit."

She was a veritable whirlwind of geniality and self-assurance as she thrust out her arms to embrace Analisa, who had just arrived in the front hall, a little breathless. Eden's mother did look very self-consciously pretty, with her hair carefully straightened and slightly darker eye makeup than normal, in a maroon shift dress with lace sleeves and simple black flats. But her attempts at elegance seemed clumsy next to Calla Thorn, who *really* had not changed at all in ten years. She still wore her copper hair in loose waves like a Hollywood actress; her green eyes were almost preternaturally striking; her bright red lipstick was the perfect contrast to her alabaster skin.

She continued her whirlwind into the living room, where Eden's father was standing patiently.

"James, there you are! I love the glasses, very distinguished. What a beautiful home you have here. I was just telling Alder—oh wait." She spun suddenly, and Eden found herself pinned by that galvanizing gaze. "Eden Rivera, by the stars, I cannot believe you've grown this much. Come here, let me look at you."

Eden inched forward, suddenly at a loss for the confidence she'd mustered only moments before. What sort of things could a sorcerer tell about a person just by looking at them? She resisted the urge to tug at her cardigan. She couldn't imagine the humiliation if Calla Thorn could somehow divine her spectacular defeat earlier that day. Why had she decided on the blue dress anyway? It was girlish and frilly, nothing like the lean, effortless chic of Calla's white silk blouse and loose black trousers that made her long legs seem even longer. She might as well have stepped right out of a Chanel ad.

Maybe it was coincidence, or maybe Calla really had divined

something of Eden's thoughts, because her eyes zeroed in immediately on Eden's shoulder.

"What happened here?" she asked. With a nude-polished nail, she nudged aside the cardigan, which, *oh god*, was probably from a bargain bin somewhere.

"It's nothing," Eden said a little too quickly, reaching up to tug the cardigan back into place.

"Training accident," said her father, ignoring the look he received from his wife. Clearly, he hadn't mentioned it to her yet.

"A burn?" Calla asked. Something twinkled in the depths of her eyes as she looked at Eden.

Eden nodded. Calla smiled. A small, conspiratorial gesture, like it was a secret just between the two of them.

"All the best slayers train with real fire, you know," Calla said. "And rightly so. Isn't that what I always say, Alder?"

She didn't break from Eden's gaze when she asked the question, but Eden turned to find Alder De Lange had entered without a sound. He looked to be around the same age as his counterpart —somewhere in the hazy territory of mid-thirties to forties—and with the same easy sophistication.

"It is indeed," he said in an urbane tenor. "Analisa, James. Good to see you again." He was white and tall, with close-cropped dark hair and the look of an actor who had gotten out of the business early and now spent his time being bored at cocktail parties and country clubs. He could have joined Calla in the Chanel ad with his black tailored suit and black shirt, the first few buttons casually undone. He, too, was exactly as Eden remembered him —vaguely European accent and all.

"Alder, so glad you could make it," Analisa said in her ebullient Hostess Voice. "I was just getting the wine. Please, you two, make yourselves comfortable."

Alder, who didn't look like he knew how to achieve such a thing, remained leaning against the mantel. Calla dropped into an armchair, instantly elevating the atmosphere with the refined languor of her posture and conversation. Eden sat down on the couch beside her father, in rapt attention. She didn't have anything to add to their discussion of the latest breakthroughs in fireproof technology or the new literature on reptilian evolution patterns, but she wanted to make sure Calla knew that she wasn't that clueless kid anymore. Her mother rejoined them and began arguing with Alder on the finer points of some article or another, and Eden felt her interest slipping.

"Eden," came Calla's voice, sliding easily beneath the debate, which James had joined now with a third contrary opinion. "Tell me what you've been up to lately. You graduated high school last year, yes?"

Eden, relieved to be back on familiar ground, started detailing her training regimen. She gave only a cursory mention of her college courses, which were all boring gen ed credits anyway. She hadn't realized how freeing it was to talk with someone who didn't need to ask what she was planning on doing with the rest of her life, and who didn't have the slightest interest in whether she was dating anyone nice, or making new friends, or any of the other irrelevant things well-meaning adults tended to care about.

And the best thing about it was that Calla actually *did* seem to care about her training—about her best times on the climbing wall, about her various weapon proficiencies. The high sorcerer. Calla Thorn. Sitting right there, listening closely as she sipped her red wine and made the occasional generous remark. Being the sole recipient of Calla's attention was a little like suddenly finding yourself at the center of the universe, with every majestic planet and burning star orbiting only you. Eden felt heady with it.

At least until Calla's next question.

"And what about your sister? Danielle?"

The cosmos spun away from Eden, and she found herself back in the living room.

She's just being polite, she told herself. Dani was still in high school, and she hadn't even cared enough to meet Calla and Alder. She couldn't be of any real interest to the high sorcerer.

"She goes by Dani, and she's at her big end-of-school bonfire tonight," Eden said, trying for a breezy, dismissive tone. "She'll be a senior next year."

"And you two train together?"

"I'm supervising her training," Eden corrected. Never mind that after today's incident, she would almost certainly be demoted back to co-pupil.

Calla's eyes were bright—probably from the wine—as she leaned forward and opened her mouth to say something more, but she was interrupted by James inviting everyone to head into the dining room. Eden hadn't even realized that the debate was over. She wondered who'd won. Both her parents seemed in good spirits, and Alder wore his same cool, faintly amused expression.

Analisa refilled everyone's wineglasses while Eden helped her father bring out the bruschetta. As Eden leaned in to put the plate of toasted baguette slices on the table, her elbow knocked Calla's glass, splashing wine onto the high sorcerer's white, no-doubt designer blouse. *Red* wine.

"Oh my god," Eden cried, lunging to right the glass, which was too little, too late. "I'm so sorry."

Her cheeks were so hot she thought she might spontaneously combust.

"I'll get something to clean it off," James said, looking mildly alarmed, which only made Eden feel worse. She was pretty sure red wine on white silk was a no-win combination.

Calla, who hadn't done more than blink at the sudden upset, glanced down at the damage and gave a careless wave.

"Don't trouble yourself," she said, to no one in particular. She smoothed a hand down the front of her ruined shirt, and the stain vanished, leaving behind only pristine white. Then she took her glass from Eden's numb fingers with a smile. "Thanks, darling."

Eden stared as the wineglass refilled itself and Calla took a sip. She opened her mouth to apologize again, but found that she couldn't speak. Realizing she was staring, she forced her feet to take her back to her chair. It was one thing to know that the woman in front of her was a sorcerer. It was another thing entirely to watch her use magic in such a mundane way, as if it were the simplest thing in the world. She sneaked a look at her parents, but they seemed neither shocked nor impressed. Eden tried to copy their nonchalance. She wasn't sure if she succeeded.

The conversation picked up where they'd left off. Her mother didn't exactly say the meal was homemade, but neither did she make any objection when Calla complimented her profusely on how much it reminded her of being in Bologna, which was apparently the food capital of Italy. Talk of traveling carried them all the way to the main course. Eden had only left the country once on a family trip to Jalisco to visit relatives, where they had spent their time connecting with fellow dragon slayers in Mexico rather than sightseeing. So yet again, she had little to contribute to the discussion, but she nodded and smiled in all the right places. Mostly she was concentrating on not dropping any food down the front of her dress and making an even bigger fool of herself. She wasn't normally clumsy, except apparently in front of powerful, important sorcerers.

When dessert arrived and the wineglasses were being refilled again, Eden saw a meaningful glance pass between Calla and Alder. She sat up a little straighter.

"It was good of you to have us here tonight," Calla said.

It was Eden's parents' turn to exchange a glance. James cleared his throat, but it was Analisa who replied.

"As lovely as the visit has been, I have to admit we're a little curious about your ulterior motives."

Calla smiled, giving no hint that she was offended by Analisa's bluntness.

"Fair enough." She paused to rearrange her napkin in her lap. "There's been talk, in certain circles, that Dani is showing a lot of promise as a slayer."

Eden almost choked on her bite of panna cotta and washed down the cream with a gulp of water.

"Eden and Dani are both well beyond the level of skill I showed at their age." Her mother's tone and expression were both frosty.

"Oh yes, I know," said Calla quickly. "There's no doubt they are both supremely talented. It's just, I've heard that Dani has a particular aptitude for it. Eden, you said you've been training her —what do you think?"

Eden's mouth dried as Calla's serious gaze swiveled to her. She took another drink of water. Her first instinct was to say no, Dani didn't have any special talent. She cared more about her stupid classes and her stupid friends and her stupid summer job than she'd ever cared about slaying. She'd never be half as good as Eden was. But not only was that petty and unfair, it was also untrue.

Eden dropped her hands into her lap and squeezed them together.

"Dani's gifted," she said, hoping that the bitterness festering in her gut wasn't seeping into her tone. "She's beaten most of my records already. If she would actually apply herself . . ." But she couldn't bring herself to go on. Surely that was enough. There was a warm brush against her knuckles and she glanced down to see her dad's hand wrapping around hers. She looked over at him, and he smiled at her. It didn't make her feel any better.

"Exactly," Calla said, "and that's why I think she should come spend some time with us at Stonecrest. Eden's already been, of course, and I think Dani could benefit from the experience. There's a lot we can show her about dragon lore and magic. It may be just the inspiration she needs."

Dani? Eden's cheeks felt hot, and she stared hard at her plate. Stonecrest, the sprawling, mountainside manor where several sorcerers lived, including Calla and Alder, still loomed large in her imagination. She'd only been nine at the time, during that visit with her parents that she still didn't know the exact purpose of. They'd left Dani with a babysitter, and it was one of the brightest spots in Eden's memory. A black limo with tinted windows. A long, winding drive. Those beautiful iron-wrought gates. Even though the night hadn't ended on a particularly good note, it still hadn't tarnished those first thrilling moments.

And now Dani was being invited personally? For an experience? What did that even mean?

She. Wasn't. Even. Here.

"I don't know," Analisa said, and Eden had a brief, shining hope that she would point out that if anyone deserved an *experience* at Stonecrest, it was Eden. But she just frowned and shook her head. "I don't think it's a good idea."

"And why is that?" Calla's tone and expression were perfectly neutral, but there was something about her demeanor that sent a chill down Eden's back.

"We have a responsibility to our fellow slayers," Analisa said.

"Most of them were against us even hosting you tonight. There's been a push to cut off all contact with sorcerers."

"I'm sure you remember what happened to Jacob Lowry and his boy a few years back," James said, fidgeting a little in his seat. He didn't quite meet Calla's eyes.

"Of course I do," she said smoothly. "Horrible business. I'm sure *you* remember that Karl Slovek was dealt with accordingly."

"It's hard to rebuild a trust broken that badly," said Analisa.

Eden thought she saw a flash of annoyance across Calla's features, but it evaporated so quickly, she might have imagined it. She didn't know what they were talking about, exactly. She knew about the Lowrys, because *everyone* knew about the Lowrys. Both were massacred by a dragon that had eluded other slayers in New Mexico for nearly a decade—the same dragon, in fact, whose skull was now mounted in the Riveras' barn. But she didn't know who Karl Slovek was, or what any of it had to do with sorcerers.

"That's why we're here," Alder said. His fingers beat a light rhythm along the side of his wine glass. "To extend the olive branch, as it were."

"Yes," said Calla, her red lips turning upward slightly. "Despite what you and your fellow slayers may believe, we don't spend our time idly at Stonecrest. We want the same things you do. There's a weapon we've been working on, for almost two centuries now, and we're close. Very close. I believe it's the key to defeating the dragons once and for all."

It was strange, hearing her toss out "centuries" so nonchalantly. Obviously Eden knew that, being immortal, most sorcerers were easily hundreds of years old—Calla and Alder being older than most. But it was still disorienting to consider it while sitting across the table from them, flesh and blood, looking younger than her parents.

"Not to belittle the work you've been doing," Alder said, "but surely you realize that picking off the buggers one by one isn't going to get the job done."

"And what do you know that we don't?" asked James, taking off his glasses to clean them, like he always did when he was peeved and didn't want to show it.

"Everything," said Calla. "Straight from the dragon's mouth —well, after a fashion."

The table was silent for a while. Eden stared hard at the few bites of panna cotta left on her plate and thought about that night ten years ago. The dank stone basement, stretching into darkness. The single dangling lightbulb. The crimson, catlike eyes. The glow, fierce and bright, of an explosion suspended in time, poised to annihilate her.

"So, what is this weapon you've been working on?" Analisa asked finally.

Calla smiled again.

"Something powerful enough that it doesn't matter how many eggs hatch, or how many dragons are still skulking around; they won't stand a chance."

"Enigmatic," remarked James dryly.

"I'm afraid it's something best kept close to the vest," Calla said, sounding genuinely apologetic. "At least until we've achieved the results we're hoping for. Unfortunately, the lack of trust extends both ways. Alder and I are keen to call that terrible incident in New Mexico water under the bridge, but most of our colleagues don't feel the same way. It's a . . . delicate situation."

Eden had always assumed that as the high sorcerer, Calla could just make whatever decisions she wanted, and everyone else would have to obey her. But maybe the sorcerers worked more like a democracy, and she was the commander-in-chief. Or maybe they had a parliament, and she was the queen. A stunning, charismatic queen to sit upon their figurative throne.

The truth was, no one really knew how the sorcerers conducted their business. They had more or less kept to themselves over the years, as had the slayers, despite their shared goal to eradicate dragons. Two factions with a singular purpose, divided by a distrust that Eden couldn't entirely comprehend.

"If you would let Dani join us at Stonecrest for a while, it might go a long way in rebuilding the trust that's been broken," Calla said. "We can give her the advantage of our experience, and help her become a truly phenomenal slayer."

"And you want to help our daughter out of the goodness of your heart?" Analisa asked, skepticism bleeding into her tone. Eden shot her an indignant look. Leave it to her mother to slap a gift horse in the face. Or whatever the saying was.

Calla offered a thin smile.

"As I said before, we want the same things you do. I see no reason why the new generation should carry the same burdens as the old."

The two women eyed each other across the table for a moment, locked in a silent battle of will. At last James interrupted with his characteristic diplomacy.

"Thank you for the offer," he said, "but we'll have to talk to Dani about it. She's pretty busy this summer with her job at the ropes course."

Calla's eyebrows raised slightly, and Eden could practically read her thoughts. *We're talking about the fate of the world, and you're worried about a summer job?* It made Eden want to scream. Calla exchanged another look with Alder, then smiled.

"Wonderful. Just let us know. We're happy to send a car for her, whenever her schedule allows." There was a tinge of mockery in her tone, but it was more amused than malicious. "Now, may I propose a toast?"

Alder and Eden's parents reached dutifully for their wine-glasses. Calla's eyes alighted on Eden.

"Ah, Analisa, James—don't you think Eden ought to join us? I know there's that ridiculous drinking age nowadays, but I think someone who's old enough to go off to war or slay a dragon should be old enough for a glass of wine, don't you?" She gave Eden a theatrical wink, and Eden couldn't help but feel the tiniest bit mollified. Her parents had one of their silent split-second conversations, and then her father went to pull out another glass from the china hutch. He wiped it out and poured a small amount of white wine.

Eden took it carefully, sitting as straight as she could and trying to affect an air of nonchalance. It was the first toast she had ever seen outside a wedding or a joke at someone's birthday party. How did Calla, standing with one hand resting lightly on the tabletop, the other raising her glass, manage to be so glamorous and so casual at the same time?

"To the end of an age-old war."

"Hear, hear," said Alder without a trace of irony.

To Eden, it felt more like the beginning of something. Like a fresh page in a dusty old tome. Like the rejuvenation of a battle cry that had been echoing faintly throughout the centuries. She didn't even care that the wine tasted awful.

Their guests stayed for coffee after dinner and more idle chit-chat. It was nearly ten by the time they made their goodbyes. Her parents saw them to the door, then headed back into the living room, still engrossed in the finer points of the most recent topic of discussion. Eden hesitated in the hall, then opened the door and ran out to the porch.

"Calla, wait," she said, rushing down the steps.

Calla was halfway to the car, a shiny black Suburban that looked so new, it might have been a rental. She stopped and turned back to Eden. In the orange porchlight, she was hazy and ethereal like a dream fading into the night.

"Did I forget something?" she asked, when Eden didn't continue.

"No, I—I just—I wanted to say—" Eden tried to catch her breath. God, why was she panting so hard? "I wanted you to know, if what happened that night when I visited—if that was some kind of test or something, and I failed—I mean, I was only nine. And I've been working so hard since then, and I promise I—"

"Eden," Calla said gently. "You didn't fail any test. What happened that night was my fault entirely. You should never have found yourself in that position."

"But . . ." Eden bit her lip. *Just go back inside.* "Then why Dani?" Even as the words came out, she hated herself for them, and shame burned in her cheeks. So much for convincing Calla that she wasn't a kid anymore. A grown-ass woman—a dragon slayer—wouldn't be out here whining about being left out.

There was a crease between Calla's brows, a pale hint of a frown.

"I never meant to imply that you aren't welcome to come to Stonecrest as well. I just assumed it held little interest for you anymore." She broke into a soft smile, though that crease hadn't quite disappeared. She lifted one pale hand and patted Eden gently on the shoulder. "If you want to come with Dani, please do. We'd be delighted to have you both."

Eden tried to force out a thank you, but she couldn't say anything past the lump in her throat. She managed a smile and a nod. Alder had started the car, and Calla waved another goodbye, navigating the gravel in her heels with masterful grace.

Eden watched their taillights disappear down the drive until the sound of the engine and rumbling tires had faded completely. Her shoulder tingled where Calla had touched her. It took her a few seconds to register that the odd feeling was just a sudden lack of pain. She carefully peeled back the edge of the gauze and found only smooth, undamaged skin.

Despite the awe at this revelation, there was a tightness in her chest that she couldn't shake. A disappointment she didn't quite understand. She'd gotten what she wanted, hadn't she? An invitation? She cast her thoughts back over the brief conversation, searching for the source of her dismay. At last, she understood. Calla's answer, kind as it was, still had a clear underlying message. Eden was welcome to come, but only if Dani came too.

She was aware once more of that shadow at her back, that sense of dread lurking just behind. She was the daughter of a legendary family of dragon slayers.

But she wasn't the only daughter. And for the first time, Eden began to wonder if the blood and sweat, bruises and burns were worth it after all. Maybe the destiny she'd been chasing all these years wasn't even hers. Maybe she was destined to be firstborn and second best.

Somewhere distant, a night bird called out, and another replied in kind. A mild breeze stirred, causing the wind chime on the porch to tinkle faintly. With a brutal effort, Eden pushed the thoughts away and went back inside. There was nothing else she could do.

THREE

Dani was pretty comfortable around fire. In a family of dragon slayers, you kind of had to be. But even she was concerned about the blazing monstrosity that her classmates had created by the time she arrived at the party. Ideally the bonfire would have been on a beach, so there could be glow-in-the-dark volleyball and drunken sandcastles and maybe some skinny dipping. Unfortunately, there was a shortage of beaches in the middle of the Great Smoky Mountains, so they had ended up on the back acreage of Andrew Melville's family's farm. It had the bonus of plenty of open space and privacy, but the downside of no bathrooms and probably a surplus of rattlesnakes.

Everyone had parked their cars in a wide circle, the headlights facing in, with the fire pit in the center. Apparently two different people had decided they wanted to be in charge of music, because something twangy and country-ish was bellowing from one truck's speakers while something poppy and techno-ish was playing from another's. From the look of things, almost everyone was nearly plastered already, even though the sun had barely set. Katie Millsap and her crew were in bikini tops and jean shorts, trying to dance like strippers on Johnny Wyatt's truck, while Johnny and a handful of other football players were hooting and filming the show on their phones. Meanwhile, Melinda Cates was holding court from the hood of her red Fiat, laughing loudly at something her best friend Kristin had just whispered in her ear. And everywhere else clumps of people were talking, drinking, dancing, throwing stuff in the fire, trying to get close enough to the roaring flames to cook hot dogs, shouting over the music to their friends, sweating profusely in the warm May air.

It was a cacophonous, wild mess, and Dani couldn't remember the last time she'd been this happy. Tomás was already there, chatting with some of the SGA preps. Dani knew most of them from helping with prom decorations that year, so she slipped easily into the conversation, which was speculation on who had filled up Mrs. Elwood's classroom with beach balls. She'd had to spend all of first period with her freshmen deflating them. (Everyone knew it was Andy Colfax, but apparently Melinda had told Kristin who had told Lily, the SGA president, that Paul West had claimed credit, and so now there were warring rumors.) And there was also the rumor that one of the freshmen had somehow sneaked a switchblade into school and had stabbed ten beach balls before Mrs. Elwood caught him and confiscated it.

Tomás was insisting that the rumor was definitely true, and Dani was in the process of pointing out that there was a new rumor every other week about a freshman stabbing something (or someone) and just how many switchblades were being smuggled into school? Then she heard her name.

"Dani! Daniiiiii. Hey, Dani!"

She turned and spotted Johnny Wyatt across the circle. He must have gotten bored of the pseudo-striptease, because he was swaying toward her. Dani had a sudden vision of him tipping over into the fire and combusting from the surfeit of alcohol in his system, so she went to meet him.

"Hi, Johnny, what's up?" She casually took his arm and guided him a few steps away from the orange flames.

"Daniiiiiii." It seemed to be all he had to say. He was grinning goofily, and Dani couldn't decide whether to roll her eyes or smile. They'd dated for less than a month, sophomore year, before he'd gotten engrossed in football and Dani had remembered that she hated football. He was cute, in a big-oafish-jerk kind of way. And not nearly as bad of a boyfriend as she might have expected.

"Hi, Johnny," she repeated.

"Hey, remember when we ditched that pep rally to make out under the bleachers?" he asked her dreamily.

"Yeah," said Dani, amused.

"That was hot. You were so hot."

"Thanks, Johnny." She gently but firmly removed the arm that he'd snaked around her waist. He wasn't dating anyone right now, but she didn't want any onlookers getting the wrong idea. "Maybe drink some water, okay?"

"God, I hate football," he said, dragging both hands down his sweat-streaked face.

"Me too."

"You don't have to play football," he said, showing admirable lucidity.

"Neither do you."

He let out a sigh that carried with it a world of woe. His breath smelled strongly of yeast and hot dogs.

"Yeah I do. My dad played football. My brothers played football."

Dani was about to point out that his family's obsession with the sport didn't mean he had to follow in their footsteps, but then she thought twice about it.

"I know what you mean," she said.

Johnny gave her a sad, wobbly little smile. He really was cute, with floppy brown hair and big brown eyes. Like a puppy. A big, loud, occasionally sexist puppy. Before he could say anything else, one of his football bros came up and slapped him on the shoulder.

"Dude," he said. "Dude. You have to come check this out. Hi, Deidre."

She didn't bother correcting him. Anyway, he was too busy dragging Johnny away to notice. Dani returned to Tomás, who had made his way to one of the giant blue coolers and was digging through the ice.

"Everything okay?" he asked, glancing up at her.

"Peachy." She grabbed a Smirnoff Ice, which she reasoned was more adventurous than a soda, but less reckless than a beer or the bottle of whisky that was making the rounds. The Smirnoff was green-apple flavored, and tasted like Easter candy.

Tomás, who had stuck with soda, popped open the can and peered at her. They were in the techno-pop half of the circle, and a song that Dani recognized but didn't know the name of blared an auto-tuned anthem about dance floors and weekends.

"Jenna texted me today," Tomás said. "I thought you didn't give her my number."

"I didn't. That's kind of creepy."

He shrugged.

"She probably got it from Melinda or somebody."

If she could have gotten it from Melinda or somebody, Dani doubted Jenna would have wasted the effort of buttering her up for the past few weeks, but she didn't say that.

"What did she say?"

"She's got an extra ticket to some band playing in Nashville tomorrow. She asked if I wanted to come."

"You have work tomorrow."

He raised an eyebrow at her.

"Thanks, Mom. That's what I told her."

"So, are you interested in her?" She handed Tomás her drink

and scrambled up to sit on the hood of someone's truck. The metal was warm under her thighs. Tomás handed her both drinks and joined her.

"I don't know." He looked skyward, though all there was to see was smoke and the occasional buzzing insect. "Do you really think she's creepy?"

Dani took another drink and held the glass bottle between her knees. There was still a tiny part of her that felt vindictive toward Jenna, but she decided to let it go. Sisters before misters, as Eden had told her once. Though Dani wasn't sure it applied to this situation, exactly, since Tomás felt more like a brother than anything else. Or maybe like the hot second cousin you have a split-second daydream about at the family reunion before remembering you're related. Her relationship with Tomás was bags of Skittles and late-night Taco Bell runs and the occasional Dungeons and Dragons game with his friends from the Catholic school he used to attend (which she enjoyed much more than actual dragon training). There had never been room for anything as complicated or time-consuming as romance.

"She's not creepy," Dani said, "but at *least* make her pronounce your name right. That's all I ask."

He chuckled.

"Fine, but if you get back together with Johnny—"

"Not happening."

"—don't let him talk you into being a cheerleader again. That's all *I* ask."

Dani made a face. She'd tried to strike that particular bad decision out of her memory. When she had still thought she wanted to make the relationship with Johnny work, she'd joined the cheerleading squad. She had lasted three days before she quit. Though she had nothing but respect for the athletic and acrobatic prowess of the cheerleaders, the last thing she wanted to add to her life was an extra layer of training, even if one was with pom-poms and the other was with boxing gloves. She and Johnny had split the day after.

"I thought we agreed to pretend like that never happened."

"No, *you* told me to pretend it never happened, and I—"

A shadow passed over them, along with a peculiarly hot wind that fanned the bonfire dangerously. Almost everyone gaped upward, pointing at a dark shape in the sky that was visible for only another couple seconds before disappearing into the night.

"Whoa," said Tomás. "What was that? A plane?"

"Pretty silent for a plane." Dani squinted into the dark, but saw nothing. It didn't seem like the shape was coming back.

"An owl, maybe?"

"Pretty big for an owl."

The mood of the party was dampened for only a few more seconds as people exchanged theories with each other, and then someone cranked up the country music louder, and the chatter and laughter resumed. Dani frowned to herself and searched the sky a little longer. A strange feeling had passed over her with the shadow, and there was a tingling sensation in her chest, like blood returning to a sleeping limb. Her first thought had not been bird or plane, but *dragon*. One of the hazards of the slayer profession. The general populace had no idea that dragons were anything more than fiction and lore, and it was part of the slayers' self-proclaimed mission to never disabuse them of that notion. The last thing they needed was adrenaline junkies with selfie sticks and animal rights extremists getting involved in the search for the last remaining dragons.

She glanced once more at the empty sky, trying to decide if she should call her parents. It wasn't like she had any real reason to think it had been a dragon passing overhead. But on the other hand, they had raised her to trust her instincts.

"Hi, Dani."

She started at the voice and looked down, then almost dropped her bottle. The girl standing in front of the truck was gazing up at her with a solemn expression. Her blond hair was a lot shorter than it had been when Dani had seen her last—almost a pixie cut. But otherwise it was unmistakably her. Pretty and fat, with a sweet snub nose and cupid's bow lips. Pale freckles across her nose and cheeks. A mellifluous, honey-smooth voice.

"Sadie," said Dani. And then, realizing that she probably needed to say more than that: "What are you doing here?"

"My dad got transferred back to his old job." Sadie hugged herself like she was cold, even though she was wearing a jean jacket over her Smoky the Bear T-shirt. Dani knew she must have picked it out on purpose for tonight, because that was her sense of humor. *Only YOU can prevent forest fires.*

"Oh." Dani had actually imagined this moment many times before—how cool and disinterested she would be. How she'd say something offhanded and clever, and Sadie would realize just how completely she'd moved on. But all that imaginary practice had deserted her, and she couldn't do anything but stare and say again, "Oh."

"Hey, I'm Tomás." He leaned down to shake her hand, though thankfully he did not abandon Dani on her perch. This manufactured distance between her and Sadie May was the only thing keeping her even somewhat coherent.

"Hi, I'm Sadie. I used to live down the road from Dani when we were kids."

"Cool," said Tomás. "Welcome back."

Dani sensed the curious glance he gave her. She'd never mentioned Sadie to him before. That was on purpose.

"Thanks." Sadie's expression had tilted into curiosity as she surveyed Dani. "Um, well, Lori Chang invited me tonight. Her mom works with my dad."

Dani had to take a sip to stop herself from saying *Oh* again.

"Cool," repeated Tomás. He was eyeing Dani more obviously now, clearly waiting for her to say something. "Lori's nice."

"Yeah." Sadie fiddled with her jacket cuff. "So, um, Dani, could I talk to you for a second?"

"No problem," said Tomás brightly. "I'll catch up with you guys later." He slid down from the hood of the truck. Dani tried to grab his shirt and keep him in place, but she wasn't quick enough. Tomás blended back into the noisome crowd, and Dani found herself alone with her ex-best friend.

"I wanted to let you know I was in town, but I didn't have your number," Sadie said, scuffing the toe of her Converse against the ground.

"Yeah," Dani said. Her dreams of wit and nonchalance were rapidly going up in smoke, as she seemed incapable of saying anything containing more than one syllable. She briefly considered rolling off the truck and fleeing into the woods to live a life of solitude, free forever from the horrible awkwardness of social interactions.

There would be a certain poetic justice to that. Four years ago, it had been Sadie fleeing the scene of adolescent angst, leaving Dani stunned and confused, her lips still tingling from her first kiss. Sadie had left without even a goodbye back then, and now here she was, wanting to talk. But Dani decidedly did not want to talk. She *had* moved on, even if her brain was having trouble expressing that. She didn't care that Sadie was back in town, and she didn't care what Sadie had to say about that impetuous kiss, or why Sadie had left without even saying goodbye.

"Look, I just wanted to say—" Sadie began, but Dani cut in.

"I have to go. Maybe we can talk later." Her tone gave no indication that that was likely. Sadie's bewildered expression made her feel a *little* guilty, so she added, "Sorry."

"Oh, um, I guess." Sadie looked like she wanted to keep going, but Dani didn't give her a chance. She hopped to the ground and headed for her car, which she'd parked outside the circle with a few other stragglers. Sadie thankfully didn't follow.

She was digging the keys to the Jeep out of her pocket when Tomás caught up with her.

"Hang on," he said, putting his hand on the door. "If you're deserting our end-of-year bash, you'd better have a good explanation."

Dani couldn't help the resulting tight smile, though it didn't exactly match any of the feelings roiling around in her stomach. At least the odd tingling sensation had dissipated.

"I'm leaving because I don't want to stay," she said, removing his hand. "But it's cute that you think you could stop me."

Tomás didn't argue with her. He was well aware of the hours she spent on the training mat with Eden, even if he didn't know the real reason behind it. As far as he knew, the Riveras were just really into mixed martial arts.

"Are you okay?" he asked, more serious now.

"I'm fine, I just want to go home," Dani said, and then, because he was still staring expectantly: "Sadie and I—it's complicated. We didn't really part on good terms when we were kids."

"Does she know that? Because she seemed pretty keen to talk to you."

"I really can't do this right now." She mashed the unlock button and opened the door. "Okay?"

"Okay." He didn't look appeased, but he didn't press it any further. "See you tomorrow?"

"Bright and early." She smiled gratefully at him and handed him her mostly full Smirnoff bottle, glad that she hadn't gone for anything stronger. "Bye."

She hopped into the Jeep and buckled up. He waved her off with his soda can before heading back into the circle. Dani took a deep breath, put the Jeep into drive, and started down the wheel-beaten track toward the road.

She made it about halfway home, windows down, music blasting, resolutely thinking of anything but Sadie, before remembering the dinner party.

"Shit." She slapped the steering wheel and tapped the brake reflexively. The winding back road she was on didn't have much in the way of convenient side attractions. No late-night coffee shops or Wal-Marts in which to pass some time. Only towering pine trees and the occasional gap through which, during the day, she would have had a stellar view of the Smokies, but at night was only blackness with a few tiny, hazy lights twinkling here and there. But there was no way she was going home this early. Mom and Dad would never let her escape to her bedroom. She'd have to glad-hand the guests, who were supposedly important sorcerers, though she doubted they could be all that important if they were wining and dining with dragon slayers. Sorcerers weren't exactly known for being chummy with anyone they considered inferior— i.e. everyone.

As if in answer to her distress, a sign appeared in her headlights. SCENIC VIEW — 0.4 MILES. Perfect.

She turned down the side road it indicated and bumped along

the rutted gravel until she reached a wide open area, also gravel. There was a long empty space along the line of trees where cars could be parked, and then a huge semicircle of railing overlooking the edge of a drop-off. She thought she could see a few of those binocular machines you drop quarters into, but otherwise the spot was barren.

She made sure her doors were locked and her taser—which her parents had bought her at the same time she got her driver's license—was on hand. Parking alone in a deserted clearing in the dark wasn't exactly the smartest move, but on the other hand, she was just as likely to be a target in a Wal-Mart parking lot, so there didn't seem to be any point in worrying about it.

For a while she just sat there, her seat leaned back slightly, listening to one of her favorite playlists and staring at the circus of insects illuminated by her headlights. How could Sadie do this to her? As if the way she'd left things in sixth grade hadn't been enough, now she had to show up again with no warning and blind-side Dani at what had been a perfectly nice party. If Dani hadn't run off, would she have apologized? Or maybe she would have just tried to pretend that the elephant in the room didn't exist.

Dani wasn't even sure which she would have preferred.

The tingling in her chest started again, and now she wondered if it had something to do with Sadie. But the longer she sat there, the less it felt like some kind of emotional reaction, and the more it felt like something visceral. Not painful, exactly, but certainly not normal.

Heart attack? She tried in vain to remember the symptoms they'd learned from health class. Pain in the left arm was the most obvious, but hadn't Mr. Griggs said something about women experiencing different symptoms? Could a seventeen-year-old even have a heart attack?

Without knowing why, she threw open the door and stepped out of the Jeep. The tingling didn't fade, but she did feel like she could breathe a little better outside. With the taser still clutched in her right hand, she walked closer to the overlook, trying to distract herself by orienting her position on a mental terrain map like her dad had taught her. She was facing west right now. Probably this spot was popular for spectacular sunsets.

The tingling was getting worse, just shy of painful. And now there was a whooshing sound in her ears—wait, no, that was coming from somewhere above her head. Another blast of hot wind hit her, seeming to originate from everywhere and nowhere, carrying with it a faint scent like burning coals. Something crunched the gravel behind her.

Dani whirled. Her brain refused to process a full picture, instead giving her flashes like rapid camera shots.

Yellow glow of headlights. Claws. Teeth. Gray scales. Trailing smoke. The leathery crinkle of wings. The hypnotic sway of a razor-sharp tail. Violet eyes, catlike and gleaming.

A dragon.

"Shit," said Dani.

FOUR

Dani didn't have time for more cursing, because in the next second that razor-sharp tail was whipping toward her chest. Her reflexes took over where her thoughts left off, though her evasive maneuver was less of an epic Matrix-style back bend and more of an epic fall—flat onto her back. For a split second she was dazed, barely registering the hiss and blur of the tail above. The gravel hurt so much more than the training room floor.

Then came Eden's voice in her head. *Move.*

Dani rolled to her feet and flung herself away from another swipe of the tail. She turned to face the dragon, some part of her still lost in the surrealism of the moment. It was like the world was suddenly underwater, every object wavering and distorted, every movement sluggish in the turbid shadows. There were so many questions—*where did it come from, what is it doing here, why did it follow me*—but they floated out of reach, distant and irrelevant. That sensation in her chest was fizzing and crackling with its own energy, somehow both painful and exhilarating.

The dragon's eyes, bright and cold as amethyst, glowed like a cat's in the Jeep's headlights as it watched her. It was small for a dragon—about the size of the Jeep, though rangier, with knobbly legs and a long, sinuous neck. That tail, edged with scales as sharp as knives, hovered at the ready, curving slightly like a scorpion's. And the scales were the least of her concerns. Her parents had been diligent in teaching her every dangerous aspect of a dragon's anatomy, and so she knew one brush of the tail would send enough volts of electricity through her body to fry every one of her internal organs.

Dani dared a single glance back, judging her distance to the Jeep. Close enough to make a run for it. Not close enough to be certain she would make it. And even if she did, she was pretty sure one swipe of its tail could bust through the windshield. And dragon flame was more than hot enough to melt the tires.

She gripped the taser more tightly in her palm. Not much, but at least it was something. The tire iron in the trunk would have been better. Like she'd told Eden just a few hours ago — it felt like years now — the dragon wouldn't be waiting for her to fetch a better weapon.

She slid her feet into a more solid stance, stubbornly holding the creature's gaze. That seemed important somehow. It started to move slowly, carefully, the tendons and muscles in its body flexing and rippling. Dani moved with it, sideways steps, to maintain the same distance between them. It felt strangely like the opening of a sparring match, circling each other, feeling each other out. The dragon's nostrils flared, and Dani wondered if it could smell fear.

She was so tense, so excruciatingly tuned in to its every move, that when the dragon finally charged, she sprang into motion with something like relief. She spun to the side, throwing out her arm as she went to ram the sizzling taser into its neck. She wasn't sure how much damage, if any, she caused, because in the next heartbeat she had to dive to miss the tail again. This time she landed on her shoulder and rolled back to her feet in one motion. Jagged pain lanced up the side of her body, and for a second she thought she'd been struck, but it was just that damn gravel.

Stay on your feet, came Eden's voice again. Dani rolled her eyes out of habit.

The dragon came at her again, and Dani realized too late that it had backed her against the front of the Jeep. She planted one foot on the front bumper and propelled herself onto the hood, flattening herself against the windshield as the dragon rammed into the front of the vehicle. She winced at the *crunch* of metal, then jumped to the side to avoid another tail swipe. No shattering glass or lick of flame. That seemed like a stroke of luck.

She decided to ignore the echo of Eden's advice in her head, as usual, and dropped to the ground again. She rolled under the Jeep as the dragon stalked around, searching for her. She held her breath as the giant reptilian claws crept surprisingly softly across the ground. She couldn't play hide-and-seek with this monster all night. Her best chance was to get to the driver's side and get the hell out of here. The road was narrow. The dragon's wingspan wouldn't let it fly easily behind her, and with the crowded trees it probably wouldn't be able to get close enough to strike from above. And her phone was on the passenger seat. Her parents would know what to do.

She did a sideways army crawl until she was right at the edge of the Jeep, then rolled out onto her back. She almost made it to her feet before finding herself flattened again. Faster than she could blink, faster than she would have thought possible, the dragon had leapt over the Jeep and landed on top of her. There were claws inches from her shoulders, and she could feel the pulsating heat from its scaly body engulf her like a furnace. Its face, somehow both reptilian and feline, prehistoric and mythical, took up every inch of her vision. Breath as scorching as a desert wind billowed over her, and deep in the back of its throat she saw a blue flare like a distant, dying star.

She threw up her hand, realizing too late that at some point she'd lost her grip on the taser. Instead her palm smacked uselessly against the base of its throat. It burned. And burned. And *burned*.

That tingling in her chest exploded into a cataclysmic blaze, shooting through her veins and muscles and sinews. Her blood burned like a river of fire. Her consciousness flew apart at the seams, and for a split second, she thought she could see the infinite cosmos, sprawling outward like an ocean of light and dark. She could see herself: so tiny in the midst of it, yet so clear and vivid on the gravel, her hair matted with sweat and dirt, her eyes wide. Then she blinked and was herself again. The gravel was digging into her back. The aching confines of her own body were oddly comforting.

She sat up. Realized slowly that the dragon was no longer on top of her. He was several feet away, crouched and wary. He'd felt it too. Somehow she knew that much. Only, for him, the boundless universe had spiraled inward, folding itself into the precious space of a moment; into the impossible complexity of a single human heart, beating steadily and relentlessly toward its own end.

Why do I know that?

She knew his name too. An ancient name, too intricate to be captured by any human language. But she searched the recesses of her mind, like it was a question with an answer that she'd learned long ago, and finally the name coalesced into something she could give voice to.

"Nox," she said.

A shudder ran through him. His pupils were dilated, so large that the black nearly swallowed the irises. She waited, not sure what she was waiting for, not sure why she wasn't being burned to a crisp at this moment or why she suddenly felt like that wasn't even a possibility. Nox crouched even lower, like he was readying himself to pounce, but instead he launched himself straight up, his wings unfurling and beating at the air with impossible ease for a creature so large. Dragon bones were harder than human bones, Dani remembered from her father's careful lectures. Strong as steel, but hollow, like a bird's.

The windstorm from Nox's wings hurled dust and grit into her face, and she threw her arms up to shield herself. By the time she had lowered them, she was alone on the overlook.

The dinner party had broken up by the time she got home. It was only ten thirty, and technically she had a curfew of midnight—not that her parents would've waited up for her, anyway—but Dani was bruised and bloodied with scrapes, and all she wanted was a hot shower and a cool pillow. Her right hand, which she was certain should've had second-degree burns, was undamaged.

Nox. The dragon's name was Nox, and he wasn't her enemy. Why did she think that? Why was she so bone-deep sure? He'd come out of nowhere and tried to kill her. He was a dragon, for Christ's sake, not a stray cat. The Riveras had been hunting dragons for generations now. She could think of at least four distant relatives off the top of her head who'd lost their lives to one of those wickedly sharp tails, one of those diamond-bright balls of flame.

Everything was wrong, but she was tired of thinking about it. So instead she stopped thinking, threw the Jeep into park, and shuffled into the house. There was a huge dent in the front of the Jeep that she would have to explain somehow. That was Future Dani's problem.

The first floor of the house was dark, though she could hear the murmur of voices and creak of footsteps overhead. Everyone was getting ready for bed. She caught a whiff of something savory and drifted into the kitchen to scavenge for leftovers. She ate cold pasta straight from a Tupperware container until the roar in her stomach had settled into a low grumble, then ripped off a chunk of French bread from the loaf that had been left half-covered on the counter.

She polished off the bread in her room while examining her battle wounds in the mirror. All in all, nothing too bad. Nothing that couldn't be explained away by training with Eden or tripping over a log at the bonfire. It took Dani a few seconds to realize that she was thinking up excuses because she wasn't planning on telling her parents what had happened earlier that night. That realization, more than anything else, was what made her world feel like it had slanted sideways—like from this moment on, something had irreversibly shifted, and she would never be able to regain her footing, no matter how hard she tried.

Something else she really, really didn't want to think about.

"I'll tell them in the morning," she told her reflection sternly. Not a very convincing lie, but it at least eased her mind enough to relax—for now. She checked to make sure Eden was shut in her room and then darted down the hall to the safety of the bathroom. After a long shower, bundled up in her terry-cloth robe and fuzzy slippers, she started to feel almost normal. Almost like she could crawl into bed and wake up tomorrow and realize this had all been a dream. Someone had spiked her drink at the party, and she'd spent all night having a bad trip.

She changed into pajamas, took a couple ibuprofen, and slid under the covers. She was just reaching to turn off her bedside lamp when there was a light knock on the door.

"Come in."

Eden was in pajamas too, her long hair pulled back in a low ponytail. Her makeup had been scrubbed away, leaving her face shiny in the lamplight, but even without the makeup her rosy brown complexion was smooth and unblemished. She'd inherited their mother's perfect skin. Dani was luckier than some of the girls in her grade, but she'd still spent the past couple years battling random splotches of acne that gleefully exploded on her face whenever it was most inconvenient.

"How was the bonfire?" Eden asked, coming to sit cross-legged on the foot of the bed. These late-night talks were something they still did occasionally, though not as often as when they were kids.

"It was fine, I guess." At least until the dragon showed up.

"You guess?" Eden scrutinized her, missing nothing, as per usual. "What's wrong? What happened?"

"Nothing," Dani said, but even she knew she wasn't being convincing. "I said, it was fine."

"Then why do you look like death?"

"Wow, thanks a lot."

"Seriously." Eden leaned forward and caught Dani's eye. "Tell me what's wrong."

Dani fidgeted uncomfortably, somehow both annoyed and relieved that Eden could still read her so easily. She thought about telling her the truth. A few years ago, she wouldn't have hesitated for a second. She'd grown up sharing everything with her sister: every secret, every hope, every heartbreak. Eden knew about the garden snake she'd kept as a pet under her bed for two weeks when she was ten, and Eden had been the one to help her tearfully release it back into the wild when she'd realized that snakes don't actually like living in shoeboxes. Eden knew about the failed spelling test she'd forged her parents' signature on in the sixth grade. Eden was the one who'd stayed up with her all night building a mousetrap car for that big science project she'd forgotten about. Eden was the only person she'd told about kissing Sadie. Eden was the first person she'd come out to.

But the years had grown between them, a subtle tangle of

changing perspectives and priorities. Dani could feel it, and she suspected that Eden could too. Now there was a lot they didn't tell each other. This dragon, and the strange, terrible connection that had been forged when she touched him, would be one of those secrets. At least for now—until she had more time to think, to figure it out for herself.

"Sadie is back," she said, since she knew Eden would keep hounding her until she gave her a reason. Too bad Sadie was officially the least of her problems now.

"Really?" Eden's eyebrows shot up.

"Yeah. Her dad's job transferred him back here."

"Did you guys talk?"

Dani's cheeks flushed. Admitting she hadn't would mean explaining that she had fled the scene, and Eden wouldn't be able to resist giving her a lecture on how immature that was.

"There was a lot going on," she said with a half-hearted shrug. "It's whatever. I don't really care. How was dinner?"

Eden watched her for a couple seconds, just to make sure Dani knew she hadn't been fooled, then gave her own shrug.

"It was whatever," she said with a little smile. But she was clearly too starstruck to keep up the mock ambivalence. "You *do* realize who Calla Thorn and Alder De Lange are, right? I still can't believe you decided to go to that stupid party instead."

Dani opted to ignore the slight to her social calendar.

"Calla is like, the queen of the sorcerers or something, right?"

"High sorcerer."

"Same difference."

Sorcerers, who kept to themselves in their secret castle, playing with their magic or whatever, had never been of much concern to Dani. It wasn't like they were carting humans off to feast on them, like dragons were. Supposedly sorcerers hated dragons too, but Dani didn't see any of *them* training for hours every day like she and Eden did, or risking their necks like her parents did, to fight the threat. Actually, she'd never even seen a sorcerer — at least, not that she knew of.

For a moment, she wished that she had stayed for dinner after all. No Sadie. No dragon. She could've had a nice, normal night playing charades with immortal sorcerers.

The errant thought made her want to laugh. Eden caught her expression, misjudged it.

"They're not a joke. It's a big deal that they came here tonight."

Dani tried to school her features. Whenever the topic of sorcery came up, it was clear that Eden was more enamored of magic than the typical slayer. Their parents had always taught them that magic was part and parcel of dragons — best left alone. But ever since they were kids, Eden had been drawn to the wild mystery of it, though she would never admit as much.

"Why *did* they come, anyway?" Dani asked.

Eden shrugged again. The earnestness in her features had slid into something more reluctant, more cagey.

"What?" Dani asked with a twinge of worry.

"Hard to say." There was a minuscule hesitation. "Mom and Dad don't really trust them. It was something to do with the Lowrys, but I don't know what. I guess there's bad blood between the sorcerers and the slayers."

There weren't many serious slayers left, and they were spread out all over the globe, though her family's closest connections were to the ones in the Americas. The last time Dani had seen any of them was six years ago at the funeral of Jacob and Aaron Lowry. She had been too young to truly comprehend the tragic circumstances, and so for Dani it was a memory awash with the other slayers' swaggering and tall tales, and the sour hard candies that

Jaime Cruz, one of her mother's oldest friends, had snuck her when no one was looking. That was the first time she remembered genuinely wanting to take up the family profession. To be one of them.

It wasn't until she was older and had accidentally made another kid cry by telling him about the dragons that were hiding in the mountains and deserts, and her parents had sat her down and explained to her the importance of family secrets, that Dani had realized being one of them would necessitate giving up everything else.

"What were they like—Calla and Alder?" Dani asked.

Eden's smug grin slid back into place. "If you wanted to know that, you should have been here to meet them."

Dani tried to kick her under the covers, but she couldn't quite reach. "If you're done gloating, I need sleep. I've got work in the morning."

Eden hopped off the bed. "You know, it would be a better use of your time to spend your summer training with me."

"Good night," Dani said pointedly.

"Good night." For once, Eden didn't push her case. By now she had probably figured out it was a lost cause. She left and shut the door behind her.

Dani clicked off her bedside lamp and flopped back onto her pillow. The conversation had left her vaguely unsettled, but she didn't know if that was because of what had been said or what had not. For a long time, she stared at the darkness overhead, trying and failing to not think about Nox, about the burn of his scales against her palm, about the strange understanding in his violet eyes. Eventually, she drifted off.

FIVE

Eden woke an hour before her alarm, dry-mouthed and groggy but unable to fall back asleep. She rolled out of bed, pulling the elastic from her wrist to twist her hair into a sloppy bun. Using the water bottle she kept by her bed, she swallowed her medication, then pulled on a sweatshirt over her pajamas and padded down the stairs. The persistent summer heat had already settled into the air outside, but her parents kept the air conditioning on so high at night that the bill must have been astronomical. Even after his years in Georgia and then here in Tennessee, James Rivera still had Scotland in his blood, and the eighty-something-degree summers were anathema to him.

Eden poked around the fridge for a while before deciding on a bowl of cereal for breakfast. She carried it into the den, where she found her dad in his favorite armchair, already dressed and shaved and tapping away on his laptop. In his deep concentration, his glasses had slipped to the end of his nose and he hadn't bothered to fix them.

"Good morning." Eden tucked her legs beneath her on the couch and dug into her cereal. Her father made a faint sound of acknowledgment that was his version of a greeting, engrossed as he was in his work. During the year, he taught a few online courses for his alma mater, but most of his energy in the past few years had been dedicated to consulting jobs for various forestry and preservation programs across the southeast. Their interests dovetailed neatly with the family business and his need to keep a close eye on wildfires, drought, and migratory patterns that could indicate dragon activity. Just last year he had tracked a small dragon to within a mile of its lair, but by the time a few slayers had narrowed down the location of the cave, cloistered in the upper crags of Mount Cheaha in Alabama, the dragon had cleared out.

Eden munched on her breakfast, content with the silence until she'd scraped up the last of the flakes from the bottom. Finally she set the bowl aside and watched her father work. The questions that had been plaguing her since the night before began to take firm shape, weighing on her tongue.

"Dad?"

"Hmm?" He didn't quite manage to tear his eyes from the screen.

"What happened in New Mexico? To the Lowrys?"

That snagged his gaze away. He blinked at her. She noticed that his eyes were reddish behind his glasses, and wondered if it was allergies or a bad night's sleep.

"Jacob and Aaron were killed by a dragon, honey. You know that."

She'd been at the funeral, so of course she knew that much. She'd been thirteen, and the funeral itself had been a short, solemn affair, in the tradition of slayers. Maria Lowry—her dark hair swept into a messy bun, her black dress powdered with flour from all the baking she'd insisted on doing that morning—had given the ashes of her husband and son to the desert's west wind. After five minutes of silence, broken only by Maria's muted sobs and the scream of a hawk overhead, they had all piled into their assortment of trucks and SUVs and driven back to the sprawling Perez homestead, where Maria's brothers and sister lived in their own houses with their families. Eden had wondered if Maria would move back to live with them, or if she would stay in her own home, alone now.

The potluck of barbecue, tacos, grilled corn, and Maria's

famous empanadas had been lively, drowned with beer and loud stories about the deceased's exploits. Children ran around barefoot in their funeral clothes, kicking a soccer ball and shrieking in fake terror when one of the slayers started throwing them into the warm, murky pond. Dani had been one of the unfortunates— though Eden had a strong suspicion she'd jumped in on her own— but her parents hadn't cared. Eden stuck close to them and listened to the stories as her mother's calloused fingers twisted idly through her hair, sending calming tingles down her neck and spine.

"But what does that have to do with the sorcerers?" she asked. "At dinner last night, you said that after New Mexico, we couldn't trust them."

Eden didn't think there had been any sorcerers present at the funeral, but they weren't always easy to spot if they didn't want to be seen.

"There was a sorcerer there, when they died," James said, after a long moment of deliberation. "He was apparently hunting the same dragon. Most people think he could have helped Jacob and Aaron, but chose not to."

"Most people?"

"Well, no one can really know for sure what happened that day." He sighed and hit a few keys on the laptop, but she'd clearly ruined his focus.

"Do you not trust Calla and Alder?"

He gave her a rueful smile.

"I find it hard to trust anyone who can do the things they can do. Sorcerers are . . . tricky."

Eden took a few seconds to mull that over. "Tricky" felt like an understatement when it came to the magic sorcerers could wield, but that magic was also the only surefire defense against dragons. Well-trained slayers could hold their own against the beasts, but sorcerers were infinitely better equipped, just by virtue of what they were. It was something Eden often thought about after a hard day's training. How incredible it must be, to carry the same magic as dragons in your veins, to be able to use that against them. How empowering it must be, to know that burns and other battle wounds were the insignificant trappings of mortality; to never be stuck in your own anxious mind, panic driving you to certainty that every cut and scrape would somehow spell your demise.

How freeing it must be, to know that death and failure are only words, and that your destiny is as infinite as you are.

"So are you going to let Dani go to Stonecrest?" she asked, trying to keep any hint of bitterness out of her tone.

"I don't know. We don't even know if she wants to go. Haven't had a chance to talk to her yet."

Footsteps on the stairs; Analisa breezed into the room in her typical uniform of running pants and an oversized T-shirt.

"Morning!" she announced. "You ready, James?"

James grunted in the affirmative and closed the laptop. He stood, stretching his arms over his head.

"Where are you going?" Eden asked.

"We have to drop the Jeep at the garage," said Analisa. "Apparently your sister had a little run-in with a utility pole last night."

"*What.*"

"Relax, we've already given her the third degree, so I don't want to hear you giving her grief."

"Maybe a little grief," James added. "It's not going to be cheap to fix."

"Teenagers have accidents," Analisa said firmly. "The circle of life and all that."

"I don't think that applies here," Eden said. She wasn't surprised that her parents weren't more worked up about it. Seeing as she and Dani spent their days training to fight literal dragons, a minor car accident was on par with a paper cut in the grand scheme of things.

"Want to come with?" her father asked, checking his pocket for his wallet. "We could stop for ice cream on the way back."

Eden was tempted, but shook her head.

"I've got some reading to get done for my comp lit course."

"All work and no play—"

"—Means I pass my courses and don't waste your tuition money," Eden finished with a smile.

"I think we've accidentally raised a sensible adult," Analisa told her husband as she steered him to the door. "Against all odds."

Eden trailed after them to the porch. The dent in the front of the Jeep didn't look as bad as she'd imagined, but it was definitely more than a tap. She wondered how Dani had managed to run into a pole. There had probably been a lot of alcohol at the bonfire, but if her parents had suspected that to be the culprit, they wouldn't be nearly as forgiving. Risky behavior was part of being a Rivera, but downright recklessness—and putting others at risk—was unacceptable. Dani had probably been distracted. Focus had always been a problem of hers.

Her father took the Jeep, and her mother followed in the silver 4Runner that had been James and Analisa's gift to themselves two Christmases ago. Eden waved them off. She had to pull off her hoodie before they'd even disappeared down the driveway, the morning was already so muggy. She wandered back inside, fully intending to pick up her reading, but instead found herself reorganizing her closet—which, she reasoned, had been on her to-do list for months, so it didn't count as procrastinating. Madame Bovary would still be there in an hour.

Elbow-deep in a pile of winter clothes that had never been

properly stored away, with a "Productive Morning" playlist blasting on her laptop, it took Eden a while to realize the insistent buzzing in the back of her mind was her phone on the bedside table. She scooped it up too late, realizing she'd already missed three calls from her aunt. She called back. If it had been her mother, she would have been anxious that something was wrong, but Frankie had never gotten the hang of texting or voicemail. Her strategy was usually to call until someone picked up. The current family record was eighteen calls to Analisa during a movie.

"Eden," her aunt declared into the phone in lieu of a greeting.

"Hi, Frankie. What's up?"

"What are you doing right now?"

Eden eyed the pile of sweaters and boots.

"Schoolwork."

"Well, stop it. I need your help."

"With what?"

"My cat, Penelope. She's stuck in a tree."

Eden laughed, but there was only silence on the other end.

"Wait, are you serious?" she asked.

"That's what I said to Penelope when I found her this morning. Up a tree."

"Are you sure she's stuck?"

"It's been hours, and she just keeps meowing. A couple times she seemed like she was trying to climb down, but you know what a little shit she is. It took her months to figure out how the cat door worked."

"Did you call Dani? Tree-climbing is more her area of expertise."

"No, I'm calling you," Frankie said, sounding mildly exasperated now. "Can you come? Now?"

Eden felt a ripple of satisfaction at that reply.

"Okay, I'll just—oh, wait—" She had just remembered that both of the cars were gone.

"What?" Frankie asked, the word carrying an extra note of stress.

"Nothing, it's fine," Eden amended. "I'll be there as soon as I can."

She hung up and sat down on the bed, weighing her options. The mechanic they used was almost an hour away, so her parents wouldn't be home for a while. Eden scrolled through her contacts before realizing that she really didn't have any friends nearby—at least, not the sort of friends you could randomly call for a favor. In the end, she opened up the Uber app and typed in her aunt's address. Frankie lived about half an hour away, but Eden had a fair bit of money saved up from the online tutoring she had done over the past year. The app spent an interminable amount of time searching for a driver. Folks didn't have much use for ridesharing in the middle of nowhere, especially not on a Saturday morning. Finally the app informed her that her driver was twenty minutes away.

She hopped up and got dressed. She had a feeling Frankie would call when she was halfway there to tell her Penelope had magically regained her ability to climb, but it had been a while since she'd seen her aunt anyway. And it occurred to her that Frankie—who had not gone into the family business per se, but had still managed to keep her finger on its pulse—might be able to answer some more questions that she had about the sorcerers.

Eden pulled on her tennis shoes, grabbed her bag, and left through the front door. Their driveway was notoriously difficult to find, so she decided it would be better to wait for the driver by the mailbox. Even in the dappled shade of the drive, she'd worked up a sheen of sweat by the time she reached the road. Summer had well and truly arrived.

She watched the little car on her phone inch ever closer to her location and pondered the need for her own vehicle — one that she did not have to share with Dani. She was just envisioning herself in something black and sleek, like Calla and Alder had arrived in the night before, when a bright orange eyesore of a car slowed to a stop in front of her.

"Eden?" the driver asked through the lowered window.

She nodded, double-checked the car's license plate against her app, and slid into the back seat.

"Hi," she said, barely glancing up as she settled herself in. The car smelled strongly of cheap air freshener with a hint of something sweet and tangy, like candy.

"Eden Rivera," the driver said as he pulled back onto the road. It took her a second to realize he wasn't just reaffirming her identity, and that he was eyeing her in his rearview mirror. Another second for her to match up those liquid brown eyes and dimpled grin to her memory.

"Nate?" she asked. "Oh my god, I didn't even — how are you?"

She was more surprised than pleased — which wasn't to say she was displeased, exactly. She had nothing against Nate Harris, who had been one of her class's star athletes all through high school. He had been less obnoxious than most of his friends, although she probably wouldn't even have known that much about him if they hadn't happened to be paired up as lab partners in chemistry during their last semester. Eden hadn't gone out of her way to be antisocial at school, but it was hard to balance any extracurricular activities without losing focus on her training, and so eventually she'd given up on everything but the required credits to graduate.

"You know, living the dream," he said, gesturing vaguely with one hand. He was still as broad-shouldered and trim as he'd been last year, though he'd let his curly Afro grow out longer. In a perfectly fitted white T-shirt and dark jeans, he had a look of easy coolness that made Eden tug self-consciously at her own faded T-shirt, which was wrinkly and two sizes too big. She'd been in too much of a hurry to put together a decent outfit. At least the stubble on her legs was only a day and a half old.

"You living around here?" she asked. Second on the list of questions that you were societally obligated to ask former classmates when trapped in small talk with them.

"For now. I took some classes at the community college this year, but I'm starting at Auburn in the fall."

"That's cool." She was afraid that sounded trite, but couldn't think of a follow-up. It had been a while since she'd had to interact with one of her peers.

If Nate sensed the awkward vibe she was emanating, he didn't let on. He flashed her more dimples in the mirror.

"What about you?"

"Oh, same."

"You're going to Auburn?"

"No! I mean—the community college—well, actually I'm taking classes online. It's not—I mean, I don't know if I—" She forcibly cut herself off mid-ramble. He was chuckling as they rolled to a stop at a traffic light.

"Chill out, Rivera. It's not a job interview. There are no wrong answers."

Eden had to resist the urge to bury her face into her hands. Dear god, when had she lost all ability to function like a normal human being? He wasn't *that* cute. Not that it mattered how cute he was. Not that she would even notice something like that. She had more important things on her mind. Dragons, sorcerers, cats in trees. No time for dimples and raging hormones.

She took a slow breath. Nate saved her from having to come up with a face-saving reply.

"You still doing that mountaineering club thing?"

It took her a couple seconds to figure out what he was talking about. She'd forgotten that in high school she'd told people she was a very dedicated member of a mountaineering club that demanded most of her afterschool hours. It was a convenient way to get out of invitations and activities she didn't care about. And it had the bonus of being a partial truth: she did spend a lot of time on the rock wall.

"Yeah," she said.

She didn't relish lying to people, but unlike her sister, who attempted an impossible balancing act between her "normal" life and her life as a slayer, Eden had just decided to forgo the normal part. She had a hard time thinking about prom and sports and friends when she knew about the world of magic and dragons that existed just outside human possibility, when she knew about the danger that lurked in deserts and caves and jungles, just outside of civilization's reach.

The wars of Tempus Dracones were over by the end of the medieval era, well before the advent of photography. Thanks to the work of dedicated slayers, by the eighteenth century, the remaining dragons had been driven into hiding. Their skill in that regard was both a blessing and a curse. On one hand, no one had ever captured an image that offered more proof of dragonkind's existence than that of Bigfoot or the Loch Ness Monster—at least, no one who had survived to share their findings—so humans were safe from the panic that a real live dragon would ignite. On the other hand, dragons were almost impossible to track, even for experts like her parents. They were fast and silent in flight, with feline stealth despite their size, and possessed the ability to magically disguise their dwellings.

Her great-grandparents on her mother's side had immigrated from Mexico, in response to the surplus of dragons and dearth of slayers in the southwest United States. They'd built an expansive network of allies and hunted dragons through the deserts and Badlands, until the Rivera name was as synonymous with dragon slaying in the United States as it was in Mexico. Her grandparents had moved to Tennessee as a young couple on the tail of a dragon they felt certain was hiding somewhere in the Smokies, but even after a lifetime they had never managed to hunt it down. Whenever a report surfaced of a missing hiker or an inexplicable plane crash in the area, Analisa and James Rivera started the hunt anew, but still without success. That was the reason Eden couldn't just give herself over to a carefree life. Dragons were out there, right under everyone's noses, and until the last one was dead, no one was safe.

Of course, that didn't mean it was always easy to be the outsider. The girl with no friends and no life outside her family.

Nate was tapping his fingers on the wheel, and she caught a glimpse of his expression in the mirror. His mouth was stretched tight, as if suppressing another laugh.

"What?" She couldn't help but smooth a hand over her ponytail, like maybe she'd sprouted antennae or something.

"Nothing. Just . . . I mean, you know everyone thought you were in some kind of cult, right?"

Dani had told her the same thing, but Eden had assumed Dani was just trying to trick her into spending less time training.

"I'm not in a cult." It came out terser than she'd intended. She crossed her arms and slumped a little in the seat, suddenly wishing she was on the rock wall instead. It was a simpler place, and she knew exactly what she was doing there.

"That's exactly what someone in a cult would say." He waggled his eyebrows at her.

Eden just looked out the window.

"Oh, come on," he said. "I'm just messing with you. Not *every-one* thought you were in a cult. I didn't."

"I don't care if you did or not," she replied lightly.

"Now you're pissed at me," he said with a rueful sigh. "I never could stay on your good side."

"What's that supposed to mean?"

"Remember when I dropped that beaker in Ms. Word's class? You about took my head off in front of everyone, and I couldn't even get you to look at me for a week after."

"Now wait a minute," Eden said, leaning forward between the front seats. "You dropped that beaker because you were showing off for Angela and her friends, and it meant we had to stay late to do the experiment over again. I had every right to be mad."

"When you put it like that, it makes it much harder for me to play the innocent victim," he said. There was another smile playing at the corner of his lips.

Eden felt her own mouth tugging upwards into a grin, and she sat back. He'd always been able to do that. Diffuse any bad mood with a few words. That week she'd spent ignoring him had been more challenging than any of her slayer training that year.

"You're something else," she said, which was what her mother always told Dani when she was being a pill.

"*I'm the only one of me,*" he said. "*Baby, that's the fun of me.*"

"That's a Taylor Swift song."

"What can I say? *I'm just a small-town boy, born and raised in South Detroit—*"

"And that's Journey."

"*Tell me something, do I make you feel the way that I do? I been uptight, you got me right, I'm back into my groove.*"

"Amber Mark," she said, amused. "You aren't going to win this game, Harris."

"Listen to a lot of music on the sides of mountains, do you?"

"Nothing better to do up there."

"*I like high chances that I might lose. I like it all on the edge just like you.*"

"Blackway."

"With?"

"Black Caviar."

"Damn, thought I had you with that one." He shook his head, his soft dark curls shivering with the movement. "I approve of your taste in music."

"Don't you mean *your* taste in music?"

"We may be out of high school, but I'm still not going to admit to liking Taylor Swift."

"Too bad. I might have to take a star off your review for that."

He laughed again, a warm, fulsome sound that seemed to rumble from deep inside him. It filled Eden up with a tingling feeling, and she realized she was smiling.

The rest of the drive flew past in a blur of jokes and band recommendations. When the phone mounted on Nate's dashboard announced that they had arrived, Eden blinked in astonishment to find herself in her aunt's driveway.

"Well, thanks for the ride," she said. For some reason, her self-consciousness from before was flooding back. "It was good seeing you again. Have fun at Auburn."

He twisted in his seat to face her.

"Hey, what do you think about—"

Her aunt Frankie chose that moment to come barreling out of the front door, draped in something flowing and flowery, her dark hair streaming behind her. Her arms were outstretched like she was a diva in an opera, greeting her long-lost lover on a windswept moor.

"Oh lord," muttered Eden under her breath, and she climbed out of the car to greet her.

"My favorite eldest niece," Frankie announced to no one in particular, throwing her arms around Eden. "Who's this? Your friend? Hello!" She was already yanking open the driver-side door before Eden could protest.

"Hi, I'm Frankie. I'm the fun aunt. Are you here to help Eden with the cat?"

"No, he's not," Eden hissed.

"I'm Nate," he said cheerily, and to Eden's dismay he hopped out of the car to shake Frankie's hand. "Friendly neighborhood Uber driver."

"You're tall," Frankie informed him, and turned to Eden. "He's tall."

Eden briefly considered crawling back into the back seat to die of embarrassment.

"Where's Penelope?" she asked instead, none-too-gently shoving her aunt back up the driveway. "Thanks again, Nate."

"She's right over here." Frankie led the way across the front yard to the biggest of her three oak trees. "See her?"

Eden followed Frankie's pointing finger and peered through the foliage to see a spot of orange among the green and russet brown. Penelope's perch had to be at least twenty feet up. She eyed the branches nearest the ground and instinctively traced the likely routes upward in her mind's eye.

"Have you tried opening a can of tuna?"

She jumped at the voice by her ear. Nate had followed them over. Just great.

"I actually did," Frankie said. "I set out a whole buffet this morning of everything I could find that I thought might tempt her, but all it did was bring the flies something fierce. The little shit is well and truly stuck."

As if in agreement, Penelope let out a mournful yowl.

"I guess that's where I come in," Eden said. She moved closer to the tree and sized up the distance to the first branch.

"I can give you a boost," Nate offered.

Normally she would have said no on principle, but she wasn't keen on ungracefully struggling her way up alone while he and Frankie watched. Also, the fact that he didn't insist on doing it himself, like she would have expected any other man to do, made her feel strangely generous toward him.

"Thanks," she said, planting her right sneaker into his inter-laced hands and bracing her hand on his shoulder. From the feel of it, he hadn't lost any of his muscle tone from high school athlet-ics. She caught a whiff of shea butter and laundry detergent as he propelled her upward.

She swung herself onto the first branch, took a moment to steady herself, and reached up for the next one.

"Wait!" Frankie called. "Hold on, wait one second." She turned and ran toward the house.

Eden waited, gripping the branch above her with both hands for balance. She pretended to be engrossed in the maze of foliage overhead so that she didn't have to look down at Nate's upturned face. Frankie returned, clutching a pale yellow piece of bunched-up cloth.

"Here, take this with you. I don't know how else to get her down." She shook it out and Eden realized what it was. Nineteen years of training to hunt and slay dragons, and she was climbing a tree to stuff a cat in a pillowcase.

Nate handed it up to her, and she tucked it into her waistband. From there, it was more or less like climbing a ladder, albeit a ladder covered in bark and the occasional bird's nest. Periodically her pulled hamstring protested when she stretched her toes, but that couldn't be helped. Sweat trickled into her eyes and down the back of her neck, making her back itch with heat.

Penelope watched her warily as she neared, tail flicking, eyes narrowed. Eden reached out a tentative hand, and the cat immediately batted it away with a hiss.

"I'm trying to help, you demonic little furball," Eden snapped, too quietly for Frankie to hear. Her aunt would be devastated if she ever found out her favorite eldest niece was more of a dog person.

She tried again, and Penelope let her get so far as a hand on her back before twisting away and jumping to another branch. She meowed plaintively.

"Dammit." Eden maneuvered until she was once again within reaching distance. Penelope waited until Eden was stretched almost to the point of losing her balance, then leapt over Eden's head and skittered down her back. Eden pitched forward. A split second of weightlessness. A crystalline thought, suspended in time: *I'll be the first Rivera killed by a cat.*

Then her reflexes took over. Her hands caught a branch, the bark scraping into her palms. The rest of the descent felt like a dream, her limbs moving without her brain telling them what to do. Her feet hit the ground, the impact reverberating through her kneecaps, and before she could snap herself back to reality, Frankie had engulfed her in another hug.

She was saying something about Eden's mother never forgiving her. Eden just stood there for a few seconds, thinking that her mother would probably be more upset that Eden had made such a stupid mistake than that Frankie might be culpable.

"I'm fine," she said, shaking the thought and her aunt away. "Seriously, Frankie, I'm okay."

"Holy shit, that was—I guess those mountain-climbing lessons really paid off." Nate was looking between her and the tree, his eyes wide.

"Well, I wasn't sure if you would catch me," Eden said, trying to sound airy and nonchalant. She was pretty sure her voice was shaking, though. She smoothed a hand over her hair, only to find that it was tangled with twigs and leaves and what felt like a spiderweb. Her hand burned in protest, and she realized both her palms were rubbed raw. Wonderful; another embarrassingly preventable injury for the list.

Something pressed against her leg. She looked down to see Penelope, no worse for wear, winding contentedly among their ankles.

"I hate you," she told the cat, without heat.

Penelope just sneezed at her.

SIX

The summer was not off to a great start. Dani's parents hadn't grounded her for the damage to the car, but she could tell they didn't buy her story about the utility pole. She had a feeling they would be watching her more closely from now on, which didn't bode well. In atonement, she'd promised to make dinner every night that week as soon as she got home from work, which was a true punishment because the last thing she wanted to do after a full day in the heat was stand over a hot stove. To make matters worse, there was apparently some new bullshit regulation at Tree Top Adventure that required all staff members under eighteen to sit through a mandatory orientation session, even if they'd worked at the park before.

So that's how she found herself slouched against Tomás on a wooden bench while Brandi Benson, who the staff secretly called Office Manager Barbie, jazzed about how awesome rules were in a tone that was entirely too cheerful for seven a.m. They were outside around the big fire pit, which was already stacked with wood for the first hot dog roast of the summer. The sun glared hotter with every second that passed, and Dani daydreamed about the (relatively) cool shade of the ropes course.

Brandi was muttering something about handouts and digging around in her massive pink bag, imprinted with the Tree Top logo, which was a staple of her daily uniform.

"Here, Brandi, you left these in your office," said a voice from behind the group. Dani jerked upright and turned, along with everyone else, to see the newcomer.

Sadie May was bounding up the gravel path with a sheath of colorful papers in hand. She was wearing a green Tree Top polo, white shorts, and baby pink Converses.

"Perfect timing." Brandi beamed. "Everyone, this is my new assistant and savior, Sadie. I'm sure you'll see her around throughout the day."

Sadie handed off the papers and gave a little wave. When she caught Dani's eye, she quickly looked away and settled on a bench on the other side of the path. Something told Dani she wasn't nearly as surprised to see Dani as Dani was to see her. The nonsensical panic that Dani had felt at the sight of her melted into a prickling irritation. Was Sadie going to invade every part of her summer? She sensed Tomás's eyes on the side of her face. When Dani refused to look at him, he elbowed her gently. She elbowed him back.

Brandi continued her speech, passing out the flyers, which had a list of emergency numbers as well as ineffectual, thumbnail-size illustrations of outdated techniques for CPR and the Heimlich maneuver. Dani folded hers up and shoved it into her backpack as the meeting adjourned. Tomás followed right behind her as she hightailed it for the path to the ropes course. She was determined not to be trapped in another conversation with Sadie.

"Come on," Tomás said, his tone dangerously close to a whine. "You can't just spend the whole summer ignoring her."

"Challenge accepted."

"Fine, but you aren't going to spend the whole summer ignoring *me*." He jogged a little to fall into step beside her on the padded pine-straw path. "And I want to know what the deal is."

"We were friends a long time ago, and now we're not," Dani said flatly. "That's the deal."

She could practically hear Tomás rolling his eyes, but she

refused to fill the silence that gaped between them as they walked. Tree Top Adventure was the Smokies' version of a theme park, boasting a ropes course, campsites, horseback riding, canoeing, fishing, and a number of other kitschy activities to amuse city folk.

By the time they reached the ropes course shed, Marcus was already geared up and fiddling with the straps on his helmet. Marcus had been the ropes supervisor for as long as Tree Top had been open, and was a fixture of the park at this point. Dani was pretty sure he slept here most nights in the summer, in the hammock that he kept slung between two trees behind the shed.

"Mornin'," he said, tossing Tomás a harness. His signature black locs were caught up in a red bandana, and he wore a ratty Life is Good shirt, cargo shorts, and Chacos. He refused to tell anyone how old he was, but Dani had managed to narrow it down to between forty and fifty, based on the stories he told about his wild college days.

She and Tomás returned his greeting in unison, and she dropped her backpack next to the shed, digging out her personal harness and helmet. From inside the shed, she heard the familiar bickering of Tippi and Anabel, a couple who had been hired a few months back. Tippi was finishing up her last year at Vanderbilt, and Anabel was doing graduate work in something biology-related that Dani could never quite grasp.

"Not that helmet, I hate that one," Tippi was saying.

"They're all the same." Anabel's dull tone was typical of the early morning. One of the first things Dani had ever learned about her was that she needed at least three cups of coffee before she was coherent, and a fourth before she was fit for company.

"No, that one's itchy. I want that one, with the scratch on the side."

"Oh my god, get your own helmet then," Anabel said. She

came out of the shed with her hands thrown up in exasperation. She gave Dani and Thomas a wan smile before snatching up her thermos to finish what was probably cup number four.

"I love you too, my darling," Tippi sang out. She bounced out of the shed with her prized helmet. Mornings weren't a problem for her. "Hi guys! How's it going?"

"It's going," Dani replied. She was used to waking up early, but it was impossible to match Tippi's enthusiasm at any time of day. There was a reason why Marcus always gave her the task of helping the guests gear up and giving them the rundown of the rules. A few more course employees that Dani didn't know very well—most of them college kids just trying to make some extra cash—showed up, and Marcus gave everyone a rundown of their day.

Tippi and Anabel headed off to their assigned stations, and Marcus walked the newbies over to give them some last-minute tips on talking panicked guests off the zipline. Dani got to work pulling on her harness. She was just tightening the straps when she realized Tomás was standing next to her, staring pointedly.

"What?" she asked.

"You're stuck on the ropes with me all day, so you might as well tell me what's going on with this Sadie chick."

"Christ, when did you get so nosy?"

"Language. And that's hilarious, coming from the girl who broke into my phone just to snoop through all my pictures."

"That was *one* time," she said. "I was bored, and it doesn't count as breaking in when you use your freaking birthday as the passcode."

"Dani, come on."

He had his Serious Face on, which was entirely unfair, because he knew that she could never hold out against that expression.

"Fine." She swiped her hand across her own face, which was

already dripping with sweat. She dropped her voice and pretended to double-check her gear, in case Marcus was watching. "Sadie and I were best friends when we were kids, and when we were twelve, we kind of . . . kissed. It was our first kiss for both of us."

Tomás raised an eyebrow but didn't say anything.

"It was confusing," she rushed on. "I mean, we were still kids, and I was just figuring out that I was bisexual, and I didn't know what to think. For the next couple weeks, I kept trying to talk to her—you know, figure things out—but she ignored all my calls and avoided me completely. And then her dad got a new job and her family packed up and moved. She never even said goodbye."

She heaved a sigh. Getting out the story was more exhausting than climbing to the top of the pamper pole.

"So at the bonfire," Tomás said slowly, "that was the first time you'd seen her?"

"That was the first time I'd heard anything from her." Dani fiddled with one of the extra carabiners she kept clipped to her harness. "Look, I don't hate her. And I know I can't ignore her forever, but . . ."

But what? She had no idea. All she knew for sure was that right now, *not* talking to Sadie was a hell of a lot easier than talking to her.

"Okay," Tomás said after a long pause. "I get it."

"Okay." Now that she'd told him, she wasn't sure why she'd been so dead set on keeping it to herself. Probably because part of her had been afraid he'd tell her the truth, which was that she needed to grow up and get over herself. And maybe he would—eventually—but for now he seemed content with giving her some space. He was good at that.

"I better gear up," Tomás said, patting her on the back. "Marcus is coming."

Tomás disappeared into the shed, and Dani started to buckle on her helmet.

"Hold up," Marcus said. "I forgot the first aid kit at the office. We had to get it restocked. Will you go get it?"

Dani made a face. Not only was it a half-mile walk back, but chances were good that Sadie would be in the office. But she also knew there was no use complaining. The only thing that Office Manager Barbie and Marcus had in common was their stringent adherence to any and all rules of safety.

"Okay," she said, tucking her helmet into her backpack and retrieving her water bottle. "But can I work the zip line instead of the grapevine today?"

"Deal," he said, waving her off.

Dani started down the path at an easy trot. Despite the heat, the dappled sun through the branches felt good on the top of her head, and the forest all around her felt lush and alive. Insects buzzed around her ears and bird calls sang from above. For a few happy minutes, she could convince herself that the summer would hold nothing more than bright sun and zip lines.

Then she heard thrashing in the undergrowth somewhere off to her right. A familiar tingling in her chest stopped her in her tracks. No, this wasn't happening. Not here. Not now.

Fearfully, she searched the path ahead and behind her. Seemed to be empty. The sensation in her chest had become a gentle, insistent tug. After an uncertain couple of seconds, she finally gave in and picked her way off the path and into the woods, careful to keep her bearings. If she got lost and had to be rescued, she would never live it down. A few hundred yards into the thick forest, she squeezed her way between two pine trees and found herself in a natural clearing, with only a few scraggly saplings and some fragrant honeysuckle bushes.

Opposite the clearing from her was the dragon.

Nox was perched on a fallen tree, delicate as a cat, his long tail sweeping slowly back and forth behind him and his wings tucked neatly against his back.

In the speckled daylight she saw that his scales, smooth and imbricate like a snake's, were not matte gray, but glimmering with a faint opalescence. He blinked slowly at her, and she was close enough to see the feline pupils of his eyes adjusting to the shade. She realized she was digging her nails into her palms and stopped.

"I know your name," she said, but her voice was barely a croak around the lump in her throat. She tried again. "Why do I know your name?"

The same reason I know yours, Dani.

The voice sounded inside her head, startling her backwards a step.

"Fuck," she said.

Nox tilted his head slightly to one side. He was amused. Why did she know that? Why did she know anything about this dragon?

My mouth isn't formed for human language. Nox opened his jaw to illustrate, giving her a glimpse of his double-rowed teeth and extra-sharp canines, as long as her forearm. His tongue was a soft pink, and narrow, but not forked like she would have imagined.

"Telepathy," she said.

I think that's your word for it.

"But why?"

He let out a warm stream of breath through his nostrils that she realized was a sigh.

It's called a soul bond, what you and I have.

"Yeah, that doesn't sound made-up at all."

He raised his chin in an almost haughty gesture and ignored her.

It's an ancient, rare connection between a human and a dragon. Our souls—and fates—are intertwined.

"Why the hell would you do that?" she demanded.

It wasn't my doing. He sounded miffed at the very idea. *It occurs when a human and dragon are hatched at the same moment.*

"Humans don't hatch."

Try not to be a pedantic twit; it will make all of this much easier.

She gaped at him, momentarily speechless. Had she just been insulted by a dragon?

The bond snapped into place last night, when you touched me. You felt it.

She nodded, even though it hadn't been a question. She wasn't sure she would ever be able to forget that cataclysmic shift inside her, inconceivable yet undeniable. Even as Nox explained it, she felt as if a part of her already knew all of this. If only she could wrap her mind around it.

I didn't choose you, and you didn't choose me. But we have each other now. Always.

He didn't speak it like a promise, but like a bald statement of fact. Dani tried to turn the concept over in her brain, but it was too enormous, too thorny with implications to process right now.

"You know who I am, right?" she asked instead. "Who my parents are?"

Why do you think I was tracking you? he returned wryly.

"You knew about the bond? Before?"

No. His violet gaze was steady. It only took Dani a couple seconds to piece together what other intention a dragon might have in stalking her. She remembered the spark of blue-hot flame deep in his throat, a heartbeat away from obliterating her.

"Oh," she said. The pause lengthened between them. And

then, even though she was aware she'd asked the same question more times in the past minute than probably the past year: "Why?"

He gave no answer to that—at least, not in words. An emotion that wasn't hers bloomed inside her, unfurling in that new, vast space that had been ripped open last night when she touched him. A tangled knot of guilt and fury and impossible heartache that seemed layered with generations upon generations of grief. The sheer enormity of it crushed her chest and choked the air from her lungs. Her knees gave out and she fell to the ground, the pine needles cushioning her fall.

Nox shook himself on his perch, and then the pain began to siphon away as if draining physically out of her body. After a few seconds, she could breathe again. She staggered back to her feet.

I'm sorry, he told her. *Our thoughts aren't the only thing we share. This is new for me too.*

"You seem to know an awful lot about it." It came out more accusatory than she'd intended. Phantom tremors of that inhuman grief were still shooting through her heart.

Dragons share a common history. I was born with the knowledge of my entire race. His serpentine neck elongated, and he ruffled his wings. He was preening, Dani realized with bewilderment.

"Good for you," she said, refusing to give him the satisfaction of her awe. "So how do we break this bond?"

Why? he shot back. *Do you want me to go back to trying to kill you?*

"I want to not be soul-bonded to a bloodthirsty dragon," she replied coolly.

And I would not have chosen an obnoxious, bony little brat, but there is no breaking a soul bond. He eyed her up and down, and she wondered if he was trying to come up with more insults to add to his list. *Besides, I need you. That's why I decided to come back.*

She considered telling him that he was shit out of luck, but her curiosity got the best of her. She could sense the barest hint of his emotions, but it was like fumbling in the dark for the edge of something intangible. She had no idea how to understand more clearly what was going on in his mind. For Christ's sake, a day ago it would never even have occurred to her that a dragon could have anything going through its head except *Kill* and *Eat*.

"Need me for what?" she asked. "I'm not letting you anywhere near my family."

I don't care about your family, not anymore. Another flicker of emotion, enough that she knew he was telling the truth, but also that the change of agenda had not come easily. But why had he been coming after her family to begin with? She'd never heard of a dragon hunting down a slayer on purpose. That was like sticking your foot purposefully into a bear trap.

"Then what?"

Nox hesitated, his eyes flashing in the dim light. Before he could reply, voices and laughter flitted down the path behind Dani. She turned in time to see flashes of color through the trees. The first guests of the day were headed for the ropes course. Dani whirled around, ready to tell Nox to get out of there before he caused a panic, but he was already gone.

Meet me at the overlook tonight, after sunset.

The descant of his voice in her head above the genial chatter of the guests was disconcerting. She peered at the snippets of blue sky through the branches, but he was nowhere to be seen.

No promises, she thought, focusing on beaming the words to him—even though she had no idea how to do that. There was no reply. With no clear alternative, she headed back to the path.

SEVEN

It wasn't until she was seated at Frankie's dining room table with a tall glass of sweet tea in front of her that Eden was finally able to rouse herself completely from the surreal state through which she'd been swimming. From the moment she'd lost her balance in the tree, it was as if her brain had decided that the notion of mortality was too much to deal with, and so had shut out reality altogether. She wasn't complaining. It was better than having a full-blown panic attack in her aunt's kitchen.

Not that the fall would have killed her, most likely. It wasn't even fear that gripped her stomach now as she sipped her tea. In fact, it was quite the opposite. She couldn't shake the desire to march right back outside and climb the damn tree as high as the branches would bear her weight, just to prove that she could.

Prove to whom, she didn't know. Frankie certainly wouldn't have let her anywhere near the tree again, and Nate had been called away by another fare while she was in the bathroom tending to her various scrapes and furiously combing the debris from her hair.

While Eden brooded over her own irrationality, Frankie had been fluttering around the kitchen like a nervous butterfly, her silk robe flapping with her movements. She set out a bowl of food for Penelope, who was acting as if nothing out of the ordinary had happened, and even seemed a little miffed at Eden for daring to sit in her kitchen. While Penelope munched, she kept shooting unhappy glances over the top of the bowl, her amber eyes narrowed and watchful.

At last Frankie sat down opposite Eden, clutching her own

glass of tea. Her glassware was decorated with purple and green abstract shapes, like something off the set of an eighties sitcom. They clashed horribly with the blue-and-yellow paisley curtains, the pale pink Formica countertops, and the foot-high Venus de Milo sculpture that served as her centerpiece. That was the way of everything in Frankie's life, though. Nothing ever quite matched up, and yet she was always so unapologetically herself that it never seemed to matter.

"Did you call your parents?" Frankie asked, watching her worriedly over the top of Venus's head.

"I texted them," Eden said. Although she had told them that she was at Frankie's and why, she had left off the conclusion to her little rescue mission. Frankie didn't need to know that.

"And you're sure you don't want to go to the doctor?"

"I'm fine," she said. "Nothing broken, nothing sprained, no head injury. There's no reason to go to the doctor."

Frankie didn't argue, but she didn't look entirely appeased either. Eden squirmed a bit under her aunt's solicitude. Neither of her parents had ever fussed much over her and Dani. Obviously, they would have been concerned if they'd watched her fall from a tree, but once it had been ascertained that there were no serious injuries, they wouldn't have kept pressing her about it. Riveras just weren't the type for hand-wringing—another way that Frankie was the black sheep of the family. Beloved by all, but undoubtedly of different stock.

Various family members had remarked before how odd it was that Eden and Frankie should get along so famously, when it was Dani who seemed determined to steer away from the family business like Frankie had. Frankie had been raised the same way that all blood-born Riveras were raised: with a knowledge of the threat that lurked around them, and the magic that teemed just out of sight; with an emphasis on the skills needed to combat that threat, to survive that unseen world. But halfway through university, Frankie had announced to the family that she was dropping out to pursue her passions. Those passions had varied throughout the years. She'd backpacked through South America, taught yoga in Bali, worked on a self-sufficient eco farm in New Zealand, and published three steamy romance novels under the pseudonym Ruby Rochester. She had moved back to Tennessee three years ago to finally settle down and be near her family again. Currently she was in the business of selling crocheted baby toys in the shape of mythical creatures — her specialty, of course, being dragons.

Unlike most of the Riveras, Dani found Frankie's newest venture endlessly amusing, but despite that, she had never made much of an effort to get to know her aunt. Eden sometimes harped at her about it, because she knew Frankie would like to see more of her youngest niece, but secretly Eden didn't mind at all. She liked having her aunt to herself.

"We need food," Frankie announced suddenly, though it was early for lunch. "Tamales?"

Eden's stomach growled at the word, and she nodded fervently. Frankie went back to darting around the kitchen. She never seemed to do anything at leisure, always brimming with energy and making more noise than necessary, as if to make damn certain that no one ever forgot she was there.

Eden flicked through her phone, half-hoping to find a message from Nate, although that would be creepy because she hadn't given him her number. Nothing. She read through a few emails regarding her online classes, unsubscribed herself from an e-newsletter about low-rate mortgages, then double-checked her messages one last time. She shoved the phone in her pocket right as Frankie sat a plate down in front of her.

On second glance, it wasn't a plate but a cardboard tray, still encased in plastic wrap. Through the heat-fogged plastic, the fare only somewhat resembled tamales.

"These aren't homemade," Eden pointed out unnecessarily.

"I didn't say they were. What am I, my mother?" Frankie's expression was indignant with only the barest hint of a wry smile.

Eden laughed.

"Mom always says that Dad is better at cooking Mexican food than any of us are."

"It's why your abuela liked him so much." Frankie leaned in conspiratorially, cheese dripping from her fork. "I'm pretty sure before she died, she gave him the family recipes."

Eden laughed again. The tamales had a tinny taste that was less than appetizing, but she kept eating, not wanting to be rude. Sometimes she felt a little pang of loss for the Mexican heritage she'd never really been a part of. Her father was white as Wonder Bread, and her mother had always been more focused on teaching her daughters the dragon-slaying aspect of being a Rivera than any other family traditions. The closest she'd ever felt to her mother's ancestry was that one visit to Jalisco, where she'd understood even less Spanish than her father had, but her older cousins had brought her and Dani under their wing, introducing them to the wonders of Jarritos soda and pollito asado — a chicken-shaped lollipop that Dani adored and Eden hated. That had been years ago. In the interim, her Spanish had improved dramatically, but they hadn't visited Mexico again.

She supposed it could be worse. They'd never even been to Scotland, and she'd only met her father's parents twice. They were content with the occasional video call, and remained blissfully unaware of the family profession their son had married into.

She and Frankie both ate in silence for a while, until Eden

finally got up the nerve to broach the subject that had been on her mind since last night. Frankie was an open book about almost everything in her life, but when it came to what she knew about the family business, she could get strangely tetchy, as if talking about it would somehow drag her back into the life that she'd worked so hard to avoid.

"So Calla Thorn and Alder de Lange came for dinner last night," Eden said, trying to sound casual.

Something flickered behind Frankie's eyes, too quick to name, and she made a noncommittal noise. She didn't seem surprised. Probably Analisa had mentioned it during one of their weekly phone marathons, watching whatever was on HGTV at the same time and talking about all the house renovations that neither of them had any intention of ever doing. Even though Frankie had dropped everything and disappeared into the wild blue yonder while Analisa was still in high school, there had never been any bad blood between them. Supposedly Frankie hadn't told anyone about her plan, but Eden couldn't help but feel that Analisa had somehow known that Frankie would be leaving, even before the decision had been made. And maybe she had. Sometimes Eden got the same nagging feeling about Dani.

"They said they want Dani to come and spend some time at Stonecrest," Eden went on, unfazed by Frankie's determined disinterest.

Frankie snorted at that, then tried to cover it by coughing into her napkin.

"You don't think she should?" Eden asked. It hadn't escaped her notice that neither of her parents had ever given an actual opinion on what they thought about Dani spending time with the sorcerers. If anything, they had been deliberately ambivalent.

Frankie took a long, slow drink of tea.

"I don't see any reason why not," she said, setting down her glass. "Doesn't seem like it's up her alley though, stuck up there in that musty mansion while the sorcerers prance around and show off their magic tricks."

Eden raised an eyebrow at that.

"Don't give me that look." Frankie shoved her empty tray aside and crossed her arms. "I know your parents walk on eggshells and bend over backwards to be polite, but the fact of the matter is that Calla and her lot are a bunch of pretentious assholes. You'd think that with all that power they'd be able to do something useful with themselves, but instead they sit up on their mountain and lord it over the rest of us. I've been all around the globe, and I've never met a sorcerer who wasn't a grade-A prick."

Eden stared at her aunt, fork raised halfway to her mouth. After a few seconds, she set it down.

"I didn't know you felt that way about them," she said at last.

Frankie shrugged.

"Well, now you do. Like I said, I don't think there's any harm in Dani going up there if that's what she wants, but I also don't see how any good could come of it." Her eyes were locked on Eden's now, in a way that made Eden feel as if she wasn't precisely talking about Dani.

"Do you know what happened in New Mexico? To the Lowrys?"

Frankie blinked, taking a moment to catch up with the sudden turn.

"Just what everyone else knows. If you're asking me if I think that sorcerer was responsible for their deaths, I don't know. No point in speculating, anyway. I hear Calla shipped him off to Alaska or somewhere, maybe as punishment for something he did or didn't do, maybe just for appearances." She tapped absently on the side of her glass, swiping at condensation droplets. "Calla is all about appearances," she added dryly.

Eden thought about the head sorcerer and her effortless chic, the graceful confidence with which she commanded a room, the smooth way she navigated every conversation. At the same time, she couldn't help but take in the cluttered, bewildering decor of the house around her, the loud, unapologetic way Frankie tackled every single interaction, with no regard for tact or etiquette, and wonder what was so wrong with caring about appearances.

"It just seems to me that it would make more sense for slayers and sorcerers to work together," she said carefully. "She also said they were close to developing a weapon that could wipe out the dragons once and for all."

"I'm guessing Her Highness didn't go into any more detail than that?"

Eden fought a sudden swell of irritation at Frankie's tone.

"If it's as powerful as she says it is, then of course it would be a secret," she said. It was difficult to keep her tone even. "And apparently the sorcerers don't trust slayers much either. I asked Dad about it this morning, but he just said it's complicated."

Frankie snorted. "That's an understatement."

"But why?" Eden's voice rose, and she had to fight to lower it. "It was terrible, what happened to the Lowrys, but even if that sorcerer was responsible somehow, he's gone now. I don't see why—"

"Escúchame," Frankie said, gently but firmly. Eden closed her mouth. Frankie's Spanish only came out on those rare occasions when she was being perfectly serious. "New Mexico isn't the reason that sorcerers and slayers are at odds. It goes back a lot further than that. Ever since the wars, slayers have passed down their legacy through their family lines, and that breeds a strong loyalty. But sorcerers are different. They're made, not born. We don't know where they come from, and we don't know where their loyalties lie. Not really."

"They are trying to hunt down the remaining dragons," Eden said tightly. "Just like we are."

"Maybe." Frankie looked like she wanted to say more, but instead she pressed her lips together and gathered up the trays and silverware.

"Now you're the one being vague," Eden said.

"I know, but I don't know what else to say. You should really be talking to your parents about this, mija. It's their business, not mine."

"Only because you decided to leave," Eden said. It came out crueler than she meant it, but Frankie didn't seem to notice.

"I did," she said, her voice strangely distant as she stared out the kitchen window, still holding the remains of their meal. "I had to. I was never going to be the slayer that your abuelos wanted, and I didn't want to live my whole life measured against someone else's expectations. Besides, they had Analisa. She was enough of a slayer for the both of us."

Eden knew that her mother had been considered a prodigy for most of her life. Talk of her in the slayer circles had probably been the same then as it was now about Dani. Was Frankie trying to tell her something? That she should give up on being a slayer now, because she was never going to be as good as her sister anyway? That if she stuck with it, she would ultimately only find disappointment?

Her stomach had begun to hurt. She didn't think it had anything to do with the tamales.

"Maybe I should go," she said, standing. The momentary excitement with the cat and the comforting familiarity of her aunt's kitchen had worn off, leaving her with the vague, jittery anxiety that she knew from experience could only be combated with a heavy round against the punching bag.

"Are you sure? I think I have some brownie mix around here somewhere."

"Yeah, I've really got to get that homework finished," she said.

"Come here." Frankie buried her in a warm hug that smelled strongly of fake Mexican food. "Thanks for your help, mija. Now give me a second to find my keys, and I'll drive you."

Eden received the hug gratefully, even though it did nothing to lift her spirits. She waited in the front hall while Frankie shifted around piles of mail and bric-a-brac on the counters.

"Oh, your tall friend left you a note," she called over her shoulder. There was no mistaking the singsong suggestion in her tone. "It's in the bowl by the door."

"So are your keys," Eden said, picking up the folded piece of paper. Scribbled on it in red pen was a phone number, and below that: *Call me maybe?*

Eden couldn't help but smile.

EIGHT

Dani had never given a lot of thought to what it might be like to ride on a dragon's back, but she had assumed it was more like riding a mechanical bull than the majestic, carefree soaring depicted in fiction. That might have been because, until the night before, the closest thing to a dragon she had experienced was El Toro. It turned out she was more or less right.

She kept her eyes squeezed shut for the first half of the journey, half-convinced that Nox was going to carry her to a suitable height and then toss her off, and it would serve her right for being stupid enough to agree to this. Despite her better judgment, she'd ridden her bike the three miles to meet him at the overlook just after sunset. Then, taking her better judgment and shooting it in the face, she'd agreed to let him carry her somewhere that couldn't be reached on foot.

I thought about it all day, he'd told her. *I know you don't trust me, and I'm not sure if I can trust you, but I want to show you the reason I need your help.*

More than anything, dragon-flying was like riding a Harley-Davidson hundreds of feet above the earth, but with the heat of the engine scalding her arms, legs, and tender parts. Nox's intricate, shifting flight muscles rippled beneath her; the wind ripped at her body, buffeting her ears, even though she kept her head tucked low and her shoulders hunched. The worst part was that there was nothing to hold on to. She could only flatten her torso as much as possible and grip with her knees until her thigh muscles sang with pain.

Almost there.

It was strange, with the cacophony of flight all around her, to hear his voice so calm and clear in her head. The faint condescension she detected in his tone was also more than a little annoying. She decided to experiment with sending him a thought of her own, loud and exceedingly vulgar, but there was no response, so she wasn't sure she had succeeded.

They banked sharply left, soaring so low across the pine trees that she was certain she could reach out a hand and bring back a fistful of green needles. He dipped even lower between a break in the trees, tucking his wings close to him like a darting sparrow. They brushed against Dani's bare arms: a soft, leathery texture ribbed with bone. She closed her eyes again, unwillingly aware of the invisible tether between them, of the way that every minuscule twitch of his body reverberated in her own. If she concentrated hard enough, she could almost believe that these were *her* muscles, powerful and precise and built to defy gravity. She could feel the heat of the dragonfire simmering in her chest, the talon-like claws that retracted with ease, the steady rhythm of wings like a heartbeat and almost as involuntary, the—

They swerved violently, and Dani fought her own momentum to keep from flying off Nox's back.

What was that? What are you doing? he demanded as they straightened back out.

"What?" she gasped out, not loud enough for him to hear, but that didn't seem to matter.

You did something. I felt it. It was like . . . I lost control.

A shiver down her spine, but she banished the notion immediately. That was ridiculous. She could barely even communicate with him.

"Don't blame me for your poor flying skills," she said, the wind ripping each word from her mouth as soon as she spoke it.

Nox didn't reply, but she thought she could feel a wariness creeping through him, tinged with something like fear. Neither of them spoke again until they had finally landed.

At first she thought they had landed in a small clearing. When she pulled out her phone and turned on the flashlight, she quickly realized that they were in fact on a very unsubstantial ledge, ringed tightly with scraggly trees and bushes that grew stubbornly out of the rock face. If she took a few steps and pushed her way through some branches, she would fall right off the side of the mountain. Wonderful; he'd brought her back to his lair to roast and eat her at his leisure.

But even as the thought crossed her mind, she realized there was no conviction behind it. Somehow, in the same way she could hear his voice in her head and occasionally feel the thrum of his emotions, she knew that Nox would never hurt her; not now. And when she let herself think about it, the idea of trying to physically hurt him was as abhorrent to her as trying to drive a nail through her own hand.

She didn't like it, this adamantine connection that had been forged between them without either of their consent. She'd been raised with the threat of dragonkind hanging over her head. Forty-eight hours ago, Nox had tried to kill her. And now she was bound to him by some ancient magic in a situation that was entirely untenable. She was Dani Rivera, daughter of a legacy of dragon slayers that went back generations. Maybe it wasn't a legacy she particularly wanted, but neither did she want to suddenly be soulmates with an actual dragon.

Are you coming?

She turned to face him and found that he was standing on the threshold of a cavern that she hadn't noticed before—no, it definitely hadn't *been* there before. She blinked hard.

It's a secret we have, Nox told her, his tone edged with impatience. *A way to protect our nests from . . . well, from you.*

She'd been told that dragons had magical ways of hiding their lairs, even though details regarding *how* were scarce. Her father would've loved to see this up close. And then the rest of his words struck her. Nests.

Dragon nests meant dragon eggs.

Her mouth was dry suddenly. She didn't know what else to do. She followed him into the darkness.

The cave was nothing like the Ruby Falls cave under Lookout Mountain, which her family had visited years ago when her parents were in one of their rare touristy moods. That cave, with its strategically placed lighting effects and walkways worn down by thousands of feet, felt almost like it had been carved specifically for visitors.

The dirt and stone beneath her feet now gave no easy passage; more than once she stumbled over holes, and sticks that she prayed really were sticks, and not bones. Holding her phone light out with one hand, she reached out to brush her fingers along the wall and found it rough and sticky with spiderwebs. She yanked her hand back and brushed it furiously against her shorts. It wasn't long before they left the outside light behind, and Nox became nothing but a suggestion of a shadow in front of her, surprisingly lithe and quiet.

Just as she was about to ask him how much farther, a faint light emanated from ahead, pale and blue like a computer screen at night. The tunnel, which to Dani's dismay had been gradually shrinking around them until Nox's back brushed the ceiling, opened back up into a cavern. It was about the size of the barn, completely bathed in that blue light. She turned off her phone's flashlight and tucked it back into her pocket. The stone walls were unnaturally smooth, shimmering with condensation. This place also felt as if it had been carved specifically out of the earth, but for a purpose more sacred than tourism.

The light was pulsating gently. Dani moved farther in, until she was standing next to Nox, and found the source of the light. Just past her toes, the stone floor sloped downward into a basin. The water was so translucent and still, it took her a few seconds to register that there was water at all. A crystal-clear pool, maybe ten feet across and of indeterminable depth. At the very bottom, dreamily distorted by the water, six dragon eggs glowed with nascent life.

The longer she stared, the more convinced she became that this was indeed a dream. How could they be real—these ageless, impossible survivors of a centuries-long war? They looked so fragile, so ethereal, glimmering like opals and radiating magic from within.

We kept them safe for so long. Nox's voice, low and haunted, drifted into her consciousness. Distantly, she wondered at that "we," wondered how many more dragons had managed to slip beneath her parents' radar, but that was a worry for another time.

"When will they hatch?" Her own voice was a bare whisper.

They can't, not on their own. That's why I need your help.

She decided not to waste time or breath protesting that she didn't know the first thing about dragon eggs, much less how to hatch them. Instead she just waited for him to explain.

The hatching of eggs requires very old, very powerful magic. There aren't any dragons left who are ancient enough to perform the ritual.

A tactful way of saying that they had been hunted to the point of extinction. Dani's stomach lurched with secondhand guilt, but she bit back an objection to the accusation that Nox hadn't made.

I can't afford to wait. Even now, it may be too late. They should

*have been hatched years ago. I don't know how much longer I can keep
them safe. The soul bond is the only other way.*

"Meaning?"

*As it strengthens between us, my magic will grow stronger in both
of us. Strong enough to hatch the eggs, as long as they are still viable.*

"Wait, magic? In me? Am I going to become a sorcerer or
something?"

He snorted disdainfully, issuing thin streams of smoke through
his nostrils as he did so.

*Hardly. The magic flows through you, but humans can't use it. It's
how we are connected, that's all. Although . . . you may find that some of
your weaker human attributes will begin to strengthen.*

"Strengthen how?" she asked. Nox hesitated, and her stomach
did a flip. "What are you not saying?"

*You will no longer age and die like normal humans. Though you
can't use magic the way a sorcerer can, our soul bond gives you life eternal — provided you don't do something stupid to get yourself killed.* His
dry tone indicated he did not find that likely.

"I'm . . . immortal?" Dani's voice, when she finally found it, felt
like it belonged to someone else.

*I suppose that depends on your definition of immortal. Once your
body reaches full maturity, it will not deteriorate with age, much like
dragonkind. But you can still die.*

His impatient explanation barely registered amidst the cacophony of shock and confusion in Dani's head. How could she be
immortal? She didn't feel any less human. She'd stubbed her toe in
the bathroom that morning. She'd pinched her skin in a carabiner
on the ropes course, and it hurt like hell, the same as it always had.

She'd only just begun to come to terms with the idea of being
bound to a dragon for the rest of her life, and now she had to deal

with the fact that her lifetime was going to be longer than she'd ever anticipated. A *lot* longer.

The dreams she had of a normal life—of normal friends and a normal job and a normal future—had begun to darken. She couldn't even begin to wrap her head around this new existence she'd stumbled into—no, that had been *forced* on her, by some ancient, merciless magic.

What's wrong? Nox asked. Dani's raging emotions were so overwhelming, she had no doubt he was feeling them too.

"I don't want to be immortal," she managed.

Of course you do. All humans want to be immortal.

"Not me. I want to be . . ." But the desire to be normal, when she'd been born into a family of dragon slayers—when she'd spent her whole life training to be one herself—suddenly felt so ridiculous, so naive, that she couldn't even say it out loud. "Never mind."

Nox eyed her, the silence heavy between them, and Dani realized that it didn't matter if she said it or not. He knew exactly what was going on in her head. She decided to change the subject before she accidentally made him privy to any more of her deep personal feelings.

"I don't think it's fair that I have to be some kind of conduit to give you extra-powerful magic, when I didn't even have a choice in the matter."

Typical human selfishness.

"Oh, don't start that misanthropic shit with me," she snapped. *Misanthrope* had been one of their vocabulary words that year, and she was pleased by how well-suited to the situation it was. "You're the one dragging me all the way out here, asking me to help you, when two nights ago you tried to turn me into the Human Torch."

That's a fine accusation, when your family and their kin are the reason I need your help in the first place. He turned so that his face was level with hers, those amethyst eyes glittering in the pale light. Heat from his breath made her eyes water.

"I've never killed a dragon," she said, crossing her arms in a protective, instinctual gesture.

And I've never killed a human.

"Bullshit."

Despite what your kind may think, I do not care about humans and their business. I care about my own kind. I care about these eggs. And if there were any other way to hatch them, I would do it. I would rather do anything than ask a slayer for help, but there is no other way. I need you.

She didn't need to read his mind to know that it was the absolute truth. Conviction was burning in his eyes, etched in every syllable.

"Is this the last nest?"

He was quiet for a long while.

I don't know, he said at last. *But it's the nest I've been charged with protecting, and I mean to see it through to the end.*

"Charged by who?"

That question he didn't answer, but she felt a ghost of that same grief from yesterday as a susurrus across her skin.

Will you help me or not?

It was a dragon asking her this question. A creature she had been taught was the sum of all humanity's fears; a pestilence her family and generations before them had spent their lives trying to eradicate. Where some children had been raised on the fire and brimstone of eternal damnation, she had been raised on the fire and brimstone that dragonkind would bring if they were ever allowed to repopulate. A second Tempus Dracones, one that would be infinitely more destructive than the first, because now humans had their own firepower, and that sort of escalation could only mean more devastation.

I can't, she wanted to say, but the words wouldn't form. Deep inside her a strange emotion pulsated in rhythm to the eggs below. Old and vast and heart-sickeningly desperate. Despite herself, she believed him when he said he cared only about his own kind, but dragonkind were nearing extinction, which made these eggs inestimably precious. The sheer weight of that burden must be agonizing.

"How?" she asked.

It was half past ten by the time Dani drudged up her front steps, bone-tired and plastered in sweat. Even this late, heat clung to the air like a bad memory.

The moment she saw her parents sitting on the couch, she remembered that she was supposed to make dinner. Plus, she had forgotten to tell them she was going out, or when to expect her back. Shit.

"Sorry," she said, not bothering with an overture.

Her dad was reading an issue of *National Geographic;* her mother was leaned against him, her bare feet tucked beneath her, reading her Kindle. At her entrance, they both glanced up, their expressions frustratingly neutral.

"The Jeep will be at the shop for a few days," Analisa said mildly. "And let me tell you how much *fun* it was, spending half our day getting that taken care of."

"I'm sorry," she repeated, plopping down in the armchair.

"It's probably my favorite part of motherhood," Analisa went on, as if she hadn't spoken, "taking time out of my day to fix my daughter's mistakes, and then coming home to find that she hasn't been able to do the one thing we asked of her, and *then* wondering where she might be and why she hasn't taken two seconds to send a text to her parents and why she isn't answering her phone and if she's dead in a ditch somewhere having her face devoured by wild muskrats."

James snickered at that, then quickly covered it with a cough.

"We were worried," he told Dani, as if her mother's quiet diatribe had needed any translation.

"I forgot about dinner and went for a ride on my bike," Dani said. "I didn't have any service. I'm really sorry."

"So you've said." Analisa closed the case on her Kindle and dropped it on the coffee table. "You can't just disappear like that, Dani. I feel like that should go without saying."

"I'll make a note for the future." Dani fought the urge to roll her eyes, and lost. Her exhaustion made her prickly, even when she knew meekness would serve her better in this instance. "Playing with guns and knives and fire is okay, but absolutely no turning off my phone."

"What is that supposed to mean?" Analisa's tone was more weary than agitated.

"It's hard to keep straight what's considered dangerous around here. Last week I was free climbing without a helmet, and this week I'm in trouble for going for a bike ride by myself."

"You know very well there's a difference between supervised training exercises and just disappearing without a word for half a day," her father said. "And besides that, dinner was your responsibility. We agreed."

Dani wanted to keep arguing, but she knew it was pointless. And she knew she was wrong.

"I know," she said at last. "I really am sorry. I had a lot on my mind after work, and I just completely spaced out. It won't happen again."

A lot on her mind: now *there* was the understatement of the century. Her mother still looked ready to hold a grudge, but her father seemed satisfied. She and Eden had both figured out a long time ago that James had a soft spot for candor, and that Analisa never stayed mad after her husband decided to forgive. Tonight appeared to be no exception.

"You should get some sleep," her father said, relaxing back with his magazine. "You look beat. How far did you ride, anyway?"

"I lost track," she said, which was the truth.

"We need to talk to you about something else," Analisa said. She eyed her daughter's state. Dani had a feeling she looked like death warmed over, because that's how she felt. "It can wait till tomorrow, though."

Dani was too exhausted, and too relieved to be escaping without punishment, to be curious. She pushed herself to her feet with effort.

"Good night," she said.

"Sleep tight," said her mother.

"Don't let the dragons bite," said her father. An old family joke. Dani couldn't help but smile as she went to the kitchen to grab a glass of water, then climbed the stairs. She was tempted to fall straight into bed, but she was sticky with sweat and coated with a fine layer of dirt and spiderwebs and whatever else had been in that secret tunnel. So she drained half her water, took a lukewarm shower to cool off, then drained the second half, along with a couple ibuprofen. She'd just pulled on a clean nightshirt and crawled into bed when there was a knock at the door. She knew it was Eden, and she didn't feel like talking to her, but she also didn't want to just tell her to go away.

"Come in," she said.

Eden, her face Elphaba-green with one of her all-natural avocado-honey-soy-whatever face masks, came and flopped onto her back at the foot of the bed.

"Mom and Dad are pissed," she said.

"Thanks," Dani said dryly. "I could have used that warning a little sooner."

"I did text you."

Which reminded Dani: she needed to check her phone. There were several texts and missed calls from her parents, a few texts from Eden, one from Marcus reminding her to bring her W-9 signed by a parent tomorrow, and one from Tomás with a screenshot of a meme that she was too tired to decipher. She plugged in the phone and dropped it on her nightstand.

"Where were you, anyway?" Eden asked.

"Went for a ride on my bike," Dani said. "Bad reception."

"And?"

"And what?"

Eden sat up and looked at her.

"So they didn't ask you about Stonecrest yet?"

"Stonecrest?" Dani echoed, confused. "Like where the sorcerers live? What about it?"

Why is your family dealing with sorcerers? Nox's sudden intrusion into her thoughts made her jump and yelp.

Shut up, she thought frantically as Eden studied her with concern. *Go away.*

"Thought I felt a spider," she said to Eden, pretending to scratch her leg under the covers.

Eden seemed to accept that and lay back down.

"Calla wants you to spend some time there," she said to the ceiling, "to learn about dragon history and magic and stuff. I guess she thinks it will make you a better slayer."

"That's ridiculous. I've never even met her."

"I know." Eden's tone had dulled. Dani tried to read her expression, but Eden's face was turned so that she could only see the side of her nose and the corner of her mouth. Her lips seemed much pinker than usual in contrast to the green mask.

You're the one broadcasting your thoughts. I'm just trying to sleep.

"You've been there before, right?" Dani asked, carefully ignoring the running commentary in her mind.

"Once, when I was a kid."

"What's it like?" She'd always imagined the sorcerers living in a medieval-style fortress, with torches and trapdoors scattered throughout.

It's nothing like that—why are humans so fanciful?

"I guess you'll find out when you go."

You can't go there. Nox's voice took on a sudden edge of fear.

"I don't want to." The response was reflexive, but fortunately it answered both Eden and Nox. She didn't know yet if she would even be able to help Nox, but she did know she couldn't just turn her back on him—not with this connection that hummed between them. She could feel it even now, beneath her breastbone like a second heartbeat. The last thing she needed was to complicate the situation even more by adding sorcerers to the mix. She was going to have a hard enough time keeping Nox a secret from her family.

There wasn't a lot of concrete knowledge about sorcerer magic, although there were rumors of telekinesis, rapid healing, super strength—basically all the superhero staples. Like dragons, they kept well out of the human eye; unlike dragons, they were a mystery to slayers as well. Jaime Cruz once told her he'd seen a sorcerer rip a tree up by the roots without so much as twitching his pinky finger. To be fair, Jaime was infamous for his tall tales, so it was hard to know how much credence to give him. Still, she figured, odds were that some level of mind reading was in their repertoire. It wasn't a bet she was willing to take.

"Of course you don't," Eden said. Her tone had a new edge to it, something like bitterness. Dani wished she could sense her sister's emotions like she could sense Nox's. She and Eden had been close enough once that she'd felt like she could, but not anymore. She was struck by the sudden horrible image of Eden growing old and decrepit, while Dani stayed the same. Would they even still be a part of each other's lives by then? Eventually her family would notice that she wasn't aging normally—would they want anything to do with her once they found out the truth? She pushed those needling thoughts aside with determination. One problem at a time.

"I've got work," she said.

"Don't worry," Eden said with another, more exaggerated sigh. "Mom and Dad aren't going to make you give up your very important job of playing in treehouses if you don't want to."

"Clever. How long did it take you to come up with that one?"

Why are you playing in treehouses?

Shut up, shut up, shut up.

"What's going on with you, anyway?" Eden asked, propping herself onto her elbows and looking at Dani with new interest. "You've never gone in for long-distance cycling."

"Nothing, I just needed some time to myself."

Eden watched her, unswayed. Dani wasn't exactly the type to go off by herself and brood. She wracked her brain for a good excuse.

"Does it have to do with Sadie?" Eden asked.

"She's working at Tree Top this summer," Dani replied, grateful for the excuse.

"You're kidding."

Dani shook her head, relieved to see the suspicion drain from her sister's face.

"She's Brandi's new assistant."

"Have you talked to her yet?"

"You sound just like Tomás."

"So that's a no."

"I'm busy in my treehouses all day. Not much time for a heart-to-heart," Dani said. She caught sight of a few angry red scratches on Eden's neck, which hadn't been there yesterday, and seized on the change of subject. "What happened to you?"

She pointed to the scrapes, and Eden touched them gingerly.

"Oh," she said, making a face. "I went to Frankie's today to save her cat from a tree."

Dani laughed. Eden just kept making the face, somewhere between a grimace and a grin.

"Oh my god, you're serious?" Dani asked.

Eden nodded and told her about how the rescue mission had turned into a battle royale, which the cat had won. Dani laughed so hard her ribs hurt, until finally Eden snatched up a pillow that had fallen off the bed and threw it at her. But she was smiling.

NINE

The first couple weeks of summer passed in a flurry of work and Nox and far too little sleep in between. Dani's agreement to help Nox hatch the eggs had been impulsive, driven by the sight of them, empyreal and lovely in their pool, and by the bone-deep emotion that seeped from Nox into her body. Once she'd had a chance to clear her head, she realized that she only had the vaguest idea what helping him actually meant. Supposedly, strengthening the soul bond was the only way that Nox would have enough power to hatch the eggs by himself. That was, assuming the eggs were even still viable. But the thought of being responsible for the hatching of six new dragons—something her family and all the other slayers had been working to prevent for generations—kept her up most nights.

More than once, she'd braced herself to tell Nox that she couldn't help him after all. That this bond between them wasn't something she'd asked for, and it wasn't something she wanted, and if he wanted to hatch the eggs, he'd have to do it alone. She was a Rivera, and that was synonymous with "dragon slayer." She couldn't nurture a soul bond with the enemy, no matter how surprisingly intelligent he was; no matter how incredibly *human* so many of his emotions felt. No matter how many times she'd felt a wisp of one emotion in particular—a visceral, overwhelming loneliness—that had made her start to truly wonder what it must be like to be one of the last of your kind.

She still hadn't managed to tell Nox any of that. She'd been born to the hunters, and now, because of this soul bond, she was seeing the world through the eyes of the hunted. It wasn't something she could unsee. Every time she found herself wanting to tell her parents or Eden the truth, she was stopped by the memory of those helpless, innocent eggs, their fragile existence protected only by the secret she and Nox shared.

She wasn't sure that what she was doing was right, but she was also beginning to suspect that there wasn't anything as simple as right and wrong when it came to dragons and slayers.

And so every spare moment she had that wasn't taken up by work or training was taken up by Nox, exploring their connection and cautiously testing the limits they found. In some ways, it was more exhausting than time with Eden on the mat. Dani had never been one to delve into the corners of her own psyche. Eden went to a therapist regularly, one who was a friend of dragon slayers and therefore well-suited to their particular needs, but Dani hadn't gotten much from the experience. Her parents had only made her go a few times before letting her stop.

And now she had to navigate how her largely unexamined inner life intersected with Nox's, and the vast well of shared history he contained. The fact that her life was now eternal—at least until she did something to get herself killed, as Nox had pointed out more than once now—only made things more complicated.

Most days she found herself wishing for a good old-fashioned punching bag. It didn't help that their progress couldn't be measured with numbers or a stopwatch. How could they even be sure their attempts at strengthening the bond were working? Despite the air of superiority Nox liked to put on, Dani couldn't help but feel that perhaps he was out of his depth as well.

"Maybe we could convince a sorcerer to help," she suggested

one early morning, when they'd met at their usual spot before she had to head to work. "If we explain everything—"

You've been talking to the sorcerers? Nox's tone was sharp.

"No. They haven't been around since they met with my parents a couple weeks back." She stretched her arms over her head and leaned back on her hands. She was sitting crisscross on the ground, despite the rough gravel. At first she hadn't wanted to involve the sorcerers at all, but the more she thought about it, the more it made sense that a sorcerer might be able to help, if they could be persuaded. They were magical beings, after all.

The high sorcerer invited you to Stonecrest.

There was a coldness in his words that sent a shiver down her own spine. She'd forgotten he had been eavesdropping on that conversation with her sister, and who knows how many more of her conversations. That wasn't something she wanted to worry about right now.

"You know Calla?"

Of course I do. She was the first sorcerer ever made.

"Made?" Dani echoed. "How are they made?"

Nox flicked his tail the way he did when he was nervous, and a frisson of reluctance passed through the bond to Dani.

It's not important, he said. And then, before Dani could call bullshit: *Stay away from sorcerers. They hate my kind more than slayers do. They can't be trusted.*

"And you expect me to just take your word for it?"

He sniffed petulantly.

I know what I'm talking about. More than you do, anyway.

"You're so full of shit," Dani said, but without rancor. She'd already begun to learn which arguments with Nox were worth pursuing and which were better saved for another time. "I don't have any plans to take Calla up on her offer. I was just trying to be proactive. As much as I love waking up at four a.m. to meet you every morning, I don't see how playing around with telepathy and sharing our feelings is making the soul bond any stronger."

It takes time, he said sullenly.

We don't have a lot of time, Dani returned, pleased with how clearly the thought flowed. She'd been getting pretty decent at speaking to him with her mind, although it was still easier to talk most of the time. *We can't keep sneaking around forever. Eventually, someone is going to notice. You're not exactly subtle.*

He shifted his weight, rearranging his claws like a persnickety cat.

There is another way, he told her grudgingly. *It's similar to the shared history we pass on to hatchlings. There have been those of my kind who have shared their consciousness with their soul-bonded human—although normally, it would take decades of being bonded to grow that kind of trust.*

"What does sharing your consciousness mean?" Dani asked, already skeptical.

Exactly what it sounds like. Right now we are linked through magic, able to pass thoughts and feelings through the connection. But it's possible to open the floodgates, as it were. To share every part of ourselves with each other. Every memory; every joy; every pain. Everything.

"That sounds terrible."

I didn't say it was a good idea, he replied, defensive. *Just that it's a way to strengthen the soul bond faster.*

"Well, I'm not doing that." She was only just starting to get used to his voice in her head and the occasional small bursts of emotion she felt from him. The notion of just opening herself up, so that he would know every single thing about her—and vice versa—was horrifying. Not least of all because of how many times in the past couple weeks she'd seriously considered giving him and the nest up to her parents. A tendril of shame curled in her belly, and she pushed it down harshly.

Nox rustled his wings in a gesture that she'd figured out was his version of a shrug.

Maybe you can't feel it, but the bond is *getting stronger.*

"I think convincing you to stop referring to me as a 'weak human' probably helped with that."

In that case, perhaps it would help even more if you would stop cursing at me.

She let out a short laugh just as her phone alarm rang in her pocket, reminding her it was time to head home to wait for Tomás to pick her up. She felt like all her time lately was spent dashing between her real life, her slayer training, and her dealings with Nox, but she didn't know how else to manage. Letting the three worlds meet at all would be disastrous. She'd always thought it was a struggle to keep the existence of dragons a secret from her normal friends, but as it turned out, that was a piece of cake compared to keeping an actual dragon a secret from her slayer family.

She attempted to climb to her feet, but her left leg had fallen asleep. She hopped ineffectually on one leg for a second, then toppled over—but was caught by Nox's tail, which hovered at waist height. After an initial moment of panic, followed by the realization that she was not, in fact, being electrocuted, she leaned on it until she was able to put weight on her foot again. She'd never noticed before how the bony, razor-sharp scales that spiraled around the tip of his tail could be folded at will, rendering them inert.

Thanks, she thought to him.

He just watched her with faint amusement as she limped over to her bicycle and raised the kickstand.

See you tomorrow? he asked.

Bright and early.

On Friday morning, Eden woke up an hour before her alarm and lay in bed listening to the muffled sounds of her sister getting ready in the bathroom. She'd started cycling every morning before work, which wasn't the type of training Eden wished she would focus on, but it was better than nothing. She considered getting out of bed and joining her, but before she could decide, she heard Dani's footsteps creaking down the stairs. She dozed for another half hour, then changed into her workout clothes and headed downstairs. Her parents were still asleep, so the house was quiet and cold from the cranked-up air conditioning.

Outside, the sun was already setting the morning ablaze, and a pleasant cacophony of competing birdsong filled the air. Eden was climbing on the ATV when her phone rang.

"Hello?"

"Eden? This is Calla Thorn."

Eden's heart stuttered at the warm, smooth voice.

"Oh hi—hello. Good morning." She swallowed the rest of the rambling that rose in her throat.

"Good morning," Calla said, and Eden could hear the smile in her tone. "I'm sorry to call out of the blue like this, but I was hoping we could meet for coffee sometime soon. There's something I'd like to discuss with you."

Dani was Eden's first thought, but maybe that was just because her sister had been on her mind recently. Dani had been acting strange for weeks now. It wasn't just that she was leaving the house earlier than usual; she was also staying out late, and acting deliberately nonchalant and vague whenever anyone asked her what she'd been up to. It wasn't like her at all.

That was ridiculous, though. It's not like Calla would know any of that, or care if she did. Maybe the high sorcerer wanted to talk more about Eden's training. Or maybe she'd changed her mind and realized that it made more sense for Eden to come stay at Stonecrest, since Dani was clearly not interested. Even as that hopeful thought swelled in her, Eden knew it was ridiculous.

No, she was fairly certain that whatever Calla wanted to talk about, it had little to do with Eden and everything to do with Dani. But even knowing that, she still wanted the chance to see the high sorcerer again, just the two of them this time.

The only issue was, she had a feeling her parents wouldn't feel the same way. Her mother would definitely see it as an attempt by Calla to go behind their backs, even if that wasn't the intention. Eden was tempted to say yes anyway—she was an adult, after all, and could make her own decisions.

But she couldn't go against her parents like that.

"Um, I'm not sure. Could I get back to you later?" She was also apparently too much of a coward to just say no to the high sorcerer. Maybe she could bring her parents around.

"Please do," Calla said. "It's rather important."

"I will," Eden said. As they hung up, she was already mentally laying out an argument to convince her parents that a private meeting with Calla Thorn was a good idea. She climbed back on the ATV, but this time before she could start it up, the back door banged open.

"Oh good, I caught you," said her mom, coming down the steps and into the grass. Her feet were bare and her hair was still rumpled from sleep.

"What's up?" Eden asked.

"Dad and I have to take a trip."

"Where? When?"

"Arizona, immediately. We got a call from Jaime. You know he's been suspicious of a young dragon in the Badlands for several months now, and last night there were a few reports of sightings. We're going to help him track it down."

Eden's pulse thrummed.

"I'll go with you."

"Sorry, not this time." Analisa gave her a rueful smile that Eden knew well. "We don't want to leave Dani here alone."

"She could go stay with Frankie."

"She has her job at Tree Top. Frankie's house is too far away."

"Frankie could stay here, then."

"Eden." Her mother's voice was gentle but firm. "Maybe next time, okay?"

"It's always next time," Eden said, her pulse thumping louder in her ears, but with anger now. "I train every single day. I don't date or go to parties or do *anything*, because all I care about is this. And still it's not enough."

"It's not about being enough," Analisa said, rubbing a hand across her back. "It's about patience. Your day will come, but it's my job and your father's to make sure it doesn't come too soon. I know how hard you work for this, mija. I know. But it's not your time yet."

"What does that even mean?" Eden cried. "You don't think I'm ready? If Dani wanted to go, you'd let her."

She knew she was sounding like a whiny brat now, but she didn't care.

"That's not true," her mother said with a sigh, withdrawing her hand. "Look, we can talk about this when your father and I get back. We have a plane to catch."

"Fine." Eden revved the ATV to life, cutting off anything else her mother had to say. She tore out of the shed and toward the barn without looking back. Her mind was a maelstrom, and it took her two tries to input the security code correctly on the door. Once inside, she stalked back and forth across the floor for a few minutes, unable to focus on anything but her own outrage at the sheer injustice of it. She gave her best, every single day, and her parents still didn't think she had what it took. Maybe they never would.

She yanked out her phone, hoping against hope to see a message from her mother, saying she'd changed her mind. But there was nothing.

Eden went to her recent received calls and hit the top number. Calla answered on the first ring.

"Sorry, I had to check my schedule," Eden said. Her voice sounded distant and strange, like it was coming from someone else. "I can meet tomorrow, if that works for you?"

"Wonderful," Calla said. "How about two o'clock tomorrow? I can send a car around for you." She spoke like it was the most natural thing in the world to send a car around for someone.

"Perfect," Eden said, trying to sound like she had people send cars around for her all the time. "I'll see you then."

"Ciao, darling." Calla ended the call without waiting for a response.

Eden carefully put the time into her calendar app with a reminder—as if there was any chance she could forget—and then pulled off her shoes. She'd intended to spend more time on the climbing wall today, but instead she wrapped her hands. She connected her phone to the Bluetooth speakers, swiping the volume up until HAYZ was blaring so loud she couldn't hear anything else. Leaving her gloves where they lay, she drove every ounce of her frustration and fury into the punching bag until her hands screamed in pain and every bone and muscle ached with exhaustion. Until her vision was blurred with sweat and tears, her lungs heaving with the effort of each breath. Until her body begged her to rest, if only for a moment. But she kept going.

TEN

Dani took a bite of her ham and cheese sandwich, glaring at Tomás while she chewed. The air conditioning of the staff room in the back of Tree Top's general store usually made lunchtime one of the highlights of her day. These days, it felt more like a minefield. Tomás, whose unerringly good nature could be more than a little annoying, had decided that being nice to Sadie was the decent thing to do. And because they were both decent people, it wasn't long before the two of them were past generic politeness and into true friendliness. And Dani couldn't blame him for wanting a new friend. Between training and strengthening her soul bond with Nox, she barely had time to see Tomás anymore.

The staff room only had a single table and four chairs — most people went off campus for lunch — so she couldn't just sit somewhere else. To be fair, after the first time Sadie had joined them for lunch, Tomás had asked Dani on the way home if she minded. But telling Tomás to *not* be nice to Sadie seemed vindictive, so of course she had said she didn't mind. Later, she realized that he'd probably arranged it that way on purpose. That was just like him, tricking her into being a good person.

She redoubled her glaring efforts as she opened her can of soda, but her heart wasn't really in it today, and Tomás was ignoring her anyway. He and Sadie were talking about books. Or at least, that's how the conversation had begun. Now they were arguing about one book in particular, *Fiends of Fire: Being a Concise History and Discourse of Dragonkind*, by Thaddeus Coombs.

"No, it was published in 1893," Tomás was insisting. "I

remember because the first copies were sold at the Chicago World's Fair."

"That was the second edition," Sadie said. "The first was published in 1890, but it was a small printing and hardly anybody read it."

"Sadie's right," Dani said, then blinked when she found them both looking at her. She didn't realize she'd said it out loud.

"You've read it?" Sadie's question quivered with cautious excitement. Dani didn't know if that was because she was excited to find another fan, or because this was the first time Dani had said anything of substance at the lunch table.

"Yeah," Dani said, figuring it was too late now to pretend she hadn't been paying attention to the conversation. "It's one of my dad's favorites." That wasn't strictly true. Her father did have a rare first edition displayed proudly in his office—the only reason Dani knew the publication date—but to say it was his favorite would be a slight on the family honor. The only acceptable opinion of Thaddeus Coombs in slayer circles was that he was a fool. More extremist views held that he was also a traitor to the cause.

A slayer himself, Coombs had immigrated to the States from England after three decades of dragon-hunting in his homeland. In his twilight years, he turned to more scholarly pursuits, gathering what would become known as the most comprehensive treatise on dragons. His work was invaluable, and for years he was a minor celebrity among slayers. Then he began spouting ideals about how knowledge belonged to the masses, and one day all those secrets were suddenly in print, available to all.

He died a couple years later, but instead of fading into obscurity, his book became an overnight sensation at the World's Columbian Exposition in Chicago. The rest was history. Or it would have been, if booksellers hadn't shelved it in the fiction section with

Shelley, Verne, and MacDonald. Gradually, through the turn of the century, *Fiends of Fire* became first a science fiction sensation, then an elusive *Jeopardy!* question, and finally a cult classic.

Dani had read it once, at Eden's insistence. It wasn't particularly useful to modern slayers, and despite the title's promise, the history was not concise at all. Dani did appreciate the irony that the secrets of her family's profession (or at least the pre-twentieth-century secrets) were being taught as classic fiction alongside *Frankenstein* and *Dracula* in universities, and pasted on websites and Tumblr posts in comparison to *Lord of the Rings* and *A Song of Ice and Fire*. Most slayers did not share her amusement.

When Dani took another bite of her sandwich and showed no signs of adding more to her brief statement, Sadie hesitantly continued, addressing both Dani and Tomás now.

"When my family visited England a couple years ago, I made them visit as many places that he mentions in *Fiends* as we could. Did you know that the house where he used to live is a museum now? It's full of old weaponry and a bunch of scientific drawings of dragons that some people think were done by Darwin, but no one knows for sure."

Sadie's round face was flushed, her big brown eyes animated. For a second she reminded Dani of the girl she had been years ago, her freckles raised by the sun, her braces as shiny as the silver barrettes she always wore in her hair to pin back her bangs. She used to coat her lips with pink-tinted bubblegum-scented chapstick, because she wasn't allowed to chew gum with her braces and she missed it.

Sadie's braces and barrettes were gone now. She still had a light dusting of freckles, but they were faded under her foundation, and the bubblegum pink of her lips had been replaced with a red lipstick that never seemed to smudge or lose its glossy shine. Dani was sad all of a sudden, and not—to her surprise—because she missed the girl that Sadie had been, but because the girl in front of her now was practically a stranger.

"Why would Darwin draw pictures of dragons?" Tomás asked skeptically. "Maybe they're just lizards that weren't drawn to scale?"

We don't look like lizards. Nox's indignant voice took her less by surprise than it once had. She'd grown used to his barging into her daily life—she didn't mind so much, as long as the interloping remained strictly in her own mind.

Stop being a baby. It's not like Tomás has ever seen a dragon before.

Dani had seen prints of the sketches Sadie was talking about, also in her dad's office. They were most definitely not lizards, but they also hadn't been drawn by Darwin, unless he had been moonlighting as a slayer. No one else could have recreated the anatomy with such accuracy.

"They're dragons," Sadie said. "I told you that no one knows if Darwin actually drew them. They're so detailed that most people agree that it had to have been someone who'd actually seen a dragon up close."

Tomás had frozen with a chip halfway to his mouth. Dani, who had been on the verge of agreeing with Sadie again, realized just in time what had given him pause.

"Wait," he said, lowering the chip. "Wait. You do know that dragons don't really exist, right? Please tell me you know that."

The color of Sadie's cheeks had deepened to crimson. Dani felt the secondhand embarrassment so keenly that she even started thinking of ways to change the subject, but Sadie set her jaw.

"I'm not a Dragon Truther or anything, but no one's ever proved that dragons *don't* exist. So I don't think it's fair to say that they are definitely a myth."

She's smart. I like this one.

Tomás opened his mouth, but Dani cut in, her interest in the conversation renewed.

"What's a 'Dragon Truther'?" she asked Sadie.

Sadie looked at her, disconcerted for a second, as if unsure whether Dani had really just spoken to her for a second time in one day.

"It comes from this subreddit," she said. "There are some people who think that Coombs's book was an actual history, not fiction at all. They think that dragons and the sorcerers he mentions are real and maybe even still around today."

"Sure, that makes sense," Tomás said, sarcastic but not mean, in the way only he could manage. "A bunch of giant fire-breathing dragons and magic sorcerers are wandering around out there, and somehow no one has noticed except Reddit."

Dani choked on a laugh and almost spewed soda through her nose. She wiped her face quickly with a napkin to hide her expression.

What is a Reddit?

I'll explain later.

"Why not?" Sadie countered. "Who's to say a sorcerer wouldn't be able to hide their magic from you, or that dragons wouldn't have advanced forms of camouflage like lots of other animals do?"

Very smart.

"She makes a good point," Dani couldn't resist saying.

Tomás, to his credit, did actually appear to entertain the thought for a few seconds.

"Maybe," he admitted finally. "But come on, you don't really believe that?"

Sadie screwed up her lips in a way that made her nose wrinkle. It was cute. With their history, Dani couldn't imagine ever wanting to kiss her again, but it was hard not to notice how she had left awkward adolescence behind and stepped into a quiet self-confidence. All her sweet quirks and mannerisms, her bright eyes, her red cupid's-bow lips—they made her into someone both approachable and alluring. Dani wasn't sure if she was jealous or captivated. Probably a little of both.

"No, I guess not," Sadie said at last. "But I do think it's fascinating. You should check out the thread sometime. Some of the theories are super well-researched and intricate. Also, there's this bar in Knoxville that I love. It's called Kaleidoscope, and it's owned by one of the original creators of the subreddit."

"Is it dragon-themed?" Tomás asked.

"No." She laughed. "But they have really wild cocktails and tons of vintage arcade games. A lot of local Truthers hang out there. We should go sometime, just for fun."

"Don't you have to be twenty-one?" Dani tried to not let it show on her face, but while a night at a cool bar sounded fun, a night surrounded by a bunch of greasy-haired conspiracy theorists who would no doubt try to mansplain dragons to her did not.

"Just to sit at the bar." Sadie's eyes were bright as she looked between Tomás and Dani.

"Sounds good to me," said Tomás with a shrug. He tossed his empty soda can toward the trash bin and missed.

"Nice one," said Dani. He made a face at her and pushed his chair back.

"I'm going to get an ice cream sandwich from the store." He dropped the can in the garbage and cleared the rest of their trash from the table. "You guys want anything?"

Sadie shook her head, and Dani waved him off.

"Hey," Sadie said once he'd gone. She swirled a finger absently through a ring of condensation on the tabletop. "You remember those stories you used to tell when we were kids?"

Dani, who had just now realized that she probably should have gone with Tomás, fidgeted in her seat.

"Not really," she said, even though she did. She wasn't at all comfortable with the conversation veering anywhere near their past. Dani had come out as bisexual years ago, and she wasn't ashamed of it in the least, but the memory of that kiss had always haunted her, tinged as it was with so many competing emotions. It hadn't even been a very good kiss. How could it have been, when it was the first for both of them—when it only happened because they had been sitting side by side on Sadie's back stoop, sharing the last red Popsicle from the freezer? Their knees had knocked together every time they giggled, and Dani's hair had been tangled and sticky from her attempts to smooth it back from her forehead.

"Here," Sadie had said, handing Dani the Popsicle. She pulled out one of the barrettes from her own hair and pinned back Dani's shaggy, dark bangs. And then they were giggling again for no reason, and Sadie's face was so very close, and the strange knotted ball of feelings in Dani's chest was suddenly all she could think about. A joy so radiant it was almost painful, like letting your eyes stray too close to the sun. A burgeoning need so visceral it burned from the crown of her head to the tips of her toes. That's when she had leaned in closer, so close that Sadie had stopped giggling, and for a few seconds there was a world of possibility between them. Then Dani had closed the gap. A wild cherry kiss, cool and sweet, while the Popsicle melted big red drops onto the wooden step between them. They both pulled back at the same time and just looked at each other, suffocating in the heat and stillness of the late summer day.

Sadie climbed to her feet without a word and ran into the house, banging the screen door shut behind her. Dani sat there for another ten minutes, until the Popsicle was nothing but a sticky puddle on the ground and a stained stick in her hand. Slowly, she took the barrette from her hair and set it on the porch next to the Popsicle stick. She had raced the sunset home on her bike. That was the last she'd seen of her best friend.

"You used to tell all kinds of stories about dragons and knights and sorcerers. I could never get enough of them. Even after—even after we moved, I used to think about those stories. I made my parents buy me every book and movie they could find that featured dragons, and I was always trying to find more. That's actually how I ended up stumbling into the Dragon Truthers subreddit a few years ago."

"Huh," Dani said, in what she hoped was a polite but noncommittal way. She actually found it kind of funny, but of course there was no way to explain the irony to Sadie. "Maybe I missed my calling as Sister Grimm."

Sadie grinned, but it faded quickly.

"Just so you know . . ." She pressed her lips together, marshaling up the nerve to finish her sentence. The rest of it spilled out in a breathless jumble. "I didn't take this job because you work here—I didn't even know when I took it. My mom knows Brandi's older sister Terri from college, and I needed a summer job, and it just kind of worked out. I know it's awkward, and I'm really sorry about—about everything, I guess. I have a boyfriend back in Ohio. His name's—well, I guess that doesn't matter, I just—" With sheer force of will, she stopped the torrent of words. Took a deep breath. Tried again.

"I'm sorry, Dani, is what I wanted to say. I'm sorry about how I left things when we were kids, and I hope we can—you know— be cool."

Dani stared at her. She had, on and off throughout the

intervening years, envisioned every possible way that a reunion with Sadie might go. Somehow it had never occurred to her that Sadie would just want to apologize and move on, without even talking about it. It seemed deceptively easy. Dani's stomach churned with emotions that were too revealing, too vulnerable to ever be laid bare. Maybe this was for the best.

She could feel Nox's curiosity burning in her head, and she silently urged him to mind his own damn business.

"Okay," she said.

"Okay?" Sadie asked a little skeptically.

"Okay." Dani slid her chair back and stood up. "We're cool, but I've got to find Tomás and get back to the ropes course. See you later?"

Sadie nodded. She hadn't moved. Dani couldn't decide if the expression on her face was relief or disbelief. She went back through to the front. Tomás was leaning on the counter with his ice cream sandwich in hand and flirting with the cashier, who seemed flattered but nonetheless refused to give him anything more than the twenty percent employee discount.

"You're gross," Dani informed him as she dragged him and his ice cream sandwich out the door and down the path.

"What? She's the one who told me I should be a model."

"She did *not*."

He grinned and took a bite. "I'm paraphrasing. Want some?"

Dani shook her head. Half her thoughts were lingering in the staff room, examining every angle of the conversation she had just left behind. It didn't take Tomás long to notice. She wasn't one to turn down free ice cream.

"What's wrong? Did something happen with Sadie?"

"She apologized." Dani's forehead creased with a frown.

"Isn't that a good thing?"

"Yeah, I guess." She rubbed her hands over her face, as if to physically scrub away her own confused misgivings. "It just caught me off guard. We're fine now, I think."

"Sweet. What do you think about inviting her to movie night tonight?"

Dani thought it sounded like a recipe for even more awkwardness, but she could tell from Tomás's expression that he really wanted her to say yes. Dani figured she couldn't say that she and Sadie were fine now, and then refuse to hang out with her.

"Yeah, that sounds fun," she said.

"Awesome, I'll ask her." Tomás munched on his ice cream, happily oblivious to Dani's unease. "That bar sounded pretty cool, right?"

"A bar full of conspiracy nuts?"

"And retro arcade games."

"You're such a nerd."

"But I make it look so good," he said, striking an over-the-top model pose in the middle of the walkway.

Dani just laughed and stole a bite of his ice cream sandwich.

You keep strange company, Nox said.

That's funny, coming from you, Dani returned.

Do your friends know that you come from a family of dragon slayers?

Of course not. A panicked thought occurred to her. *You'd better not be planning on any surprise appearances.*

She sensed, rather than heard, Nox's indignant snort.

"You okay?" Tomás asked around a mouthful of ice cream.

"What? Yes—why?" she replied, with zero smoothness.

Tomás eyed her skeptically.

"You looked like you were freaking out about something," he said.

"I'm not," she said, and then, because she knew that wasn't

going to fly: "I was just thinking about all the chores I have to do when I get home."

You're a rather poor liar, Nox observed dryly. *I am amazed you have managed to keep any secrets at all.*

"Shut up."

"I didn't say anything," Tomás said.

"Sorry, not you." *Shit.* Dani stopped walking, trying to untangle the competing conversations in her brain.

"Are you sure you're okay?" Tomás stopped too and turned to face her. His skepticism was edging into concern. "If you want to talk more about Sadie, we can—"

"No," she broke in, a little too desperate. She was too frazzled to carry on a normal conversation, much less delve into the complicated feelings about Sadie's apology that she'd already decided to bury forever.

Tomás was watching her with open concern now. Dani took a deep breath. Told herself to focus.

"I'm okay," she said, trying to relax her expression in a way that reflected that. "Just a lot on my mind."

She started walking again, hoping Tomás would drop it. He did not.

"Are you sure you don't want to talk about it—whatever it is?"

"I'm fine. I promise."

She smiled winningly at him. He didn't look completely won over, but he didn't press any further, just silently offered her another bite of ice cream.

I'm sorry, Nox said, in a rare moment of meekness. *I wasn't trying to make things harder for you.*

Could have fooled me, Dani thought, then immediately felt bad for the barbed response. *It's okay. Tomás is my best friend. He's seen worse.*

Nox didn't reply, but she felt a new understanding click into place between them. Another puzzle piece in the tenuous connection they were building.

Because she didn't feel like stopping off at home to change clothes and possibly be bullied by Eden into an afternoon training session, Dani rode with Tomás after work straight to his house. The Vasquez homestead was in a subdivision of brightly colored houses from the eighties with yards bedecked with kid's toys, abandoned sports equipment, and kitsch lawn ornaments. It was the sort of place that hosted a block party every couple of months and held a neighborhood-wide yard sale once a year.

Tomás pulled into the driveway of 43 Watercress Lane, a two-story white colonial. It boasted a mailbox with hand-painted birds on it, and three cherry trees that covered the front lawn in a pink-petal carpet every spring.

"Is Sadie coming?" Dani asked, half-hoping that she wouldn't be.

"Yeah, she's just got to run by her house first. She said there's a movie streaming on Netflix about dragons that's supposed to be really good."

"As long as it's not a documentary," Dani said dryly. Tomás just laughed.

Movie nights were traditionally held in the basement of the Vasquez house, which doubled as a family room and game room. They had a huge television with surround sound and an impressive array of electronics, not to mention a full-size Ping-Pong table and basically every board game ever invented. There were few things Dani loved more than curling up on the familiar old couch and laughing while Tomás got his ass handed to him by his sisters on every video game they owned, or munching on Skittles and talking through some movie they'd seen a dozen times before. She didn't know how to feel about Sadie invading this sacred space.

Judging from Sadie's nervous fidgeting as she arrived and sat down on the couch, she didn't quite know how to feel about it either. She gave Dani a little smile and wave but didn't say anything as Tomás fiddled with the sound system. In her galaxy-patterned leggings and loose purple tank top, she was more casual than she'd ever been at work, but there was still an effortless chicness about her that Dani couldn't help but envy.

Unable to stand the awkward silence, Dani hopped up and went to the kitchenette to pop some popcorn and grab some drinks from the fridge. She also found a half-empty bag of Skittles on the counter that she dumped into a bowl. She paused to reply to a text from Eden asking where she was.

Movie night with Tomás and Sadie. I told you this morning.

It only took a few seconds for Eden to reply.

I thought you'd come home for training first.

A wave of irritation washed over Dani, and she decided to ignore the text, sliding her phone into her back pocket.

"Perfect," Tomás announced as she carried her bounty to the coffee table.

"I love Skittles," Sadie said, reaching for some.

"A woman after my own heart." Tomás dropped down on the couch between them, and instantly his presence made everything a little less awkward. Gradually, Sadie loosened up, and Dani found herself in a better and better mood as they joked about the latest set of ridiculous rules Brandi had come up with at Tree Top, and shared their funniest stories of people freaking out on the ropes course. By the time they finally started the movie, Dani had begun to forget why she resented Sadie being there in the first place.

What is this nonsense? Nox demanded at the first image of a dragon onscreen, making Dani jump. Luckily, her friends didn't notice.

It's just a movie.

It's a mockery.

"Wow, this CGI is terrible," said Tomás.

See? said Nox. *Even your friend agrees.*

You don't even know what CGI is, Dani shot back. She'd already missed most of the opening dialogue. Hopefully it wasn't anything too important. *Now hush.*

He obliged, but not without sending her a wave of prickly irritation. Dani was able to focus on the movie—or more accurately, focus on roasting it with Tomás and Sadie. She got another text from Eden about half an hour in.

We can just do a double training session tomorrow to make up for it.

So generous, Dani typed back with spiteful jabs of her thumbs. Then she put her phone on silent mode and tucked it away.

Sadie and Tomás were both laughing at something a character had just said, a joke that Dani had missed while focusing on her sister. She jammed some Skittles in her mouth to soothe her frustration and tried her best to forget about everything outside the basement. She only wished there was a way to set Nox to silent as well.

What does that even mean? Nox asked, radiating indignance.

Nothing. Never mind. I'm trying to watch this movie.

Fine. I'll be silent so you can enjoy this exceedingly offensive depiction of my kind.

She knew that wouldn't last long, and unfortunately the next time he chose to interject was at a jump scare, right as the hero turned to find himself face-to-face with a snarling dragon.

Is it over yet?

Dani swore and upturned the popcorn bowl in her lap. She

clutched her pounding heart while Tomás and Sadie—after a split second of shock—both burst into laughter at her reaction.

"Do you need to hold my hand?" Tomás asked.

"Shut up." Dani gave him a shove, her face flushed. But she couldn't bite back a grin herself as her heart rate settled.

"We can turn the lights back on if it's too scary for you," Sadie said.

Dani flicked some popcorn at her over Tomás's head, then on second thought threw some popcorn at him too. Sadie giggled and flung a Skittle that hit Dani in the nose.

"Hang on," Tomás cried, throwing his arms over his head to protect himself. "I'm the one who's going to have to vacuum all this up."

"All the more reason for us to enjoy ourselves," said Dani, grabbing up more popcorn.

I don't understand you humans, Nox said sullenly.

Dani ignored him, but in the back of her mind she wondered for the first time if the dragon ever felt left out of the life she led apart from him, while he had to spend most of his time secreted away in that cave to guard the eggs. Not that he would ever admit it if she asked. But maybe it was a good reason, apart from her sanity, to start practicing the ability to keep her thoughts and experiences from leaking haphazardly into his consciousness, which he'd promised her was possible.

For now, though, she decided to focus on her friends. And on winning this food fight.

ELEVEN

Remedy Coffee, which was in a squat brick building across the street from a cemetery in Knoxville, was not the sort of locale Eden imagined someone like Calla Thorn would frequent. Even so, she couldn't help but feel incredibly chic when the driver of the black Mercedes stopped right in front and rushed around to open the door for her. A few people were staring at her through the giant windows and nudging their companions, probably assuming she was some kind of celebrity.

As she used the front-facing camera on her phone to check the status of her lipstick one last time, Eden was glad she'd taken twice as long as usual to get ready, striking the perfect balance between sophisticated and casual. She'd picked out a breezy cream-colored blouse tucked into a pair of high-waisted jean shorts with a narrow red belt and leopard print flats. Then she'd watched a YouTube video three times to get her "daytime smoky eye" just right, and borrowed one of her mom's nude lipsticks to pair with it.

All in all, she was pleased with how she looked, and only a little nervous about the upcoming conversation. No matter what happened, she was determined that this encounter would leave no doubt in the high sorcerer's mind that Eden was a real dragon slayer now, not just a kid who got left behind.

Just before she pocketed her phone, it buzzed with a text message from Nate. She grinned automatically. They had been texting for a couple weeks now, mostly increasingly obscure song lyrics in a continuation of their game. She knew it was silly to keep texting him in the first place when she didn't have time for anything outside her training, but it was hard to ignore him when he turned on the charm. She made a mental note to reply later, set the phone to silent, and tucked it in her purse.

She entered the shop and pushed her sunglasses up on her head, giving an embarrassed smile to the heads that swiveled in her direction. Calla was lounging at a table in the corner, one leg crossed over the other, talking rapidly into her phone in French.

When she caught sight of Eden, she smiled and waved. She snapped one last sentence into the phone and dropped it on the table. Eden couldn't help but notice as she sat down that the phone screen was black. Whoever Calla had been talking to, she hadn't been using technology. She couldn't help but wonder if sorcerers had been relieved or annoyed when the marvels of modern science began to catch up with their magic.

"Thank you so much for coming," Calla said. "I know it's a bit of a trek, but you really can't beat the coffee here."

"No problem," Eden said, setting her pocketbook and her sunglasses down on the table in a neat row. "Have you already ordered?"

"Not yet." Calla raised a hand and waved down a barista who was wiping a table. Eden could see other patrons lined up at the counter to place their orders, and was about to point that out to Calla, when the barista popped over with a smile.

"What can I get for you today?" she asked.

Eden was surprised that she hadn't just told them to order at the counter, and she could see over the barista's shoulder that the hipster guy manning the cash register was giving her a strange look. Calla, nonplussed, rattled off a complicated order that Eden wasn't even sure was entirely in English. The barista absorbed it without blinking and turned to Eden. There was an odd quality to her smile, like the corners of her mouth were straining with the effort.

"I'll just have a flat white." Eden couldn't help but fidget in her seat under the glare of that unyielding smile. "Thanks."

The barista left. Eden looked at Calla, who was examining one of her wine-red nails with a frown, even though Eden couldn't see even the slightest chip. She fidgeted some more, then forced herself to still. Behind the counter, the barista and her coworker exchanged a heated conversation in whispers that the patrons in line strained to overhear while pretending not to notice.

"Here's the thing," said the high sorcerer without preamble, gazing at Eden and tapping her perfect nails on the tabletop. "I'm a busy woman, and I know you are too. So I'm just going to tell you straight why I wanted to meet today. I don't have any use for small talk."

Her tone was clipped but not harsh. Eden sat up straighter in her seat.

"You want to talk about Dani," she said. The disappointment wrapped up in the words was mitigated by the brief slash of surprise across Calla's face, followed by a slow smile.

"Just so," she said, inclining her head slightly. Her copper hair was wound into a loose bun at the nape of her neck, with a few artful tendrils escaping by her ears. In her black stilettos, black ankle pants, and silky forest-green blouse, she could have just stepped out of a board meeting in a plush office somewhere. And Eden was pretty sure she'd seen a glimpse of some trademark red soles. "I'm assuming your parents have at least mentioned my invitation to her?"

Eden nodded. Her mom had finally broached the subject with

Dani at dinner, the night after Eden had told her about it. Dani's answer remained unchanged, and neither Analisa nor James had put any effort into convincing her otherwise. Eden had tried to understand her parents' distrust of the sorcerers in the context of what Frankie had told her, but she still didn't get why they were so blasé about the situation. God knows how many dragons—and dragon eggs—were out there, and her parents were turning their nose up at help from the only living beings as powerful as dragons. The sorcerers had been keeping to themselves for so long, and now they were finally reaching out a hand—if not as friends, then at least as allies. Eden couldn't believe her parents were ready to let that slip away.

"We all talked to her about it, but Dani isn't interested," she said carefully.

Tap, tap, tap. Calla's fingernails clicked on the tabletop one by one.

"That's disappointing," she said at last. "Can I ask why?"

There was a latent danger in her voice that made Eden glad the barista interrupted with their coffee. Hers had an intricate white flower swirled into the top, and she had to resist the urge to pull out her phone and snap a picture. Frankie would have loved it. She had a thing for what she called "fresa white-people drinks," which included anything from fancy coffee to neon cocktails to Pinterest-ready milkshake concoctions.

"Dani is really talented, but she's not as dedicated as—" *Me.* "—as she should be."

Calla appeared to ponder this as she took a sip from her white porcelain cup.

"I thought your parents, of all people, would run a tight ship," she said, almost to herself.

"It's not their fault," Eden said with a rush of defensiveness. "Dani just . . . has other priorities. She trains with me, but Mom and Dad aren't going to force her to do anything."

"Priorities," Calla echoed mildly. A dense silence expanded between them, until finally Calla spoke again, her tone just as mild as before. "Can I show you something, Eden?"

Eden swallowed down the other arguments she had primed in her parents' defense and nodded wordlessly. Calla leaned forward and extended one hand across the table. She tapped one delicate nail on the rim of Eden's cup. Instantly, the liquid rippled as if someone had slammed a hand down on the table. Eden stared down at it, mesmerized as the latte art began to stir and reshape itself. This wasn't something the marvels of modern science could do.

Calla leaned back, crossing one leg over the other and taking another sip of her own drink.

"It was about two hundred years ago," she said, glancing briefly skyward as if trying to remember what she'd had for breakfast yesterday. "I lose track of the precise date—those sorts of details stop mattering when you've been around as long as I have. I was living in Ireland at the time, just outside a gorgeous little village by the sea. There was talk, like there always was back then in rural parts, of a dragon in the area. I thought it was just folk blaming the supernatural for their bad harvests and dead cattle. I had 'other priorities' then, too. His name was Josiah."

Eden watched as the story took shape in the cup in front of her. On its tiny round canvas, the velvety micro-foamed milk painted itself into a heart-stopping vista of Irish cliffs overlooking a thunderous sea, into a cottage grown beautifully wild with flowers where a goat munched happily in the yard, into a man's face, broad and grinning, his nose a little crooked, his eyes wonderfully kind. Calla, though she didn't look down at the scenes her magic was illustrating, smiled softly, sadly. There was a dreamy glint in her eyes.

"I know. It's the worst of clichés. And I knew even then that it was a terrible idea to get involved with a human, but so it goes. He took up all my time, all my attention. Looking back, I think I was so consumed with him *because* of how fleeting his life was compared with my own. That's not important, though. One night I woke to the smell of smoke. I thought it was my house at first, then I realized the smoke was drifting downwind. I could see it all from my back garden, the entire village engulfed in flames."

Eden watched in mute horror as the image bloomed in front of her. She tried to tell herself she was just imagining the acrid smoke tickling her nostrils, the distant sound of screams.

"Dragonfire is different than regular fire, you know," said Calla, her tone curiously light. "It burns hotter and faster. It can devour a human in the blink of an eye, a house within a minute, a whole village in less than an hour. By the time I arrived, there was nothing—and no one—left to save. The other folk who lived outside the village didn't dare come near. They must have seen the shadow tearing across the moon, heard the awful shriek like a massive bird of prey."

A dragon took shape in the foam, its wings extended, its tail and claws poised to strike. And beneath it was a tiny figure, her hair streaming loose, her fury and sorrow so complete, so earth-shattering, that Eden could feel them vibrating through her own body.

"I could have killed it," Calla said, no hint of pride in her dull tone. "Sometimes I still think I should have. In that moment, though, I realized that my revenge would only be for this one village, for one man, and there would be more, all across the world.

There would always be more. I wanted to find a way to rid the world of dragons for good, and for that, I needed to know more about them than anyone ever had before."

Chains lashed out from the tiny sorcerer's hands, binding the dragon, dragging it down to the earth.

"Everything okay over here?" came the cheerful voice of the barista.

Eden jumped in her seat, looked up guiltily at the barista, and then looked back down at her drink, only to find that the surface had melted into nothing but a shapeless whirl of white and brown.

"Yes, thank you," said Calla with a languid smile, unmoving.

The barista drifted away, and Eden took a few seconds to straighten her thoughts. She tried a sip of the coffee. It was still hot.

"The dragon I saw at Stonecrest," she said, choosing each word with painstaking care.

"The very same." Calla's smile hadn't shifted, and she directed it at Eden. "I knew that night you must have an instinct. Only a born slayer would be able to home in on a dragon so perfectly."

It hadn't felt like an instinct; it had felt like a nightmare. She'd been nine years old and just starting to come into an understanding of what it meant to be a Rivera. Dani, only seven (*and a half*, as she insisted on correcting everyone), had been left with a babysitter, so for the first time in her memory, Eden had her parents all to herself. The shine of it had worn off pretty quickly though, once dinner was over and the grown-ups were talking in low, serious voices about serious subjects that Eden didn't care about. She'd used the bathroom down the hall, but instead of making her way back to the glowing parlor and familiar voices, she'd tiptoed in the opposite direction.

Her exploration was a blur now, even when she let herself dwell on it. The memory was a long streak of wood-paneled corridors, and musky bedrooms with furniture draped in white sheets, and then that door. Secretive and metal and inscribed with a symbol she didn't know, in paint as red as blood. There were locks and bolts on it, but it had been left open—just a crack. Beyond the door were stairs, cold and stone and winding down, down, down. She'd felt like an adventurer in a story, a warrior on her way to fight a terrible monster.

Of course, when she'd reached the bottom, her whimsical fantasy had dried up and blown away, leaving her alone in a cavernous room lit only by a single bulb dangling from a wire overhead. Beyond the warm circle of light, she could see nothing but shadows that seemed to squirm and slither with their own life. She made herself hold her ground and stare into the black, fists clenched at her sides, because her baby sister was the one who was afraid of the dark. Not her.

Other shapes took form slowly, but nothing she could make out with any certainty. Then, a few feet in front of her, just outside the ring of light, another shape emerged. Red eyes that glinted like rubies. Black scales that seemed birthed of the shadows. A scalding puff of breath that made her eyes water and her cheeks burn. She took a step backwards and found herself hemmed in by a black tail as thick as she was, sliding across her shoulder blades. When she turned her head, she saw the dagger-like tip hovering at eye level, like it was waiting for her to make the first move.

She told herself to scream, but no sound would come. She told herself to duck and run, but her muscles were frozen. All she could do was stare in sick fascination as the dragon opened its mouth horribly wide, flashing rows of wicked white teeth. In the back of its throat gleamed a ball of blue flame, jewel-bright and lovelier than anything she'd ever seen in her life.

Then came a blast—not from the dragon, but from behind her. She had no idea what it was. It sizzled and sparked like electricity, but left her colder than the time she'd fallen into a snowdrift and had to wait for her dad to fish her back out again. It seemed to move straight through her, but hit the dragon with a force that knocked it back into the shadows until it had vanished completely. There was an awful crash and a wail that she sometimes thought was the dragon's and sometimes thought must've been her own.

After that the memory grew fuzzy again. Calla, so tall and beautiful, without a hair out of place, asking her if she was hurt. Another voice, a man's it sounded like, using language that her parents called "swearing" and Frankie called "please-don't-tell-your-mom-I-said-that-in-front-of-you." She couldn't see the source, glued now as she was to Calla's side with her face buried in the woman's hip.

The voices had pinged back and forth, cutting and angry, their words coming back to Eden only in brief snatches.

"He wasn't going to—"

"—that filthy, pathetic excuse for a—"

"—fucking *kill* you."

"You're welcome to try, darling, any time you like. Just remember that failure has consequences."

For some reason, that last reply from Calla stuck with Eden in its entirety. She didn't know if it was because the tone, slick and sinister as poison, had sent shivers down her spine. Or if it was because of the bleak, hollow silence that followed, filling up her ears until all that anger had been replaced with emptiness.

The next thing she remembered was being outside the parlor again, though she had no memory of the climb back up those stairs. Calla smiled at her and winked, like they shared the best secret in the world, and they had gone back in together. Though Calla had never actually asked her not to, Eden had never told a soul.

"You've had a captive dragon for over two hundred years?" Eden asked, not sure why she felt the need to force the question out. Hadn't Calla just told her as much?

"Tricky beasts," said Calla. "Took us nearly that long to even begin to learn anything useful."

"So the weapon you told my parents about . . ."

Calla smiled and tapped the side of her nose.

"All in due time," she said. "Meanwhile, we need to focus on training up the best and the brightest."

"That's why you want Dani," Eden said, hating herself for the glumness in her voice.

Calla eyed her for a second over the rim of her cup before taking a long drink and setting it back down. She leaned forward, crossing her arms on the table.

"I don't know what your parents have been telling you, Eden, but it's clear to me that you're already past training. You're a dragon slayer now. The sooner you accept that, the better off the world will be."

Eden's heart thrilled, and she had to retrace her way through the words just to make sure that she'd understood correctly. That Calla Thorn, the high sorcerer, considered her a bona fide slayer. No longer a kid in need of training. No longer a liability to be left behind.

"I want to bring Dani on board, because we need more like you," Calla went on. "The dragon population has been culled quite low, but it's begun to level off because the true slayers are becoming few and far between. If we aren't careful, we'll find ourselves back in the middle ages, with a dragon for every city."

Eden recalled the scent of smoke and those screams echoing from a memory that wasn't hers. She gripped her cup tightly.

"I understand," she said. "I'll talk to Dani again. I'll get her to at least come visit you at Stonecrest."

Calla sighed in obvious relief.

"That's all I ask," she said. "Thank you. I truly mean it."

Eden crossed one leg over the other and tried to look gracious and nonchalant as she finished her drink. Hipster Guy had left the barista in charge of the cash register and made his way over to their table.

"Can I clear these up for you?" he asked, in pleasant enough tones, though Eden could see irritation seething beneath the surface. She handed over her cup and saucer and looked down, embarrassed. He took Calla's empty cup as well and then set down a small piece of paper in the middle of the table. "Your bill. People usually pay at the register."

There was no missing the pointed jab there. Eden's cheeks flushed warm, and she reached for the bill, but Calla waved her away.

"Don't worry about that," she said.

Eden opened her mouth to politely protest, but before she could say anything, Hipster Guy had scooped back up the bill and crumpled it in one hand.

"Don't worry about that," he repeated, his broad grin twitching at the corners.

Though her cheeks were still hot, Eden shivered. The man walked away, bearing their dishes and the unpaid bill back behind the counter.

"Well, this was lovely," Calla said, standing up and stretching as if nothing were out of the ordinary.

Eden realized she was staring at the sorcerer and jumped to her feet, gathering her sunglasses and pocketbook in shaking hands.

"It was—thanks—I mean, we should do it again soon." She had no idea what one was supposed to say in this situation.

"Absolutely." Calla stepped forward and gave her a peck on each cheek, leaving Eden feeling both very stunned and very European. "I have some other business to take care of, but the car will be waiting for you. Good luck with your sister."

They walked out the front together and sure enough, Eden saw the black Mercedes cruising down the street to stop in front of the shop. The driver popped out to open the door for her. Before she climbed in, Eden turned to give a final goodbye to Calla, but the high sorcerer was already gone.

Dani and Sadie both spent the night at the Vasquez house. All three of them stayed up most of the night playing games with increasing levels of caffeine-induced delirium until finally they collapsed into sleep. Dani couldn't remember the last time she'd had this much fun, even with the stubborn nudge of Nox's presence in the back of her mind as a reminder that this world of Ping-Pong and Skittles wasn't one she could stay in forever.

They passed most of the next day in a sleepy haze, playing video games with Tomás's sisters and watching more terrible dragon movies that Sadie recommended and Nox, of course, hated. At around four in the afternoon, Dani's phone pinged with a message from Eden.

I'm here. Hurry up.

It took Dani a few seconds to recall that she had texted Eden the night before and asked for a ride home the next day. She said her goodbyes, but then Tomás insisted on walking her to the door, no doubt because he knew Eden was picking her up. They had to make a stop in the kitchen for Dani to say goodbye to Mrs. Vasquez, who tried in vain to convince her to invite Eden in for dinner. When Dani held firm to her polite refusal, Mrs. Vasquez compromised by heaping two servings of leftover chili from lunch into a Tupperware and pushing it into Dani's hands. It was next to impossible to leave the Vasquez house without a container of food—not that Dani was complaining.

Once on the front porch, she saw the Jeep parked in the street, windows down and music blaring. Tomás immediately made a beeline across the lawn for the object of his long-unreturned affections. Dani rolled her eyes, even though there was no one to see it. Eden had turned down the stereo and was chatting pleasantly with Tomás through the passenger window as Dani neared. They were talking about some band or another. Tomás thought Eden was some kind of musical goddess, just because she listened to all the same weird hipster bands he did. Dani had tried pointing out before that Eden was just as likely to listen to Lizzo or Taylor Swift, but to no avail.

"Excuse me," Dani said, bumping Tomás with her hip so she could open the door and climb in.

"I'll send you the link to the new album," Tomás said, still clinging to the open window as Dani pulled the door shut behind her.

"Awesome," said Eden. Dani knew that Eden had, of course, noticed a long time ago that Tomás had a crush on her. It's not like he was ever actually subtle about it. She treated him with perfect civility, like every other guy in high school who had mooned after her before figuring out she didn't have time for them, no matter how rich or ripped or smart they were. That was when the rumors about her being in a cult had started. Dani had thought it was funny at first, when the rumors filtered down to her year, but then it had begun to piss her off. She didn't like the habit boys had of coming up with elaborate reasons for why a girl didn't want to date them, and then using those imaginary excuses as weapons against her. Especially when that girl was too nice to wreak any revenge on them, and doubly especially when that girl was Dani's sister.

Tomás had always been perfectly content with the occasional smile and brief conversation he shared with Eden, which was the only reason that Dani was okay with the crush continuing. At this point, she had a feeling it was more of a habit for him than anything else. Eden had been his first real crush, and so she would always hold a special place in the lofty reaches of his mind—like the first concert you ever attended, or your favorite movie-theater candy.

"See you tomorrow," Dani told him pointedly. Tomás flashed her sad puppy eyes, but then he grinned and stepped back, waving them off.

"He's so sweet," Eden said as she backed out. "And cute."

"I'm glad you think so," Dani said. "Go ahead and start dating him so I never have to buy him another birthday or Christmas present again."

Eden let out a short laugh.

"God, you two are so weird."

"Why?"

"You've been attached at the hip for years. Are you seriously going to pretend like you've never thought about dating?"

Dani shrugged.

"We're best friends. I don't want to date him, and he doesn't want to date me. I don't get why that's so hard for everyone to understand." She didn't add that the last time she'd tried romance with her best friend, it hadn't ended well. Even if she did one day find herself the victim of hormones in Tomás's vicinity, she wouldn't risk losing him the way she'd lost Sadie, just for the sake of some short-term excitement. And it *would* be short-term. She knew Tomás well enough to understand that their friendship was not one that would survive the tangle of romance. With a soul-bonded dragon and immortality to deal with, Dani wasn't willing to make her relationships any more complicated. She didn't know how long she could possibly keep up this charade of a normal life, but she was going to try.

"Okay," said Eden in a way that told Dani she was already thinking about something else.

Dani turned up the stereo again and examined the scrape on her elbow. Or at least there had been a scrape there yesterday. She'd tripped over a root at Tree Top and used her arm to avoid face-planting in the dirt. Now it was barely a red mark on her skin. She swiped a finger over it, and then it was gone. Nox had told her that the stronger their soul bond grew, the less she would be plagued by "weaker human attributes" like scrapes and bruises. Without direct access to magic, she'd never be as strong or fast as a sorcerer, but she would be a lot harder to kill than the average human. That might come in handy, at least.

"Mom and Dad had to leave on a trip," Eden said after a while.

"Yeah, Dad texted me." It had given Dani a moment of panic at first, the mention of a dragon sighting, until she saw that it was in Arizona and therefore couldn't be her dragon. It also gave her a second moment of panic when she realized that at some point she'd begun to think of Nox as *her* dragon. Did he think of her as his human? She couldn't decide if the thought was disturbing or comforting.

It occurred to her that the last time they had gone on a

trip—which is what they always called their hunts—their parents had promised Eden she could go with them the next time. Dani opened her mouth to ask Eden why she hadn't gone, but then, in a rare moment of clarity and self-preservation, thought better of it and shut her mouth.

"So you'll never guess who I had coffee with today." Eden's voice had a strange, forced brightness to it.

"Who?" Dani asked, instantly skeptical. She eyed her sister, noticing for the first time that she was in something other than her workout clothes, with her glossy hair straightened and her makeup on point.

"Calla Thorn."

"Seriously, why?" She knew Eden probably expected a more appropriate level of awe in her response, but Dani couldn't muster up the effort. Also, she couldn't help but think of Nox's reaction to Calla's name. He hadn't been very forthcoming at the time, but whatever he knew about the high sorcerer, it wasn't flattering.

"She asked me," Eden said with a smidgen of petulance. "She sent a car and everything."

"Wow." Dani couldn't help the sarcasm that dripped from her voice.

"She really wants you to visit Stonecrest." Eden hesitated, and then reached over to turn down the volume. "I think you should go. It'll be good for you."

"Good for me how?" Dani asked. "It's not a health spa."

"I'm being serious. I know you think that dragon-hunting is some big joke that you can laugh away, but dragons are a real problem, Dani. They're dangerous, and they hurt people. If you ever saw one, you'd get it."

Dani thought of the wickedly sharp scales on Nox's tail, which had evolved solely for the purpose of swift, merciless pain. Then she thought of the way those same scales had folded away, harmless, when his tail wrapped softly around her.

"I get it," she said. The reckless fun of the night before and the lazy indulgence of earlier that day seemed far away now. She was back in her family's world, where laziness was an anathema; where recklessness could get you killed.

"If you did, then you'd be serious about your training. You'd realize that Calla is trying to help you. Sorcerers understand dragons better than we ever will."

"And why is that?" Dani asked.

"What?" Eden was caught off-guard by the question.

"Why do they understand dragons so well?"

"They've been fighting them for thousands of years," Eden said after a pause.

"So have slayers."

"They both use magic."

"Haven't you ever wondered why sorcerers exist? Why they can use magic in the first place?" It was something that had been nagging at Dani ever since Nox had explained their connection to her. How his magic flowed through her, but she couldn't use it the way a sorcerer could. What made a sorcerer different? Nox had said they were made, not born. But *how*?

She couldn't quite wrap her head around it, but she knew without a doubt that the answer to that question was important somehow. Necessary, even.

"I don't see how that matters," Eden said, but her tone had lost its know-it-all strictness.

"I think it does," Dani said, trying to keep her voice even. She didn't want to argue with Eden this time. She wanted to actually talk to her. "I'm not sure I trust them—the sorcerers, I mean."

"Why? What are you—"

"Just hear me out," Dani pleaded. "Think about everything we know about dragons. It all comes from research by slayers or sorcerers. Nothing from the dragons themselves."

"They're just animals, Dani."

"If that were true, they would have gone extinct a long time ago. You can't claim that they're dangerous and clever and magical, and also just dumb animals. You can't have it both ways."

For a second she thought her sister was going to keep arguing, just to be contrary, but Eden pursed her lips together and nodded once. Her hands were gripping the wheel tightly at ten and two, and her eyes were glued to the road, as if she were in the middle of a driving test.

"The history of Tempus Dracones has been passed down for generations," Dani said slowly, determined to get this right, to somehow use the perfect words to make Eden understand. "But it's only one side of the war—the winning side. What if there's more to it than that? What if the story we've been told about dragons is wrong?"

Eden was quiet for a long time. The only sound was the hum of the engine and the low melody from her Spotify, some sort of ballad, all strumming guitar and scratchy singing.

"What, then?" Eden's voice was barely louder than the music. "You've decided you feel sorry for dragons now, so the rest of us must be the bad guys? Jacob and Aaron Lowry? The Morenos? Kara Baker? Jon Evans? Emily Naviasky?"

"That's not fair," Dani murmured, her stomach turning at the list of names. All of them had been killed while dragon-hunting.

You know, my kind have our own list of the slain, Nox's voice broke in peevishly.

"I think their families are the ones who would say it isn't fair,"

Eden said. Her voice, while not harsh, was unrelenting. "Dragons are almost extinct now, thanks to slayers like them—like our parents, and grandparents, and great-grandparents. We haven't had to witness any of the destruction, so it's easy to say that they aren't that dangerous. Mom and Dad always skip over the worst of the damage, but I've read the reports that Dad has on his computer. In Bolivia in the seventies, nine people were killed over the course of a month before they finally tracked the dragon to its lair. New Zealand, in the early 1920s: there were two young dragons, barely the size of mountain lions, that still managed to kill two children and maim their parents. In the Rocky Mountains, a dragon was picking off hikers for almost a decade before it was caught."

Is this what you tell yourselves? Nox asked, his irritation bleeding into anger. *What of the crimes of slayers? My kind has done what we must to survive.*

Can we please talk about this later, Dani pleaded, her focus painfully split between the two harsh realities.

I do not like your sister.

"I get it," Dani said aloud to Eden, but Eden didn't stop.

"Multiply that by every new dragon that's hatched, and soon we'll be back in the nineteenth century, when dragons were burning down entire villages." Eden slowed, catching her breath. The song had changed over to something with a staccato beat and too many horns. "There aren't a lot of true slayers left. That's why I'm always pushing you to be better. That's why Calla wants you to come to Stonecrest."

Stay away from sorcerers, Nox said. It was a warning he'd given her before. When it was just her and Nox it had seemed an obvious precaution, but now that she was with Eden, everything felt twisted up. She felt that Nox was right to distrust sorcerers. She felt that Eden was right to distrust dragons. She felt like her head was going to explode. The line between her two lives was blurred and tangled and she couldn't navigate it by herself, not anymore.

"Turn here," she said suddenly, jabbing her finger at the window, where a brown sign announcing the scenic overlook had just come into view. "I want to show you something."

"I've seen it before," Eden said tiredly. "I want to go home."

"Please, just a few minutes?" Dani had no idea what she was doing. Or rather—*why* she was doing it.

Nox, can you come to the overlook?

Now? With her?

Please. Just trust me.

He gave no reply, but she could feel the answer in her bones. He trusted her.

All she could think was, if Eden could just meet Nox, could just see that he wasn't a ravenous wild animal, that there was so much intelligence and hope and grief all bound up inside him, then she would realize there was more to the Tempus Dracones than they had been told. And maybe with Eden's help, they might be able to figure out how to strengthen the soul bond and hatch the eggs before they were discovered.

The thought of having her sister on her side, of no longer being alone with this lifelong burden of a secret, was such a relief that Dani almost wanted to cry. Eden pulled off and followed the rutted gravel road through the trees. The overlook was empty, thank god, so she didn't bother pulling into a parking space. Clearly, she was hoping this wouldn't take long.

"There's something I have to tell you," Dani said aloud. Her voice was thick with emotion, and she dug her nails into her thighs to steel herself.

"Oh god—you're pregnant."

"No." Dani winced. At that moment, pregnancy actually

seemed like an easier secret to share. "The night of the bonfire, when I was on my way home, I pulled off here, and there was—I met a—"

Dragon. She couldn't force the word out. It seemed so big and grave and ridiculous, all at once. She felt the telltale tingle through the bond, and she knew that Nox was close. Maybe it would be easier to just show Eden. With a *whoosh* and a *whump*, Nox landed on the gravel in front of the Jeep, his head cocked slightly to one side, his eyes sparkling in the dying daylight.

"Shit," said Eden.

TWELVE

"It's okay," Dani said, throwing open the car door. "He's not going to hurt you."

"Dani, get back in the—"

"It's okay," Dani insisted, her tennis shoes crunching on the gravel as she hopped out and walked toward Nox. Judging from the alarm in Eden's voice, maybe a dragon suddenly descending from the sky wasn't actually the best way to introduce her to this part of Dani's life, but it was a little late for hindsight.

Why are you doing this? The doubt in Nox's tone was unmistakable.

I think you two need to meet, said Dani. A wave of antipathy from Nox revealed his opinion of this in no uncertain terms, but she pressed on. *She can help us.*

Are you sure about that? He sniffed and looked over her shoulder, an unsettling glint in his eye.

Dani turned, expecting to see her sister staring at them from the Jeep, but the driver's seat was empty, the door open. Had she run away?

Dani realized what a stupid question that was as the same moment she heard the telltale *click-clack* of a bolt action rifle being loaded. Eden stepped out from behind the Jeep, the rifle already shouldered, her movements as sure and fluid as a dancer's. Her focus was through the scope, and Dani knew she only had seconds before Eden found her shot and took it. She ran forward to block her sister's sightline. All the confusing emotions of moments before had streamlined themselves into a single driving force: panic.

Because, in her desperation and naiveté, Dani had forgotten one simple, transcendent fact. Nox was a dragon, and Eden was a born dragon slayer.

"Dani, move," Eden said, her voice strangely calm. She hadn't lowered the rifle.

"No," Dani said, throwing out her arms in a way that felt overly dramatic, even for her. "You're not shooting him. Put it down."

Eden raised her eye slightly to look over the scope at Dani. Her finger was off the trigger, but the gun was still raised, still ready. It struck Dani what a beautifully terrifying sight her sister was in that moment—looking for all the world like one of the indie pop darlings she so admired, wielding a Weatherby Mark V rifle as naturally as if it were a guitar.

"What's going on?" Eden's keen gaze darted from Dani to Nox. There was an edge to her voice that frightened Dani more than the finger that hovered near the trigger.

"Please, just put it down, and I'll explain," Dani said, and then to Nox: *Go, now.*

I can't just leave you here. She has a gun.

"She's my sister!" Dani whirled around to face him. She hadn't meant to shout, but her heartbeat was hammering in her throat, making it hard to speak without forcing the words out.

"Dani," said Eden.

Dani, said Nox.

Dani put her hands to her head and tried to think.

"His name is Nox," she said aloud, not sure else where to begin. "He's not going to hurt us."

"What the hell are you talking about?" Eden ground out through clenched teeth. Too late, Dani realized she had closed the gap between them, her prissy leopard-print flats silent on the gravel. Eden grasped the back of Dani's shirt with her left hand

and yanked her backwards. Then she had the gun raised again, zeroing in on her target with the cool composure she'd learned from their mother.

"No!" Dani threw herself onto Eden's right arm, slamming the gun's barrel downward at the same second the sharp report echoed through the valley. Gravel fragmented where the bullet hit, right between Nox's front claws. To her utter dismay, Nox did not take flight and retreat like any intelligent creature. Instead, he squared himself to face Eden head-on, the razor-sharp scales on his electrified tail flaring out, blue flames licking through his bared teeth.

What are you doing—stop! Dani abandoned her attempt to protect Nox from Eden and focused on protecting Eden from Nox, leaping in front of her sister.

She tried to shoot me.

Dani couldn't believe he had the nerve to sound hurt, as if she was supposed to feel sorry enough for him that she'd let him roast her sister alive.

"Just stop it," Dani cried to both of them.

"What's going on?" Eden's tone was strained to the point of snapping. She had raised the rifle again, though her finger stayed off the trigger—for now.

"Nox and I have a—" Dani's face flushed at the absurdity of the words about to leave her mouth. "We're connected by something called a soul bond."

Eden said nothing. Her gaze flicked momentarily to Dani, but her focus remained on Nox and the flame simmering behind his teeth.

"It's something that happens when a human and dragon are born at the same time. We can hear each other's thoughts. He's just as intelligent as any human."

Nox snorted in disdain at the comparison, and Eden's finger leapt to the trigger in reaction, though she didn't fire.

"It's tricked you somehow," she said, "with magic."

"I'm not under a spell," Dani said, a little miffed. "I know what I'm doing."

Debatable, said Nox.

"Debatable," said Eden at the same time.

Fair enough, since she had thought it was a good idea for some reason to introduce a dragon to a slayer with no warning and expect them to play nicely, but Dani wasn't about to admit that.

"Just put down the gun," she said. "He's not dangerous."

"No way," said Eden. "Get in the car."

"No! You're not listening to me."

"You're not making any *sense*, so get in the goddamn car before this dragon kills us both."

"He's not going to hurt us." Dani shot Nox a pointed look, and he begrudgingly extinguished his flame and lowered his tail. "You don't have to trust him, but you can trust me."

"Why should I?" Eden asked.

Dani's indignation deflated. Her voice, when it finally came, was distant to her own ears.

"What?"

"You don't know anything about dragons, Dani. You never pay attention, you half-ass all our lessons, and now you expect me to trust your judgment here?"

"That's not true," Dani said, ignoring the inner voice whispering that it might be. Indignation filled her again in a heady rush of heat. "And just because I don't care about being the next great dragon slayer, that doesn't mean I don't know what I'm talking about. Nox is my friend. He's more than that. He's not going to hurt you, and I'm not going to let you hurt him."

"That's not up to you." Eden's voice was like iron. She pushed Dani aside, raised the rifle, and fired.

Dani might have screamed, but she couldn't be sure with the gun's report exploding in her eardrums. Nox's pain imploded inside her, hot and glistering. Dragon scales were hard and resilient, but the Weatherby Mark V was meant for big game. It wasn't fatal for Nox, but it wasn't exactly a mosquito bite. And if Eden was able to hit any weaker points, like his eyes or throat, she could do some real damage. Dani wasn't about to let that happen.

Still reeling from the shock, she staggered forward and clambered onto Nox's back. He gave her a boost with his tail, and seconds later they were airborne. Eden was shouting her name, but Dani only tucked her head down against the wind and urged Nox to go. Her sister wouldn't risk a shot now—of that Dani was certain—but everything else she thought she knew was spiraling away from her as they left the earth behind.

How could everything have gone so wrong, so fast?

Eden's head ached at the very thought of the clusterfuck she was in. Her throat was raw from screaming for Dani to come back until she and the dragon were just a dark blot against the pale blue sky. She sank to the ground, her back against the wheel of the Jeep, her knees hugged to her chest. Everything was wrong—so, so wrong. Shaking, she picked up the rifle and slid it into her lap. She turned on the safety. Double-checked it. Triple-checked it.

The compulsion gave her something to focus on, but it did nothing to soothe her mounting panic. She knew she needed to get up, retrieve her phone from the car, and call her parents or Frankie or *someone*. She needed help. She needed to fix this.

But the thought of trying to explain any of this to her parents was nauseating. It was her fault. She was supposed to take care of Dani, but instead she'd lost her cool and exploded the delicate situation into bits. Telling Dani she didn't trust her was exactly the wrong thing to say—she'd known it even as the words left her mouth—but she hadn't been able to stop herself.

Everyone thought Dani was going to be the next great dragon slayer—even Dani took it for granted that the title was hers for the taking—but she didn't even want it. And not only that, she went out of her way to prove to Eden that it didn't matter to her. That this destiny, which to Eden was a precious, feverish dream, was less important than bonfires and summer jobs.

But flouting everything Eden had worked so hard to achieve wasn't enough. Now Dani wanted to convince Eden that dragons were victims in need of saving. And not only that, Dani herself was the savior, with this "soul bond" to a dragon she claimed was her friend? The notion was a spike of white-hot fury through Eden's chest.

Dani didn't know what she was talking about. Of that, Eden was certain. But she shouldn't have said as much to her. Now Dani was god knows where on a dragon's back, possibly being flown back to its lair to be devoured, because whatever its intentions were in enthralling her sister, they weren't friendship and harmony.

Eden checked the safety again, unable to stop herself. The anxiety pounding in her chest and swirling in her brain had found itself an outlet, and she was powerless to control it.

She needed to call her parents. The pressure redoubled. How could she even begin that conversation? How could she admit that, less than twenty-four hours after their departure, she had let Dani get bespelled and kidnapped by a dragon? It wasn't Eden's fault, but it was her responsibility. That's what her father would say. Her mother wouldn't say anything, but her jaw would tighten and the vein in her forehead would bulge and her eyes would flash dangerously. Eden's fingers strayed to check the safety again. She told herself to stop, but she couldn't.

Calla would know what to do.

The thought flashed lightning-bright through her mind, and she seized on it. If she could enlist Calla's help, then she could call her parents with a plan of action already in place and prove to them that she could handle a crisis. The more she considered it, the more it seemed like the only choice she had. Eden had learned tracking from her father, but she wasn't good enough to track a single dragon through the mountains—at least, not quickly enough to help Dani. Sorcerers had more resources at their disposal. Magical resources.

She climbed to her feet and returned the gun carefully to its case in the trunk. Despite the hot frustration washing over her, she couldn't resist checking the safety one last time before she slammed the back door of the Jeep. In the driver's seat, she fished her phone out of the cupholder and opened her text messages. After typing and deleting multiple iterations, she finally settled on something simple and direct, which she knew Calla would appreciate.

I need your help. My sister has been taken somewhere by a dragon she thinks is her friend.

The wait was interminable. Anxiety was twining around her lungs and clawing up her throat, and she forced herself to focus on her senses. One: the feel of the leather steering wheel clenched in her hands. Two: the sight of the reddening sun falling steadily toward the horizon. Three: the stale smell of the Jeep's evergreen-scented air freshener. Four: the sweet, chemical tang of her lip gloss. Five: the chirp of a new text alert.

She snatched up the phone. Calla had replied.

Come to Stonecrest. I'll send a car to your house.

Eden took a deep, trembling breath and turned the key.

THIRTEEN

Stonecrest was by all appearances a palace, insofar as palaces could exist in the middle of Tennessee. There was no telling how long ago it had been built or what the full measure of it was, because no blueprints had ever been filed with the city; no permits had ever been obtained; no construction companies, present or past, could claim the craftsmanship of the pristine limestone facade, French-Renaissance-style turrets, flowing tracery, gargoyles, and the lavish fountains and gardens that decorated the estate.

Eden had only seen it once before, from the back seat, as the car driving her and her parents crested over a hill. That brief, shining glimpse was all she needed to seal it in her memory forever. Later, she had searched obsessively on Google's street and satellite views, trying to find it again, but it was no use. Stonecrest was a place that could only be found if you already knew where it was.

The car Calla had sent was another glistening black luxury number with a driver who didn't speak or make eye contact the entire trip. When they arrived, he opened the door for her, and once again she found herself standing at the base of the mansion's broad front steps. The car pulled away, and she turned to take in the view of the massive, immaculate green lawn that was encircled by the gravel drive. At its center was a fountain that appeared to be a scale model of the Fontaine Des Mers in Paris, with stern oceanic figures and playful water-spouting fish. Anywhere else it would have been kitschy, but the solemn grandeur of Stonecrest demanded nothing less than history's most mythical architecture.

"Welcome back," said Calla. Eden whirled to find the high

sorcerer standing at the top of the steps. "I hope you don't mind if we save the tour for later. I'm afraid we're on a bit of a tight schedule."

Eden followed her wordlessly inside, drifting as if in a dream through the airy main hall and long corridors, which were familiar only as sense memories. The tapping of her footsteps on the marble floors, the glint of the gilded frames on the walls, the smooth mahogany grain of closed doors, the cool, crisp air in defiance of summer's humidity. When they reached a set of double doors at the end of a corridor, Eden expected a dining room or some sort of grand ballroom, but Calla led the way into a study that put her father's little office to shame. Bookshelves lined the walls from floor to ceiling, like a librarian's fantasy land. The center third of the far wall was taken up by a huge stone fireplace, flanked by two overstuffed leather armchairs. In between the chairs was an antique table on which lay a book, face-down to save the reader's place.

As Calla crossed over to the antique bar cart in the corner, Eden inched close enough to the small table to read the book's binding, only to find that it was in Cyrillic. She wondered if mastery of languages was part of sorcerers' magic, or if it was just that their unnaturally long lives gave them plenty of time to learn.

"Have a seat," said Calla, unplugging a crystal decanter of amber liquid that Eden assumed must be Scotch, or something equally classy. "Do you want something to drink?"

As tempted as she was to blend in with the classiness, she remembered that her first taste of hard liquor had ended with an embarrassing amount of sputtering and coughing. Not something she wanted to risk in front of the high sorcerer.

"No thank you." She sat down in one of the armchairs, trying in vain to smooth the wrinkles and dirt from her blouse.

Calla sat down beside her, crossing her long legs and sipping from a glass tumbler.

"You said you could help my sister," Eden said tentatively, when it became apparent that Calla wasn't going to speak first. She recounted the events that had just transpired with as much accuracy as she could muster, despite her flaming embarrassment that she hadn't been able to keep things under control. Calla listened without comment or expression, her only movement the occasional sip from her glass.

When at last Eden had finished, she gulped some air and forced herself to fall quiet. It wouldn't do to start rambling nervously. Calla remained silent for a while longer, deep in thought. Eden tried not to fidget.

"I was afraid this would happen," Calla said at last.

"What?" Eden hadn't expected dramatics from the high sorcerer, but she also hadn't expected this calm prescience.

"It's rare for humans to be able to communicate with dragons, and I've suspected for some time that Dani might have the ability. That's why we've been keeping close tabs on her."

Of course they had. Of course Dani was special enough to have sorcerers keeping watch over her. Special enough that she could communicate with dragons.

"She called it a soul bond," said Eden. "Is that a real thing?"

"Yes," Calla said. "She and the dragon only recently discovered their connection, but I could sense the magic of the soul bond, even before it was properly forged."

"Is it dangerous? For Dani?"

"It can be." Calla was staring straight ahead now, the afternoon light painting her profile in shades of gold. "How can a human ever fully trust a dragon? How long can you be connected so intimately to another creature before losing yourself completely?"

Eden couldn't help but feel that she was missing something, that the sorcerer was lost in her own private musings. On another day she might have been curious, but today she had watched her sister fly away on the back of a dragon, so that was the only thing on her mind.

"It must have tricked Dani into trusting it," she said aloud as the welcome thought occurred to her. "Or threatened her, or something like that. She wouldn't betray us." *She wouldn't betray her family.*

Calla cocked her head to the side, sweeping a wintergreen glance over Eden. An expression flitted across her features, too quickly for Eden to identify.

"Maybe you're right," Calla said. "I'd like to believe that you are, but either way, we have to track them down. Fast."

"Do you have any idea where they could have gone?" Eden asked.

"No," Calla said, and Eden's stomach fell. She'd thought that the sorcerers would have some supernatural means of finding them. "Dragons have the means to hide themselves from our magic. That's why we're going to need your help."

Eden blinked.

"Me?"

"With your parents gone, you're the only dragon slayer in the tri-state area," Calla said with a thin smile. "If we're going to track a dragon, we need the skills of a slayer."

Eden swallowed hard against the flurry of emotions tickling the back of her throat. For a split second, she forgot all about Dani. The sorcerers needed her. Calla needed her.

"Okay." It was a far cry from the cool, collected reply she had been aiming for. More of a squeak, really.

"It's not just that." Calla was studying her more intently now, the wrinkle of a frown in her forehead. She rubbed her finger across the bridge of her nose, deep in thought. "I have a proposition for you."

Eden straightened in her seat, stricken by the new gravitas in Calla's tone.

"What is it?"

"I want to make you one of us. A sorcerer."

Eden was certain she had misheard. She couldn't conceive of a world in which Calla Thorn had just offered to make her, Eden Rivera, into a *sorcerer*. She couldn't even wrap her mind around what that meant.

"The weapon I spoke of before is not a weapon in the traditional sense," Calla went on. "I've perfected a way to turn any human into a sorcerer."

"How?" Eden wasn't even sure what made someone a sorcerer. Were they born that way? Was it something that happened naturally at some random point in a person's life? She had no idea what natural occurrence could grant magical powers and immortality. Mutant spider bite? Falling into a vat of radioactive waste?

"By transferring a dragon's magic into them." Calla swirled the liquid in her glass absently, as if they were discussing something mundane. "Imagine it, Eden. The ability to hand-pick the best and the brightest, to form an army of sorcerers—and if some of those sorcerers are slayers as well? We will finally be capable of wiping out the dragon population once and for all."

A sorcerer and a slayer. The thought sent a shiver down Eden's spine. In a strange way, it felt right to her. She'd been poised between the two worlds in her mind ever since that night at Stonecrest: born a slayer, but enamored with the power of sorcery. She pressed her palms into her thighs, then winced. She'd forgotten she scraped her hands falling from Frankie's tree.

Calla downed the rest of her drink and set it on the table between them.

"For a while now, I've thought your sister might be the perfect candidate. You've said yourself that she has an extraordinary natural aptitude."

Eden said nothing and wondered how, even in this magic castle miles from civilization, she still couldn't escape her least favorite subject: how fabulously talented her little sister was at everything. Then immediately a rush of guilt overtook her, because she was here *for* Dani. To save her from whatever plight she'd found herself in.

"Now I'm thinking I was mistaken," Calla said, tilting her head to meet Eden's eyes. "Talent is all well and good, but for this sort of opportunity, dedication and drive are much more important. You're a smart woman. Smart enough to see the bigger picture. Smart enough to understand what needs to be done."

Her heart thrilled at the praise. More than anything, Eden wanted to believe her. The desire burned deep in her stomach. She wanted to be the person the high sorcerer said she was. Smart enough, strong enough, driven enough.

The brief elation from Calla's words faded. It didn't matter how much she wanted it. She wasn't that person. Dani was talented and special, but what was Eden? Firstborn and second best.

She could scale a rock wall in record time, hit a bull's-eye with a pistol at fifty yards, and take down someone twice her size in hand-to-hand combat, but she couldn't make it through the day without medication; couldn't keep her own mind from devolving into helpless panic, even in the face of perfect, undeniable logic. That had to be the real reason her parents kept leaving her behind. She *was* a liability. There was no escaping it.

"Listen, Eden." Calla reached over and gently touched the

back of Eden's hand. "I know what it's like to feel out of control, to feel like your own mind is working against you."

"I'm fine." The reply was mechanical. A habit honed over the years.

"You don't have to lie to me." Calla gave her a small, soft smile. "And it doesn't have to be this way. Magic fixes what's broken."

Eden dug her nails into the tops of her thighs to stop herself from replying immediately. She took a slow breath.

Calla removed her hand and leaned back in her chair. "The reason I bring this up now is that I think we'll have a better chance at finding her once you've reached your full potential. You're in a unique position to track your sister. I want to put you in an equally unique position to bring her in and free her from whatever connection she has with this dragon."

She made it sound so easy. As if having magic—becoming immortal—was a simple decision.

Maybe it was.

Magic fixes what's broken.

Eden took another deep breath, this time to steel herself as she met the high sorcerer's gaze. Dani was in over her head, and this was the best way to save her. Eden was the firstborn, but she'd always been second best. Not anymore.

"Tell me what I have to do."

It was nearing seven o'clock, and Dani was stuck, in more ways than one. Nox had taken her back to the cavern where the nest was hidden. He said it was the only place he knew was safe. The problem was that once they were safe, he staunchly refused to leave, which meant that Dani—who was a good rock climber, but not good enough to scale an overgrown cliff face without equipment— couldn't leave either.

Eden didn't trust her. It was that fact, even more than the gunshot, that she couldn't get out of her head. She'd done everything she could to explain, and still Eden had refused to listen. What did that mean for her and Nox? What would Eden tell their parents? Half of her wanted to stay here forever in hiding. The other half knew she had to get back to civilization, find Eden, and figure out how to mitigate this disaster.

She tried berating, begging, and threatening—both verbally and mentally—but Nox wouldn't be moved. He'd gone into the depths of the cavern to nurse his wound, which he insisted was barely a scratch. Dani, who couldn't deal with him anymore, stayed at the mouth of the cave. She'd given up on magical aid, and was pinning her last hope on technology. She stalked for several minutes around the small outcropping with her phone held aloft before finding one precious bar of service.

After some deliberation she tried her parents, but neither answered, which wasn't uncommon during their trips. She didn't leave a message. While she was trying to figure out how to phrase a text to her sister, she managed to achieve a second bar of service. With that, three notifications for voicemails dinged in rapid succession, their timestamps spread across the last hour. The first two, unsurprisingly, were from Eden. In the first, the engine of a car revved in the background, and Eden was demanding in a strained voice that Dani come home immediately. In the second she heard the sound of a door slamming, and Eden, a little calmer, said she was meeting Calla at Stonecrest and Dani needed to call her back.

A stone dropped in her stomach as Dani selected the last message. It was an unknown number, and the unfamiliar voice that came through was low and svelte.

"Hello, Dani darling. This is Calla Thorn speaking. Your sister is safe and sound with us here at Stonecrest. Perhaps you'd like to join us before that changes. You have my number."

That was all. Dani stared blankly at her phone screen for a few seconds, her thoughts skittering in a dozen different directions. She listened through all the messages again, searching for some kind of clue, some kind of reassurance that Eden was fine, that there was nothing to worry about. Trembling, she called her sister, but it went straight to voicemail. She tried again. And again.

Defeated, Dani dropped to the ground and cradled her head in her hands, trying to convince herself that she was overreacting. Maybe the high sorcerer hadn't intended her message as a threat. But no matter how hard she tried, she couldn't shake the grim certainty that Calla Thorn had chosen every word with careful intent. If anything did happen to Eden, it would be her fault. Nox was her secret—her responsibility—but she hadn't been able to keep her mouth shut, and now Eden was caught in the middle of it.

It's not your fault, came Nox's voice, drifting into her consciousness.

Everything was fine until I brought Eden to the overlook. I don't even know why I wanted to tell her the truth. I guess I was just tired of feeling alone.

As soon as she thought the words, she cringed, worried that Nox would take offense. After all, wasn't the whole point of a soul bond that she was never alone? Instead, she felt a thin trickle of understanding between them. Nox knew what it was to be alone.

I don't think the sorcerers have any reason to hurt her, he said.

Calla wants me there for some reason.

She wants you there because she wants me *there. I've told you before, sorcerers hate my kind more than humans do. The high sorcerer has made it her mission to kill us all.*

So had Dani's family, but she decided not to point that out.

We won't give her the chance, Dani thought firmly. *You don't need to come with me, but I have to help Eden.*

You can't find Stonecrest without me, he shot back. *And I'm tired.*

A strangled laugh escaped Dani: half disbelief, half exhaustion. *You think I'm not?*

You're not the one who has to do all the flying. There was a distinct strain of petulance in his tone, one Dani had come to recognize.

Stop being a baby, she told him without any real vitriol. She could sense that something had tipped the scales in her favor, either her frantic phone calls or her own wretched conscience. He was changing his mind.

And what, pray tell, would be your plan? Knock on the front door? Climb through a window and wander the grounds until you get caught? You won't last five minutes.

Excuse you, I'm a fucking Rivera. I think I can handle some minor breaking and entering.

What you are is a pain, he grumbled, but she could hear the rustling deep in the tunnel that signified his return to the outside world.

"How are the eggs?" she asked, feeling the need to be polite since she was getting her way.

Same as they always are. He emerged onto the ledge, giving his wings a shake.

"Do you"—she hesitated, but went on—"do you feel like you might be strong enough to hatch them soon?"

He eyed her for a few seconds. For all his reptilian and feline features, there was a certain quality of the canine in his face. She'd noticed that he had eyebrow muscles, which she had read somewhere that dogs had evolved in order to communicate better with humans. As of yet, Nox had not attempted to sway her with puppy-dog eyes. Mostly he used his expressive eyebrows to glower at her, which lost most of its sting when she could feel that his underlying emotions were generally a rueful acceptance of her human foibles, rather than any genuine aggravation.

Not yet, he said, *and I never will, if you insist on expending all my energy to save your sister—who, I might remind you, tried to kill me.*

"You tried to kill me, and we managed to work it out," said Dani. "Think of this as a team-building exercise. We'll save my sister and strengthen our bond at the same time."

I don't like it, he told her, but he lowered one wing so she could climb on his back. *I've got a bad feeling about this.*

"Okay, Han Solo. Your concern has been noted."

What is a Han Solo?

"All the knowledge of dragons past, and you don't know *Star Wars*?"

He made a sniffing sound that meant she'd offended his dignity, and jettisoned them both into the air without bothering to warn her first. Dani scrambled to get a good hold. She was pretty sure she'd left her stomach behind on the cliff. Within minutes, they were soaring across the Smokies. From this height the mountains were more like rolling hills, furred with pines and veined with creek beds and electric lines. They were flying due east with the sun sinking low behind them, siphoning the last of its golden light from the sky.

Dani tried to appreciate the view, but she couldn't pull her mind away from her sister or their confrontation on the overlook. Maybe it was naive of her, but she really thought that she could have brought Eden around—if only they'd had more time.

The high sorcerer's veiled threat felt like a bad dream. She'd always thought of sorcerers as posh aristocrats from a bygone era, sitting in their hidden mansions and congratulating themselves on how superior they were. But if Nox was to be believed, they were the real enemy—and not only for dragons.

She wondered if the story she'd grown up with—the story of how humans valiantly overcame dragons during the dark Tempus Dracones, and generations of slayers since then had tirelessly worked to rid the world of the monsters for good—was really a load of bullshit. What if the real story was about a timeless struggle between dragons and sorcerers, both creatures of magic, both fighting for dominance, with humans on the fringes, lucky enough to be left out of the fray?

You aren't far off, Nox told her, and she started.

Don't do that.

Do what?

Listen in on my thoughts! I wasn't talking to you.

Well, keep your thoughts to yourself, then.

She rolled her eyes, and then paused.

Wait, what do you mean—I'm not far off? About what?

Early humans and dragons coexisted for thousands of years with very little strife. It wasn't until the first sorcerer was made that things went wrong.

Dani closed her eyes briefly and hunched her shoulders higher in a vain attempt to keep out the wind buffeting her ears.

Tell me, she thought. *I want to know everything.*

She could sense Nox's desire for a sarcastic reply, no doubt an observation about human brain capacity, but to his credit he kept that to himself.

There were more soul bonds back then, simply because there were more dragons. It wasn't a common thing, but it wasn't unheard of. Then came the day—I suppose it was inevitable—when a dragon died before their soul-bonded human. If the human dies first, the magic that's shared with the human is absorbed by the dragon. Since we are born with magic anyway, the physical effect is not great. The dragon might be weaker than they were with the soul bond, but they will survive.

And when the dragon dies first? Dani prompted him.

Humans are not born with any magic, and they were never meant to carry it themselves. When the dragon in a soul bond dies first, their full magic transfers into the human. Assuming the human survives it, they will not be the same. There is something inside them that shatters under the strain. Their own soul, perhaps. I don't claim to be an expert on humans. But that's how sorcerers are created, and that is why they can't be trusted. They lose their emotions, their empathy, their capacity for love—everything that made them human. That is what's sacrificed to make room for the magic.

Nox fell quiet, and Dani let his words settle in slowly. It all made a strange sort of sense, despite how fantastical it was. She wondered why he hadn't told her any of this sooner—the information would have been useful for her to have. Instead, he'd carefully sidestepped any discussion about the origin of sorcery. It occurred to her that any human with a soul bond who wanted to gain the power of sorcery would only have to kill their dragon.

Now that their lives and emotions were intertwined, Dani couldn't imagine hurting Nox, even with her years of slayer training and deep-seated family loyalty. But throughout history, there must have been more ambitious, callous humans who'd considered it—who'd even gone through with it. Had Nox been afraid she was one of those humans?

She must have been broadcasting her thoughts again, because she sensed a faint affirmation from Nox, tinged with guilt. In the beginning, he *hadn't* been sure how much he could trust her, and Dani could hardly blame him. Hadn't she felt the same? But things were different now.

Calla Thorn, she thought, feeling again the ripple of hatred run through Nox at even the mention of the name. *She was one of the first sorcerers, wasn't she?*

The very first, as far as anyone knows. In the Middle Ages, she gathered her kind together and started the war with the dragons. There weren't many sorcerers back then, but there were enough. They enlisted humans as well, using manipulation and fear-mongering, until the only humans left on the dragons' side were the ones with a soul bond. And they were the ones who Calla and her ilk targeted first.

Dani didn't want to ask what that meant. All of a sudden, she didn't want to know any of this. It all felt too big, too terrible. A war of a thousand years, and for what?

Why? she asked. *Why do the sorcerers hate dragons so much, when they were once soul-bonded with them?*

Nox wasn't her favorite most of the time, what with his endless preaching and fragile ego, but he and she were connected on a level that superseded mere emotions. The link between them was more than just an accident of birth: it had become a living, breathing bond. Their lives were intertwined, for better or worse, and she couldn't imagine hating him enough to want to wipe out his entire race. She couldn't imagine hating anything that much.

I don't know, he replied, *but if I ever get the high sorcerer beneath my claws, I intend to find out.*

FOURTEEN

Dani's first glimpse of Stonecrest, materializing out of the peachy sunset haze like a mirage in a desert, made her think of a royal palace in the English countryside. That illusion was hard to maintain, what with Nox's own feelings about it leaking into her subconscious. It was more than his contempt for the residents that colored his view. There was something more elusive, a foreboding that settled into the pit of her stomach and wouldn't go away.

Something's wrong here, Nox told her. *I can feel it.*

My sister is in danger.

No, it's something else. Like a memory from my kind's shared history, but not. I can't explain.

Dani took a slow breath, focusing on the opalescence of his smooth scales beneath her fingertips to center herself. She remembered the last time Nox had accidentally let the full weight of his feelings drain into her. It wasn't a process she was eager to repeat, and yet she found herself saying:

Show me.

She didn't have to say more. Nox knew exactly what she meant, of course. After a brief hesitation, he did. It was like floodgates opening. A cacophony of emotions and sensations and even flashes of images against the insides of her eyelids. Chains, curiously light but somehow unbreakable. Darkness. Damp. The festering, unbearable desire to spread her wings and take flight. Blinding light. Agony. A young man's face, his eyes glinting onyx, and words, like a promise, like a mantra, like a comfort in the coldest part of the night. *It won't be forever.* Then the face of a woman she knew to be Calla Thorn, her eyes green as gemstones and twice as hard. A loss. A falling away into nothingness. A resurfacing. A return into the darkness and chains and cold and agony. *It won't be forever.* But more and more, the words felt like an empty prayer.

Dani gasped like she was coming up for air as Nox closed her off from the nightmare. She pressed her forehead against his warm back and tried to breathe.

"Oh god," she whispered.

Are you sure you want to—

"Yes," she said. Now more than ever, she was determined to get in there and find Eden.

As for a plan on how to accomplish that, one still had not presented itself. Tomás played a lot of *The Legend of Zelda* video games and as far as she could tell, Link's general strategy for entering forbidden places was to walk up the front steps. She had a feeling that if she suggested that, Nox would simply turn around and go back the way they came. As they neared the mansion, Nox began to circle in wide swoops, and Dani got a better idea of the estate's layout. There was a grand lawn with a circular drive leading to the front of the mansion. To the west was a series of terraced gardens in a riot of colors. Attached to the eastern facade was a courtyard that featured a series of colonnades with gleaming white pillars and roofs draped in rich green moss.

The cover provided in that courtyard was the best option by far, and she told Nox so. He did not express much optimism, but he did dip lower. As much as she would have preferred to have the razor-tailed, fire-breathing dragon at her side for her foray into the sorcerers' stronghold, Nox couldn't exactly traipse down the palace corridors. In fact, he informed her, the longer he stayed on the premises, the more likely it would be that one of the sorcerers would sense his presence. She would have to go this alone.

It did not dissuade her.

Not bothering to close off his flurry of disapproval from her, Nox stretched his wings and glided downward. Dani drew up her knees, braced herself on her palms, and forgot to breathe. The moment Nox alighted on the roof of the middle colonnade, she slid off his back, landing on her toes and crouching down. A gust of wind from his wings stirred the moss and blew loose strands of hair across her face, and then he was just a shadow fading into the dusky sky.

I won't be far, he promised her.

She allowed herself almost a minute to readjust, finding her balance and keying her senses into her surroundings, the way her father had taught her. When you got right down to it, this wasn't so different from being on a wilderness trail. She squeezed the rooftop's moss between her fingers and pressed into it with the toes of her shoes. She breathed in the earthy scent of it, detecting the traces of sweet summer blossoms from somewhere nearby, as well as the pungent tang of sun-baked stone. She strained her ears into the quiet, searching for identifiable sounds. It took her a while to catch on to the reason for the new unease welling in her chest. It wasn't just quiet here. It was silent. No singing birds, no chirp of crickets or cicadas, no distant hum of traffic or air conditioning. Stonecrest existed in its own bubble of perfect, unnatural stillness.

Not ideal for stealth.

She inched to the edge of the roof and peered over. It was only about ten feet to the neatly trimmed grass below. She listened a little longer for any sign of activity in the courtyard, then finally slid off, hanging first by her hands and then dropping to the earth. She stayed low, keeping close to the bushes instead of the walkways. She couldn't decide if she felt like a spy or just felt ridiculous.

I think it's safe to assume you look ridiculous, Nox intoned dryly.

Dani, with great effort, ignored him.

There was only one set of doors into the palace that she could see, glass-paned and half-hidden behind vines that dangled from the trellis overhead. She began to wish she'd learned lock-picking at some point in her life. It seemed like a more useful elective for schools to offer than Pilates or show choir. But on the other hand, locked doors seemed like the sort of simple security measure that sorcerers would overlook.

She crept closer and peered around a pillar. All she could make out in the gloomy interior were white-and-black tiles and a series of abstract sculptures. Some sort of gallery. She searched for movement but saw none. She took a deep breath to steel herself.

"Who the hell are you?"

The voice made her jump. She whirled, one hand over her pounding heart. The source of the near-heart attack was a man on the other side of the colonnade, framed by two pillars. He must have come across the grass from the rear of the house, but she still couldn't believe she hadn't heard him. So much for being aware of her surroundings.

"I was invited by Calla Thorn," she said, which had the benefit of being absolutely true.

He eyed her wordlessly as he stepped onto the terra cotta walkway. Dani was uncomfortably aware of how little she resembled the sort of person who would be invited to this grand estate. She was still in her work clothes: jean Bermuda shorts and a sweat-stained pink tank top with ON WEDNESDAYS WE WEAR PINK printed across the front. Her hair was pulled into a messy bun on top of her head and was no doubt littered with bits of nature.

"I'm looking for my sister, Eden," she said, unable to bear the lingering quiet. "Have you seen her?"

The man was younger than she'd first thought. A shaft of the last golden daylight slanted across his pale face, and she realized he was probably around Eden's age. The illuminated features also sparked recognition in the back of her mind. At first, she thought she must have seen him in a movie or online—the memory was vague and secondhand. He was near enough now that she could see the way his inscrutably dark eyes absorbed the light rather than reflected it.

Then she knew. She wondered wildly if the vision Nox shared with her had somehow summoned him. *It won't be forever.*

"You need to leave." The clear timbre of his voice was unmistakably the same—not that it gave her any hint about who he was, exactly. He had to be a sorcerer, or else he wouldn't be here. He was wearing heather-gray slacks and a black dress shirt with the sleeves rolled up to his elbows. All he needed was a silk tie and jacket, and he would fit in at any highbrow corporate function. His hair, jet-black, was neatly combed in a side part, just touching the tips of his ears. Over his right temple was a premature streak of silver that really only made him seem younger by contrast.

He was also disturbingly attractive—but that, Dani told herself firmly, was neither here nor there.

"As soon as I find my sister," she said, keeping her tone pleasant and airy. Somehow, without her noticing, his careful steps had placed him between her and the door. She swore inwardly and moved onto the walkway, trying to keep her own pace casual and nonthreatening, but there was no ease in the tense line of his shoulders and the light furrowing of his forehead. He was taller than her by several inches, but wiry and gaunt in a way that suggested malnourishment rather than genetics. She wasn't worried, as long as he didn't conjure any magic. She'd never seen magic, and wondered if it was a showy affair with flashy lights and colors, or more of a subtle, sneaking thing that she wouldn't notice until her nose had fallen off or something.

What on earth is going on? Nox's voice shook her out of her ill-timed rabbit hole, and she refocused. She didn't reply to Nox—she still wasn't skilled enough at multitasking to carry on two conversations at once.

Although it wasn't much of a conversation on this end. The boy hadn't said anything else. He just watched her, like he expected to ward her off by the strength of his glare alone. Not hardly. Dani decided for the direct approach, which had served her well before. She brushed right past him, hoping against hope that the doors would be unlocked.

His fingers closed around her wrist. Dani reacted with blind instinct, twisting her arm to break his hold and spinning with her fist aimed at his throat. To her shock, he caught her wrist again, right before she made contact. She saw her own shock reflected in his eyes. Neither of them had been expecting the other.

For a few seconds, their gazes remained locked, as if waiting for something. Then the fragile moment snapped, and everything was impulse and impact, blow and counterblow. It was nothing like the training mat. Proper form fell away in favor of speed, and despite all her conditioning, Dani quickly became aware that she wouldn't be able to keep this up for very long.

She threw her weight into a roundhouse kick, hoping to elude his guard by forcing the trajectory downward at the last second. The Brazilian kick was a technique that had worked on Eden more than once, but her opponent was ready for her. He stepped into it and caught her thigh, planted his palm against her sternum, and threw his own weight against her. A second later she was on her back staring at the roof of the colonnade, the wind knocked from her lungs, the collision radiating through her bones. She tried to push herself upright, but her right ankle was trapped under his arm. He crossed his leg over hers and dropped to the ground, slamming her into a leglock.

She would have cried out in pain, but her lungs had been robbed of air. She'd thought she would be pitting her superior mixed-martial-arts training against haphazard street fighting. It hadn't occurred to her that he would be able to counter her techniques with his own. She raised her hand to tap out, before remembering with an awful jolt that this wasn't a sparring match. This was for real, and he was going to break her leg if she didn't break the lock first.

Focus, whispered a voice in her head, and she didn't know if it was Nox's, Eden's, or her own.

With both hands she pushed against the side of his right knee with every ounce of strength she possessed. It was enough, barely, to shift his weight so that she could yank her leg free. In one smooth motion, she rolled to her stomach, channeling the momentum into the swing of her other leg. Her heel smashed directly into his cheekbone. He swore, and Dani couldn't help a grim smile of satisfaction as she made it back to her feet.

He was still on his back on the ground, and she closed the gap without thinking, her adrenaline-spiked mind racing through the potential moves to end the fight. That voice again—it was definitely Eden's this time— *Think before you move.*

But it was too late. She'd put herself in a vulnerable position without a plan, and as her sister had always promised it would, it bit her in the ass. He sat up, thrusting his hands against her knees, and just as she registered that his ankles were hooked around the backs of her own, she lost her balance and was once again flat on her back.

She expected him to straddle her, and was already raising her knees to block the mount, but he came at her from the side, jamming his arm beneath her head so that the back of her neck was squeezed into the crook of his elbow.

Fuck, she thought wildly, recognizing too late the opening salvo of a Kesa-Gatame hold. She threw her right arm up and clamped a hand on the side of his neck, knowing that her best chance of escape was to set up a frame to hook her left leg around his head and force him into an armlock. He was ready for the countermove and made her pay for it in swift, exacting fashion. He clamped a hand on her tricep and slid forward until both her neck and arm were crushed between his, their heads mashed tight together. From there he locked his hands and twisted her into a chokehold that demanded that she struggle if she wanted to breathe, but promised to break her arm if she did so. It was a brutal submission.

On the mat she would have tapped out immediately, but all she could do now was try to suck in whatever oxygen she could manage. Her arm was going numb. His face was close enough to hers that through the ringing in her ears she could hear his own rapid breathing.

"I did tell you to leave," he said, but it seemed to come from a great distance. Dani's vision was darkening at the edges. She didn't have much longer before she passed out. All those years of training, of Eden and her parents drilling technique and proper form into her, and it still wasn't enough. Her mother had warned her many times that there would always be someone better than her. It was just Dani's luck that she'd happened upon him today. Didn't seem fair.

A violent shudder wracked her opponent. All at once, his grip slackened. Dani's brain was so muddled from lack of oxygen that it took her several seconds to realize she could breathe again, and then a few more to register that she was no longer in a hold. She rolled away from him and scrambled to her feet, trying to catch her breath and at the same time prepare herself for whatever was coming next. She faced him, half-certain that this was some kind of cruel cat-and-mouse routine, but he was still on the ground. His body had gone rigid, hands fisted shut, face contorted in silent pain. Some kind of seizure?

Then a faint red glow materialized, shimmering across the surface of his skin, wisping in and out with his ragged breaths. It was like nothing she had ever seen. He made no noise, but his agony was a palpable thing, sloughing off him in waves. Despite everything, Dani felt the urge to try to help. She couldn't make her feet move.

"Dani, just *go*," he gasped out, his dark eyes fluttering open for the briefest moment. Tears streamed down his cheeks, and his jaw clenched against any further words.

Dani threw herself forward out of her horrified reverie and to the glass doors. The handle turned and let her in to the cool, dim interior. She didn't know where she was going, but she knew she didn't have much time, so she ran. She didn't look back, and she didn't let herself wonder why the boy had known her name.

The corridors of Stonecrest were no less vaulting and endless than they had been in Eden's memories, even though she was ten years older now. The metal door with its crimson inscription in crusty red paint was even more portentous now than it had been when she was a kid. No doubt it was some kind of ancient ritual, meant to protect the rest of the world from what lurked at the bottom of the winding stone steps.

When Calla touched the door, the locks and bolts sprang open immediately, and the hinges creaked ominously. Some part of Eden wished that her sister was here after all. She would make a crack about haunted-house sound effects, or something, and lighten the bleak mood. Eden said nothing as Calla led the way down the stairs. The only light came from the open door behind them, so they descended into darkness, until Eden was certain she would topple headfirst down the stairs and take the high sorcerer with her.

Fortunately, before it came to that, a light flared to life in front of Calla. Eden watched in fascination as Calla cupped the orb in her hands. It gleamed a spectral silver like moonlight and expanded slowly to the size of a balloon. Calla released it and it floated ahead, matching their pace like a ghostly guide.

Soon enough they had reached the base of the steps, and with the benefit of their miniature moon, Eden was able to see everything that had been blanketed in shadows during her first visit. The basement was entirely gray stone, with high, vaulted ceilings in a spiderwebby architecture that reminded Eden of a cathedral. But there was nothing sacred down here, only a distinct chill and an accompanying foreboding that clung to Eden's skin and sent convulsive shivers down her spine.

"Stay close," said Calla, her voice a slender thread connecting Eden to the real world beyond this beautifully crafted tomb. "It's a bit of a maze if you don't know the way."

Eden stayed as close as she could without stepping on Calla's heels. They passed between carved stone pillars that were set at regular intervals. There were branching corridors, each identical to the last, with the same arched ceilings and elegant pillars. Occasionally Eden caught glimpses of what she thought might be doors or stairwells, but she couldn't be sure. With the light drifting along overhead, her eyes were playing tricks on her with the shifting shadows. Calla led the way without faltering through a series of these corridors, until finally ahead Eden saw another source of light spilling around a corner, this one bolder and tinted a sickly yellow.

Calla stopped suddenly, and Eden barely avoided walking into her.

"I want you to understand something before we continue," said the high sorcerer without turning around. "These aren't children's games we play down here. The stakes are always life and death, and the toll can be dear. You have to be ready to accept everything you witness tonight, Eden, no matter how it may offend your sense of decency. If you truly want to be one of us, you have to accept the cost."

Eden shut her eyes briefly against the words. Nausea threatened to overtake her. A part of her—a large part, if she was being honest—was desperate to turn around and go back the way she'd come. But when she thought about going home, when she really thought about it, she couldn't bring herself to want it. The same four walls of her bedroom, closing in while she tried to sleep. The same bed that felt at times like a prison, at times like the only world she could survive in. The mats of the training barn, slick with her own sweat and blood and tears, as she pushed, pushed, pushed, and yet never seemed to go anywhere.

How could she go back to that, now that she'd been given a chance to step into a new, better version of herself? To shed everything she despised about Eden Rivera and transform at last into someone she actually wanted to be?

"Is it worth it?" The question escaped before she could second-guess herself.

At that, Calla did turn, just enough that Eden could see her regal profile and the slender curve of a smile.

"More than you can possibly imagine."

"Then I'm ready."

The decision was made. No turning back now. She followed Calla into the light, breathing easily for the first time in what felt like years. A calmness settled over her, an embracing of the inevitable. Whatever came next, she had chosen it, and it would be worth it in the end. There was nothing left to worry about.

They turned the corner, and Eden absorbed the scene with her newfound equanimity. It was a cavernous room, easily the size of the school gymnasium. Around the walls were various tools and devices that Eden didn't look at too closely. She focused on the center of the room, where Alder De Lange was sitting on the edge of a sturdy oak table, fiddling with something long and slender that glinted darkly in the light. And just behind him, on a dais raised a few feet above the ground, was the dragon.

Eden had been ready for it, but she still stopped in her tracks at the sight. Dangerous as they were, there was no denying that dragons were awe-inspiring creatures. This one was much larger than the one on the overlook, as big as a bus, with long horns that curved back like a ram's and claws as long as her arms. It raised its head slightly when they entered, steam billowing through its nostrils, but Alder didn't even glance back.

Eden forced herself to keep walking, trying to keep her expression neutral as she surveyed the dull black of its scales, scarred pink in several places along its back and sides. It was lashed down from neck to tail with iron chains that must've been enchanted somehow, because the individual links were only inches long—surely not strong enough to hold the beast with their own strength. When its ruby eyes met hers, dull in the grim light, she couldn't help but wonder if it remembered her. She looked away.

"Finally," said Alder in an elegantly bored tone. He slid off the table and held out the object in his hands to Calla. It was a long, wickedly sharp dagger.

A sick feeling rushed up the back of Eden's throat, but she swallowed it down hard. Calla ignored Alder's comment and took the dagger. The dragon shifted on the dais, but made no effort to strain against the chains. Eden hadn't thought it possible for their reptilian features to show emotion, but she could have sworn his expression was one of sorrowful defeat.

The stakes are life and death, she reminded herself. This was no time to devolve into fanciful sentimentality.

"Eden, over here please," said Calla, in a voice as pleasant as a nurse's in an exam room.

Eden went to the spot where Calla pointed, a circle about four feet wide carved into the stone floor. When she took her place, she was directly in front of the dragon, with barely more than an arm's length between them. She looked at Calla so that she didn't have to look at the dragon.

"What do I have to do?" she asked, hating the way her voice quivered.

"Nothing at all." Calla smiled with a warm reassurance that eased the tension knotted between Eden's shoulder blades. "Just stay in that circle, and Alder and I will do all the work."

She wanted to ask if it would hurt. The question was poised on her tongue, but she bit it back. What did it matter if it hurt? The stakes were life and death. The decision was made.

Alder and Calla exchanged a low conversation, then broke apart. Alder pushed the table out of the way, its legs screeching on the stone. Calla moved to stand at a diagonal from Eden, only a few feet away from both her and the dragon. Alder stood across from Calla. Their loose square formation reminded Eden of when

Hacky Sack had been all the rage during P.E., and she had to cough into her hand to smother the absurd giggle that accompanied the thought. She knew it wasn't really amusement that was bubbling up in her chest, but nerves.

Calla held the dagger between her teeth and combed back the hairs that had fallen from her bun, redoing it quickly but no less neatly than before. Then she nodded at Alder. He lifted his hands, cupped together with palms up, and began to murmur. Eden was pretty sure it was Latin, but she thought she could hear some other languages tangled in there as well. Or maybe she wasn't hearing any human language at all, and her mind was just finding associations where there were none. Instead of another orb of light, a dark liquid began to pool in his open palms. At first she thought it was black, but it was not as simple as that. Colors swirled in the depths of it, as ethereal as the Aurora Borealis splashed against the night sky.

Eden caught her breath at the sight of it. The dragon breathed out more steam, accompanied by a sound almost like a whimper. Calla laid the flat of the blade across Alder's hands, and the liquid swarmed to the steel as if magnetized. When Calla raised the dagger again, the blade was coated thickly, the oily black shimmering its rainbow of colors without a drop spilled. Calla was speaking now, her voice clear and rhythmic. The words reverberated deep in Eden's chest, but when she tried to parse them out, they slipped just out of reach.

The high sorcerer's next movement was so smooth, so devoid of the gracelessness of violence, that it took Eden a few seconds to realize that Calla had slit the dragon's throat.

The dragon keened, a low, aching sound that pierced Eden's heart as easily as a blade. *Life and death,* she told herself, clenching her hands into fists. *Life and death.*

Blood began to flow, crimson intermingling with black as it drip, drip, dripped to the stone. Calla tossed the dagger carelessly away, and it clattered on the ground. The steel gleamed, unnaturally bright and clean. The dragon made no further sound and only rested its head on the stone, the heaving of its chest the only sign of distress. Its eyes met hers again, but there was no reproach in them, no rage or malice, which Eden expected—maybe even hoped—to see. Instead all she found was an infinite weariness that seeped right into the marrow of her bones.

In her mind, dragonkind had always been the enemy, feral and bloodthirsty and bent on destruction. Slaying them was supposed to be both her duty and honor as a Rivera. But standing here, face to face with a dragon for only the third time in her life, watching the lifeblood flow from its neck, there was no sense of triumph, no sense of rightness. Dani had asked her only a few hours ago, *what if the story we've been told about dragons is wrong?*

Eden was too afraid to consider the answer.

The dragon closed its eyes. The blood was pooling, flowing through grooved channels in the ground, until the circle in which Eden stood began to run red. Calla had fallen silent. For an interminably long minute, the only sounds in the vast chamber were the dragon's labored breaths, Eden's own pulse pounding in her ears, and the sick wet sluicing of the blood.

As the dragon's breaths began to taper off, a faint red shimmer rippled across its scales, from head to tail, vibrant against the black. Eden blinked hard, certain she had imagined it, but the shimmering swelled in intensity until the creature was covered in a fine, glittering mist. And as the dragon stilled at last, the mist began to rise.

Calla began to chant softly, her hands raised as if in worship. Eden's own hands were trembling at her sides, and she clasped them together tightly. The mist swirled overhead, forming a galaxy of ruby-red stars. Calla traced a shape in the air with her finger, over and over again. Slowly, tentatively, the mist began to snake toward Eden in a scintillating river. Her instincts screamed at her to run, but she didn't move. She couldn't look away.

It coiled around her like a living thing, dazzling her vision until she couldn't see anything else. As the mist settled onto her body, every inch of her skin exploded with a pain that was somehow both debilitating and exhilarating. She felt it in her muscles, in her bones, in her lungs and veins and nerves and sinews. She looked down at her hands, watching in mute fascination as the scrapes on her palms evanesced into nothing.

Something burned inside her. Some indefinable part of herself, deep beyond the physicality of her body, burned and burned and *burned*. That inner flame grew, fanned by her gasping breaths and fueled by her pumping blood, until there was nothing else left. There was a *crack*—soundless, yet obliterating in its resonance. It was a bursting of a dam, a toppling of a foundation. Eden fell to her knees, clawing at her chest as the flame flared white-hot through every corner of her being. She thought she was dying. She thought she was disintegrating.

Then, with nothing left to consume, the flame died out, leaving behind darkness inside her, smooth and sharp-edged as obsidian. For a moment she knew only regret, and reached in vain for the light, for the precious piece of herself she'd just lost. And then even that was gone.

Eden fell unconscious.

Dani ran as fast as she could without knowing where she was going or how to get there. That didn't slow her down.

Was that you, back there? she thought to Nox, though she felt sure she would've known if it had been. She would have felt it somehow.

No, something is happening—I think it must be underground. I can sense magic far below you. A lot of it.

Dani slowed her pace just enough to start searching her surroundings for any hint of where she might find stairs leading down. A house this big had to have a basement, but there were so many doors and corridors, she could spend hours searching it.

Stop—go back the way you came, Nox told her. *It's growing fainter the farther you move in the direction you're going now.*

Dani stopped and turned around, forcing herself to slow to a walk even though she was convinced that at any second, another sorcerer—or the same one from before—was going to come across her. Nox nudged her in another direction, and soon they were playing the world's most bizarre game of Hot and Cold.

Keep going that way.

There's a wall there.

Well, find a way around the wall, then.

No need for that tone.

I'll take any tone I like. You're lucky I don't just leave you there. You would deserve it, you know.

Dani knew he didn't mean it, but she did force herself to feel some gratitude for him, just in case.

She managed to find the door she needed in less than ten minutes, though it felt much longer, exposed as she was amid her decadent surroundings. Most of Stonecrest's furnishings and decor were of a solidly Victorian feel, as if the owners had never bothered moving into the twentieth century, much less the twenty-first, but the door to the basement was straight out of a medieval legend.

"Christ," Dani muttered under her breath as she pushed at it cautiously, careful not to touch what she was pretty sure was dried blood smeared across it in a strange, pagan-esque symbol.

The stairs leading down did nothing to dissuade her sudden anxious visions of torture chambers and oubliettes, scattered with the rotted bones of everyone else who had sneaked into Stonecrest.

What are you waiting for? Nox asked, though she knew he must have sensed the fear clawing up her gullet.

She pulled out her phone, which had been cracked during her little tussle but thankfully still worked. With the flashlight on, she started down the stairs, reminding herself with every step that she was here for her sister, that Eden would do the same for her, that she had come too far now to go back.

The Gothic maze she found herself in once she reached the bottom could have come straight from a Dungeons and Dragons manual. Maybe the sorcerers had hired Gary Gygax as their interior decorator. At least there were no bones that she could see.

Nox guided her through a couple turns, but fortunately it wasn't long before she could see a faint light ahead. She followed it to the source, slowing when she heard the murmur of voices.

The flow of magic has stopped, Nox told her.

Dani crept forward, glad she was wearing rubber soles. She knelt down at the end of the corridor and peered around the corner. Once her eyes adjusted to the light and she could make out the scene before her, it still took her a long time to come to terms with what she was seeing. A massive black dragon—at least twice the size of Nox—chained and limp, blood running from its throat to the stone floor. Her sister, limp but unfettered, lying in the center of a circle of blood. A man and woman, standing nearby, whispering to each other with the casual air of two theatergoers waiting for the movie to start.

Dani pressed both hands over her mouth to stop herself making a sound. Panic and revulsion roiled in her stomach, hers or Nox's or possibly both. She thought she might be sick.

"Dani. I thought you might be along soon." The voice was muffled through the blood rushing in her ears, and at first Dani thought it was Nox. But no, it had been a woman's voice. A faintly familiar one. Calla Thorn.

She closed her eyes for a second, then stood up.

What are you doing? Nox demanded.

She ignored him and turned the corner, keeping her chin high and her hands clenched at her sides to conceal their shaking.

"I came for Eden," she said aloud, relieved that there was no tremor in her tone. "I'm not leaving without her."

"No need for the dramatics. Eden is free to leave whenever she wants," Calla said with an amused smile. She followed Dani's nervous gaze to her sister's prone form. "She's perfectly fine, I promise. She should wake up any minute now."

"What did you do to her?" Dani edged a little closer to Eden, who she could see now was breathing steadily. As much as she wanted to check on her, she couldn't bring herself to cross that river of blood. The cloying, coppery smell of it was heavy in the air, coating the back of her throat. Bile threatened to rise.

"I imagine she'll want to tell you herself," Calla said.

That was when Eden began to stir, and Dani swallowed her nausea enough to run forward. She stepped carefully over the blood and crouched beside Eden, grabbing her arm and helping her sit up. Her skin was ice cold.

"Are you okay?" Dani asked, unable to prevent the tremble in her voice now. "What happened? What did they do?"

"What are you doing here?" Eden asked, staring at her in

confusion. Not the confusion of someone just waking from uncon-sciousness, but as if she couldn't think of a single reason Dani might have to be here. "Get off me."

Eden shook her hand away and stood up, dusting herself off. Then she studied her hands as if fascinated by them, though Dani couldn't see anything different about them. There *was* something different about her sister, though. Something in her voice, in her eyes. Something strange and unsettling.

"What happened?" Dani asked again.

Eden just kept looking at her hands. Dani was just about to take her by the shoulders, to shake her out of it, when suddenly a red light blossomed in her sister's palm. Dani jumped back in sur-prise, barely avoiding stepping in the blood. She whipped her gaze toward the sorcerers, but both Calla and the man who must have been Alder De Lange were just standing there. Alder was smirk-ing, and Calla's thin smile bore a hint of pride.

Eden juggled the magical orb gently between her two hands, the light gleaming in her eyes. She tossed it up high and it exploded overhead, raining showers of sparks down on them. Dani shielded her head reflexively, but Eden stood with her face upturned, a broad smile growing on her face.

She's a sorcerer, came Nox's voice, giving the chilling confirma-tion to what had already begun to take root in Dani's mind. *Some-how they've made her into a sorcerer.*

"Eden," Dani said, struggling to get words out. "What have you done?"

Eden finally looked at her. The smile had not dimmed.

"I'm the first of my kind," she said simply. "A slayer and a sorcerer."

You have to get out of there, Nox told her. *Now.*

But Dani couldn't make herself move. Couldn't drag her gaze away from her sister. Couldn't wrap her mind around what all of this meant.

"Goddamn it, Calla." A voice behind her finally spurred her into motion. She turned. It was the boy from earlier, his appearance altogether less fastidious after their encounter, but otherwise recovered from whatever magic had assailed him. "You could have waited for me."

Dani braced herself at his approach, but he stalked right past her without even a glance in her or Eden's direction. He went straight to the lifeless black dragon, kneeling down by the head and glaring at the high sorcerer.

"Kieran darling, I've told you before not to take that tone with me," she said, her own tone deceptively light. "Don't mistake my forbearance for tolerance."

"He shouldn't have had to be alone." Kieran brushed a hand, whisper-soft, along the dragon's scaled cheek. There was a tenderness to the moment that cut Dani to the quick. Calla did not look to be similarly moved.

"I think he's rather accustomed to it by now, don't you?"

Kieran's dark eyes flicked at her with a vitriol so potent that Dani was convinced he couldn't be a sorcerer after all, because if he had any measure of magic, surely that look would have melted Calla on the spot. He snapped something in a language that Dani didn't recognize, and Calla replied in kind, utterly unfazed by his anger. The exchange went on for a few seconds longer, Calla clearly keeping the upper hand.

"Just bring him back," Kieran said abruptly in English. "We only have a few minutes."

"Yes, I'm aware of how my own magic works, thank you." Calla nodded to Alder, who walked over to the dragon's side, flexing his hands and rolling his neck like he was stepping up to bat. "Eden, Dani, you two will want to step back. Necromancy can be a fiddly business."

She paused and looked at Eden pointedly, silent for a long while, and Dani couldn't shake the feeling that the two of them were communicating telepathically. But about what? Eden nodded at last, her gaze flicking to Dani as she grabbed her wrist and tugged her a good ten feet back from the dragon. Dani let her, not sure what else to do. It was just now occurring to her that, though Calla had said Eden was free to leave any time she wanted, she hadn't promised the same for Dani.

But I'm safe with Eden, she thought fiercely to herself.

Nox's skepticism vibrated through the bond, though he managed to stay silent. Dani wouldn't let herself think about what it meant that a part of her agreed with him.

The sorcerers were standing to the left and right of the dragon. In unison, though they wouldn't have been able to see each other over the slope of the dragon's back, they began to trace shapes in the air. Dani watched in reluctant awe as the symbols glowed green, rotating slowly as they hovered, as if drifting in the eddies of a breeze. They were intricate, beautiful things, but carried with them an aura of something primeval and forbidden. For some reason, that was the first moment Dani actually comprehended what was happening. Necromancy, Calla had said.

There was a jolt of pain through her head and she averted her eyes from the ghastly symbols, focusing instead on Kieran, who hadn't left the dragon's side despite Calla's warning. He stroked the side of the dragon's neck with the soothing motion of a parent comforting an ailing child. The sorcerers were chanting now, ancient words that sent chills down Dani's spine and fired up every survival instinct she possessed. But even so, she found she couldn't look away from Kieran, from the expression on his face that was so different from the cool edge she'd seen in the courtyard. It was fury tempered with fear, love poisoned by regret. A heartbreak so keen and enduring that all its tears had been shed long ago.

They're bonded, Nox said.

Really? Are you sure?

Can't you sense it?

Now that he asked, she felt that maybe she could. Not in the immediate way she sensed Nox's presence, but with a more abstract knowledge.

That can't be right, she thought, trying to keep up with her own spiraling thoughts.

Dani's mind raced backwards to the sight of Kieran, immobilized by the gleaming red energy, wracked in agony as if life itself were being forcibly drained out of him. She looked down at Eden's hand, still firmly clasped around her wrist. The hand that only minutes ago had conjured magic with ease. Nox began to put the pieces together at the same time she did. His own revulsion entwined with hers.

They found a way to divert the dying dragon's magic to someone other than his soul-bonded human. She had to think each word carefully, because otherwise she couldn't be sure it even made sense. *Is that even possible?*

Apparently so.

But if they killed the dragon to create a sorcerer, then why are they bringing him back to life?

A silence. So long that the sorcerers' soft chanting wormed into her head and set off a dull ache in the base of her skull. Nox's reply, when it finally came, was so low and strangled with fury that she could barely make it out.

So they can do it again.

Dani's heart began to pound.

I have to get out of here, she thought, glad that Nox at least had the decency to not say "I told you so."

I told you so.

Or not.

Slowly, Dani tried to pull free from her sister's grip, keeping her expression as neutral as possible. Eden's hold only tightened, and she shot Dani a glare.

"You're staying right here," she hissed. "Haven't you caused enough trouble for one day?"

"I'm not the one who murdered a dragon so I could have magical powers," Dani shot back. She cast a nervous glance toward Calla and Alder, but they were trapped in their own orbit of glowing symbols interwoven with their rhythmic chants.

"It's a monster," Eden said. "If you weren't so obsessed with your pet, you'd see that. You know it tried to kill me when I was little, when I came here with Mom and Dad?"

"They're the monsters," Dani whispered, flinging her free arm in the direction of Calla and Alder. "They killed that poor creature, and now they're bringing him back to life so they can do it *again.*"

"We're not playing games here," Eden said softly, in a voice that didn't sound entirely like her own. "When the stakes are life and death, you have to make sacrifices."

"Well, it looks to me like the dragon is the one making all the sacrifices, while your precious sorcerers are the ones reaping all the benefits."

"I'm a sorcerer now." Eden's voice was as flinty as her gaze. "I'm your family. We've spent our whole lives training for this moment. Now it's time to decide whose side you're on."

"Now it's time for me to get the hell out of here," Dani said, twisting and yanking her arm to break Eden's grip. She started to run, but Eden was lightning fast—faster than was humanly possible—and slammed a fist into her stomach.

Dani doubled over with the impact, involuntary tears springing to her eyes. With brutal efficiency, Eden grabbed the back of her head and rammed her knee into the side of Dani's face. Dani's vision exploded into light and pain, and she only vaguely registered that she had somehow ended up face-down on the stone ground.

Oh fuck, was all she could think.

I'm on my way, said Nox, but she barely heard him.

She tried to get up, but found herself pinned with Eden's knee in her back. An arm snaked around her windpipe, pulling her into a headlock.

"Just stop, Dani," her sister said into her ear. "You can't beat me. Not anymore. And where would you go if you could? Stonecrest let you in because Calla wanted you here. It's not going to be so quick to let you out."

She's right, Dani thought hazily. Eden had always had the superior technique, and now she had superhuman strength and speed to go with it. Dani couldn't compete with that. She blinked rapidly, trying at least to clear her eyes of tears. The sorcerers were still enmeshed in their spell, apparently oblivious to the drama playing out a few feet away. Her eyes locked with Kieran's. He hadn't moved, but he was watching her with a faint wrinkle in his brow, like there was something he couldn't quite figure out. Then slowly, deliberately, his eyes shifted toward the wall on Dani's right. He cocked his head in that direction, so slightly that she couldn't be sure she hadn't imagined it. In the next second, his attention was again fixated on the dragon.

Dani strained her eyes to survey the wall without moving her neck. There, maybe twenty feet away, was a metal grate set into the wall. There were multiple channels carved into the stone floor converging at its mouth. A drainage tunnel of some sort. That would make sense. Murdering innocent creatures did appear to be messy work.

But an escape route didn't do her any good if she couldn't break away from Eden. Her sister's form, as always, was flawless, leaving no weaknesses for Dani to exploit, no tactics for her to employ.

Then again, Dani realized she was still thinking like she was on the training mat. She was trying to beat Eden at her own game. She was following rules that, as she had complained often enough, didn't actually apply in the real world. *I'm not like you,* she'd told her sister once—it felt like a lifetime ago now. *I fight to win.*

Time to prove it.

She managed to turn her head a few degrees and tucked in her chin against Eden's arm. Then she opened her mouth and bit down as hard as she could. Eden shrieked and tried to yank her arm away. Dani was pretty sure she tasted blood, but she wouldn't let herself think about that now. The second she had a bit of leverage, she reached back, grabbed her sister's ponytail in an iron grip, and pulled. She rolled at the same time, absorbing blows and curses from Eden, until Eden was the one on the ground. Dani threw her full weight, knee first, into her sister's stomach.

She could have done more damage, but that wasn't what she wanted. She just wanted to get away. She shot to her feet and sprinted, breathless but fueled by adrenaline and desperation. Hopefully that well wouldn't dry up any time soon.

She stuck her fingers through the metal grate and yanked back on it. For a heart-stopping second it didn't budge, but then it came loose with a rusty squeal. The drain was just tall enough for her to stand in, as long as she stayed bent forward. It was dark beyond. She didn't have time to fish out her phone. She was just going to have to trust that the tunnel would lead her somewhere safe. She was going to have to trust Kieran, who less than an hour ago had nearly choked her into unconsciousness.

She plunged in.

The slick stone beneath her feet gave no purchase, and after the first few feet, the tunnel curved steeply downward. She began to slide, grabbing uselessly for a handhold, suddenly sure that she was going to end up broken at the bottom of a dark pit. The slope gradually leveled out, until finally she had enough traction that she was running downhill again instead of sliding.

Footsteps pounded behind her. Eden wasn't far behind. Dani picked up her pace despite the pitch-dark blackness, praying there wasn't anything for her to trip on. There was a fizzing sound, followed by a red explosion against the tunnel wall just beside her. She could feel the sting of electricity and the shower of rock shrapnel, but it hadn't been close enough to hurt her. Not that time, at least.

The second explosion was practically on her heels, and the blast flung her forward. She skidded on her hands and knees, crying out from the ragged pain, but her adrenaline and desperation hadn't deserted her yet. She made it back to her feet and kept running.

Please tell me you're close, she thought to Nox.

I'm almost there.

More fizzing. Dani flattened herself against the tunnel wall and the orb sailed past, detonating on the ground a few feet ahead. In its violent light, Dani saw that the tunnel was widening and coming to an end at another metal grate, this one much thicker and heavier than its counterpart. Beyond, she thought she could make out the midnight blue of the night sky and the shadowy outline of treetops.

When she judged she was close enough, she stopped running. A part of her hoped that she was wrong, that Eden wouldn't take the opportunity to fling another blast of magic, knowing that at this distance it would seriously maim Dani, if not kill her. But even as she thought it, there was the telltale *fizz* and swoop of the orb soaring right for her back.

Dani hit the deck. The orb collided with the grate in a furious clash of magic and metal. The magic won, leaving behind it a twisted gap just large enough for a person to squeeze through. Dani climbed to her feet, lightheaded from exertion and pain.

"Dani, it's a hundred-foot drop," Eden said—not with concern, but smugness. "You're done."

Are you here yet? Dani asked.

Almost.

Good, because I'm about to do something stupid.

A pause.

Do it.

Dani ran and scrambled through the hole, ignoring the sharp metal teeth that ripped at her skin and clothes. There was a tiny lip of stone extending past the grate, just enough to stand on, but Dani didn't stop there. Without a heartbeat's hesitation, she hurled herself off the edge and into the night.

FIFTEEN

Upon watching her sister take a running leap to certain death, the only thing that Eden could think was, *How typical*. Dani had never been able to do anything the easy way. Everything had to be a statement. She couldn't grasp the beauty of simple efficiency.

There was another, vaguer notion that she should probably be concerned about her little sister jumping to her death, but there was no underlying emotion to grant it any urgency. Either Dani had just died or she hadn't. There wasn't anything Eden could do about it now.

She walked to the end of the tunnel and peered into the murky night. For a few seconds, everything was quiet. Then there was a *whoosh* of wings and hot air, and the ghostly gray outline of her sister's pet dragon—Nox, was it?—rose into view. Perched on his back, very much alive, was Dani.

Yet another statement.

Eden didn't hesitate to summon an orb of energy into her palm. It was easier than she'd thought it would be. It was like the magic knew exactly what she wanted, and all it needed was for her to call it forth. She had no particular desire to kill Dani. In fact, it wasn't her intention at all, but Calla had told her to keep her sister here at any cost. Eden was confident that the high sorcerer could rectify any maiming or dismemberment that ended up being necessary. Even death, as it turned out, was negotiable.

Eden didn't hesitate, but neither did the dragon. Before she could launch her attack, Nox had unleashed his own. He roared a firestorm toward the tunnel, so dazzlingly bright that the whole world seemed to ignite. Eden let the orb dissolve, and instead threw her concentration into shielding herself. Again, the magic seemed to know what was needed; all she had to do was conjure it into existence. A crimson bubble expanded around her, shimmering and translucent. The dragonfire whorled around her, battering at her defense, but she held steady. The flames couldn't reach her, but the heat quickly became unbearable. Just when she thought she couldn't hold out another second, the flames died down.

She kept up the shield, though it was now costing her some effort, and looked out the mouth of the tunnel. The dragon and Dani were gone.

She dropped the shield and swore. Calla wasn't going to take this well.

A few hours ago, the prospect of disappointing someone, especially Calla Thorn, would have sent her into a spiral of panic and self-loathing. She knew that about herself. Her therapist had pointed it out enough times. Recognizing the pattern was supposed to be the first step to combating it, though most the time it just meant she was panicked, full of self-loathing, *and* acutely aware of how irrational it all was.

Things were different now. She was different. All those old patterns, stitched as they were into the fabric of her being, had been ripped out. She'd been sewn back together with better pieces, stronger thread. She was no longer at the mercy of her own discordant brain. The gift that the sorcerers had given her was perfect clarity. A clinical understanding of the universe, a way to bring order to all the chaos.

Dragons were chaos. To her, it was obvious, but Dani needed some convincing. How could the world thrive while these leftover monsters of a primeval age were allowed to roam free, wreaking havoc as they wished? Humans had ways of taming nature, staving off disease, and protecting themselves from almost everything—including other humans—but they had no way to conquer dragons. That was a job for the sorcerers and the slayers.

And now that Eden was both, she refused to let Dani's stubborn antics get in her way. Her sister needed to be brought to heel. She needed to understand her place in this world. It was all so very simple.

Eden closed her eyes, wondering if her magic was up to the task of something more complex than destruction and defense. She focused on the way it hummed through her body, vibrating power through her pores. She familiarized herself with the weight of it, the taste of it, the way it clung to the very core of her, filling up every empty space, intertwining with who she was on the deepest level. It had belonged to that dragon, not so long ago. But it was her magic now. It was her.

She trained her thoughts on where she wanted to go, and her magic obliged. When she opened her eyes, she was back in the basement chamber with Calla and Alder. The ritual was apparently complete. The dragon, despite its lifeblood still pooled and sticky on the stone floor, was alive again. They had removed the chains that kept it trapped on the dais, though a single iron cuff was still attached to its right foreleg. Eden could tell by looking at the cuff that it was spelled to dampen magic, including electricity and dragonfire. With the cuff in place, the dragon was no more a threat to the sorcerers than an oversized house cat—albeit one with a razor-sharp tail.

The young man who had come in after Dani and yelled at the high sorcerer—Calla had called him Kieran—was still by the dragon's side, one hand on the side of its neck. He wasn't speaking, but Eden had a feeling they were communicating with each other somehow. Interesting. She still hadn't quite figured out Kieran's purpose here, or why Calla had let him speak to her that way.

"Where is she?" Calla asked, turning to Eden. A sheen of sweat glistened on her face, and loose tendrils of her normally immaculate hair clung to her neck and cheeks. Necromancy was obviously not as simple and intuitive as the magic that Eden had practiced thus far.

"Her dragon was here. They got away." Eden braced herself for outrage, but she should have known that wasn't the high sorcerer's way.

Calla let out a long sigh and began the tedious process of fixing her hair.

"I'd hoped you might prove marginally more useful than that," she said.

"I did warn you she wasn't the right material," Alder said. Eden shot him a glare, but he didn't notice. He was checking his shoes for blood. "It took the dragon's magic almost three years to regenerate this time. Who knows how long it might be until there's enough juice to try for another sorcerer?"

"Which is why we have other irons in the fire, my dear." Calla gave Eden a once-over, her keen eyes seeing everything but her expression giving nothing away. "At least you're catching on quickly. That's something, I suppose."

"I'll find them," Eden said. Disappointing Calla might not send her into a tailspin of anxiety anymore, but that didn't mean she was content to have the high sorcerer think she was a waste of effort. Magic had given her the tools to finally explore her full potential, but she would still have to prove herself. That was fine. Proving herself had been her full-time occupation since she was nine.

"I'd rather you stay out of our hair until I find some use for you."

Calla nodded at Alder, and before Eden could reply, the two of them vanished. Clearly there was to be no orientation course for the newbie sorcerer. She realized she was alone now with Kieran and the dragon whose magic now coursed through her own veins. The dragon, curled up in a way that did absurdly resemble a house cat, appeared to be sleeping. She could see the fresh scar along its neck where the blade had cut. From the way Alder had spoken, that was probably not the only scar layered there.

Kieran was staring at her with open hostility.

"What do you want?" she demanded.

"I was about to ask you the same thing," he replied, standing up. "Don't you have someplace better to be?"

She did, in fact, but she didn't appreciate his tone. He wasn't a sorcerer, as far as she could tell, and no slayer would ever show that much concern over a dragon.

"I can be anywhere I please," she said.

"Haven't you done enough here?" His strident voice echoed through the chamber, and he strode two steps forward, stopping himself with what seemed to be a great effort of will. His hands were clenched into fists at his sides. "Can't you just leave us alone?"

Eden didn't have a reply. A flash of red caught her eye, and she saw that the dragon had opened its eyes. It did not stir, but its long tail snaked out and curled around Kieran's waist. With the razor-sharp scales folded down, the gesture was a gentle one, almost like a parent nudging their child away from a stranger.

Maybe the dragon spoke to him in their silent language, because Kieran muttered something she couldn't make out and turned away from her to return to the dragon's side. He sank down to the floor and leaned against the scaly flank, his head tilted back in a picture of exhausted defeat. The dragon's tail remained draped across his lap, a comforting barrier between him and the rest of the world.

Eden's eyes met the ruby-red gaze once more, and though no words were formed, she heard the message loud and clear. What had been a protective gesture to Kieran was a warning to her. The dragon might not have its magic anymore, but there was plenty of damage to be done with its other faculties. It was, after all, an ancient beast, and Eden had been a sorcerer for all of half an hour.

Part of her rankled at the threat, but she also knew there was no reason to stay here and exacerbate the situation. Especially since she had to track down her sister, hopefully before Calla started to regret the decision to make her a sorcerer instead of Dani. Eden squeezed her eyes shut so she could focus on the top of the basement stairs. She wasn't sure yet how far her new magic could take her, but she intended to find out.

Nox's landing in the tree-circled clearing was clumsier than usual. Dani could sense that his exhaustion was as crippling as her own, and knew that he wouldn't be able to make it all the way back to the cave tonight. Overhead the brilliant stars blanketed the sky. They were miles from the artificial lights of civilization, and far away from Stonecrest. The chirruping of crickets and rustling of night creatures had resumed.

As soon as they were on the ground, Dani stumbled toward the edge of the clearing on shaky knees and retched until she couldn't breathe. Her adrenaline had deserted her, leaving behind a trembling weakness that coiled around her bones. She spat the acidic taste of bile out of her mouth and crawled a few feet away, pulling her phone from her pocket. She wiped hot tears from her eyes and called her parents. Straight to voicemail. She texted them both to call her, then tried Jaime Cruz, but reached his voicemail too. It was normal for them to be out of touch during a hunt, but still her heart clenched as various scenarios filled her with dread, each more far-fetched and unlikely than the last. What if the sorcerers had done something to them? It was clear that whatever Calla had planned, it wasn't anything as benign as a friendly partnership with the slayers.

After a few seconds of thought, she called Jaime's husband, Luis, who she'd only met a handful of times. The only reason she had his number was because her parents were big believers in emergency contacts. Luis must've had her number saved as well, because he greeted her by name.

"I was just wondering if you'd heard from Jaime or my parents recently?" she asked.

"¿Puedes repetir eso?" There was a crash and chorus of laughter on his side, followed by his muffled shouting in Spanish. Dani could only make out pieces of what he was saying—someone had either broken a plate or robbed a cat. Her mother only spoke Spanish when she was around her side of the family, so Dani hadn't learned much growing up. She and Eden had both taken the elective in school, but while Eden had studied and practiced enough outside class to be conversationally fluent, Dani had barely passed the final exam. Tomás had offered several times to practice with her, but between school and slayer training, there never seemed to be any time for mastering a second language. Like so many other things in her life, she'd consigned it to the hazy territory of "maybe one day."

"Sorry," Luis said at last into the phone. "I've got some friends over. What was that about Jaime?"

"I just wanted to know if you've heard from him or my parents," she repeated, trying to sound casual. It was a little disorienting to be reminded that, for most people, this was a typical Friday night.

"Oh, not since he left, sorry. Something wrong?"

"No," she said quickly. "I just had to ask my parents something. It's okay. I'll try them again tomorrow."

There was a hesitation, and Dani wondered if her worry and exhaustion had bled into her voice after all.

"Dani, are you sure—" Another crash and bout of laughter. More muffled shouting.

Dani took advantage of his distraction to say a quick goodbye and end the call. She glanced over her shoulder, where Nox was already lying on his side in the grass. For a long time, she stared at her aunt Frankie's name on her contact list, her finger hovering over the call icon. Frankie was family, but Dani didn't know her very well. Certainly not enough to trust her with a secret as big as Nox. And she didn't see any way to explain the mess with Eden without explaining how she'd ended up at Stonecrest in the first place. And Eden had been there the day before, hadn't she? Was it just to help with the cat, or did Frankie have something to do with Eden deciding to become a sorcerer? A litany of increasingly ridiculous conspiracy scenarios began to play in her mind, before finally she canceled the screen.

Her phone vibrated a low battery warning, and she switched it to power-saving mode before sending off one last text to both Marcus and Tomás, telling them she had to take Saturday off. She decided on a case of pinkeye as an excuse: contagious, but not serious enough that Tomás would want to check up on her.

Then she crossed the field, back to Nox. He had battered down the long grass in a huge circle all around himself, creating a serviceable bed. She sank down to the ground beside him. For the first time, she was glad for the warmth that radiated from him. Despite the mild summer night, she was shivering slightly in her shorts and tank top.

Neither of them said anything. There didn't seem to be much to say. Dani knew she couldn't avoid the day's events entirely. At some point she had to come to terms and decide how to move forward, but right now she couldn't bring herself to do anything but rest.

Which was easier said than done on the lumpy ground. The flattened grass was probably much more comfortable for Nox, with his thick scales, but Dani could feel every individual stem jabbing into her body, as well as about six different rocks that were probably smaller than quarters but might as well have been daggers in her back. She tried to remember the last time she had gone "roughing it" with her dad, and realized it must have been three or four years ago now. She had grown soft and spoiled in the interim.

The constellations overhead blurred, and she realized she was crying again. Furiously, she wiped at her eyes and sat up. Beside her, Nox stretched his legs while his jaw stretched wide with a raspy sound that Dani guessed was a yawn. Then he shifted his weight enough to unfurl his wing across the ground.

Come on, then, he said, in that determinedly cross way of his that meant he wasn't really cross. *If you're going to be flopping around and crying all night, I won't get any sleep.*

"I'm not crying," Dani said automatically, briefly forgetting that he would know she was lying. She eyed the ribbed expanse of his wing with some trepidation before resting one palm on it, then the other, then crawling the rest of the way. Despite its leathery texture, the wing was as soft and warm as a heating pad, and she found that if she curled between two of the bony supports, it was no less comfortable than a sleeping bag under the stars.

"I don't want to hurt you," she said, surprised by the drowsiness already slurring her words.

Nox was miffed at the notion.

My wings are fireproof, and strong enough to withstand hurricanes.

Dani smiled to herself at his tone. She could already feel her muscles relaxing from the heat.

Thank you for saving me. It was easier now to offer the sincere gratitude, snug as they were, well beyond all pretense of ego.

I would never have left you there.

I know. And she did know, like she knew her own mind—better, even. For the first time, she'd begun to understand how a soul bond might make you stronger in more than a physical sense. Unlike everyone else in her life, she didn't have to keep any secrets from Nox. In fact, until she had better control over her half of their telepathic bond, she *couldn't* keep any secrets from him. At first, she'd thought that would be suffocating, but it had turned into a kind of shelter. Her family and friends meant everything to her, but the division she kept between her slayer life and her normal life was a gulf inside herself. To let the two worlds meet would be putting a fuse to the flame.

There was no division between her and Nox, just a harmony that sang through her marrow. The more she opened herself to it, the more invincible she felt. She was more than whole: she was safe.

As the prickling discomfort of the ground faded, sleep began to take its place. She was just drifting off when Nox's voice slipped through the cracks in her consciousness.

I'm sorry about your sister. I know what it feels like to lose family.

She's not dead, Dani returned, not quite awake, not quite asleep. *I'm going to bring her back.*

Nox said nothing else, but Dani carried the cold weight of his doubt into her dreams.

Stonecrest felt smaller, now that her nerves no longer aggrandized it into mythical proportions. The stately corridors didn't stretch on forever. The spectacular view was really just the same mountains she'd grown up with. As she listened to the rhythm of her own footfalls, she imagined the rest of the world shrinking as well, diminishing in importance until it was nothing but a snow globe in her palm. That's what it meant to be a sorcerer. The world was finally in her hands.

"You're looking entirely too satisfied with yourself," came a voice from farther down the corridor. She blinked out of her reverie to find Alder leaning against the wall ahead of her, arms crossed, as if he'd been waiting for her.

"I'm sorry," she said without slowing. "I think you've mistaken me for someone who cares what you think."

The readiness of the curt reply shocked her. Not so long ago, she wouldn't have even been able to muster a complete sentence in the face of Alder's smug air of authority, much less breeze right past him and feel nothing but a hint of disdain.

He fell into step beside her, giving no indication that he'd even heard her barb.

"You should know that I don't have anything against you," he said, tucking his hands into his pockets with calculated nonchalance. "I'm actually rather pleased you turned out to be so incompetent. It's not often I get to prove Calla wrong."

The remark needled her pride, which was clearly his intention, so out of spite she kept her expression neutral.

"If you were so competent, Calla wouldn't have needed to recruit me in the first place," she said. "Dani got lucky. It won't happen again."

"I doubt you'll get the opportunity to test that theory. Calla doesn't give second chances." He stopped at a set of double doors at the entrance to a grand dining room and nodded in the direction of the diners. Maybe a dozen sorcerers in all. They were absorbed in their conversations and dinner, ignoring the harried serving staff who fluttered around them filling wine glasses and whisking away empty plates. "Stonecrest is full of sorcerers that Calla thought would be worthy additions, but most of them let her down in one way or another. If you're not careful, you'll be one of them. Eternity is a long time to be a disappointment."

Eden stared down the long table, trying to envision what it was like to be just one face among the many. Was it possible to be extraordinary in a room full of extraordinary people? Didn't that just make you ordinary?

"Your concern is touching," she said. She could feel Alder's eyes on the side of her face, studying her reaction. "I'll keep it under advisement."

"No concern," he said. "Just giving you the lay of the land." He gestured toward an austere white-haired man in a black suit, gray-striped vest, and tie, who was surveying the dinner proceedings from the corner with the attention of a hawk. The man immediately made his way over to them and proffered a small bow.

"How may I be of service, Master De Lange?" he asked with the nasal politeness of a Hollywood butler.

"Miss Rivera needs a room," Alder said, giving her a dismissive wave, as if she were a stray dog that had wandered in. She resisted the urge to bare her teeth. "Take care of it, will you, Paulson?"

"Of course, sir." Paulson offered a second bow, this time angled to include Eden in his obeisance.

Someone at the table called for Alder, and he wandered away without a parting word. Eden shot a glare at his back, then followed Paulson back down the corridor. The room he showed her was exactly what she would have expected from Stonecrest. All Victorian elegance and moneyed charm. There was a connected bathroom, and she thought she caught sight of an actual claw-foot tub.

She sat down on the foot of the bed, realizing for the first time how exhausted she was. It was more bone-deep than physical exertion, like the magic had taken something extra out of her.

"Wait," she called to Paulson when he tried to bow his way out of the room. "I need to go somewhere tomorrow morning."

"Breakfast is served at nine," he said gravely. "If you wish, I can have a car waiting for you after."

She nodded and waved him off without a thank you, which was something else that a few hours ago she wouldn't have been able to do as nonchalantly. Manners, like proper fighting techniques, were non-negotiable in her family. But now those niceties felt so useless. A waste of breath in the scheme of things. Paulson's feelings were no more important than those of an insect buzzing by.

That particular spot inside herself where goodwill and humility used to shape her thoughts was emptied and bare now, leaving space for her to flex her new power. It was freeing. Intoxicating.

Once the door shut, she flopped backwards, staring at the draped forest-green canopy over her head. She never would have let him know it, but Alder's words had spurred a panic inside her. Not the uncontrollable, mind-consuming anxiety that she'd grown up with, but a new understanding that if she didn't prove her merit now, she might never get the chance again.

Nineteen years of blood, sweat, and tears, and she'd made it this far. She was in Stonecrest with real magic coursing through her veins. She wasn't about to stop now.

SIXTEEN

If Dani had been hoping that the clear light of day and the benefit of Nox's dragonly wisdom would help dissuade her from the fear that she was caught in a complex web of danger and intrigue with no one left to trust, she was sorely mistaken. Nox seemed convinced that sorcerers were behind not only the near-extinction of dragonkind, but also everything from global warming to the sinking of the Titanic.

"Good god, you sound like one of Sadie's conspiracy nuts," Dani said around a mouthful of breakfast burrito.

Isn't Sadie the smart one?

She ignored that and took another massive bite. That morning, in the first rays of dawn, Nox had dropped her about a half mile from her house. She'd hiked down the bike trail that led into their back forty and sneaked into the house. She'd been half-convinced that Eden and her new friends would be waiting for her, but either sorcerers weren't fans of the early morning, or no one thought she would be stupid enough to go home. The Jeep was in the driveway, but she was alone. She couldn't resist a five-minute shower to rinse off the sweat, outdoors, and musty memories of the Stonecrest dungeon. Then she grabbed her portable phone charger and her wallet.

Before she left, she nuked three frozen breakfast burritos in the microwave and filled up her water bottle with cold water. She couldn't find the keys to the Jeep, so she shoved everything into a backpack and cycled back to Nox, figuring she could hide her bike in some underbrush to retrieve later. Funny how quickly she had come to think of dragon flight as her primary mode of transportation.

They returned to the cave, where Dani set herself up on the ledge. The ethereal tranquility of the eggs in their pool didn't seem like the sort of place where you charged your phone and inhaled breakfast. Nox flew off to find his own food. Apparently the deer-hunting was good this season—a fact that Nox felt the need to share with her right as she was unwrapping her first burrito. She tried to kick him, but he'd already taken off. Despite his attempt to ruin her appetite, Dani made it through two burritos and was starting on the third—she kind of wished she'd grabbed a fourth—when he returned.

Calla Thorn has been around for over a thousand years, Nox said, turning up his nose at her in a gesture that seemed so human Dani had to resist a laugh. *It's well within her wheelhouse to devise complex plots. She's already come up with a way to create sorcerers at will.*

"You don't have to remind me." The talk of conspiracy theories had given her the first inklings of an idea. She turned it over in her head while she polished off the rest of her breakfast and drained half her water bottle. The sun had just crested over the pine trees, haloing them in orange and pink. Her phone buzzed and she checked it eagerly, but it was only a text from Tomás lamenting that she'd left him alone with Tippi and Anabel, followed by a GIF of Robert Downey Jr. rolling his eyes in exasperation. She responded with a GIF of Justin Bieber dramatically wiping away a tear and pocketed her phone.

"I have an idea," she told Nox. "You're going to hate it."

An idea about what?

"About how to help Eden. Or at least find someone who might know a way to help her."

He just stared at her, and something dawned on Dani.

"You don't think I should try to help her."

Help her how? She's a sorcerer. It's not something you can cure.

"If there's a process to turn her into a sorcerer, then there has to be some way to reverse it."

And how do you intend to accomplish this against her will?

"I don't know, but I'll figure it out. As soon as I find a way to reverse the process. Calla tricked her into doing this somehow. That girl in the dungeon wasn't the Eden I grew up with."

I've told you before, when a dragon's magic transfers into a human, their soul shatters. That is *your sister, minus her humanity.*

Then I'm going to get her humanity back. Dani glared at him. *If you don't want to help, then fine. But I'm not going to sit on my hands and do nothing.*

I'm not doing nothing, he shot back. *I'm trying to protect these eggs. I'm the only one who can hatch them now.*

"Oh, don't be so dramatic. You're not the last dragon on earth."

That's not what I meant.

Another flash of that phantom grief she'd felt the first time she'd spoken with him. Garbled with it were images — memories that weren't hers — of the eggs being lowered gently into the sacred pool, of another dragon's face, dark gray scales and amber eyes.

"Tell me," Dani said, as she absorbed the scattered images and emotions.

A long stretch of silence.

There was another of my kind. Nox's tone was low and tremulous. *She was with me from my birth. Her name was Polara.*

Without thinking, Dani stepped forward and slid her hand along the curve of his shoulder, hoping the touch might impart at least a little comfort.

She had charge of the eggs. We lived far to the west then, in a place of canyons and red sand.

"New Mexico," Dani whispered. Her hand had stilled. She was starting to realize where this was going.

We hoped to hatch them eventually. It would take years with just the two of us, but we had time, as long as we stayed hidden. Nox released a heavy stream of smoke through his nostrils. *Then a slayer started getting too close. It's dangerous to move a nest, but we couldn't risk it being discovered. Polara sent me back here with the eggs. She had lived here many years ago, before a family of slayers moved into the area — it must have been your kin. This cave was still infused with her magic, and was the only other place suitable for the nest. So I brought them here.*

"And the slayers tracked down Polara," Dani said softly. The Lowrys.

I don't know exactly what happened. Across that distance, I couldn't sense her at all. Then one night, I could. It was weak, but she was getting closer. I thought she'd come to tell me it was safe, that we could go back home. I flew out to meet her. Instead I found her skull being unloaded from a truck.

Dani dropped her hand. A chill ran through her blood. She remembered that night. It was nearly midnight, but Frankie had let her and Eden stay up late because their parents were coming home. It was a couple weeks after the Lowrys' funeral. Analisa and James had stayed in New Mexico, determined to track down the dragon that had gotten the best of their fellow slayers. Their return home was a victorious one. Jaime and Luis had met them in New Mexico and helped them make the cross-country drive with a rental car and a U-Haul truck.

To Dani, it had felt like a party. Despite the late hour, everyone had been laughing and hugging, and her parents were flushed with pride and excitement as Jaime raised the roll-up door of the truck, which they had backed all the way up to the barn doors. The skull had been packed carefully in quilted padding and wooden pallets. It had taken all the adults nearly half an hour to unload it, as Dani and Eden did their best to stay out of the way while also never losing sight of the wondrous trophy.

When she had touched it for the first time, her own bones had quivered with the power of it. The thought of her parents being able to bring down a monster so enormous, so terrifying, had filled her with her own pride and excitement—especially when she thought about how they would soon be teaching her to do the same.

Now, in the place of that childish flurry of emotion, was a sick, empty feeling in the pit of her stomach. She wanted to say she was sorry, but what good would it do? She hadn't been the one to kill Polara, and nothing she could say would bring her back.

I wanted to raze everything—the barn, your house, all of you—to the ground, Nox said in a disturbingly matter-of-fact tone. *But Polara charged me with the safety of the eggs, and I couldn't risk bringing the attention of more slayers. So I decided to bide my time, to learn what I could about your family, to wait for my chance.*

"That's why you were following me that night," Dani said. "The night of the soul bond."

I'm not going to apologize, he said tartly.

"I'm not asking you to." Dani told herself to stay calm, to not rise to the bait of another spat. "You're right. The eggs have to be protected, but I'm not going to turn my back on my sister either."

So where does that leave us?

Dani considered for a few moments.

"You stay here with the nest, and I'll try to find a way to help Eden," she said. "I promise if I don't have any leads in a day or two I'll come back here, and we can sing 'Kumbaya' or something until you feel like you're strong enough to hatch the eggs."

What is "Kumbaya"?

"Guaranteed to strengthen our soul bond," Dani assured him. "It's summer-camp-tested and approved."

Sometimes I don't think you are taking this seriously enough.

"Now you sound like my sister," she said, stuffing her discarded burrito wrappers into her bag. "I don't take anything seriously enough. It's not personal. Now, can I get a lift back to civilization?"

Eden kept to herself at breakfast, and the few other sorcerers who attended didn't seem to mind ignoring her as well. Calla and Alder were both absent. They weren't the type for communal meals. As Paulson had promised, there was a car with a driver waiting for her out front. She slid into the back seat and gave the address to her house. The night before, she'd lain awake for hours piecing together a plan for how she would find Dani and bring her back to Stonecrest. It wasn't as foolproof as she would like, but she did have one advantage on her side. Dani had never been any good at planning ahead, and Eden suspected that she would prove equally useless at laying low.

She didn't expect to find Dani at home, but she searched the house carefully just in case, including Dani's room for any clues of where she might have gone—not that she had any idea what those clues might be. She took her time showering and changing into more suitable attire, foregoing the cute, summery pieces in favor of her favorite boots, dark jeans, and a black asymmetrical tank top in the back of her closet that she'd never had the guts to wear. She pulled a necklace from the bottom of her jewelry box that she'd also never worn: a piece of iridescent dragon scale, filed down to the size of her finger but retaining its razor-sharp edge. It felt more fitting now than it ever had before.

She charged her phone while rifling through her father's office in search of anything about soul bonds between dragons and humans. She found a couple obscure references, but there was no additional explanation or details, and finally she tossed the book away in frustration. She'd hoped to have a better idea of why Dani had decided to attach herself to this dragon, but it wasn't strictly necessary. Eden could always ask her when she was ensconced once more at Stonecrest.

She leaned back in the desk chair and spun back and forth absently with one toe on the ground. The motion brought back the times when she would sit on her father's lap while he worked, trying hard to be quiet and still so he wouldn't make her leave. Once, her mother had come in with a tub of ice cream and four spoons, announcing that she wasn't in the mood to cook dinner, so they were going to have dessert instead. Dani had tumbled in a few minutes later, covered in leaves and dirt from outside, earning a chuckle from Analisa and an exasperated sigh from James. They had passed the tub around, one bite at a time, until it was gone. Eden remembered laughing until her stomach hurt, though she couldn't remember why. It was a distant memory now, like something that had happened to someone else. She had been so very happy that day, but that emotion belonged to someone else too.

She left the office, shutting the door behind her, and retrieved her phone. It was time to leave.

She'd misplaced the keys to the Jeep in the past couple of days, which was such an ordinary inconvenience in the light of everything that was happening, she almost wanted to laugh. Almost. Instead, she glared at the useless hunk of metal with increasing frustration until something occurred to her. She concentrated with her hand on the door, focusing her thoughts on the locking mechanism. It took a few seconds, but her magic responded, feeling its way out of her fingers and through the metal of the door. She smiled at the satisfying *click*.

Tree Top Adventure was only a twenty-minute drive, but she made it in twelve. Again, she didn't expect to find Dani, but it was worth checking out. The bored college student manning the general store begrudgingly made a few radio calls before confirming that Dani was off sick that day. Eden was about to leave, when a thought struck her.

"Is Tomás here?" she asked. "Tomás Vasquez?"

The clerk barely managed not to roll her eyes as she dragged her gaze up from her phone again.

"He's probably at lunch," she said. She waved indistinctly to the back of the store. "But the break room is employees only."

Eden didn't think that the clerk would do anything to stop her if she just marched back there, but she decided to try a different route. She leaned forward, propping her arms on the counter. She could already feel the magic fizzing through her veins in readiness.

"It's okay, I'm allowed to go wherever I want," she said. She pushed her own certainty outward and watched in fascination as it washed over the clerk.

The woman frowned, slowly lowering her phone. Her mouth fell slightly agape, and her pale eyes glazed over.

"I think—" But she couldn't seem to figure out what she was thinking. Eden patted her arm and found it easier to channel her will that way. At last, the clerk's lips dragged into a strained, tremulous grin. "It's okay; you're allowed to go wherever you want."

"Thank you."

Eden turned and headed for the back. The power thrilled through her, increasing with every step when she wasn't called back. It was easier than she'd imagined it would be, and a hundred times more satisfying. She reveled in the uncomplicated elation of it.

Tomás and a blond-haired girl were the only ones in the break-room, chatting over the remains of the lunch. Their conversation broke off when she entered.

"Eden? What are you doing here?" Tomás asked.

"Hello to you too," Eden said, dropping smoothly into the chair beside him.

"Oh—I mean, hi." His blush was visible even in his tan cheeks, and he swiped a hand through his already messy hair.

She'd never given much thought to Tomás's crush on her. It had always seemed cute and harmless, since he wasn't the type to be obnoxious about it, and she'd assumed it would fade eventually. So far, that didn't seem to be the case. Now that puberty was done with him, he at least had the eye-candy thing going on. Eden wondered, with faint amusement, how much it would piss off Dani if she kissed him right now just for the hell of it.

The blonde was looking between them with a mix of surprise and consternation.

"Hi, Eden," she said haltingly. "You probably don't remember me. I'm Sadie May. I was friends with Dani when we were kids?"

Eden glanced at her with revived interest.

"Of course, I remember you," she said. "You ghosted my sister. Fucked her up pretty good."

It was Sadie's turn to blush, her pale skin flaming scarlet.

"Um—well—I—"

"Is Dani doing okay?" Tomás asked, very valiantly coming to the rescue. "She said she had pinkeye."

"Is that what she told you?" Eden examined their faces, hoping for a hint that they knew something she didn't. Blank confusion stared back at her.

"She doesn't?" Tomás asked.

"She's playing hooky," Eden said, amused by the frown that overtook Tomás's face as he realized Dani had lied to him. "That's why I'm looking for her. I'm guessing you don't know where she is, then?"

Sadie and Tomás both shook their heads.

"Any ideas?" Eden pressed, trying to keep the impatience out of her tone.

Tomás pulled out his phone and called her.

"Straight to voicemail," he said, ending the call and opening his messages instead. "I'll tell her to call me."

"I hope she's okay," Sadie said.

"I'm sure she'll be touched by your concern." Eden stood up, suddenly bored. "If you hear from her, let me know right away."

She started to say she was worried, but wasn't sure if she could pull off the lie just then, so she settled for an entreating smile.

"Of course," said Sadie, either immune to Eden's pointed sarcasm or ignoring it completely. She was eyeing Eden with a strange expression, her light blue gaze sharper than her cherubic features would suggest.

"Do you want a drink or an ice cream or something?" Tomás stood up next to her, eager in a way that would have been endearing if it weren't so pathetic. "It's hot out there."

"I'll pass." Normally she would have at least been friendly about her refusal, for Dani's sake if for no other reason. But now she couldn't see the point. He must have figured out by now that he didn't have a chance with her.

"Good to see you again," Sadie said, managing to actually sound sincere.

Eden ignored her and left. The cloying politeness and naiveté in the room was overbearing. She hated the smallness of them. Their pointless feelings and petty embarrassments.

The general store was packed with patrons when she left. A raucous bunch of men in khaki shirts and polos and women with high ponytails and expensive sunglasses were all talking over each other and making jabs about someone named Johnson failing the trust fall. Probably a corporate retreat of some kind. Eden automatically braced herself for the anxiety that always clawed its way up the back of her throat in the midst of crowds, with their sharp elbows and blunt shoulders and grating conversations. But as strangers milled all around her, that new, calm center inside herself remained unruffled. The people might as well have been on the other side of glass, an exhibit she could examine at her leisure with clinical detachment. She was safely apart from them. She was untouchable. And she was unimpressed.

She took a soda from the cooler and left the store. In the parking lot, there were a few other folks clearly from the same group heading toward their luxury cars, all of which were out of place in Tree Top's potholed gravel parking lot. One car in particular caught her eye: a sapphire Porsche that looked like a traffic ticket waiting to happen.

She crossed the lot to where the apparent owner was talking too loudly into his cell phone with the smarmy, unmistakable tone of a salesperson. He used the word "synergy" no less than three times before finally ending the call.

"718 Cayman GTS. Gorgeous, isn't she?" He patted the top of the car and flashed Eden a pearly grin that made her kind of want to slap him. She decided on another tack.

"Absolutely," she said, stepping closer. "I'd love to take a ride in a car like this."

He gave her a once-over, obviously weighing his chances of getting lucky against how likely it was that she was underage.

"Hey, if you want to go for a spin," he said, "I'm happy to oblige."

"Really? That's so sweet." She touched his arm. Her magic responded like an eager friend, gleefully lending her power to bend the world to her will. "But wouldn't you rather just give me the keys?"

He blinked, smile faltering.

"What?"

Convincing someone to give up their seventy-thousand-dollar car was a little trickier than convincing a bored clerk to bend some rules. Eden was up for the challenge. She focused on her own desire and pushed it into him, forcing the magic throughout every inch of his body. He faltered physically, like he might fall, but managed to stay upright. His eyes were glazed and unseeing.

"You want to hand me the keys and let me take your car," Eden said. "It's not a big deal."

"It's . . . not a big deal." His grin returned, but it was different now, too wide and trembling. He lifted the keys and dropped them into her outstretched palm.

"Wonderful," she said. "Now go away."

He hesitated, but only for a second, and then wandered away like a lost duckling in search of its mother. Eden slid into the car, set her soda in the cupholder, and adjusted the seat and mirrors. Her phone buzzed in her pocket and she dug it out, expecting it to be her parents. It was Nate, with another stupid song lyric. Nate was the furthest thing from her mind, and she didn't have time to deal with him in any case. She ignored his message and opened the Find My Friends app instead. Dani's location was currently unavailable, as it had been all day. She doubted Dani would have thought to turn it off. Probably she was outside of a service area, or her phone was dead.

Eden double-checked that her own location wasn't being shared and leaned back against the leather headrest. Even as she tried to brainstorm options, she couldn't get Alder's warnings out of her head. *An eternity is a long time to be a disappointment.* It hadn't occurred to her before that there could be fates worse than death. She was free from her old anxieties, but maybe that was only because they had been eclipsed by new ones. She found herself naturally gravitating toward her five senses as a distraction from the troubling notion. The Porsche still had the faintly chemical new car smell. The sunlight was glaring through the windshield, heating up the interior until sweat prickled her forehead. The birdsong outside—no. When she realized what she was doing, she shut it down with a wave of panic. She was supposed to be beyond all that now. Magic was supposed to fix what was broken. She didn't need her old coping mechanisms. She *didn't*.

She ground her back teeth together and forced herself to refocus on the matter at hand. After a few minutes of contemplation, she decided that perhaps Nate might be useful after all. Eden hadn't told Dani about them reconnecting, which meant Dani wouldn't be suspicious of him. She opened Nate's message again and replied:

Want to hang out tonight?

It was only a few seconds before his response pinged.

Sure! Dinner and then a movie or something? I can come by your place after work.

Eden smiled as she typed. This was easier than she'd expected.

How about I pick you up? Just got a new ride.

SEVENTEEN

It was more difficult than Dani had expected to bring Sadie and Tomás on board with her spur of the moment plan. For some reason, texting them out of the blue to suggest they accompany her that night to Kaleidoscope, the Dragon Truther bar Sadie kept talking about, did not result in their immediate and enthusiastic acceptance. In fact, Tomás replied to ask her where the hell had she been, and why had she lied about having pinkeye? A couple seconds later, Sadie added that Eden was looking for her.

Dani's heart leapt into her throat, and she typed a reply with trembling thumbs.

Please DON'T tell Eden we're talking. I'll explain later.

Are you ok? came Sadie's response.

Yeah but I really need a night out. Pls?

It took a few minutes, but finally Tomás replied that he was in. Sadie was in as well. Since Dani didn't have the Jeep, and Sadie's brother had already laid claim to the car they shared for the evening, Tomás agreed to drive.

Dani knew it was smarter to go alone to the city. The kind of questions she needed to ask the Dragon Truthers who supposedly frequented the bar weren't subtle, and trying to learn what she could about how sorcerers were made—and how they could be *unmade*—was going to be that much more difficult with Tomás and Sadie around. In spite of that, she convinced herself that she needed Tomás's car and Sadie's knowledge of the subreddit.

Deep down, she knew it was just because the thought of going it alone was paralyzing. Nox couldn't risk getting close to a bustling city full of people and their camera phones, and she wasn't sure how many miles their mental connection could stretch. She hated that she was scared, but after what had happened with Eden, and with her parents still out of contact, she was utterly adrift. All the familiar, regimented routines of her life had been decimated, leaving her with no foundation, no safe haven.

She promised herself that she would keep her friends well clear of her real intentions at the Truthers' bar. There was no reason to believe that they would be in any danger there, in a public place surrounded by people. And she didn't think the sorcerers had any magical means of tracking her down; otherwise, they would have already found her.

And so, after a flurry of texts and meeting times and adjusted meeting times and convincing Tomás not to wear his T-shirt with the dragon printed on it that said #SLAY, which Dani had bought him as a birthday present last year, the three of them were on the road north just before sunset.

Dani had let Sadie sit up front, since she was navigating, but soon began to regret the decision. Tomás's erratic driving style was a thousand times more nauseating from the back seat. To her relief, neither of them had broached the topic of Eden just yet, though she knew better than to think that the forbearance would last all night. Sadie, who had also taken control of the playlist, insisted on Top Hits, much to Tomás's vocal dismay.

"Not liking something just because it's popular is so overrated," Sadie informed him, turning Young Thug's beat up louder as if to punctuate her point.

"That's not why I don't like it," Tomás said. Dani couldn't help but notice that his fingers were tapping out the rhythm on the steering wheel. She also couldn't help but notice that Tomás and Sadie had developed a suspiciously easy rapport over the past few weeks.

"We'll listen to your music on the way home." Sadie patted his shoulder in a sympathetic fashion. "You big baby."

"Rude," said Tomás, but he was smiling.

"So do you think there will be any of these Dragon Truthers at the bar tonight?" Dani asked, popping her head in between the seats.

"Are you buckled up?" Tomás asked, shooting her a look in the rearview mirror.

"Yes, Mother." Dani patted the lap belt. "A crappy Corolla is not how I plan on dying."

"Rude."

Sadie giggled and pulled down the visor to check her makeup in the mirror. She had managed a perfect cat eye, which until then Dani thought was only possible in beauty magazines. In her flowy blue-and-white striped blouse, jean shorts, and signature pink Converses, she looked like summer itself. Light brown freckles played around the dimples in her cheeks, and her plump thighs were rosy with a sunburn that she'd insisted would turn into a tan within a few days.

"I think the owner actually bartends most weekends," she said, once she was satisfied with the mirror. "He's the one who started the subreddit."

"Cool." Dani tried not to sound too interested, but Tomás gave her another look.

"Are you thinking about converting or something?"

"It's not a religion," Sadie said.

"Maybe I am," Dani said. "I'll trade in my Bible for *Fiends of Fire* and start saying 'Hail dragons' every night before bed."

"You don't even have a Bible," Tomás said.

"So I'm already halfway there."

"Heathen."

Dani clasped her chest in mock injury and flopped back in her seat.

"Just don't come crying to me when our dragon overlords begin their fiery reign," she told him.

"You guys need to stop," Sadie said, her voice shaking with suppressed laughter. "Some of these Truthers take it very seriously. You're going to piss someone off."

"I would never joke about something as serious as dragons," Dani said.

They reached the city around seven, just as the night life was beginning to rouse itself. Market Square was humming with people, and she could hear strains of music from buskers and the colorful pianos set up beneath the big events pavilion. A man with a tip jar stood in the midst of dozens of hula hoops that kids and adults alike were making use of, to varying degrees of success. Tomás insisted that they try it out. None of them were any good at it, but by the time they finally gave up Dani was breathless with laughter and had almost forgotten the reason they were in the city in the first place. Sadie put some cash in the tip jar, and the man offered to take a photo of the three of them. They brandished their hula hoops like champions.

Kaleidoscope was only a few blocks away from the square, but it was on a street that Dani had never gone down before. The Georgian brick and stone facades of the buildings mostly belonged to offices with dark windows, but sandwiched between an austere accounting practice and chiropractor was the glass window display of a guitar shop. The store was closed, but the merchandise artfully arrayed in the windows was lit up with Christmas lights. Just above the store was a small metal sign that said KALEIDOSCOPE in rainbow letters.

"Come on," Sadie said with barely contained excitement. She led them to a doorway that a couple holding hands had just gone through. Dani realized that there were stairs going up. The bar must be above the guitar shop. There was no railing, and the walls of the stairwell were plastered with old band posters and neon fliers advertising everything from clearance sales to PSYCHIC READINGS — ONLY $40 A SESSION!

The interior of Kaleidoscope was dimly lit with Edison bulbs dangling from exposed ceiling beams. Mismatched tables and chairs filled up the front half, and beyond that was the Technicolor flashing and beeping of arcade games. The bar was to the right, lined with metal stools, and on the wall behind it were metal shelves packed with liquor bottles and a few abstract sculptures that looked to be made entirely of bottle caps.

"Hi there, you can take a seat anywhere," a waitress told them as she breezed past with a full tray. "I'll be with you in a sec."

There were fewer than a dozen patrons, so it wasn't hard to find a suitable table. They sat down near the back, close to the games and an old coin-operated jukebox that was currently blasting "Barbie Girl."

"I love this place," Sadie said. She was holding a paper menu, but her eyes were roaming the room.

"It just looks like a normal bar," Tomás said with a note of disappointment.

"What were you expecting?" Dani asked. "Wizard robes?"

"That's him," Sadie hissed suddenly, nudging Dani. "Mack Jeffries. The owner."

She gestured furtively toward the bartender, a man in his forties with a shock of red hair and a mustache that curled up at the ends. He was joking about something with a patron and grinning wildly. Under his black apron he was wearing jeans and a T-shirt that had what appeared to be the TARDIS on it. Dani liked him immediately.

The waitress arrived then to take their orders. She seemed mildly relieved when they all ordered soda. Dani wondered how many teenagers they got in here who were trying to get away with buying alcohol. All the food items on the menu were bad puns, like Fry me a River and Cheese Stick It to the Man. They each picked an appetizer to share. Tomás immediately hopped up and headed for the change machine.

"Skee-Ball, anyone?" he asked.

"Ooh, me," said Sadie.

"Maybe in a minute," Dani said. "I'm going to wait for our drinks."

She watched the two of them head off, chatting together happily and walking so close that their elbows touched. She rapped a knuckle hard on the table and told herself to focus. There were only a few people sitting at the bar right now, and likely it would get busier as the night went on. If she wanted to talk to Mack, now was the time. She waited until she was sure Sadie and Tomás were engrossed in their game, then made her way to the middle of the bar, where Mack was busy drying a glass.

"Sorry, hon," he said, barely glancing up. "Gotta be eighteen to sit up here. Twenty-one to drink."

She was a little offended that he immediately assumed she couldn't be eighteen, but then realized that in her basic shirt and shorts, with no makeup and her hair pulled into a rough ponytail, she would be lucky if she even looked old enough to drive.

"I'm not sitting," she said, propping her arms up on the counter. The top of it was made of colorful mosaic tiles, arranged in vibrant fractals that must have been inspired by the bar's name. "Are you Mack?"

He slowed his drying efforts and eyed her more closely now.

"Yeah," he said. "Can I help you with something?"

"I have a few questions to ask you," she said, then hesitated and pitched her voice a little lower. "About sorcerers and dragons?"

He raised an eyebrow at that, but set down the glass and moved closer.

"You on the subreddit, then?"

"Kind of. I was hoping you could tell me what it is that makes someone a sorcerer?" She had decided on the ride there that this was the best question to start with. If he didn't know anything about how sorcerers were made, then he wouldn't know how to unmake them, and she wouldn't need to waste any more time.

"Strange question for a Saturday night." He was studying her now, scratching the cleft of his chin in thought. Dani wondered if he would start twirling the end of his mustache. "I've got some theories. Even met a sorcerer once. Real piece of work, that guy."

"He told you he was a sorcerer?" Dani couldn't help the skepticism bleeding into her tone.

Mack shook his head.

"Saw him light a cigarette without a lighter. Just, poof, it started burning. I tried to cozy up to him, you know? See about getting some questions of my own answered." He sighed and grabbed a new bottle of beer from the cooler to pass to the man sitting a few seats down. "Not a very friendly dude. In fact, if I hadn't left when I did, I'm pretty sure he was about to do some kind of mind wipe on me or something."

"When was this?" Dani asked.

"Last year. Haven't seen him since. Not sure if I would go near him if I did."

"Sorcerers ain't all that," said the man with the beer, slamming his bottle on the bar. Dani hadn't realized he was listening, and shot him a sharp look that he didn't appear to notice. He was a white guy around Mack's age, his head shaved to disguise his balding crown. He was wearing a shirt with a glaring golden eagle on it that probably said something obnoxious about freedom. "You can bet those pussy motherfuckers wouldn't be so tough looking down the barrel of my shotgun."

Dani decided to just ignore him.

"So what are some of your theories?" she asked Mack.

Before Mack could reply, their new friend had swapped bar stools to the one beside Dani.

"Here's the thing about sorcerers," he told her, as if he'd been part of this conversation from the beginning. "They only live forever if you don't kill them first, and all *that* takes is the right firepower. Same goes for dragons." He pointed his finger down the bar like a gun and mimicked firing a few shots.

Mack rolled his eyes and gave Dani a small apologetic smile.

"That so, Dick?" he asked.

"Name's Richard."

"That's what I said. Come across a lot of dragons in your line of work?"

"As a matter of fact . . ." Richard leaned his elbow on the bar and cocked his head at Dani with a grin that made her take a half-step back, and not just because of the stale beer smell of his breath. "Look here, sweetheart. Take a look at this."

He tapped his forearm, where a tattoo of a badly drawn dragon breathed orange fire toward his palm.

"Cool," she said, with absolutely no interest, because he was waiting for a response.

"I'm a dragon slayer," he told her in a conspiratorial undertone.

"This tattoo is what we get when we kill our first dragon. Mack spends all his time on the internet looking for breadcrumbs, but what I got is real firsthand knowledge. I'll tell you anything you want to know."

He tapped the side of his head smugly. Mack got called down to the other end of the bar by a patron, and Dani watched him go with no little regret.

"I thought dragonfire was blue," she said.

Richard gave her a smile that was so condescending, she ground her back teeth.

"You read that on one of your little blogs?" he asked. "Trust me, I've seen enough dragonfire to know what I'm talking about. Even got some burns from some close calls on my back, but you wouldn't be interested in seeing those, would you?"

He asked it in a way that said he'd very much like her to be interested in him taking his shirt off. She tried not to gag at the thought and inched farther away from him.

"I really just want to know about sorcerers," she said. "Thanks, though."

"I've come across a few of them too," he insisted. "It's in the eyes, you know. You can always tell by their eyes what they are."

"What's so special about their eyes?" she asked, watching for when Mack would be returning, but more and more people were coming in and placing orders.

"They glow in the dark."

Dani snickered, then realized Richard was dead serious. Of course he was.

"Wow, I've never heard that before," she said truthfully. "How'd you figure that out?"

He grinned again and took a swig of beer.

"Well, if you really want to know . . . it was a couple years ago. I meet this gorgeous woman right here in this bar. She tells me she's a model and she's only in town for the night. And we talk all the way to last call, and of course I'm ready to head home, but this woman is all over me, and she wants to go back to my place. So what am I supposed to do? I take her home, thinking I'll pour her some wine, romance her a little—she's clearly desperate for the attention—but this chick, honest to god hops straight into my bed, ripping off her clothes." He gave Dani an exaggerated wink. "Of course, a gentleman doesn't kiss and tell. But it's not long after that, the lights are off and she's looking at me, and I realize what she is. Pulled my Glock out of the night-stand. She's crying and begging and promising me eternal life— the whole nine yards—but sorcerers can't be trusted. Besides, I've got a duty to mankind."

Dani stared at him. The whole story was such a sordid mix of obvious lies and plot points from a bad porno. And then there was the way Richard was leering at her, like he was getting off on telling her. She felt the sudden urge to jump into a scalding shower.

"I find that difficult to believe." A dry voice came from the other side of Richard.

Richard scowled and jerked his head around to the interloper.

"Like I said, sorcerers aren't so tough when you got a Glock shoved in their face."

"No, the part about a woman wanting to get in bed with you."

Dani swallowed a surprised giggle and peered around Richard to see who the voice belonged to. Tailored slacks, dark button-up shirt, black hair in sharp contrast to his pale skin. It was Kieran.

He was hunched over the bar, fingers tapping the side of a glass tumbler with ice cubes melting in amber liquid. Had he been there the whole time? She hadn't been paying much attention to the other people sitting at the bar. He didn't seem shocked to see her. In fact, the blank look he gave her was the same you might give a mailman or a passing cyclist.

"Private conversation, asshole," said Richard.

Kieran's bored expression didn't waiver. He shrugged and returned to his drink.

Dani tried to move around Richard to reach him, although she had no idea what she planned to say or do when she did. But she found Richard's arm around her instead. He'd slid off his stool and had squeezed her in a side hug like they were the best of friends.

"Come on, sweetheart," he said. "Let's get a table, and I'll answer more of your questions."

"I don't have any more questions," Dani said, cringing at the dampness of his armpit sweat against her shoulder. "Please don't touch me."

She shoved his arm off, and he raised his hands in surrender, still holding his beer bottle.

"Calm down," he said. "I'm just trying to help. No need to get all psycho on me."

"I don't need any help, thanks," Dani said, trying to keep her voice even.

"Just being friendly." He shrugged. "You're too serious. Why don't you try a smile?"

He reached out and attempted to push a strand of hair behind her ear, in what he probably thought was a suave gesture. The moment she felt his fingertips on her skin, she reacted. One warning was all her mother had taught her to give.

She rammed her knee into his groin. Simple, but effective.

He doubled over with a rodent-like squeak. Dani caught his bottle before it hit the ground. Over Richard's back, Kieran was watching her, his lips quirked in a vague hint of a smile. She set the beer back on the bar. All eyes swiveled in their direction as

Richard gasped and grunted and tried in vain to regain his dignity. Mack hurried back over.

"Did you . . . see . . . what that . . . *bitch* . . . just did?" Richard demanded, his voice a full octave higher than it had been previously.

Mack looked between him and Dani, his gaze dark, and for a second Dani was afraid she was about to get kicked out of the bar.

"Sorry, Dick," said Mack finally. "Didn't see a thing. But I think you're done for the night. Why don't you come with me to the cash register to settle your tab, and then you can go on home."

"You'll probably want to put some ice on it," Kieran said mildly.

Richard cursed some more, but Dani was relieved that all his bluster appeared to be just that. He wouldn't even look at her as he limped over to where Mack was waiting to take his payment. She was glad that she didn't have to walk back to the car alone, though. He was a lying scuzzball, but she didn't doubt that he probably had a shotgun in his truck.

"Are you okay?"

After a two-second delay, she realized that Kieran was talking to her.

"I'm fine," she said, just now noticing the jackhammering of her heart, the sudden weakness in her knees as the adrenaline evaporated. "What are you doing here?"

He didn't look like he believed her, and he also didn't seem interested in answering her question. He picked up his glass and took a sip. Although he was possibly old enough to sit at the bar, Dani didn't think there was any way he was old enough to be drinking.

"Are you following me?" she asked, moving to stand beside him, though she still didn't sit down.

His mouth twitched at the suggestion, and he gave her a sideways glance.

"I could ask you the same question," he said. "I'm just here trying to relax. You're the one coming in asking about sorcerers and dragons and assaulting people."

"Not people," she said with a frown. "Just a creep who deserved it."

"Fair enough."

"You helped me escape Stonecrest."

"Is that a question?"

"Why?"

"You may recall that I also did my level best to stop you from getting into Stonecrest in the first place," he said. "Helping you get out was just rectifying my initial failure."

Dani opened her mouth to say more, but was interrupted by Sadie's stage whisper behind her.

"Oh my *god*, what happened?"

Dani turned to find her and Tomás both staring at her with wide eyes. She glanced toward the door, where Mack was standing, arms crossed, as Richard made his sullen exit.

"People were saying you stabbed a guy," Tomás said.

"Sounds like me," she replied. "It's not a big deal. Is our food ready?"

Sadie nodded, her eyes still round. Her gaze flicked momentarily to Kieran, which gave Dani an idea.

"Kieran, these are my friends Sadie and Tomás," she said, stepping aside to introduce them. She smiled broadly in return for the glare that Kieran gave her. "Guys, this is Kieran. An old family friend."

"Hi," Sadie said.

"Nice to meet you," Tomás said. "I'm guessing you're not the guy she stabbed, then?"

"Night's still young," Kieran replied.

"Are you meeting someone?" Sadie asked. "Why don't you come sit with us? We got plenty of food."

"Yes, Kieran," Dani said sweetly. "Why don't you come sit with us? We've got so much catching up to do."

For a second she thought he might tell her to go screw herself, but then he stood up slowly, taking his drink with him.

"Sure," he said, his enigmatic gaze resting on Dani. "Why not?"

It was easier than Eden had expected to convince Nate to spend their date night tracking down her sister instead of doing dinner and a movie. Early that evening, when Eden had just struck out on the last of Dani's usual haunts, the Find My Friends app had finally given her some good news. Delighted, she'd zoomed in on the icon of her sister's face to see that she was moving north along US-129, in the direction of Knoxville.

Nate had been very concerned when she spun her story about Dani falling in with the wrong crowd and going on a bender in the city, and he'd been very sympathetic when Eden told him how desperate she was to bring her sister back home before their parents returned. And he had very readily agreed when she asked for his help in doing just that.

The hour-long drive to Knoxville flew by, with her new Porsche smoothly devouring the miles. She'd never felt more in control of her life than she did right then, her hands clutching the leather steering wheel, the engine purring beneath her, and Nate sitting next to her, stealing infatuated glances every chance he could.

This was who she was supposed to be.

"You look really nice, by the way," Nate said, rubbing the back of his neck.

"I know," she said with a smile. He didn't look too bad himself in his loose white dress shirt and beige linen pants, smelling of the perfect amount of soap and aftershave. She couldn't help but feel that she had won some sort of prize.

The stereo crooned a haunting female cover of Johnny Cash's "I Walk the Line." Eden could see Nate mouthing the words to himself from the corner of her eye.

"Will you check the app again?" she asked. They were only a few minutes out from the city.

He nodded and dutifully refreshed Dani's location on Find My Friends.

"She's right off Market Square. The building is labeled Reno Guitars, and something called Kaleidoscope? A bar I guess?"

"Look it up."

He tapped the screen in silence for a few seconds, scrolling through the results.

"Yeah, a bar," he said. "Huh, that's weird."

"What?"

He grinned to himself as he skimmed.

"There's this article about how the owner of the bar is this guy who's obsessed with dragons."

"What?"

"Like, he thinks they're real. He apparently started this sub-reddit about how there's some big conspiracy to cover them up or something. This is wild."

"What's his name?"

"Mack Jeffries."

His name wasn't familiar, so it was unlikely he was a slayer. But then why had Dani gone to his bar? It couldn't be a coincidence. Unease prickled at the base of Eden's skull. How could she be sure she wasn't walking into some sort of trap? Or at the very least, into a place where Dani would have allies on her side? She couldn't let her sister slip away again. The longer she and her dragon were on the run, the further Eden would fall from Calla's good graces. This had to end, tonight.

"I don't like the idea of Dani holed up with a bunch of delusional freaks," she said at last. "If she's on drugs or something, she might not come willingly, but I don't want the cops to get involved."

At least if Dani made a scene, Nate would assume it was because the influence of drugs and conspiracy theorists, as opposed to any real danger.

"Yeah," he said thoughtfully. "Okay, I have an idea. What if you wait outside the back door of the bar? Those buildings downtown usually have an alleyway in the back for the dumpsters. I'll go in the front and see if I can find her, and I'll just tell her you and I are on a date and you're on your way in. If she seems cool, I'll text you. If she tries to bolt, she'll probably go out the back, and then you can try to calm her down outside."

Eden had been toying with a similar scheme since the moment she enlisted Nate's help—she knew she would need a friendly face to catch Dani off-guard, because if Dani caught so much as a glimpse of Eden, she'd run again. Nate's plan was perfect. Eden would be able to subdue her with no one around, and then Nate could drive while Eden made sure Dani stayed quiet.

"That could work," she said, trying to sound like an anxious older sister. "Thanks so much for your help, Nate."

The gratitude sounded wooden, even to her own ears. She hadn't anticipated how difficult it would be to fake emotions that had always come naturally to her before. In order to make it more believable, she reached out and touched his knee gently.

"You're welcome," he said. After a short hesitation, he slipped his hand in hers, gripping it lightly. Eden let him hold it until they reached the city. With the heightened senses the magic gave her, she could feel the rapidity of his pulse and the rise in his body temperature. She gave him a sweet smile and heard his breath catch, felt his heart skip a beat. It was almost funny, how easy it had been to wrap him around her finger.

Kieran showed better manners than Dani had expected. Actually, his manners were so painstakingly polite, it was like he'd stepped out of Downton Abbey or something. He ate very little of the greasy smorgasbord of appetizers, and gave only the vaguest answers to any questions posed to him. He did accept when the waitress offered him a refill for his Scotch and soda.

Sadie and Tomás both exchanged a glance at that, no doubt sharing Dani's skepticism that he was of age, but neither of them said anything. Once the food had been thoroughly picked over, Sadie announced that she had to prove to Tomás that she could, in fact, kick his ass at *Tekken*—Dani gathered that it had become a point of contention during their Skee-Ball game— so the two of them headed back to the arcade, nudging each other playfully as they went. Neither of them were any good at trash talking, but they did their best, and Dani couldn't help but smile.

Then she realized that she was alone with Kieran again, which was what she had been angling for, only now that his dark eyes were locked on her, she couldn't remember what her reasoning had been. He was obviously not inclined to break the silence, and instead let it lengthen between them to an almost painful degree.

"I'm sorry about what happened to your dragon," she blurted out, unable to bear it any longer.

For the first time, she saw him flinch.

"I'm not going to talk about Zephyr with you," he said.

"I'm soul-bonded with a dragon too." She dropped her voice to just above a whisper. She had no idea why she was telling him this, but it was too late now. "His name is Nox."

"Good for you," Kieran said, but something in his flippant tone rang false. He wasn't looking at her anymore. Instead he traced shapes in the condensation his glass left on the table.

Dani hesitated. She hadn't expected instant camaraderie or anything, but she'd hoped for at least some indication that he cared what she had to say.

"My sister, Eden—they turned her into a sorcerer."

"I know."

She winced. Of course he knew. They'd killed his dragon and transferred his magic into Eden.

"How many . . ." She wasn't sure she could finish the question. She took a deep breath and pushed the words out. "How many sorcerers have they created that way?"

He still didn't look up. "I told you, I'm not going to talk about Zephyr," he said softly.

She gritted her teeth and tried to regroup. Glancing down, she saw that she'd shredded the napkin in her lap into tiny pieces without realizing it. She gathered them up carefully and crumpled them into a ball on her empty plate.

"I need to find a way to change Eden back to normal," she said. It took great effort to keep her voice steady.

"What makes you think there's a way to do that?"

"Are you saying there isn't?" she demanded.

He was quiet for a long while, staring into the last inch of watery Scotch in his glass. Finally, he raised his eyes to meet hers.

"I'm not saying that."

Hope billowed in her chest. She was so caught up in the heady rush of it, she didn't realize at first that someone was calling her name from across the room.

"Another friend of yours?" Kieran asked wryly, looking over her shoulder.

Dani twisted in her seat. It took her a few seconds to put a name to the face. Nate Harris had been in her sister's grade, but she'd talked to him a few times during her brief stint as a cheerleader. He'd always seemed like a nice guy.

"Hey, Dani," he said as he came up to the table. "Haven't seen you in a while! How's it going?"

"Going good," she said, forcing a smile. "How are you?"

"Great! It's the craziest thing. I'm actually here on a date with Eden. We had no idea you were in town."

Dani stiffened, her body tensing into fight-or-flight mode as she searched the bar behind him.

"Eden's here? Where?"

"She's on her way up. She was just finishing a phone call."

"Sorry, I have to go check on my friends," Dani said, standing up. Her hands and brain seemed to be working on two totally different levels, as she fished her last three twenties out of her wallet to throw on the table while simultaneously plotting the best escape route. There had to be a back door. They could leave that way and be halfway to the car before Eden knew she was here. "Great to see you, Nate."

He looked worried by her abrupt demeanor but didn't make any protest as she headed for the arcade, where Sadie and Tomás were embroiled in their *Tekken* grudge match.

"Guys, we have to go," she said, trying to keep her voice quiet while still injecting the right amount of urgency.

"What? What's going on?" Tomás asked, clearly too entranced by his angry, karate-chopping avatar to care.

Sadie was a bit more concerned, actually giving Dani a brief glance, but still keeping the bulk of her focus on her own avatar, a scantily clad woman with impressively round breasts that surely needed better protection than the bikini top she was wearing.

"Is something wrong?"

"Please," Dani said, grabbing their arms. "Please come on. I'll explain in the car. We have to *go*."

"Dani, what the hell?" Tomás complained as his ninja succumbed to a flying roundhouse kick. "We're in the middle of a game."

Sadie had seen Dani's expression, and the gravity of the unnamed situation settled on her.

"Okay," she said. "Let's go, Tomás."

She wrapped her arm around his and tugged him away so calmly and efficiently that Dani wanted to hug her. No time for that, though. She led the way back to a metal door that said EMERGENCY EXIT ONLY. Dani thought that this qualified.

"Wait." The voice gave her pause just before she pushed the bar to open the door. She turned to find Kieran standing just behind them.

Sadie stepped a little closer to Dani, maybe thinking that Kieran was the reason they were fleeing the bar. It would have made more sense to her than the real reason, anyway.

"I can't wait," Dani said.

"Don't you think it's a little odd that your sister shows up here on a date the day after she tried to—"

"So what are you saying?" Dani asked, cutting him off before he could say anything that would *really* confuse Tomás and Sadie.

"I'm saying if I were her, I'd be waiting right outside that door," he said coolly.

Dani looked back at the door, which suddenly seemed more like a trap than salvation.

"But what if she isn't," Dani said, "and I walk out the front door and right into her arms?"

"Wait, is Eden here?" Tomás asked, trying desperately to catch up.

Kieran contemplated for a second, then seemed to reach some private conclusion.

"Follow me." He took a left and headed up a set of narrow stairs that had a paper sign taped to the wall beside them with BATHROOMS scrawled on it in Sharpie and an arrow pointing upward.

"Seriously, what's going on?" Tomás asked as they filed up the stairs.

"I promise I'll explain later," Dani said. "We just have to get out of here." And then she had to come up with a plausible explanation for why she was running away from her sister like her life depended on it.

At the top of the stairs was a dim corridor with peeling paint. Boxes of paper towels, toilet paper, and napkins lined the walls. There was a door with another BATHROOMS sign, while the rest of the doors all said STAFF ONLY. Kieran walked straight to the door at the very end of the hall and opened it to another set of stairs, even more cramped and dark than the ones they had just climbed.

"Where are we going?" Sadie whispered, but Dani didn't have an answer. She was just relieved that her friends kept following her up the dank stairwell to a metal door at the top. Kieran reached up and pulled out what appeared to be a wire over the door frame— probably an emergency alarm. Then he pushed it open, and the warm, sticky summer air swept over them. A few seconds later they were all standing on the roof.

"Whoa," said Tomás. He walked to the four-foot wall around

the roof's perimeter and looked out over the lights of the city. They were only three stories up, but there was still a decent view.

"Is this legal?" Sadie asked, though she also moved forward to admire the panorama.

Dani went to the wall along the back of the building and peered very carefully into the alley below. And there was Eden, standing at the base of the steps outside the back door, arms crossed. Waiting.

Dani jerked backwards and swore under her breath.

"How do we get down from here?" she asked Kieran, though her friends seemed content to keep enjoying the view.

He pointed in the direction of the neighboring roof, which appeared to only be separated by the one wall.

"All the roofs connect. There's a fire escape at the end of the block."

"Spend a lot of time escaping from buildings?" she asked, trying to mask her pounding panic with humor.

He shrugged. "I always know where the exits are," he said. He didn't seem amused. "I don't like feeling trapped."

"Come with us," she said impulsively.

"Why would I want to do that?" Now there was a faint flicker of amusement in his expression. It was strangely incongruent with his features, as if his straight brows and firm lips were made only to be solemn.

"Because I have a hunch that you're not supposed to be here, either," Dani said. "And it's not going to take Eden long to find you once we're gone."

The amusement sharpened immediately into irritation—whether at the predicament itself or because she had correctly guessed it, she wasn't sure.

"Fine," he said. "Let's go."

There was a certain illicit thrill in running across the flat roof-tops and hurtling across the low divider walls, kicking up loose gravel while the rest of Knoxville enjoyed their Saturday night on the streets below. Tomás was singing the *Spider-Man* theme song under his breath, and Sadie was torn between laughing at him and cringing about all the laws they were breaking. The fire escape was more rusty and rickety than it had any business being, and the whole contraption swayed ominously under their combined weight as they made their way down. The ladder that was supposed to slide to ground level got stuck about halfway down, so one by one they had to climb to the last rung and drop the rest of the way to the grimy concrete.

Dani could barely breathe as she watched the others go first, positive that someone was going to break an ankle. They all made it down unscathed, except for a long rip in the sleeve of Sadie's shirt and a welt on Tomás's hand where it had been pinched between two joints of metal.

For a few seconds, they all just stood there in the shadow of the building, panting and coughing. Dani knew that if she looked around the corner, she'd probably see the shape of her sister at the far end of the alley. Best not to think about that.

"Come on," she said, when she could breathe without her sides hurting. "The parking garage is that way."

"I can't believe we just did that," Sadie kept saying as they maneuvered through the rows of cars.

Tomás hit the unlock button on his key fob, and his car beeped helpfully with a flash of lights farther down the row. Dani kept searching over her shoulder, half-expecting Eden or another sorcerer to jump out from between two cars.

"You've got to be kidding me," Tomás said.

Dani jerked her attention forward again, and her stomach fell.

Tomás was bending over to examine the rear right tire of his car. It was flat.

"This one's flat too," Sadie said, from the other side.

"They all are," said Kieran.

"Who would do something like this?" Sadie hugged herself and looked around them with a light frown, like she expected the perpetrator to be laughing maniacally in the distance.

"Eden," said Dani. Her fingers and toes had gone numb. She must have guessed they would park here, and she'd seen Tomás's car enough at home to recognize it immediately.

"Are you serious right now?" Tomás asked. "Why would Eden slash my tires? And why are we running away from her?"

Shit. She'd hoped to have more time to come up with a good explanation.

"Not here," she said helplessly. "We need to go—"

"I'm not going anywhere until you tell me what the hell is going on," Tomás said. He was wearing his Serious Face.

Shit, shit, shit. *Think, Dani.*

"Eden's in a cult," she said. As soon as the words left her mouth, she was mortified. And then a second later, she was relieved, because it actually was the perfect way to explain all this.

"What?" Tomás and Sadie asked together.

"Yeah, this mountaineering club she was a part of turned out to be this weird cult where they believe in, like, worshiping rocks and assimilating people and . . . I don't know what else, but it's really scary stuff, and she hasn't been herself the past few days." Dani carefully avoided looking in Kieran's direction, because she had a feeling he was smirking at her.

"She seemed fine today," Tomás said. "Kind of rude, I guess, but I figured she was worried about you."

"She's good at pretending around outsiders," Dani said. "But then she started trying to convince me to join and dragged me to one of their meetings, and it freaked me out, so I've been avoiding her."

"Should we call the police or something?" Sadie asked, alarmed.

"No!" Dani cried, with more force than she intended. She told herself to breathe. "No, my parents will be back from their trip soon, and they'll know what to do. I just need to stay away from her until then."

"Why didn't you tell me any of this before?" Tomás asked in a quieter voice. She saw the confused concern in his eyes, and the thought of how much more she was keeping from him made her head ache.

"I'm sorry," she said. "I didn't realize how bad it was until it was way out of hand. Can we just go now? She's going to catch up."

"Go where?" Tomás asked, patting the trunk of the car mournfully. "I don't have four spare tires."

"I have a car," said Kieran.

"You do?" Dani asked.

"Well, I didn't walk here," he said. He didn't roll his eyes, but she could tell he wanted to. He started toward the other end of the parking deck without waiting to see if they would follow him.

"Who did you say this guy is, again?" Sadie asked in a whisper, looping her arm through Dani's as they walked. "There's something . . . off about him. No offense."

"Yeah, he's kind of weird," Dani said, not caring if he heard her. "But he's okay. I trust him."

She wasn't sure if that last part was true, actually, but at this point he'd given her more reason to trust him than to not. After all, he'd only attacked her to stop her from going into Stonecrest, which *had* turned out to be a bad decision on her part. And technically speaking, she'd attacked him first.

There was also something about his bond with Zephyr that made her feel a strange kinship to him. She couldn't stop thinking of the gentle way he'd stroked the dragon's neck, of that poignant expression on his face. Surely he hated the sorcerers even more than she did, after all they'd done to him and Zephyr. And a common enemy made them, if not friends, then at least allies. Didn't it?

Kieran's car looked like it had been jacked from the grand estate of Stonecrest. It was a sleek black Maserati GranTurismo with a red leather interior and a dash display that looked like something out of a spaceship. Dani leaned the passenger seat forward so Sadie and Tomás could climb into the back, and then slid in herself. She could hear their suppressed silence as they marveled at the car and tried to be cool about it. Or maybe she was the only one doing that.

Kieran hit the button to start the engine and whipped so neatly out of the parking spot that she barely saw him change gears. She gripped the handle above the window while they ripped out of the deck and into the Knoxville streets. Riding with Tomás always felt like the car was taking them for a spin instead of vice versa, but Kieran's control over every inch of the vehicle was as fastidious and coolly confident as his fighting technique. She released her grip after thirty seconds or so, and they sliced through the city traffic with the ease of a hot knife through butter.

"It would help if I had a destination," Kieran said.

Dani blinked and realized she'd been mesmerized by his smooth handling of the wheel and the acute focus in his eyes as the passing headlights slanted golden across his flinty features. Her cheeks were hot, and she fumbled to get her phone out of her pocket.

"I don't know," she said. "I can't figure out how Eden knew where to find me in the first place. Did you guys tell her? Or post anything online about tonight?" She glanced over her shoulder, and her friends both shook their heads.

Her biggest fear was that Eden *did* have a way to track her through magical means. And in that case, she had no idea how to evade her. The hope that had blossomed early had already begun to shrivel. How was she supposed to figure out a way to help Eden if she was spending all her time running away from her?

"Let me see your phone for a second," Sadie said, reaching forward.

Dani unlocked it and handed it back. Sadie tapped around for a few seconds, then shook her head with the air of an exasperated kindergarten teacher.

"You guys follow each other on Find My Friends," she said. "Her location is turned off, but yours is on."

"Oh my god," Dani said. She snatched her phone back and stared in disbelief at the screen. "I completely forgot about that stupid app." She disabled the "Share My Location" function, and then for good measure she turned off her phone's location services altogether.

"What a magical era we live in," said Kieran.

She'd lost Dani again.

The simple, hateful thought turned over and over again in Eden's mind, expanding until there was nothing left but her own fury. She was the firstborn of a family of world-class slayers. She was a sorcerer with fresh magic flowing through her veins. And somehow her hotheaded, careless little sister had bested her a second time.

She'd waited in that filthy alley for nearly ten minutes before Nate had finally texted, asking how it was going with Dani.

"She headed straight for the back as soon as I said you were on your way," Nate had said when she stormed into the bar. "Do you think she's okay?"

His innocent concern, which once upon a time she might have found adorable, now only made her want to smack him across the face.

"She didn't go out the back," was all she could manage through gritted teeth.

"I was right here the whole time. Where else could she have gone?"

Useless. He was utterly useless. She should have known better than to bring a clueless layman into something like this. She'd thought he would be a good distraction, but all he'd turned out to be was a tip-off for Dani. She left the bar, studying the map on her phone, refreshing madly. It looked like Dani was still at the parking garage, which she wouldn't be leaving any time soon. Eden had taken care of that.

The deck was nearby, but her car was just across the street, and it would be faster to drive. She strode across, ignoring the violent honking of a car that had to slam on its brakes to avoid hitting her. The driver stuck his head out the window and called her a crazy bitch. She shot him the bird without slowing down, and a second later smoke started streaming out from under his hood. She slid into her own car and checked her phone again. She'd just turned on the ignition when the map with Dani's face disappeared suddenly. At the bottom of the screen, "Location Not Found" appeared under her name. Eden swore and hit refresh. She swore again.

Perhaps the magnitude of her failure had resonated all the way to Stonecrest, because she suddenly heard Calla's voice in her head, as clearly as if she were in the passenger seat.

Eden darling, you're needed back at Stonecrest.

That was all. No rebuke. No indication that she knew what

Eden had been up to. Eden wanted to protest, although she wasn't quite sure how to transmit her thoughts back to Calla. Maybe somehow she did because a single word rang out in response.

Now.

Eden bit her lip and gripped the steering wheel so hard she thought for a second she could rip it off completely. She closed her eyes. Found the cold, hard center of herself, where everything was quiet and empty; where she was infinite miles away from everything, and nothing could touch her. That was better.

When she opened her eyes, she saw Nate standing with the driver of the smoking car, both of them examining under the hood, scratching their heads and offering each other suggestions. Impatience curdled with disgust in her chest. She lifted her hand to honk her horn and wave at Nate to hurry up, but then thought better of it.

She pulled up her playlist, starting the music where it had left off previously. Billie Eilish was singing in murmuring tones about being that bad type, make your mama sad type. Eden threw the car into drive and sped away. She didn't so much as glance in the rearview mirror, and when her phone lit up with a picture of Nate's grinning face and started buzzing, she flipped it on silent and threw it in the back seat. Then she turned up the volume until the music was all that was left inside her head.

EIGHTEEN

When she arrived back at Stonecrest, Calla was waiting for her in the basement. The dragon was curled up in the corner, eyeing them like a suspicious cat. The single black metal cuff was still on its front foreleg. Eden eyed it warily.

"Don't worry," Calla said with a careless wave. "That metal band is charmed to dampen magic—not that our dragon friend has any left to speak of at the moment."

She even had her back to the beast, and was leaning over an open leather-bound tome on the table. Above their heads hovered a bright white orb of light, illuminating the entire chamber with radiance greatly disproportionate to its size.

"Will the magic regenerate?" Eden asked, joining Calla at the table, though she still kept one eye on the dragon.

"Eventually. At first it was a week or two, but now it takes years." She smiled up at Eden as beatifically as if they were discussing tulip season. "Dragon magic is technically an infinite resource, but that doesn't mean it never weakens."

"Doesn't the dragon ever try to escape?" Eden lowered her voice, though she wasn't sure why.

"Oh, not for a long time now. He used to make an attempt every couple of days or so, but we eventually drilled the lesson into him and Kieran."

"Lesson?" Eden asked, even though deep down she already knew the answer. It whispered to her across time and memory: a cold, cold voice in a dark, dark place.

"Failure has consequences," said Calla.

Eden swallowed hard and looked down. The stone beneath her feet was smooth and unstained, though yesterday it had run red with blood.

"Let's not dwell on the past," Calla said, shoving the book toward Eden. "I called you back because I need your help refreshing the spell on the cuff. Since you have the same . . . shall we say, *brand* of magic as the dragon, the dampening charm is much more effective if you set it."

Eden opened her mouth, but Calla waved her silent.

"I'll walk you through it. It's simple enough."

Eden pulled the book closer and examined the pages before her. The paper was yellowing and curled at the edges, and the handwritten ink was smudged in several places. There were blocks of writing in a language she didn't recognize, interspersed with sketched symbols.

"I can't read this," she said.

"It's my birth language," Calla said. "These days, scholars refer to it as Old Irish."

"You wrote all these spells?" Eden flipped a few pages forward. The entire book was a collection of the same handwriting and similar symbols.

"Of course I did," she said. "Other sorcerers have come up with their own spells since, in their own languages, but mine are the first and remain the best." Her tone was matter-of-fact, without an ounce of pride, as if this were all common knowledge.

"I don't suppose you have this one in English or Spanish?"

"It's not a matter of translation." Impatience edged her voice. "Language and symbols create a conduit for the magic and shape it into the desired form. It took me years to perfect these spells as they are, working only by instinct and trial and error. If I just wrote the spell out in English, it would become useless drivel."

"So you expect me to learn how to read Old Irish in the next few minutes?"

"I liked you better when you were a sniveling little sycophant," Calla said flatly.

The comment stung. Not her feelings, but her pride.

"I liked *you* better when you were pretending not to be a bitch," Eden replied. She knew there was a good chance she was about to get her own taste of the high sorcerer's wrath, but she couldn't help herself.

A pause. Then Calla smiled, amused.

"You trace the symbols with me and release your magic," she said. "I'll speak the spell and channel it."

Eden nodded and leaned over to study the symbols more closely. There were only three of them. With Calla's guidance, she practiced tracing them in the air with her finger. In the corner, the dragon shifted and ruffled its wings. She'd nearly forgotten it was there. The narrowed red eyes watched her steadily, burning a hole through her careful focus. She screwed up the same symbol twice, and Calla slapped her hand, bringing her back to task.

"You said your spells were the first," Eden said, as she repeated the motions. "Does that mean . . ."

"I was the first sorcerer."

"How?" Eden realized that even though she was one of them now, she had no idea how sorcerers came about naturally—they weren't all products of the violent, bloody process Calla had created.

"I had a soul bond with a dragon, in my first life. No, not like that, like this." Calla corrected her movement over one of the symbols. "If a dragon in a soul bond dies before the human, then their magic transfers."

Which was the process she had manipulated and replicated with Kieran and his dragon, in order to create new sorcerers as she wished. Eden tried to imagine Calla Thorn as a human with her own dragon, connected to it in the same way that Dani was to Nox, but it was too strange to comprehend.

"What happened?" Eden asked.

Calla pressed her lips together as she watched Eden's hands. She obviously wanted to tell her to stop asking questions and focus, but Eden was still diligently practicing the symbols, and Calla couldn't seem to find anything to critique.

"We were flying during a storm," she said finally. There was an odd, strained quality to her normally self-assured tone that Eden had never heard before. "A bolt of lightning struck her through the heart. A freak accident. As we fell, I could feel her magic flowing into me. By the time we hit the ground, she was dead, and I was this."

Calla lifted one hand with studied calm, and Eden watched the green sparks dancing along her pale, slim fingers. She couldn't remember much about her own transformation, except for that split second when her entire existence had contracted into nothing but a single moment of aching regret. She wanted to ask if Calla had felt the same, on that fall from the heavens that must have felt like eternity. Did she regret the loss of everything she'd had, everything she'd been? Or had what she become outweighed all the rest?

"Do you miss her?" The words slipped out of their own accord.

Something between surprise and sorrow flickered across the high sorcerer's features, too fleeting to pin down. Then her expression hardened again.

"She was just an animal. Too weak to survive in a world that favors only the strong. Why should I miss a millstone around my neck?" Her voice was as callous as her words, but Eden couldn't help but feel that there was a prick of guilt in the question, as if Calla herself wasn't convinced. "As a sorcerer, I can change reality to suit my needs instead of the other way around. The best thing she ever did for me was die."

Eden realized her hands had stilled, but Calla hadn't seemed to notice.

"Dragons are only worth the magic they can give us," Calla said. The sparks along her fingers had faded, and she met Eden's gaze with cold certainty. "Survival belongs to the strongest species, and that is us, Eden. Don't forget that."

Humans, was Eden's instinctual thought, but then she understood. Not humans. Sorcerers.

"There was never a Josiah, was there," she said. It was so obvious now. The sob story that Calla had swirled into that coffee cup had been nothing but a lure, a way to get her claws into the soft underbelly of Eden's oh-so-human sympathy.

"Does it matter if there was?" Calla asked, unruffled. "You're here now. You've made your decision."

Eden didn't have an answer for that, so she said nothing. Calla must have been satisfied that Eden knew the symbols, because she summoned the dragon with a snap of her fingers. The gesture made Eden start. Once again, she had forgotten the dragon's presence, silent as it was. Had it been listening to their conversation?

"Hurry up," Calla said, as if she were scolding a reluctant child. "I haven't got all day."

The dragon heaved a sigh, jettisoning smoke through its nostrils. Then it lifted its massive body and slunk toward the raised dais, where just yesterday it had been killed and resurrected in the course of an hour. It was strange, seeing such a powerful creature cowed by simple commands. Eden stared at the raised scars along its flank and neck and wondered exactly what sorts of consequences the high sorcerer's lessons had entailed.

When the dragon was in place, Calla moved to stand in front

of it. Eden faced her, in the position where Alder had been last night. Quietly, Calla began to chant. Eden mimicked the motions of her hand, determined to get the symbols right. At the same time, she pushed her magic outward, almost like she had for the clerk and the Porsche owner, but without any specific purpose this time. She just pushed and pushed and felt, with a stifled gasp, when Calla caught hold of it and started shaping it to her will. It was like nothing she'd ever felt before. A brutal, vulnerable kind of intimacy, both disturbing and exhilarating.

A shiver rippled down the dragon's back as the cuff around its leg shimmered with a faint red glow. Eden didn't have any control over what was happening, but at the same time she sensed the fervency of her magic as Calla sealed it into the metal.

The spell ended, and the glow around the cuff faded slowly away. Calla nodded in satisfaction. Eden could tell that was the closest she would get to a pat on the back.

"I want you here tomorrow afternoon," said Calla. "Your sister can wait. We have more important plans to discuss."

"What plans?"

Calla ignored the question and scooped up her book.

"It's no accident that I chose now to bring you into the fold," she said, giving Eden a slow once-over that made Eden straighten subconsciously, like a schoolchild under scrutiny. "Tempus Dracones has run its course. Now I intend to usher the world into Tempus Magus."

And with that, the high sorcerer vanished. Eden let out a long breath and relaxed marginally. Her body still hummed with magical energy, burning behind her eyes and tingling at the base of her neck.

You were here once before, came a voice inside her head: not

Calla's. It was a low, gravelly bass that resonated in her skull. *You were smaller then.*

She turned to face the dragon, which was still on the dais. Its eyes were rounder now, bright with something like curiosity.

"You tried to burn me alive," she said.

It cocked its head slightly in thought, and then let out a rumbling sound that after a few seconds she realized was a laugh.

I was yawning.

She blinked, thinking back to the flash of white teeth, the gem of fire in the back of its throat. There had been a flame, hadn't there? But Calla had arrived in the nick of time. Calla had rescued her. That was what had happened. It had to be.

"I don't believe you," she said. "How are you speaking inside my head?"

The same way other sorcerers can. We're both creatures of magic, are we not?

"So you can talk to Calla and the others?" she asked, frowning.

When I choose to. A thin, tired strain threaded through its tone. *They don't always choose to listen.*

"Maybe I don't want to listen, either," she said, but she didn't move. "You aren't going to trick me into helping you."

I'm beyond help, little one. There was a quiet resignation in those words that ached in her chest, burrowing deep into the emptiness inside her.

"Do you have a name?" The question left her lips before she could think better of it, before she could figure out why she even cared.

Not one you can pronounce. I'm called Zephyr, in your tongue.

"Where's Kieran?" She looked around, half-expecting him to be skulking in the shadows somewhere.

Zephyr said nothing, just shook his head slowly. She wasn't sure if that meant he didn't know, or he didn't want to answer.

"I'm not sorry," she said suddenly with a vehemence that she didn't entirely understand. What did she have to prove to this dragon? "I've been training my whole life to be a slayer. It's all I've ever wanted. I deserve to be here."

We all do what we think we must.

Magic fumed in her hand, summoned by fury, by an abrupt need to lash out. She flung it, shifting her aim at the last second so that it hit the wall beside Zephyr. It exploded in red sparks, chunks of stone spraying outward. Zephyr watched the impact without flinching, then turned his solemn gaze back to her, silent. Eden didn't know why she was angry, why her carefully cultivated control had begun to slip away, and that only infuriated her more.

A million words pushed at her lips. Cruel, nasty, devastating words. In that moment, unleashing pain felt like the only way she could regain her equilibrium. But something stopped her. Maybe it was the unnerving steadiness of Zephyr's eyes. Maybe some part of her realized that there was no peace to be found in inflicting pain, no matter how satisfying it might be.

Instead, she said nothing. She turned on her heel and stalked away. And as she went, she extinguished the orb of light with a flick of her hand, leaving Zephyr in the dark.

It was a quarter till midnight, and Dani was in the nicest car she'd ever been in, beside a boy she barely knew, parked in the lot of a twenty-four-hour gas station. She had a feeling it would be a good time to reevaluate her life choices, but she also suspected it was too late for that now. They had already dropped Tomás and Sadie off at their houses. Tomás had tried in vain to convince Dani to stay for the night. She was sorely tempted by the offer. She loved the Vasquez house, with its pile of shoes in the front hall, its overstuffed floral couch from the eighties, its kitchen that always smelled faintly of roasted garlic, and the murmur of the telenovelas that were constantly playing in his abuela's bedroom.

But she wasn't about to let Kieran out of her sight, not when he had practically told her he knew of a way to cure Eden. She had to see this through.

"We can't just sit here all night," Kieran pointed out finally. "I have to get back to Stonecrest before they notice I'm gone, or—" He cut himself short, lips set in a grim line.

"Or what?" she asked.

He was quiet for so long, she thought he had decided not to answer.

"Or Calla will take it out on Zephyr," he said softly.

Dani pressed her own lips together and looked down at her hands. A faint ripple of repulsion from Nox was her first hint that she was back in range of their telepathy.

"Please just tell me," she said. "Do you know of a way to reverse what they did to my sister?"

"Maybe. I don't know for sure."

"What is it?" She met his eyes, which glistened darkly in the fluorescent glow from the gas station.

"I can't help you, Dani," he said. His voice was tight. "I won't do anything to jeopardize Zephyr, and if Calla even suspects—"

"Please," Dani said, not caring how pathetic she sounded. "I can't just leave Eden with those monsters. I'll do anything. Just tell me."

"Eden's the one who decided she wanted to be a sorcerer."

He's got a point, said Nox.

"I don't care," she said to both of them. "I don't care what she's done. She's my sister, and I have to bring her back."

Don't you think we should be more concerned about the dragon that's been imprisoned for over a century?

Dani crossed her arms, unhappy that some part of her agreed with him. Not that she would ever admit it. Eden was her priority; she had to be. Kieran stared straight ahead for a while, then shook his head and shifted the car into reverse.

"I'm taking you home," he said.

Dani reached over and covered his hand with hers, shoving the gear stick back into park.

"Wait," she pleaded. "Just wait."

We have to help Zephyr, said Nox. *We can't leave him there.*

Dani's thoughts ricocheted wildly, until an idea occurred to her.

"Help me, and I'll help you get Zephyr away from Stonecrest," she said. "Nox and I—we can help you."

Kieran froze at that. She saw his Adam's apple bob with a swallow.

"It's impossible," he said, but his voice—barely above a whisper—was desperately void of conviction.

"We've escaped Stonecrest before," Dani said. "We can find a way to do it again."

"I don't know that the ritual would actually work—I've never heard of a sorcerer becoming human again."

"I'll try it. I'll try anything."

The car's engine hummed quietly while Kieran considered, a thin furrow between his brows. Dani realized her hand was still on his, and she pulled it back to her lap.

"It's a manuscript—or, pages from one," he said, catching her gaze for a fleeting moment before looking away. "Thaddeus Coombs's original *Fiends of Fire* manuscript had several pages of rituals that he hypothesized could be used against sorcerers. He never proved that any of them worked—at least, as far as anyone knows—and his publisher left the pages out when it was printed because they were too bizarre, even for Coombs."

"And one of the rituals is for turning a sorcerer back into a human?"

He nodded.

"If I help you get the pages, you'll help me free Zephyr?" he asked.

She hesitated, in a rare moment of common sense. Was this a good idea?

It's a terrible idea, said Nox wryly. *But say yes.*

"Yes."

Kieran held her gaze for a long time, searching—for what, she didn't know. He must have found it, because he shifted the car into reverse again and spun out of the parking space.

"Where are we going?" Dani asked, as they sailed down the highway.

"Nashville."

NINETEEN

It was a three-hour drive to Vanderbilt University, but seeing as Kieran was pushing ninety miles per hour on the interstate, she was pretty sure they'd make better time than that. The manuscript pages depicting Coombs's rituals were supposedly on display in the library's Special Collections Reading Room. Dani vaguely remembered her parents discussing some previously lost work by Coombs that was donated to the university, but she hadn't paid much attention at the time. It had hardly seemed relevant to her life. Now she wished she'd been listening more closely. Had her parents said anything about how likely the rituals were to work? She couldn't remember.

She'd started calling them and Jaime every fifteen minutes or so, still with no luck. She knew Kieran had noticed her preoccupation with her phone, though he hadn't said anything about it. They drove in silence. There was a *ding* from her phone, and she scrambled to unlock it, but the message was from Tomás, not her parents.

I'm worried about you.

The simple honesty of it, uncoupled with any emojis or tongue-in-cheek GIFs, struck a chord in Dani, and she found herself hesitating over her reply. There was so much she wanted to tell him, but she'd already made the mistake of sharing Nox with her sister. She wasn't going to make that mistake all over again and drag her best friend into this mess as well — at least, not any more than she already had.

She leaned back against the headrest and concentrated on reaching through the nebulous distance to Nox. There had been too much happening in Knoxville for her to worry about him, but now that everything was quiet except for the hum of the wheels on the asphalt and the occasional bug smacking into the windshield, she missed the constant comfort of his presence in her mind.

Is it time for "Kumbaya"? His dry tone drifted into the edges of her consciousness, faint but unmistakable, and she couldn't help but smile.

Not just yet. She chanced a look at Kieran, but his focus was on the road. She wondered if he and Zephyr had the same kind of running communication. Was Zephyr equally pretentious, or was that unique to her dragon?

I heard that, Nox snapped.

Sorry. She suppressed another grin and looked down at her phone screen. Tomás's message glared back at her, and her amusement evaporated. Her thoughts drifted back to the Vasquez house, to the smell of frying onions and garlic at dinnertime, to the uncomplicated joy of living without dragons and sorcerers on the periphery of her life—never quite far enough away. She thought about how easy it would be to tell Kieran to turn around, to leave Eden to the fate she'd chosen, to bury herself in the safety of that normalcy for as long as she possibly could. The craving for that life was like a hollow place inside her, a space she could never seem to fill, no matter how much she surrounded herself with friends and work and school.

Is that really what you want? Nox asked. There was a ghost of hurt in his tone, but it was crowded out by genuine concern. He could feel that hunger, that hollowness, as if it were his own.

Yes, Dani thought. *No. I don't know.*

Being bonded with Nox was its own kind of safety, but it was too new, too fledgling of a feeling to truly fill the emptiness inside her. She wanted her family and the legacy she'd been born into, but she also wanted her friends and the life she'd carved out for herself. She was a Rivera, but that wasn't all she was, and more than ever the tension was threatening to tear her apart.

Does it have to be one or the other? Nox asked.

Yes. Of that she was certain. Splitting focus in a game of magic and fire was the ticket to a swift demise, and she refused to risk her family or her friends by making that mistake.

Nox was quiet for a long while, and she could feel the strain of his own conflicting emotions. He needed her to fulfill his quest, to hatch the eggs. He was not an impartial bystander in this struggle. But he did not remind her of that, or her promise to help him, like she expected he would.

I'm sorry this is so difficult for you, he said softly. *I truly am.*

Dani's chest swelled with new warmth toward him. It gave her the strength to type a reply to Tomás.

I'm going to be ok. I promise.

It might have been easy to walk away from this, but it was impossible just the same. She couldn't abandon Eden to the devices of the sorcerers. She couldn't break her promise to Nox. If that meant everything else had to fall by the wayside, so be it.

The longer they drove, the weaker her connection to Nox felt, until she couldn't hear him at all, no matter how hard she tried. She wondered if strengthening their bond would strengthen their telepathy as well. Without Nox, the quiet of the car ride once again became interminable. She longed to play some music to break the monotony, but she wasn't sure she could decipher the car's space-age technology without breaking something.

About an hour into the drive, she couldn't stand Kieran's reticence anymore, and risked a question.

"How long have you been . . . living . . . at Stonecrest?" The word *guest* felt too friendly for the situation. *Captive* felt too high-seas adventure.

"I don't keep track anymore."

He must have been very young when he first got there, then. Could he have been born there?

Kieran obviously had no problem with the lingering silence, and made no efforts to continue the conversation. She studied his profile in frustration. In the hazy interstate lights, the slash of silver above his ear was like a moonbeam across his night-black hair. She felt the strangest urge to brush her fingers against it.

"Why are you staring at me?" he asked without glancing away from the road.

"I'm not." She sat on her hands, just in case they tried to betray her, and stared straight ahead. "I'm just trying to figure you out."

"I'm not very complicated."

Somehow she doubted that.

"You're not a sorcerer?"

"No."

She almost made a smart-ass remark about his penchant for unsatisfying answers before remembering that the reason he wasn't a sorcerer was the gruesome cycle of death and resurrection that he and Zephyr were trapped in. When it came to Kieran, it seemed she was destined to keep putting her foot in her mouth.

She decided to stop asking questions and busied herself Googling "Thaddeus Coombs magic rituals" instead, not because she expected to learn anything useful, but because it was better than attempting a conversation that wasn't awkward or insensitive or both.

Traffic was negligible in Nashville, and they made it to Vanderbilt without trouble. Kieran parked in the lot right next to the Central Library. A hundred feet away, occasional headlights flashed on 21st Avenue, despite the hour.

"Are you planning on just walking in the front door?" she asked in disbelief.

"What's your suggestion? Tunnel in from the basement?"

"There's probably a security system. Alarms, cameras, guards."

"So be quick, keep your head down, and run faster than anyone who starts chasing you." He popped the trunk and climbed out of the car. She sat for a few seconds longer, trying to figure out if he was joking, and then got out.

"This is absurd," she whisper-yelled at him across the top of the car.

"So is sneaking onto an estate full of sorcerers, and you didn't see any problem with that." He retrieved something from the trunk and started walking toward the sidewalk. A tire iron.

Dani stared after him, open-mouthed, and then jogged to catch up. She had already pulled up the library website on her phone and studied the very convenient floor maps, so she knew that Special Collections was just inside the terrace that faced the street. The outdoor tables, which during the day were probably all packed with students, stood abandoned, surrounded by huge stone planters and a metal railing.

They stayed close to the building, away from the view of any passing motorists. When they reached the doors, Kieran didn't hesitate to smash the tire iron into the glass. It took him a couple good hits to clear a hole large enough to reach through and unlock the door. Dani was torn between watching his calm progress in shock and trying to keep a lookout for any security guards. No blaring alarm sounded as they slipped into the building, but that didn't mean anything. Right that second an alert could be going out to the security company. Police would be called. Sirens and flashing blue lights would fill up the night. She wondered if Tomás would have enough money to post her bail.

Dim safety lights and the pulsing LED glow from the power indicators on the front desk's computer lit their path. Dani started for the corner room that had been marked on the map, but Kieran caught her arm and pointed across the two rows of tables: an alcove of glass display cases. She turned on her phone's flashlight and they made their way around the alcove, scanning the texts on display.

"Here it is," Dani whispered, unable to quell a frisson of excitement when she caught sight of Thaddeus Coombs's name on the white information placard. There were six pages resting on wooden reading stands, each sheathed in its own thin glass sleeve. Most of the text was from a typewriter, though there were some hand-drawn sketches of symbols as well.

Dani started feeling around the case for some kind of latch, and when she couldn't find one, opened up the camera on her phone. Her attempts to snap photos only resulted in a blinding flash and pictures of the sharp glare on the glass, no matter what angle she tried. She leaned over the glass, trying in vain to somehow memorize the pages of words and meaningless symbols. Then Kieran stepped up beside her and she jumped back with a yelp as he brought the tire iron down on the case, showering the floor with shattered glass.

"What is *wrong* with you?" she demanded.

"Remember the part about being quick?" He stacked the glass sleeves one on top of the other and handed them to her. The thought of their impending arrest prompted her to give up any attempt at photos. She shoved her phone in her pocket and hugged the pages to her chest. She couldn't believe she was holding Eden's salvation. She wouldn't let herself think that it could be anything else.

They ran all the way back to the parking lot. Despite the short distance, her heart was pounding in her ears, and her lungs seized up with every breath. Kieran was already tearing out in reverse by the time she got the door shut, the glass pages sliding and clinking together in her lap. They pulled onto the street just as the wail of sirens reached them from around the corner. Kieran kept to the speed limit as the patrol cars zipped past them on the other side of the road, then once the library was out of sight behind them, he laid on the gas.

Dani waited until they were back on the interstate before she let herself breathe properly. It was a few minutes before she regained her calm enough to be a functioning human again. She turned on the car's interior light and started studying the pages

"They're in English, but none of it makes any sense," she said. It was like reading something that had gone back and forth through Google translate too many times. Some of the words seemed to go together, but others read like a random string of nonsense.

"Not really surprising. Coombs was practically a basket case by the end."

"These symbols though, they look familiar. They look like some of the ones that Calla and Alder were drawing during the — in the dungeon." She was doing her best not to bring up the subject of Zephyr and necromancy. She didn't want Kieran to shut down completely, the way he had in the bar. "If Coombs knows some of the sorcerers' symbols, then there's a good chance he was actually on to something, right?"

"Maybe. Or maybe he was just copying what he'd seen. Calla had him as a guest at Stonecrest once, you know. She thought he might have some insight into dragons that she could exploit. Once she realized he was mostly a blowhard, she cut him loose."

"You talk like you were there."

"I was."

Dani's finger stilled where she had been running it along a line of text. Slowly, she looked up.

"Thaddeus Coombs lived in the nineteenth century."

Kieran didn't reply. Dani tried very hard to keep her breathing calm, her voice even. For some reason, despite so recently coming to terms with her own immortality, it hadn't occurred to her that Kieran could be much older than he appeared. Aside from his eerily calm demeanor, he seemed so . . . normal.

"How old are you, exactly?"

Kieran sighed, tapping his thumbs against the steering wheel. She couldn't make out his expression, fragmented as it was by shadows.

"I was born in Ireland. I forget the exact year. It was right after the union with Great Britain."

History wasn't Dani's strongest subject, but she was pretty sure that was at least a couple hundred years ago. She remembered that Kieran had said he'd lost track of how long he'd been at Stonecrest. Suddenly, those words took on a whole new meaning. Her stomach turned.

"How . . . how did you end up at Stonecrest?"

He was quiet for a while. He changed lanes to pass an eighteen-wheeler, by all appearances utterly absorbed in the task of driving.

"Zephyr and I found each other when we were ten years old," he said at last. "During the day I helped my parents on the farm, and at night I would sneak out to be with him."

His tone never changed from its tempered, steady rhythm, but Dani could see that his grip on the wheel was white-knuckled.

"I don't know who it was that found out about Zephyr, but the rumor started going around the village and the neighboring farms. And then someone saw me with him, and that made it into the rumor mill as well. Not long after, Calla showed up. She had a reputation, even then, and we Irish were already a superstitious lot. As soon as I heard that she was looking for Zephyr, I left to warn him. We hid in the woods until nightfall. We were going to go north, to Scotland."

He fell silent, eyes fixed on the road ahead but mind traveling back to that distant place. When he spoke again, there was a new note in his voice, acrid and raw.

"What I didn't know was that she was searching for me too. She burned down the whole village trying to find me. She killed my family when they couldn't tell her where I was. Zephyr tried to fly us to safety, but she shot us right out of the sky. My leg and arm were both broken, and Zephyr was hurt. He tried to fight her off, but . . ." He trailed off and swallowed hard. He shot through the gap between two cars to get past a slow driver in the left lane, barely missing its rear bumper. Dani was too shell-shocked to even brace herself.

"She wanted to use your bond to create more sorcerers?" Her throat was so dry the words cracked as they left her mouth.

"It was just a theory she had back then. I'm assuming you know how sorcerers are created? The natural way, not Calla's twisted little horror show."

"When a soul-bonded dragon dies before their human does. The dragon's magic shatters their soul or something, and they become powerful and completely fucked up."

His mouth curved slightly in something not quite a smile.

"That's the gist of it. Calla created a spell to transfer the dying dragon's magic into someone other than their soul-bonded human, giving her the ability to change anyone she wanted into a sorcerer. She'd already found Alder at that point, and a few others, but it wasn't enough for her. She wanted her own army of sorcerers. Zephyr and I were lucky enough to be her test subjects." There was a tremor in his tight jaw, but his voice didn't falter. "She killed Zephyr right in front of me. I felt the life go out of him. I felt all of his magic flow into me. It reset my bones, healed all my wounds from the fall, and then it began to break me apart from the inside."

The road stretched on ahead of them, a ribbon of asphalt through the endless trees, but Dani was somewhere else entirely, trapped in this nightmare of a story. She wished suddenly, fiercely, that Nox was here so that she could touch him, just rest her hand on his warm scales, just hear the comforting lull of his voice in her head.

"I'm sorry," she whispered. She wasn't sure what she was apologizing for, exactly.

"Calla and Alder siphoned the magic away from me into their new recruit. I don't remember much of what happened next, but when I woke up, we were in Stonecrest and Zephyr was alive. At first, I thought it was over. Calla was quick to disabuse me of that notion. In the beginning, the only time they would let me see him was when they were ready to do the ritual on a new sorcerer. You'd think eventually I would start to get used to it, but it hurts the same each time."

She didn't know if he meant the ritual itself or having to watch Zephyr die. She didn't dare ask.

"Eventually they grew more lax. Sometimes I was able to sneak down to the dungeon to spend time with him. I think Calla knew, but she didn't care, as long as we kept serving our purpose. I can get away from Stonecrest sometimes too, like tonight. They don't pay much attention to me anymore. They don't even need me there for the rituals, really."

She almost asked why he even went back. Why, if he could leave Stonecrest, didn't he just run and keep running? But then she realized she already knew the answer to that. Zephyr.

"Your bond with Zephyr is still intact," she said. "I could feel it."

"The bond reforms when they bring Zephyr back."

She tried to imagine what it would feel like, to have that indescribable connection between her and Nox severed and stitched back together, over and over again. For two centuries.

"But you're not a sorcerer?"

"I'm completely fucked up, to use your terminology," he said lightly. "But I don't have any magic. Calla's ritual grants me all the existential crises of a broken soul bond and none of the power. Honestly, I don't even know if I believe in the soul as a concept, but if I ever had one, it's long since been destroyed."

Nox had told her that humans weren't meant to carry a dragon's full magic—that absorbing it shattered something vital inside them. Is that what happened to Kieran every time Calla performed her ritual, before Zephyr's magic was then transferred to someone else? No wonder the process had appeared so excruciating.

"You're like, two hundred years old," she said, remembering the revelation that had sparked this entire conversation.

"Is that seriously your only takeaway from this?"

"Two hundred years!" She squeezed the bridge of her nose between her thumb and forefinger. "This is some real Twilight shit."

"I'm not a vampire."

"That's exactly what a vampire would say."

Annoyance flashed over his features, but his grip on the wheel had relaxed, and the tense line of his jaw had softened.

"Important question," she said, after some thought. "Be honest. Did people really used to talk like they do in Charles Dickens novels?"

"I'm not doing this."

"Did everyone really think aliens were invading during the 'War of the Worlds' broadcast?"

"We're done talking now."

"Were the Mets ever actually any good?"

"I'm about to leave you on the side of the road."

"Was Paul McCartney replaced with a body double?"

"Actually, I think that one's true."

"Wait, really?" Dani blinked and looked over. He was wearing a thin smile, possibly the first one she'd seen from him. "If you're British, I'm pretty sure it's against the law to joke about The Beatles."

"I'm Irish."

"Same difference."

"Spoken like a true American."

She rolled her eyes, but she was smiling too. They lapsed into silence again, but it wasn't nearly as uncomfortable this time, which made it that much harder for her to work up the nerve to say what was on her mind. She let the quiet stretch into minutes, until finally she couldn't hold back.

"My sister almost killed me." Just saying it out loud was like some kind of betrayal to everything she'd once held dear.

If he was caught off-guard by her sudden change of topic, he didn't show it.

"I know."

"Nox told me that losing the soul bond is like losing your humanity." She wracked her brain, trying to recall his exact words. "Empathy, emotions, the ability to love—he said it all gets destroyed. Is that what happened to you? Is that what happened to Eden?"

The car swayed as Kieran effortlessly maneuvered through a group of slower cars. His grip on the wheel was tight again.

"I don't know what you want me to say."

"I want to know what happened to my sister, what it really means."

"I told you, I don't know if I believe in a soul." He hesitated and ran a hand through his hair, leaving it disheveled. "But I lost a part of myself that night—the first time Calla performed the ritual. And every time after. I don't know what it was, exactly, or how else to explain it. I'm not who I used to be. Zephyr's the only one I have left, and I don't care about anyone else. I haven't felt anything but angry in a very long time."

Dani thought of Eden in the dungeon, playing with her new magic in a circle of fresh blood. She thought of the cold emptiness in her eyes, like she'd been replaced by a stranger, like she'd been replaced by something inhuman.

"You helped me escape," she said softly. "You didn't have to do that."

"I helped you escape to piss off Calla."

She closed her eyes, wishing she didn't believe him, but knowing he had no reason to lie. She pressed her palm against the cool glass in her lap. The answer was somewhere in these pages. It had to be.

"Will they miss you, if you don't go back tonight?" she asked, not opening her eyes.

"I don't know. Probably not. Calla's preoccupied these days."

"Then stay." She couldn't stand the thought of sending him back into that place, after everything she'd just heard. "Just until tomorrow."

She felt his eyes on her then, for the first time since they'd started driving. Only now, she couldn't bring herself to look back. The quiet between them was fragile and waiting, and when Kieran finally replied, his voice was feather-light.

"Okay," he said. "I'll stay."

TWENTY

At three in the morning, the subdivision where the Vasquez family lived was utterly asleep, except for the occasional barking of a dog and the whirring of automatic sprinklers. Kieran and Dani parked on the street in front of Number 43. She sent a text and waited until the porch light flickered on and off three times.

"Let's go," Dani said, climbing out of the car. That was the signal she and Tomás had agreed upon when she'd called him half an hour ago and asked to take him up on his offer to stay the night, with a plus one. He was less welcoming after being woken up from a dead sleep, but he at last agreed to sneak them into the basement's family-slash-game room. In the morning, they'd figure out something to tell his family.

They crept through the side gate and into the backyard. Tomás was waiting at the sliding glass door in his pajamas, yawning wildly.

"You really owe me for this," he muttered to Dani as he ushered them down the basement steps.

"Thank you," she said.

"I mean big time."

"You know I'm good for it."

Tomás was too sleepy to play host, but Dani had spent enough time playing Ping-Pong and video games with Tomás and his family that she knew where to find anything they might need.

"If one of my sisters finds you in the morning, they'll probably cause a scene," he informed them from the base of the steps, but did not follow up with any advice on how to prevent it. "Good night."

"Good night. Thanks again." Dani gave him a little wave as he left. He hadn't asked her anything about Kieran, but she knew he was just saving his questions until he was more awake and could grill her properly.

The family room had two ratty leather armchairs and a huge L-shaped sectional that could easily fit the two of them lying down. Dani pointed out the bathroom to Kieran and went to work gathering throw pillows and pulling down blankets from the closet. Once she had everything arranged, she went to the kitchenette in the corner and filled up a glass of water that she drained in three huge gulps.

When Kieran came out of the bathroom, his hair was damp, and he'd taken off his shoes and dress shirt, leaving his white undershirt untucked. It was the most undone she'd ever seen him. For some reason, it made her feel annoyingly self-conscious. She skirted around him and locked herself in the bathroom. She ended up hopping in the shower for a quick rinse. Fending off bar creeps and breaking into prestigious university libraries was sweaty work.

By the time she finished up, Kieran was stretched out on the couch under a blanket, his face turned away. Dani padded around for a few minutes, plugging in her cell phone and trying her parents again, getting another glass of water. Then she turned out the lights and curled up beneath her own blanket, breathing the worn, familiar scent of the Vasquez house. She was only a foot or so away from Kieran, and she squinted in the darkness at the top of his head, trying to guess if he was asleep.

"You're staring at me again," he said without moving.

Dani cringed and pressed the side of her face into her pillow.

"No I'm not," she said, not very convincingly. "I'm trying to sleep."

He made a soft sound that could have been a snort, but didn't reply. Dani pulled her blanket up over her head, as if that would protect her from her own awkwardness, and closed her eyes.

"Thank you," she said impulsively, "for helping me tonight."

A pause.

"I didn't do it for you," he said. "I did it for me and Zephyr."

She thought of the vision Nox had shared with her outside Stonecrest. The hopelessness of captivity without end, the agony of unnatural death and resurrection, that she knew now must belong to Zephyr. And Kieran's voice, diamond-hard with determination. *It won't be forever.* A promise that she wasn't supposed to hear, a secret that she had no right to carry.

"I know," she said. The blanket was swiftly becoming suffocating, so she pulled it back down to her chest. "What will you do, when you and Zephyr are free?"

Another pause, longer this time. She waited for him to shut down the question. But, not for the first time that night, he surprised her.

"Disappear. Someplace so far off the map that we'll never be found." He drew in a slow breath, an expansive sound in the quiet darkness. "Someplace where Zephyr can fly again."

Dani rolled onto her stomach and propped her chin onto her folded arms.

"Tell me what it was like, when you first discovered the soul bond." She didn't know if it was the lulling familiarity of the Vasquez basement or his moment of candor that was making her so bold, but she didn't want this brief, tenuous connection between them to end. Kieran was the only person she knew who could truly understand the strange magic of the soul bond, and she needed more.

After a long moment, he rolled over as well. They were face to face, close enough that Dani could see the sheen of his eyes from the dim glow of the bathroom's night-light. The nearness sparked a frisson along her skin that she couldn't attribute to a chill. She licked her suddenly dry lips.

"You first," he said. The subtle timbre of his voice eased her further into the dreamlike cocoon they were wrapped in. The outside world with all its problems was muffled and distant.

"Nox attacked me," she said. Though she had often done so in her own memories of the incident, right now she didn't want to embellish her own prowess during that fight. "The bond snapped into place before he could finish the job, thankfully. When it happened, it was like I was seeing everything through his eyes, like I could feel through his skin. It was . . ."

Impossible. Breathtaking. World-shattering.

"Weird," she finished weakly.

Though his features were shrouded in shadow, she thought she could make out the lilt of a smile on Kieran's lips.

"I found Zephyr hiding in our barn loft, buried under the hay one winter. I don't know if I was drawn to him or if he was drawn to me. Maybe both." He spoke with the gentle rhythm of a cherished memory. He'd told her that he hadn't felt anything but angry in a long time, but his words were shot through with something untouched by anger. "When I first saw him, I was so startled I fell off the loft. He caught me with his tail, and that's when the bond forged."

"Was it the same?" she asked.

"Weird, you mean?" He was definitely smiling now. "It was. I felt like I was both of us at once. Like for that split second, we were the same being."

A depth of connection she'd never felt before and doubted she would ever feel again. Maybe once was enough for a lifetime.

Or maybe not.

Carefully, uncertainly, Dani slid her hand across the short distance between them, palm up in invitation. She didn't think before she moved, didn't consider anything beyond the simple yearning to touch him, skin to skin. For an interminable moment, he didn't move, didn't react. Yet again, she had put herself into a vulnerable situation without a plan. It was becoming a habit with Kieran.

Then he shifted, and his hand met hers in the middle, fingers twining together in a nexus of exquisite sensation. His hand was colder than she'd expected, sending shivers up her arm and down her spine. She was conscious of her calluses, earned on the rock wall and the grips of weapons—and how they rasped against his own, in different places, earned in different ways. She wanted to know where each one came from. She wanted to know what thoughts were hidden behind his night-black eyes. She wanted to know everything about him.

"Tell me about Zephyr," she said at last.

Kieran stiffened, and she thought she'd pushed too far. But then he sighed. The sound carried with it a soft release of tension.

"He's kinder than me. And more generous—always has been." His thumb traced idle circles on the back of her hand, leaving trails of effervescence on her skin. "Snores like a locomotive and nags me constantly about how much sleep I'm getting. And he's curious about everything. It can be pretty annoying, actually."

The fondness in his tone draped warmly over her, and she was brought back to her night with Nox under the stars. How sheltered she had been. How tranquil.

"It's my fault," Kieran said, and she was so entranced by the intimacy of the moment and the hypnotic motion of his touch that it took her a few seconds to fully register his words.

"What is?" she asked.

"Everything. That we were captured in the first place. He

stayed to protect me after Calla shot us down. I'm the reason he was trapped." His thumb had stilled, and a hairline fracture ran through his voice. "Sometimes I wish that fall had killed me. It would have been easier."

Dani's heart twinged, and she gave his hand a squeeze.

"What Calla did isn't your fault."

He was quiet for a long while, his expression unreadable in shadow, their hands locked together like a pact between them. For an unbearable moment, Dani felt the weight of the two centuries of trauma that had trapped him in this emotional stasis, unable to change the past, unable to move forward into the future.

"I wish I could believe you," he said, his tone brittle as glass. He pulled his hand away from hers and rolled over, hiding his face again from view. "Good night, Dani."

Dani bit her lip against the wave of protestations that rose in her chest and buried herself under the blanket again. After what felt like ages, she heard Kieran's breathing ease into the deep rhythm of sleep. Her own body was so exhausted it was painful, but she couldn't make sleep come. Her head was too full of the images of Stonecrest, the blood and chains and death.

Nox? she thought. *Can you hear me?*

There was a long pause, but then, finally:

What's wrong?

Nothing. The comforting sound of his voice instantly began to edge out the intrusive memories. *I'll see you tomorrow. Just . . . be safe?*

She sensed his curiosity swelling at her odd mood, but he didn't ask her about it.

You too.

After that, the anxious hitch in her chest eased, and she finally drifted off.

• • •

Her eyes snapped open with a start. She wasn't sure at first what had woken her. It took her sleep-logged brain a few seconds to process where she was and why she was there. The basement was still dark, with only a faint glow emanating from the night-light in the bathroom. She'd kicked off her blanket. Tomás's parents were stingy about air conditioning, even in the summer.

Then she registered a soft, strained noise near her head. Kieran. She propped herself up on her elbows. He looked to still be asleep, but his hands were clenched into fists: one was tangled in his blanket, the other shoved between his teeth like he was trying not to scream. He made a small gasping sound and twitched restlessly.

Dani had seen a night terror before. There was a period in their childhood when Eden had suffered from them multiple times a week. Dani would hear her murmuring and whimpering and tiptoe into her bedroom. She would squeeze into bed beside her sister and stroke her face gently until Eden came back to consciousness, panting and crying.

"You're safe," she would whisper, as Eden's psychologist had suggested to their parents they should. "You're safe, and you're not alone."

Carefully, she rolled off the couch and knelt down next to Kieran. After a moment of hesitation, she reached out and brushed her fingers lightly across his sweat-soaked forehead. He shivered at her touch, but didn't wake. Another strangled cry ripped from his throat.

"Kieran," she whispered, sliding her hand more firmly against his cheek. "Kieran, wake up."

Faster than she could blink, he jerked awake, his hand catching her wrist in an iron grip.

"It's okay," she said, not trying to pull away. "Everything's okay. You're safe."

He was gasping for breath, his eyes glistening wetly as he frantically searched the darkness. His gaze settled on hers. Gradually, his hold loosened and his breathing began to steady. His head fell back against the pillow, eyes squeezed shut. Dani rested her palm on his chest, over his heart, feeling the staccato rhythm.

"You're safe," she repeated, her voice low and soothing, the words a mantra that she'd memorized long ago. "You're safe, and you're not alone."

TWENTY-ONE

There was a strange air of celebration among the sorcerers that Eden didn't quite understand. Nearly a dozen had returned to Stonecrest for lunch that day, buzzing with an undertone of excitement as they bragged about their latest endeavors, told jokes at each other's expense, and made the occasional sly remark in Eden's direction. She was the youngest by far, not only in magic but in appearance, and even though she gave as good as she got, she couldn't help but feel that none of them were taking her seriously.

The notion burned in the pit of her stomach. Hadn't Calla chosen her specifically? And after years of training to bring down dragons with only human strength and ingenuity, wasn't she twice as deserving as any of them to be invited here? To her dismay, as the meal went on, she found herself prickled by familiar insecurities — tiny fluttering anxieties that she thought had been annihilated by her new power. She viciously sliced a knife through her steak and told herself to get a grip.

"Karl, it's been so quiet here without you," drawled the woman across from Eden, her plum lips twisted in a smirk. "You really have to tell us all about Greenland. I hear yak-fucking is a national pastime over there."

The man she'd addressed was a few seats down from Eden. He was built like a linebacker, wearing a polo shirt with sleeves that looked ready to burst at the seams. He took a swig of wine and smirked right back at her.

"Six years with nothing but a yak to fuck, and you still couldn't pay me to hop into bed with you, Priscilla."

Everyone laughed except Priscilla, whose glare turned to daggers.

"Watch it, Slovek," she said primly. "Calla might have lifted your exile, but you're still on thin ice."

A few sorcerers looked perturbed by the mention of the high sorcerer, even though both she and Alder were absent from the meal. Something itched in the back of Eden's mind. Karl Slovek? Where had she heard that name before?

"I'm not going anywhere," Karl returned evenly. "I've paid my dues."

"You're the one who killed the Lowrys." Everyone turned to looked at Eden, and to her shock, she realized she'd been the one to speak.

"Who?" Karl asked impatiently, giving her the same look that you might give a fish flopping around in the bottom of a boat.

"The slayers in New Mexico." Calla's voice rang down the table before Eden could reply. Everyone scrambled to their feet as the high sorcerer strode into the room, Alder just behind her. "Try not to be such a ghoul, Slovek. It's terribly lowbrow."

She took her seat at the head of the table with the disdainful grace of a queen and waved at them to get on with their meals. No one had been expecting her and Alder, even the serving staff, judging by the way they tripped over themselves trying to set new places.

Karl muttered something vaguely apologetic and gave Eden a look that informed her she'd managed to make an enemy with a single question. It bothered her more than she would have liked, as did the fact that he hadn't even known the Lowrys' names.

"Don't worry about Karl," said Priscilla in confidential tones, leaning forward to address Eden as the rest of the table moved on to different topics of conversation. Her ebony hair was fixed in tiny intricate braids that were wrapped on the top of her head in a complicated bun. "He's just a washed-up old fool. No matter what he thinks, Calla's never going to forgive him for fucking up so badly in New Mexico."

It seemed that in making an enemy of Karl, Eden had made a friend of Priscilla.

"What happened?" she asked, trying not to seem too interested.

"There were rumors going around that this Lowry kid had gotten friendly with a dragon—can you believe that? A family of slayers, and he goes out and makes nice with one of them. Anyway, Slovek thinks maybe the two of them have a soul bond and he can impress Calla by bringing them in."

"You need another dragon and human with a soul bond?" Eden asked, but it wasn't really a question. She wasn't a fool. She'd figured out that Calla's obsession with Dani had nothing to do with her skills as a slayer, and everything to do with her pet dragon. The realization was more than a little gratifying.

"The dragon down there right now is losing its juice. I'm sure you've seen his bonded human moping around—real moody little brat."

"Kieran."

Priscilla nodded.

"Most of us have Calla to thank for our magic, same as you." She paused. "Well, technically I suppose we owe it to Kieran and his dragon—it's really their magic. He's a huge pain in the ass about it, though. I guess I would be pissed too, if I had to watch everyone else get the power that was supposed to be mine."

She shrugged to herself and took a bite, chewing thoughtfully.

"Anyway," she said once she'd swallowed, "Slovek goes to New Mexico, and it turns out this kid doesn't have a soul bond at all—just a bleeding heart. At that point all Slovek had to do was take care of the dragon, because it's useless to us without a soul bond, but this kid gets in the way, and then the kid's father shows up and wants to protect his son, even if it means protecting the dragon too. And poor idiot Karl just completely lost control of the situation. He ends up killing the two slayers, which wouldn't have been a big deal, except he let the dragon get away in the process. Calla nearly blew the roof off the place when she found out."

Priscilla snickered to herself.

"A couple of other slayers hunted down the dragon and killed it before Karl could even get his head out of his ass long enough to track it," she went on. "Of course, that pissed Calla off even more."

"My parents," Eden said, but her voice came out as a whisper. She cleared her throat. "My parents were the ones who killed it."

"Huh, good for them," Priscilla said, mildly impressed. "Wait, so did you know the Lowrys?"

Eden remembered the funeral, the grim faces of her parents, the heavy heat of the day. She remembered Maria Lowry sobbing as the desert wind carried the ashes of her son and husband into the bright, desolate air.

"No," she said.

Priscilla shrugged again and went back to her meal, apparently bored with the conversation. Eden tried to follow the other threads of discussion being carried on around the table, but she couldn't focus. She stole a glance at Calla, who was swirling her wine absently in her glass and nodding at something Alder was telling her. The high sorcerer had told James and Analisa that Karl Slovek had been dealt with accordingly, but for what? For killing two innocent slayers, or for having the audacity to fail?

Failure has consequences.

Six years in exile and now he was back, sitting at the table, enjoying the expensive wine and gourmet food, not even recognizing the names of the people he murdered. Those were Karl Slovek's consequences. And meanwhile, Maria was alone in the house she and her husband had built, where they had raised their son, where they had taught him the empathy and compassion that would later get him killed.

For the first time since her transformation, Eden felt something in that hollow core inside herself. Not an emotion, but the absence of one. A keen sense of loss, of a missing piece. She'd made the decision to give up everything for the magic, and now there was no retrieving it. She slid her chair back and dropped her napkin on the table. No one spoke to her as she left the dining hall. She wasn't even sure they noticed that she was gone.

She refused to decide on a destination, but her feet didn't falter on their way down to the dungeon. She could summon her own light now, a pale red orb that hovered above her, casting long, eerie shadows that stalked her through the passageways. In the central room, Zephyr was back in his corner, lying with his feet tucked beneath him, his tail twitching occasionally. At her approach, he raised his head slightly, eyes flashing in the ethereal glow; then he tucked it back into his side.

She waited for him to say something, but he didn't. So she opened her mouth to speak, only to find that she had nothing to say. Slowly, she came closer. He watched her through slitted eyes but didn't move. With painstaking care, she lowered herself to sit on the ground—not near enough to touch, but near enough that she could feel the warmth that radiated from his body, a haven in the vast, cool darkness that surrounded them.

She still couldn't think of anything to say, of any reason to give why she had come down here in the first place. So she said nothing at all. Gently between her fingers, she spooled her magic like string, appreciating for the first time the delicate nature of it, so different from the violent explosions and bold manipulations that it had created before. It was bold and violent, but it could also be soft. Serene.

She explored it with her hands, wholly entranced and desperately grateful for the comfort of Zephyr's silence, of his warmth. She wouldn't let herself think about why it was that she needed comfort at all.

Dani didn't wake up properly until almost noon. She staggered to the bathroom to use the toilet and splash cold water on her face. She brushed her teeth with her finger and did her best to comb out the tangles in her hair with her hands before pulling it into a ponytail. She padded back into the family room, yawning but actually feeling mostly awake. That was when she noticed Kieran was gone. His blanket was folded neatly on the foot of the couch, his pillow stacked on top.

She grabbed her phone, but there were no missed calls from her parents, just two text alerts: one from Sadie, one from Tomás.

Sadie: *Are you going to be at the barbecue today?*

Tomás: *Text me when you wake up.*

"What barbecue?" Dani muttered to herself as she replied to Tomás and then shoved her charger into her backpack. The manuscript pages were still in there, winking at her promisingly. She dug around for a mint that she thought she'd seen at the bottom of one of the zippered pockets, but came up empty.

The door at the top of the stairs opened and Tomás came bounding down. He was wearing a black shirt with a white twenty-sided dice and the words CHAOTIC GOOD on it. Another present from Dani. She wasn't very creative when it came to gift-giving. Once she found something that worked, she stuck with it.

"Good morning," he announced. He checked his watch. "Well, for a few more minutes anyway."

"What's going on up there?" Dani asked. Voices and laughter were filtering down through the open door. It sounded like a lot of people, even for the Vasquez house.

"So it turns out my parents are having a neighborhood barbecue today that my mother insists she told us both about, even though I have no memory of it."

Dani frowned and thought back. She could almost remember the idea of a barbecue being tossed around, but if she'd ever known the exact date, it had obviously slipped her mind.

"Mom also told me to tell you that you better not even think about leaving before you come and eat something and say hi to everyone."

Dani groaned.

"I can't. I'm tired and gross and I have stuff I have to get done today."

"Well, you can make all those excuses to my mother," Tomás said. "I'm not going to take the blame for you sneaking out. I already had to do some fast talking this morning about why you and some strange guy were sleeping in our basement."

Dani made a face, not at Tomás specifically but at the situation in general.

"Fine, but do you think Alicia will mind if I borrow a clean shirt? And a hairbrush?" Tomás's sister was a couple years younger than them, but wore the same size as Dani and often lent out her closet when late-night gaming or study sessions turned into all-nighters.

"Go ask her. She's probably still in her room getting ready," he said, with a vague wave in the direction of the stairs. "Sadie and her parents are here, and so is half the neighborhood. Get your game face on."

He grinned at her, and she wrinkled her nose.

"The best I can give you is Non-Resting Bitch Face," she said.

"Wouldn't that be Active Bitch Face?"

"Exactly." She grabbed up her backpack, winced at the clattering of the glass, and set it back down. Probably better to leave it down here for now.

"So are you ever planning on telling me who this Kieran guy is?" Tomás asked, eyeing the backpack and then her.

"I told you, he's an old family friend. He's dealing with some . . . trouble at home, right now."

"Okay, and what were you two doing until three in the morning?"

"Jesus, are you *trying* to sound like my dad?"

"Language—and I think it's a fair question. You drag us out to a bar at the last minute, then drag us out of the same bar to flee across rooftops like criminals, and then you tell us your sister has turned into some kind of tire-slashing, rock-worshipping cultist, and *then* you disappear for hours with this guy I've never even heard of before. What the hell is going on with you?"

My soul-bonded dragon and I are being hunted by my sister, who is a sorcerer now, and I just promised to help Kieran break his own soul-bonded dragon out of the sorcerer's evil lair. Oh, and by the way, dragons and sorcerers exist. Also, I'm immortal now. Surprise!

"Nothing," she said weakly.

"Look, Dani, if you don't want to tell me, just say so, but I—"

"I don't want to tell you."

He stared at her, clearly caught off guard. Tomás was the second person she'd come out to, even before her parents, and ever since then there hadn't been anything in her life that she didn't want to tell him. Except, of course, that one all-important thing at the center of her life. Her family's secret had never been anything but a burden for her, and now that she'd let herself get sucked into their world, things were only going to get worse. She couldn't take him with her.

"I'm sorry," Dani said. "I just . . . can't."

Tomás nodded slowly, but there was no understanding in his eyes.

"Okay, whatever," he said. "Just don't leave without talking to my mom."

With that he turned and went back up the stairs. Dani wanted to call after him, but she didn't have anything more to say, so instead she waited until he was gone, then headed upstairs herself.

As Tomás predicted, Alicia was still fiddling around with her makeup in the bedroom she shared with Beatriz, the youngest. She was more than happy to lend out a sleeveless cambric shirt with faint white flowers on it, as well as a brush and straightener so that Dani could get her hair under control. She also tried to talk her way into doing Dani's makeup, but Dani made a polite escape. She wouldn't have minded some light cosmetics to spruce up her haggard appearance and hide the dark circles forming under her eyes, but she also didn't trust Alicia near her face with a makeup brush. The girl was far too fond of neon lipsticks and colored eyeliners for Dani's taste.

The barbecue in the backyard was in full swing. Mateo Vasquez was flipping burgers on a giant grill while other dads stood around him drinking beer and making approving comments. A sprinkler in the corner of the yard was on, and little kids in their swimsuits were running through it and shrieking gleefully. Dani went to one of the blue coolers and fished a soda out of the ice. The liquid hit her empty stomach, reminding her she hadn't eaten anything since the shared appetizers at the bar. She searched the yard for Mrs. Vasquez, determined to discharge her social obligations as quickly as possible. She needed to get back to Nox.

Lara Vasquez found her first, enveloping her in a bear hug and chattering excitedly about anything and everything. She was a short, bubbly woman with dark, curly hair and a fondness for white jeans and statement jewelry. Dani had loved her from the moment they first met, when Lara had informed her that in their family, pizza and ice cream was a Friday night tradition, and just as important as Mass on Sunday.

Dani patiently answered her inquiries about her health, her family, the summer job, the likelihood of rain tomorrow, and whether Captain America was Chris Pine or Chris Evans because Lara had been having a debate with Susan from next door.

"Thanks for letting me crash last night," Dani said when she could get a word in edgewise. It felt like the right time to start wrapping up the conversation.

"Anytime, honey, you know that," she said, tugging on her chunky lemon-yellow necklace to ensure it was straight. "Although I'd appreciate a little warning if you're going to bring friends along too."

"Yeah, sorry about that." She'd kind of hoped that Kieran had left before anyone had been the wiser. Apparently not.

"Not a problem. He seems like a very nice young man, and he was able to talk World War II trivia with Mateo."

"I'll bet he was." Dani suppressed a smile.

"You know how that man loves his trivia. Anyway, it looks like Tita has him cornered, so you should probably rescue him."

At first Dani thought she was talking about her husband, but when she followed Lara's gaze she found Kieran instead, holding a bottle of Cheerwine like a lifeline and nodding dutifully at whatever Tomás's grandmother—Tita, as she insisted everyone call her—was saying.

"Oh," Dani said. She couldn't think of another reply.

She crossed the yard, wishing that she had let Alicia put some makeup on her and then immediately feeling stupid for wishing that. She took a gulp of soda to clear the lump in her throat. Kieran caught her eye over Tita's shoulder, and his expression was one of such helpless pleading that another smile curled her lips. He could break into a library with a tire iron without even blinking, but an eighty-year-old woman regaling the epic tale of her bunions had him at a complete loss.

"Hola, Tita." Dani insinuated herself between them and gave the old woman as big a hug as she dared, seeing as her hunched body always felt so frail.

"¿Qué onda?" Abuelita said without slowing her story. "And that's when I went to the specialist, or they say he was a specialist, but he was very young with a baby face." She pinched Dani's cheek as if to make a point.

"Ow," Dani said.

"He has a name like a frog, Croaky or Croaker, no lo recuerdo. And he tells me that I must have the surgery on my feet, but I tell him that—"

"Tita!" came a voice across the yard. Beatriz, in her pink-and-green swimsuit, was jumping up and down and waving her arms. "Tita! I can do a cartwheel! Come see!"

Tita looked stricken by the thought of having to choose between her youngest granddaughter and her bunions.

"You should go watch her," Dani said generously. "We have to get going anyway."

"It was nice to meet you," Kieran said, managing not to sound relieved.

Tita murmured something in Spanish about old bones and too many children, but nonetheless looked pleased as she tottered off to join her granddaughter.

"I thought you'd left," Dani said, as they watched her go.

"I tried. Mrs. Vasquez is very . . . determined." He gave a rueful half-smile. "She wouldn't let me leave until I'd eaten something."

"Yeah, she does that." Dani pressed the dripping can against the side of her face—the heat was already growing unbearable. She felt strangely giddy all of a sudden. She couldn't help but think that despite Mrs. Vasquez's efforts, Kieran could have already left. If he'd wanted to.

"What is it?" he asked.

"What is what?"

"You're smiling."

"I'm not allowed to smile?"

He didn't reply. but only watched her with a look of suspicion that made her smile even more.

"You need to relax," she told him. "You're acting like we're at an execution. It's a barbecue, for Christ's sake."

He cast a glance over the bustling yard: the hollering kids, the dads huddled up around the grill, the moms huddled up around two infants, and a handful of teens, including Sadie and Tomás, in the process of setting up the cornhole boards. She studied his expression as it melted from suspicion into something more like puzzlement.

"You've never been to a barbecue before, have you," she said.

"When would I have been invited to a barbecue?" he replied testily.

Dani raised her hands in mock surrender. "Point taken." She finished off her soda and tossed it into the garbage can that had been set up next to the food table. "I'm just saying, you can quit acting like you're waiting for something terrible to happen. You're safe here."

Kieran stiffened. Dani bit her lip. She hadn't intended to echo her words from the basement. The carefully constructed walls he'd hidden behind since the day she met him, which had just begun to lower, snapped back into place. Once again, the thoughts behind his shadowy eyes were unreadable. Dani tried to think of something to say, to either gloss over it or to somehow make him understand that trauma wasn't the same thing as weakness, and he didn't have anything to be ashamed of. But the words wouldn't come.

"I need to go," he said, not looking at her. "I shouldn't have stayed this long."

"Wait." She grabbed his sleeve. "We have to talk about Stonecrest. We have to come up with a plan."

He didn't pull away, but he gave her a wry look.

"I don't think now is the best time, unless you were hoping to get some ideas from Tita too."

She surveyed the yard and realized he was right, but she only tightened her grip and marched him toward the side yard. It was mostly concealed by two wooden trellis archways on each end that Mrs. Vasquez had planted with thick climbing vines she never got around to trimming. There were some bushes along the tall wooden fence that were also in need of a trim, but were nonetheless covered in white fragrant blooms and buzzing insects.

Once they were safely ensconced, Dani released his arm and turned to face him, but drew up short when she saw how close he actually was, with only inches between them. He was staring down at her with a new intensity that made the hairs on the back of her neck stand up. She swallowed and broke away from his gaze, but found she didn't know where else to look. His lips, soft and parted ever so slightly, were a definite no-go. Her eyes traced down the column of his throat, the sharp edge of his collarbone just below his open collar, the spot over his heart where hours ago, in another life, she'd rested her hand and felt the rhythm of his pulse.

"How are we going to get Zephyr out of the dungeon?" she asked his chest.

"We have to get the metal cuff off his leg. It's spelled to stop him from using magic or fire. If we take it off, Zephyr will be able to burn his way out."

She hadn't heard of dragonfire being hot enough to melt stone, but then again, Zephyr was two centuries old. There was no telling what he was capable of.

"All right, how do we break the cuff?"

"I don't know."

Of course he didn't know. If he did, he wouldn't still be a prisoner after all this time.

"I don't suppose there's another spell book in a library somewhere we can steal?" she asked.

"I doubt it. This is Calla's spell that she wrote herself." He hesitated. "But I might be able to get ahold of *her* spell book."

Dani looked up to find his gaze still steady on her face. She told herself the heat creeping across her cheeks was from the sun.

"I'm listening," she said, conscious of the wobble in her voice.

"I need a distraction. Big enough to keep everyone—but especially Calla—busy so that I can find the book in her study."

"Nox and I can do that," she said. "How long would you need?"

He considered for a moment, worrying the corner of his lip between his teeth. Dani remembered that she wasn't supposed to be looking at his mouth and forced her eyes upward.

"Half an hour?" he said.

"We can do it," she said, showing more confidence than she

felt. "Tonight? It's supposed to rain later, and the mountains usually get foggy. That would be good cover."

He nodded absently, and Dani realized that his eyes were on *her* mouth. The blush that was decidedly not caused by the sun began to creep up her ears.

"I really need to go," he told her, but he didn't move. If anything, he was leaning closer to her. Her stomach did a somersault.

"Then go," she said, the words barely a breath escaping her lips. He was so close now, and despite the garish daylight, his eyes were like the night sky: a dark infinity illuminated from within by countless burning stars.

"I really want to kiss you first."

"Then do it."

The instant she spoke the words, their mouths were crushed together. She didn't even know who closed the gap. She didn't care. She was enveloped by the sensation of him, the pressure of his hand on the small of her back, pulling her in, the trails of tingling warmth left by his fingertips across her cheek and through her hair. He kissed like he drove: utterly, unerringly in control. Dani gripped the front of his shirt with one hand and slid the other behind his neck, suddenly desperate to keep him there.

They parted for breath, came back together, found a rhythm with their lips and tongues. He tasted of Cheerwine and confidence. She dissolved into the kiss, lost track of everything that came before and whatever might come after. For just this moment, none of it mattered, and all she wanted was him.

Then, perhaps inevitably considering where they were, came the crunch of footsteps through the archway and a startled sound. Kieran pulled away so fast that Dani teetered dizzily before finding her bearings. Her lips felt hot and swollen, and she pressed the back of her hand against them as she turned to see the unfortunate interruption. She was terrified that it would be Tita. It wasn't, but it was the next worst person. Sadie.

She registered that she was still clutching the front of Kieran's shirt, and she released him.

"I'm sorry," he said in a choked voice, though she didn't know what *he* was apologizing for. "I have to leave."

"Kieran, wait," she called after him, as he headed for the front of the house.

"Tonight," he said, without slowing down and without looking back.

Dani stared at his retreating form, struggling to return to her senses. She spun around slowly and found that Sadie was still hovering awkwardly in the archway.

"I'm so sorry," she said. It was more of a squeak. "Mrs. Vasquez asked me to come find you. The burgers are ready."

"Wonderful," Dani snapped. She knew she was being unkind. It's not like they had picked an entirely private spot, and it's not like Sadie had stumbled upon them purposefully.

"I'm sorry," Sadie repeated. "I didn't know—are you guys—"

"We're not anything," Dani said. And then, because she still couldn't bring herself to be charitable: "It's none of your business, anyway."

"No, I know," Sadie said quickly. "I just thought—I mean, I was afraid that you . . ."

"That I what?"

"That you had a crush on Tomás." Sadie's cheeks flamed red, and she twisted her hands in the hem of her shirt.

"I don't. Why does everyone assume that?" It was a pointless question, because she knew why everyone assumed that. Tomás was attractive and thoughtful and funny and genuine. The sort of person she was supposed to want.

But apparently, she had a weakness for rude and sardonic and emotionally inaccessible. Kieran *was* attractive, at least. In a brooding, sharp, lethal kind of way. A girl had to have standards.

She didn't have time to ponder her own stupidity, because something else had just occurred to her.

"Wait, why were you afraid I had a crush on Tomás? Do *you* have a crush on him?"

By now Sadie was cherry red from her neck to her hairline.

"I don't know, maybe," she managed. "We've been talking a lot lately, and last night at the arcade was really fun—I mean, until the whole running away thing."

"You told me you have a boyfriend back in Ohio."

"I did! But . . ." Sadie grimaced and ducked her head. "We actually broke up when I moved back here. Lori told me at the bonfire that you had come out as bisexual a few years ago, and I guess I just didn't want you to think—I didn't want to make things awkward."

Heat washed down Dani's back, and not the pleasant kind.

"For Christ's sake, Sadie, were you scared I was going to jump your bones or something? I'm bisexual, not a raging sex animal."

"I know! I'm sorry!" Sadie took a hesitant step forward, her hands clasped together as if in penance. "I know that. I just, I was worried about how things would be between us. I didn't know what to do."

"Leaving aside the fact that you just assumed I've been carrying a torch for you all these years, after one stupid kiss—"

"I didn't—"

"You could have just told me you aren't interested in girls, or me, or whatever. Or better yet, you could trust that I would catch on when you, you know, didn't act interested in me?"

Sadie was miserable by now, and she looked so much younger, so much like the best friend that built blanket forts and watched TV way past their bedtime and slurped popsicles on the back stoop. It was almost enough for Dani to feel sorry for her. Almost.

"I'm sorry," Sadie said for what felt like the thousandth time. Her voice quivered, but she wasn't crying. "I was wrong. The truth is, that kiss when we were kids really freaked me out for a long time. I couldn't figure out what I felt about it. I think I was scared to figure it out."

"And now?" Dani asked, the ire draining from her tone. She should have known that the tangled mess of their friendship couldn't just be smoothed out with a smile and a handshake. She'd been fooling herself that it would be that easy.

"I think it's really great that you are confident in your identity," Sadie said. "I'm just . . . not there yet, and I'm okay with that. I'm okay with taking my time to figure things out."

Some part of Dani wanted to keep yelling, but deep down she knew that there was nothing left to fight about.

"I get it," she said, wrung out. "You can stop apologizing. I get it."

Sadie studied her for a few seconds, her brow wrinkled in worry. Finally, whatever she saw in Dani's face eased her concern. She smiled, just a small one.

"So you really don't have a crush on Tomás?"

"He's my friend. I don't care who he dates."

"Even if it's me?"

"Are you saying you want me to care?"

"No, I just . . . I don't know. I want things to be simple between us again. I guess that's not possible."

It was Dani's turn to study her. She gathered her memories of the girl she used to know, with her silver barrettes and wide-eyed fascination at stories of dragons and knights, and she took in the reality of the Sadie who stood before her now, smart and earnest and entirely adorable in her baby pink Converses. Then she bridged the gap and saw, for the first time with clarity, that she and Sadie May really could be friends.

"Simple is boring, anyway," she said, moving forward to loop her arm around Sadie's. "Now let's go eat. I'm starving."

Their shoulders knocked, and they fell into step together, and it was like no time had passed at all.

TWENTY-TWO

Dani polished off two burgers and way too much potato salad before finally deciding that it was time to leave the enchanted bubble that was the Vasquez house. She and Nox had work to do. She said goodbye to Tita and Tomás's parents, but Tomás was nowhere to be found and Sadie had also slipped off at some point during the meal. Dani tried very hard not to speculate, though she did steer clear of the secluded side yard, just in case she'd given Sadie any ideas. She retrieved her backpack from the basement, double- and triple-checked that all the pages were still there, then left through the front door.

On the porch, she remembered that Kieran had been her ride. Shit.

She considered tracking down Tomás after all, but after their less-than-fruitful discussion in the basement, she didn't think asking for a ride would go over well. In the end, she stole Tomás's bike out of the garage, sent him a text to let him know she'd return it later, and headed down the street.

Meet me at the barn behind my house in an hour? she asked Nox.

She sensed his hesitation and knew he was thinking of what he'd seen the last time he found his way to the Rivera barn. That was something she intended to rectify. No time like the present.

I'll be there, he said.

Dani pedaled harder.

She took the forest trail onto their property again, not sure she felt safe cruising up the front drive. She spent several minutes in the cover of the foliage, studying the back of the house for signs of movement. Everything was still and peaceful. She hopped back on the bike and rode the rest of the way to the barn. She felt Nox's presence before she saw him, and when he appeared she still wasn't entirely sure where he had come from. His arrivals and departures were so quiet that she was sure he utilized some sort of magic when he flew. He had hinted before at some sort of camouflage that kept him invisible to all but the most discerning eyes—slayers and sorcerers, mainly.

I don't like it here, he told her simply, wrapping his tail around himself like it was a barrier to the evils of the Rivera estate.

"I know, I'm sorry, but can we please go into the barn? Anyone could see us out here."

His distaste at the mere mention of setting foot inside washed over her, but he didn't refuse. Dani tapped the code on the keypad and opened both doors for him to enter. She pulled them shut behind herself. Nox was already in the center of the training mat, staring up at the skull of his mentor and friend.

The sorrow and fury that had become so familiar to Dani flooded the connection between them, wrenching at her heart and drawing tears to her eyes. She swiped the back of her hand across them.

"Do dragons bury their dead?" she asked.

We burn them. The reply was soft and aching. His gaze was still fixated on the bleached white bone, the empty eye sockets, the teeth exposed in a lewd grin.

"Can you help me get her down?"

It took a long time for Nox to come back from wherever he'd gone in his mind. Slowly, as if moving through molasses, he turned his head to look at her.

Why?

She understood what he was really asking.

"I can't change what my family is," Dani said. "I can't change what we've done, but Polara isn't a trophy. She shouldn't be trapped up there forever. She deserves to be free."

He said nothing, but she could feel his reply emanating through every corner of her being. She went to the utility closet and dug out the ladder that was buried in the back, behind old cans of paint and broken tools that her dad always claimed he could fix but never did.

Nox wasn't particularly dexterous, given his relatively short limbs and lack of opposable thumbs, but between the two of them they managed to get the skull off the wall and onto the mat. It was as tall as Dani and nearly twice as long, but the hollow dragon bones lessened the weight dramatically. Even so, when it was safely on the ground, Dani dropped her hands to her knees and panted for air. Her shoulders and arms blazed with pain. Not ideal.

They stood facing the remains of Polara for several minutes, saying nothing. They were both completely absorbed in the moment. Or at least, that's the only reason Dani could think of later for why neither of them heard the barn door open.

"Jesus Christ."

Dani spun around. Found herself face to face with Tomás. She stared at him while he stared at Nox, and for a brief eternity, the whole world came to a halt. And then:

"Language," said Dani. There wasn't really anything else to say.

Tomás blinked hard, twice, three times, then looked at her. Another shape appeared in the doorway behind him.

"Are you sure she's back here—" Sadie stopped. Stared. "Jesus fucking *Christ*."

"Language," Tomás and Dani said together.

This . . . is bad, said Nox.

Yeah, no shit, Sherlock.

What?

Never mind.

"I can explain," Dani said out loud, and then realized they were both staring at a real, live dragon, and that was kind of the only explanation there was to give. "This is Nox."

More staring. More silence.

"I just won so many standing bets," Sadie said at last.

Tomás gave her the same look you might give a chipmunk that started singing. Nox shifted slightly, and both Sadie and Tomás jumped back a step.

"He's not going to hurt you," Dani said quickly. "Don't freak out."

"Too late," said Tomás, his tone surprisingly even. He was definitely in shock.

"This is amazing," Sadie said. She hadn't taken her eyes off Nox. She may have been in shock as well, but hers was the shock of all her wildest dreams coming true. "Can I . . . touch him?"

Nox gave his petulant snort. Dani nudged him with her shoulder.

Be nice, she thought.

"You can ask him," she said to Sadie. "He can understand you."

Sadie's round eyes somehow widened further.

"Oh my god," she breathed. Her hands fluttered from her sides to her hair, to her collar, back to her sides, like she didn't know what to do with herself. "Hi, Nox. I'm Sadie."

Can you make them leave? asked Nox.

"He says it's nice to meet you," Dani said. Nox's tail whacked her lightly in the back, and she glared at him. "He can't talk, but he and I can sort of . . . hear each other's thoughts."

"Oh my god," Sadie repeated, clapping her hands together. "There was speculation about this on Reddit. You two are linked somehow, right?"

Dani nodded, suddenly desperately glad for Sadie's strange obsession. It was making all this so much easier, especially since Tomás was still just staring blankly, his mouth slightly ajar.

"It's called a soul bond," Dani said. "We were born at the same time — or something. I don't know. It's kind of new to me too."

"How . . ." Tomás seemed to struggle with what exactly he was trying to ask. "How long?"

"We only officially met a few weeks ago," Dani said. Something in her twinged. "But, well . . . I guess I have a lot to explain."

Dani had often thought being a dragon slayer was a lot like being in the CIA. Technically no one could stop her from telling anyone she wanted about her family's profession, but it also wasn't the sort of thing she wanted most people to know. She always assumed that the only person she'd tell would be her spouse, if she ever decided to marry. Analisa liked to tell the story of when she'd first brought James in on the secret, a year after they started dating, when she realized that he was going to propose soon and that she wanted to say yes. She'd decided to break the news by taking him on a dragon hunt that she pretended was a camping trip.

"When we spotted the dragon on the ridge, James didn't try to run, didn't make a sound," Analisa would say with a dreamy glint in her eye. "He just lifted his camera and snapped a picture. And that's when I knew he was perfect."

Eden liked to point out that she probably could have guessed his reaction, seeing as James had also believed in the existence of Bigfoot and the Loch Ness monster — still did, actually, much to his family's collective amusement.

Dani had never seriously considered telling the truth to

anyone, even Tomás, although sometimes she had fantasized about how much easier it would be to not have to come up with excuses for why she couldn't blow off a training session for a movie, or why their barn had a high-tech security system. But in the end, the truth always felt like more trouble than it was worth.

Now that she had no choice but to give her friends a real explanation, she found that she couldn't stop herself from explaining *everything*, starting with Tempus Dracones and the sorcerers and then moving on to the Rivera legacy and discovering the soul bond. She ended with the real reason she was running from Eden. The only things she purposefully left out were the dragon eggs and Kieran and Zephyr, deciding that none of that was her story to tell.

Sadie absorbed every word with ravenous attention. Dani got the feeling that if she'd had a notepad and pen she would have been taking notes. Tomás looked a little green around the gills, but he didn't interrupt or fall into hysterics. Dani thought that all in all, the situation had come off pretty well.

You won't be saying that when they run to the newspapers with their story.

"They won't do that," Dani said, "and no one reads newspapers anymore."

It took her a second to realize she'd said that out loud. Her friends stared at her in confusion.

"Sorry," she said. "Nox is worried you'll go to the media or something."

"Like they would believe any of this," Tomás muttered.

"You guys understand why you can't tell anyone, right?" Dani asked, as Nox's worry gnawed at her gut. "It's not safe for Nox and the other dragons out there."

"How many are there?" Sadie asked.

"Not many." Dani bit her lip. That was thanks in no small part to her own ancestry. "Please, promise me you won't tell anyone. *Anyone.*"

Sadie and Tomás exchanged a look. Sadie looked slightly crestfallen; maybe she'd already been composing her post for the Dragon Truthers thread. But she nodded.

"Promise," she said.

Tomás said nothing for a long while, his gaze flicking between Dani and Nox.

"Can I talk to you?" he asked Dani at last. "In private?"

He shot another look at Nox, as if wondering if such a thing were even possible. Dani didn't bother to assure him that Nox wouldn't listen in, because that would be the day hell froze over, but she did walk outside with Tomás, leaving Sadie to gleefully launch into what was doomed to be a one-sided conversation with Nox.

"How could you keep this from me?" Tomás asked, his carefully neutral tone giving her no indication of whether he was hurt or angry.

"I've kept this from everyone," she said. "Dragons and sorcerers aren't the kind of thing you share at show and tell."

"I'm your best friend." His voice cracked, both hurt and anger creeping through. "Aren't I?"

"Of course you are," she said. He had been from the moment he'd handed her that first bag of Skittles, but her family's dragon-slaying legacy had been with her since birth. "But I didn't want to risk you and Sadie getting caught up in all this. It's dangerous."

"You already dragged us into it," he said. "You made us go with you to that bar without telling us about Eden. You brought a sorcerer to my *house.*"

"Kieran's not a—"

"I don't care. Don't you think it's a little condescending to act like I don't know what danger is? We do active shooter drills twice a year at school. Half the time, I can't even talk Spanish with my family at the grocery store without some pendejo threatening to call ICE or some shit."

Dani opened her mouth with a response, but found she had none to give.

"I'm your friend," Tomás said. "If this dragon-slaying thing is part of your life, then I'm already caught up in it. I just didn't know it before."

She wanted to argue with him. She'd been so diligent for so many years to keep her normal life separate from her family life, but maybe that division had never been as clear-cut as she hoped it was. Maybe it had been naive or ignorant of her to think that she could—or should—keep them apart. Tomás was right. He was already a part of this.

"I'm sorry," she said. "I wanted to tell you sooner. I wish I had."

Tomás studied her for a second; then his expression relaxed and the tightness in his shoulders eased slightly. He clapped an arm around her shoulder, and they went back inside. The familiar weight was more comforting to her than she could have imagined.

"So does that mean you'll stop sneaking around?" he asked. "I think we deserve to know what's going on."

"You're the ones who followed me back to my house like a couple stalkers."

"Only because you were being so weird," Sadie said. "We were worried about you."

"Fine," Dani said. "I'll do my best."

Tomás didn't look entirely appeased by that, but he didn't push the matter.

Is this the part where we sing "Kumbaya"? Nox asked.

Dani didn't quite manage to bite back her laugh. Sadie and Tomás exchanged another look.

"There's actually something you can help us with," Dani told them, once she'd composed herself.

"What?" asked Tomás.

Dani stepped forward and ran one hand gently over the top of Polara's skull.

"A funeral pyre."

TWENTY-THREE

The flight to Stonecrest felt longer this time around, maybe because Dani now knew exactly what was waiting for them there. Every ounce of her being revolted at the thought of returning, but Kieran had held up his end of the bargain. She would hold up hers. Then, once Zephyr and Kieran were free, she would find a way to help her sister.

It was well past sunset by the time she and Nox were finally airborne. The rain had started in the middle of Polara's long overdue funeral, though the water had done nothing to douse the dragonfire as it gave Polara's skull back to the earth. After changing into some dry clothes and a rain jacket, Dani had said goodbye to her friends. They both insisted on waiting at her house until she and Nox returned, and after a long, pointless argument, Dani finally gave in, as long as they promised to lay low and run like hell if anyone but Dani herself or her parents showed up. Then she and Nox had returned to the cavern and nest to make sure the eggs were still safe, although she'd figured out quickly that Nox had an ulterior motive in bringing her there first.

You should stay here, he told her, stalking around the edge of the shimmering pool. It was still sprinkling, so they had gone into the cavern to stay dry. *It's safer, and I can create a distraction on my own.*

"The hell I will," Dani said, crossing her arms. "Maybe *you* should stay here. Protect the eggs in case something goes wrong."

The last time you went to Stonecrest on your own, it didn't turn out so well.

"I'm not staying here. I'm the one who made the promise to Kieran, and I intend to see it through."

Nox glared at her, but a perk of the connection they shared was that he could feel how deep her stubbornness truly ran, and he knew he wasn't going to win. So instead of wasting more time arguing, they had come up with a plan.

It wasn't much of a plan, Dani had to concede to herself, now that she could feel their destination looming ahead. Guerrilla tactics, which had been in an essay question on her history class's final exam that year, seemed like the best option. They could bring the sorcerers outside with a few strategically placed fireballs, and then draw them farther and farther away from Stonecrest, while never actually getting too close to their deadly magic. It had stopped raining, but the foggy forests and mountain slopes around the mansion would provide plenty of cover. With any luck, they could give Kieran much longer than the half hour he needed.

Dani, who had designated herself as lookout so that Nox could focus on the business of flying, braved the gusting wind to sit up straight and peer into the night. She wasn't entirely sure how the magic concealing Stonecrest worked, but she suspected it was similar to Nox's camouflage, in that you had to know what you were looking for in order to see it.

Sure enough, as she squinted at the dark, faint lights became visible, glowing brighter with every second, until the windows were beacons shining out of the mansion's palatial silhouette.

The eastern side, she told Nox. It at least had the benefit of being familiar to her.

He tucked his wings and dove in a graceful swoop that sent Dani's stomach clawing up her throat. She shivered, momentarily regretting the decision to leave her jacket at the cavern, but it was bright yellow and red. Not exactly ideal for stealth. They approached in a silent arc. Dani felt a rumble beneath her as Nox's internal flame flared, ready to be released. She held her breath, waiting for the blast.

The world exploded around her in a cataclysm of heat and pain and a violent, blinding green that seared the insides of her eyelids. Her head was spinning—no, it was everything else that was spinning.

She was falling.

She didn't have time to fully process the thought before her body shut down, her mind folding in on itself in a primal panic. She could have been falling for minutes, hours, days. She waited for her life to flash before her eyes, but there was only darkness.

And then warmth. A cocoon of scales and claws and leathery wings. An impact that juddered her bones and pummeled her organs. A thick, coppery liquid filled her mouth and drained down the back of her throat. She'd bit her tongue.

She gagged and coughed and struggled to breathe.

Nox, she thought wildly. *Nox.*

He released her from the folds of his limbs and wings, and she rolled onto singed grass and retched. Every inch of her body screamed in agony, and inside she bore the terrible magnitude of Nox's injuries too. She slid her hand across the ground—she couldn't seem to lift it—and pressed her fingers against his scales. Somehow the contact made it better. The cacophony of their combined pain quieted, just barely, just enough for Dani to hear the clear, cold voice of Calla Thorn resonating around them.

"And here I thought I was going to have to find you and drag you here myself. Silly me."

She shot us right out of the sky. The memory of Kieran's words wrapped around her mind, wouldn't let go. Calla's obsession with getting her to Stonecrest was finally making sense. She couldn't believe she hadn't put the pieces together before. She'd been too distracted by Eden, too obsessed with finding a way to save her.

Nox, you have to get out of here, she thought desperately.

She could tell he was conscious but wasn't sure how much he was comprehending. She wasn't even sure he could stand, much less fly.

Calla couldn't get her hands on him. Dani couldn't let it happen.

Distraction. That's what they had come here to do. She would stick with the plan. Give Nox a chance to get away.

With an effort that had her gritting her teeth so hard she was afraid they would crack, she climbed to her feet. Her knees tried to buckle, but she refused to let them. She refused her body every one of its current demands—to fall, to cry, to black out completely—and stood her ground.

"I didn't peg you for a cheap shot, Calla." Her words were slurred slightly, and she spat more blood to the side.

The remark, rather than needling the high sorcerer, seemed to amuse her. She was maybe ten or fifteen yards away on the wide, immaculate lawn, with at least half a dozen sorcerers and the imposing geometry of Stonecrest at her back. The area was lit by pure white lights that Dani thought at first were lampposts, but realized were orbs hovering all around them like fireflies.

"I wasn't about to let you two ruin the landscaping," Calla said. Her smile was like a knife, hard-edged and deadly. "This is twice now you've invited yourself onto my estate. I thought this time you might like to stay a while."

"Technically, you invited me first." Dani forced her feet to move a few steps, back and to the right, trying to increase her distance from both Nox and the sorcerers.

Nox, please get up, please get out of here.

"It could have all been very civil." Calla shook her head regretfully.

"There's nothing civil about torturing innocent dragons."

Nox, please.

I'm not leaving you here. The sound of his voice gave her a rush of relief, but it didn't last long.

You're not strong enough to carry me, she told him. *Just go. Protect the eggs. I can take care of myself.*

I'm not leaving you.

She had never thought she would meet anyone as stubborn as herself, but she could trace his conviction down to the core of his very being, and she knew she couldn't win. She closed her eyes. Felt the slow, steady drum of his heart, pumping blood and hot pain through his body. Felt the weakness in his limbs. Felt the tremors rippling through his wings. That was the blood that Calla would spill, so that she could break this bond between them and twist it for her own purposes. Those were the limbs that would be shackled with unbreakable bonds. Those were the wings that would wither away over the centuries, unused and useless.

Kieran had told her he wished he had died, rather than let Zephyr be captured.

But maybe there was another way.

Dani's mind didn't know what it was doing, but there was some part of her that did. Something deep and instinctual had been awakened at the same time as the soul bond.

I won't let them take you.

She took a deep breath, wrapped her will around the bright blue spark of eternal flame burning in Nox's throat, and released it.

The night erupted with dragonfire, arcing across the line of sorcerers. Most managed to shield themselves in time, though not all, and cries of agony mingled with the roar of the flames. Dani pushed herself further into that strange, dreamlike place where she and Nox were one, and thrust out her wings. Hot air flurried around her as she willed the wings to beat.

Nox was fighting to regain control—she could feel it—but he'd forfeited too much of his strength in protecting her when they fell from the sky. Dani fought harder.

I'm sorry, she thought, wretched with guilt at this violation of his trust. *I'm so sorry.*

But she didn't release him. The other sorcerers were still trying to extinguish the dragonfire that encircled them, but Calla was already clear of it, her focus zeroed in on Nox. Dani forced Nox to fly higher and faster as she threw herself forward, full tilt into the head sorcerer.

She hadn't expected to make contact, but Calla must have been just distracted enough, because Dani's shoulder slammed into her side and knocked her off balance. She refocused on Dani, who kept sending Nox higher and faster, farther and farther. Calla sent her crashing to the ground with barely an effort, but Dani knew how to take a hit. She rolled with the impact, pushed herself onto the balls of her feet, and made a second charge.

She wasn't actually trying to hurt the sorcerer. She wasn't even sure that was possible. But every second Calla was beating the shit out of her meant more distance between Nox and this terrible place. Calla merely flicked her wrist and a wave of energy slammed into Dani, throwing her bodily across the lawn.

Her face was full of grass and dirt. Her consciousness was swirling around the single, inescapable concept of *pain*. For a few moments, she began to lose her hold over Nox. She felt him struggling to turn back, ready to dive back into the fray, no matter the cost.

Dani dug her fingers into the earth and dragged her mind into focus. She regained control.

Hazily, she heard Calla snapping orders to the sorcerers behind her, but she couldn't latch on to any words. Somehow, despite the screaming complaints of every bone in her body, she registered something flat and hard pressing into her ribcage. Her phone had slid out of her pocket. With only the most abstract of thought, she managed to grab hold of it and cradle it in one hand, curling around it in the fetal position, her back to Calla and the others.

Her finger shook so hard that it took her three tries to unlock it. There were several missed calls from her parents and Frankie, but it was too late for them to help her now. Calla's footsteps were coming closer. She was running out of time. She flipped wildly through the different screens, searching for the right app, cursing herself for never deleting old ones she didn't use anymore. *There.*

She managed the last few taps on the screen, then shoved it face-down in the grass, where hopefully the navy blue case would blend into the shadows. Then she climbed to her feet and ran at the high sorcerer for a third time.

And for a third time, Calla sent her to the ground. This time Dani stayed there, executing a floor sweep with her right leg. She was so caught off-guard when it worked that she didn't even try for a second strike, just watched the shock and outrage battling for dominance on Calla's face.

She regretted it a second later when the sorcerer was on top of her, one hand clamped around her neck, the other sparking green like she was getting ready to shove the explosion right down Dani's throat.

"Go ahead," Dani managed to gasp. "But when I die, so does your chance at Nox's magic."

Calla's nostrils flared. She shifted her glare upward—to an empty night sky. Nox was distant enough that Dani had lost her last vestiges of control over him, but he was safely away. She really hoped he wasn't foolish enough to come back. Surely once his head cleared, he'd realize the futility of it; he'd realize that if he returned, he was giving the high sorcerer exactly what she wanted.

Calla leaned down, so close that Dani could see the poison green of her eyes, could feel her warm breath on her cheek.

"You're going to regret this." Her voice was soft as a lullaby. Her punishing grip on Dani's throat hadn't loosened.

"Nobody . . . likes . . ." Dani wheezed out each word with vigor. ". . . a sore . . . loser. . . ."

After that, everything went black.

A thrumming ache on the side of Dani's face pulled her back into consciousness. Calla must have hit her hard enough to knock her out. The thought of the high sorcerer losing her perfectly controlled temper was almost enough to make Dani smile. If only her face didn't hurt so damn much.

The other side of her face was pressed against something hard and cold. Stone. She curled her fingers and felt the roughness of it drag along her fingertips.

Voices. Arguing.

"You said you'd release us. You *swore*."

"I said I'd release you when you brought me the girl and the dragon. In case it slipped your attention, I have a girl here, but no dragon."

"It's not my fault she outplayed you."

A smack. It was a sound she'd heard often enough on the training mat to recognize easily, even in her dreams. Flesh hitting flesh.

"You know how I loathe common violence, Kieran darling, but when you speak to me like that, on top of the day I'm having, I really can't help myself. Now, go pout somewhere else; my guest is waking up."

Footsteps ringing on the stone, echoing in her ear. Then a grip on her ponytail, wrenching her head up.

"Welcome back," Calla said. "Why don't you make yourself comfortable? You and I are going to have a chat about your pet dragon."

Dani cried out as Calla dragged her up by the hair. She scrabbled to find her balance while clawing at Calla's arm. She might as well have been fighting against a tornado for all the good it did her. Calla flung her back and she landed hard in a chair, nearly tipping over before catching herself.

Her whole body was still sore, but it was bearable at least — she was getting a lot of mileage out of the rapid healing aspect of the soul bond. Even so, all she wanted to do was close her eyes and lie back down. Pretend none of this was happening. Pretend she was far away from here.

She forced herself to survey her surroundings. She was back in the Stonecrest dungeon, which was no surprise. Calla, of course, stood before her. Alder was to Dani's right, his fine gray suit and coiffed hair still immaculate, untouched by the showdown up above. She could see a hulking shape in the corner and knew that Zephyr was still here. The wooden table was just behind Calla, laid out with a black leather tome that she guessed was the spell book that had started all this. Next to the book was a dagger, a bottle of wine, and two glasses. Perhaps Calla and Alder needed some refreshment amid all the murdering they had to do.

She didn't see Eden anywhere. She wasn't sure if that was

cause for relief or another reason for worry. Did her sister know about all this? Did she even care that Dani was down here, bruised, bloodied, and alone? Dani didn't think she wanted the answer.

Even as she shied away from thoughts of her sister, it took all of her willpower to set her eyes on the last person in the room. The last person she wanted to be there. The last person she wanted to see.

Kieran stared back at her, his expression unreadable. His cheek was red where Calla had struck him, but otherwise he was as unruffled and punctilious as ever. She tried to tell herself that it was an act, or that maybe Calla had caught him during his attempt to steal the book, and he'd made a desperate deal. She tried to somehow explain this all away, to somehow soothe the twining betrayal and fury that held her heart in a vice grip.

But no. Their meeting in the bar had been no accident. She could have seen it if she hadn't been so hellbent on saving Eden, if she hadn't been so entirely out of her depth. And if the bar had been a setup, then so was everything that came after. Everything.

Slowly, deliberately, Dani pivoted her gaze back to Calla.

"I don't have anything to say to you."

"That's a pity," Calla said, propping herself on the edge of the table and crossing her arms. "And after Kieran went through so much trouble to get you here."

Dani winced, then regretted it when Calla's predatory smile widened. How much had Kieran told her? That night in the basement, that kiss in the bower—those ardent memories had gone gray and cold.

"Calla," Kieran started, but she raised a hand to silence him.

"Our discussion is closed," she said without so much as a glance in his direction. "If you want to make yourself useful, why don't you explain to Dani how unpleasant I can be when someone crosses me?"

"Is this you being pleasant?" Dani asked, and Alder cuffed her on the back of the head. She clung to the sharp physical pain. It was better than losing herself to the gaping hole that had ripped open inside her chest. It was better than letting herself fall prey to the barbed regret that was wrapping around her lungs, choking the breath out of her.

"I don't want any part of this," Kieran said. "I already did what you wanted. Now release Zephyr like you promised."

Kieran, don't push her.

Dani blinked at the new voice in her head, low and rumbling, and saw Kieran's eyes flit momentarily in the dragon's direction. She'd known that Kieran and Zephyr must speak through their soul bond the same way she and Nox did, but she had no idea why she could suddenly hear Zephyr. Was he purposefully letting her hear him? Did he expect her to intervene between Kieran and Calla somehow?

Whatever Kieran's response was, she couldn't hear it, but Zephyr shook his massive head.

It's not worth it.

"I really have been too soft on you," Calla said with a mournful note in her tone, apparently unaware of the silent exchange, "if you think that you can give me orders."

"I'm done with this, Calla." Kieran's voice was quiet but steely, determination etched into every word.

Calla's eyes flared, her thin patience worn away, and she whirled to face him. Dani flinched, expecting her to strike him again, but she only stepped closer. Kieran held his ground.

"That's not your decision to make," she said, her tone as level as his. "I own you, and I own your pathetic dragon, and the only reason you're standing here defying me instead of languishing in a dark pit somewhere is because I made the mistake of dangling the carrot when I should have kept using the stick."

Don't let her bait you. Please, Kier, just drop it. Please. There was a thread of despondency in Zephyr's voice now. He must have been able to sense the fatalistic gleam that Dani could see in Kieran's eyes. Some part of her also wanted to speak up, echo the dragon's concern, but she held her tongue.

"Since you hate me giving orders so much, I'll phrase this as a strong suggestion," Kieran said. "Why don't you take your stick and shove it up your—"

It happened so fast that Dani's brain took a second to process what she'd just seen. Calla raised her hand casually, as if getting a waiter's attention. A cord of glowing green coiled around Kieran's neck and pulled taut like a noose. He rasped for air and struggled to pull free, but his fingers found no purchase on the incorporeal rope.

Dani didn't realize she'd jumped to her feet until Alder's hand on her shoulder shoved her back down into the chair. Zephyr's roar seemed to rattle the very foundation, and in one lethal motion he leapt to his feet and lunged. Calla's head snapped in his direction, and she threw up her other hand. The blast sent Zephyr sliding backwards into the opposite wall, his claws screeching on the stone.

And while Calla's attention was on the dragon, tensed for another attack, Kieran snatched the dagger off the table and aimed it at her heart.

From her angle, Dani couldn't see how close the dagger actually came to hitting its mark, but it must have been close. So very, very close.

Kieran was hurled backwards, his body hitting the ground

with a terrible *thump*. The dagger, its blade still clean, clattered and slid across the floor. Kieran lurched to his feet, gasping for breath now that the noose was gone. Calla strode toward him, incandescent with a singular purpose. She thrust her hand forward and Kieran flew back again, this time slamming into the wall.

"Time and time again, I've told you." In Calla's right palm, an orb began to form, expanding from a pinprick like an explosion in slow motion. It was made not of light but blackness, its surface rippling with an oily rainbow sheen. "Failure has consequences. I think that's a lesson you need to learn one last time."

Kieran sagged against the wall, his features glazed with pain. His eyes fixed on the orb, but instead of fear, his face softened into something like relief. Dani wondered if he was thinking the same thing she had before—that if the human in a soul bond dies first, the dragon's magic is safe from sorcery. She wondered if that's what he had been thinking all along.

"Do it, then," he said to Calla, without even a tremor in his tone.

Calla released the orb. Dani squeezed her eyes shut, bile and panic rising in her throat.

The sound was like a crashing of waves against jagged cliffs, violent and inevitable. Then another sound—a powerful shudder, a great collapse. Dani forced herself to open her eyes. She saw Calla, her empty hand dropped to her side. She saw Kieran, his back against the wall. And prone on the ground between them was Zephyr, silent and still.

TWENTY-FOUR

Dani launched out of her chair and ran forward. Maybe Alder was stunned, because he didn't even try to stop her. When she reached Zephyr, Kieran was already kneeling beside him, trying to assess the damage. There was no visible wound, but an oily sheen rippled across his flank, melting into the dull black scales. The brightness of Zephyr's ruby eyes had faded, and he peered at Dani through slitted eyelids.

I'm sorry it came to this, he told her. And with a devastating groan of effort, he tucked his head to the side, nestling Kieran against his flank.

"Zephyr." Kieran's raw whisper carried with it such impossible grief that Dani had to look away from the intimacy of the moment. "Please . . . I didn't—I can't—"

Don't worry, little one. We'll be together again someday. Zephyr's eyes were closed now, his wheezing breath coming in shorter and shorter gasps. *It won't be forever.*

He let out one long, rattling sigh that carried with it tar-black smoke and the weight of two hundred years of darkness. And then he was gone.

A strangled sob erupted from Kieran's throat, and he pushed his forehead against Zephyr's for a long, aching moment. Then his head snapped back, his gaze locking on Calla's. His eyes were wet with tears, but the fury emanating from him was palpable.

"Bring him back."

Calla laughed shortly.

"Is that a suggestion or an order, darling?" she asked, in an arch tone. "Either way, I'm afraid I'll have to decline."

Dani was glad that Kieran was still lodged in place beside Zephyr. Otherwise, she was certain he would have gone for Calla's throat and gotten himself killed as well. She couldn't tear her eyes away from the dragon's lifeless features. In death, he looked peaceful at last. But he'd left behind him a grief two centuries in the making. The soul bond ran deeper than thoughts, deeper than emotions. He was Kieran's everything, and now he was gone.

Dani's throat burned with tears she refused to shed. She wanted to reach out, to entwine her fingers again with Kieran's, to somehow impart to him a modicum of comfort in this moment of anguish. But she couldn't stop thinking about Nox, and how close he'd come to being trapped down here with her. Kieran had been the one to lead them here, right into Calla's waiting arms.

Seeing Zephyr so scarred and broken, she knew without a doubt that she would have done the same for Nox. But that didn't mean she could forgive Kieran. How could she, when his traitor's kiss still stung her lips—when she could still feel Nox's panic as she'd stolen his control, mastered him against his will? Betrayed him, in order to save him? That was the position Kieran had put her in.

No, she couldn't forgive him for that.

"Calla," Alder said quietly, coming to stand beside her. "Do you think that's wise?"

Calla gave her lieutenant a look that would have made a lesser immortal flee.

"Am I to start taking orders from you as well, De Lange?" she asked.

He held her glare for barely a second before shaking his head and dropping his eyes in obeisance.

"No, of course not. I'm just concerned about wasting a perfectly good soul bond."

Calla snorted, contempt souring her features.

"Their bond wouldn't be strong enough to give us another sorcerer. I could feel it during the last ritual. You can only break something and glue it back together so many times before it's too fragile to be useful."

"So what are you suggesting we do?" Alder asked.

"Exactly what we came here to do." She turned to Dani, the contempt in her face turning her smile into a sneer. "Replace it."

When Eden arrived in the dungeon, it took her nearly a minute to take in all that she had missed. Calla had ordered her to remain inside while she and a few other sorcerers went out to capture an unsuspecting Dani and Nox. The assumption that Eden would somehow be a liability chafed at her pride, but she also had to admit to herself that she didn't actually want to go. Dani had turned her back on her family and generations of slayer legacy. She was stubborn and spoiled and too arrogant for her own good, and she deserved whatever consequences Calla deemed necessary. That didn't mean Eden was eager to witness the scene for herself.

After half an hour, when there was still no word from downstairs, she had started to get antsy and overwhelmingly curious. All the other sorcerers in Stonecrest had gone to search for the dragon that had somehow managed to escape their grasp. And since Calla had issued no orders about staying away from the basement, Eden decided that that was tacit permission to join them.

Zephyr was dead. That was the first thing she realized, the first thing she had to wrap her mind around. Zephyr was dead, and Calla seemed to have no interest in raising him. A bileous taste filled her mouth at the thought. Perhaps it was a reaction triggered by the magic that had once been Zephyr's. The only other possibility was that she cared that the dragon was dead, and she didn't. She couldn't.

Dani was not dead. Despite Calla needing her alive in order for her soul bond to her dragon to be any use, Eden had still thought there was a strong chance her sister would get herself killed. There was no way she would have come quietly. She was sitting straight-backed in a chair, her arms and ankles bound with lucent green restraints.

She glared up at the high sorcerer, her chin jutting out in that dauntless way that was so familiar to Eden.

"I do regret how messy tonight's events have become." Calla's arms were crossed, and she lifted one hand lazily to examine her cuticles. Eden saw Dani flinch at the movement, and then double down on her ferocious stare. Calla didn't seem to notice. "So I'm going to try to be civil and ask you nicely, Dani. One more time. Where is the dragon?"

Dani said nothing. Calla sighed.

"For heaven's sake, girl. The filthy beast abandoned you here. Why are you protecting it? The reality that you need to come to terms with is that you aren't leaving here alive. But how you choose to spend your time here—as a guest or a prisoner—is entirely up to you."

"Yeah, it's a real country club vibe you have going on here," Dani said.

"I know what you've seen here tonight has been frightening for you," Calla replied, unfazed. "But the truth is, Kieran has always been treated very well—when he follows the rules. There's no need for you to suffer unduly, if you're prepared to do the same."

"Thanks, I'll pass."

"Fine," Calla said with a delicate shrug. "We'll do it the uncivil way. Alder."

Alder stepped forward, his expression impassive, almost bored. He held no weapons or tools of torture. He simply lifted his hand, palm up, as if waiting to catch a raindrop. A ghostly yellow substance, somehow both viscous as ink and ethereal as smoke, swirled around his fingers. The magic slithered through the air toward Dani like a living creature on the hunt. She jerked her head to the side, eyes and mouth closed tightly, but the fluid didn't slow. Eden cringed despite herself as it forced its way into Dani's nostrils. She gasped, choked, and then cried out sharply in pain.

Calla turned suddenly to Eden. The high sorcerer seemed neither concerned nor surprised to find her there. In fact, Eden could have sworn that a smile was playing around her mouth.

"The useful thing about magic," Calla told her, quite conversationally, "is that it can cause such exquisite agony without physically damaging the subject."

As if to punctuate the point, Dani let out a scream, muted behind her stubbornly sealed lips. She tried to double over, but the restraints held her fast. Eden's pulse quickened.

"See?" Calla asked with clear satisfaction. "It can be tricky, but Alder has truly made an art form of it."

"Thank you," said Alder.

"You're welcome, darling. I think she might be more amenable now, don't you?"

Alder nodded and closed his fist. The magic drained out of Dani's nose and mouth, vanishing almost as soon as it hit the air. Dani was trembling and coughing wetly, tears streaming down her cheeks. Her head hung low.

For some reason, Eden wanted to shake her, tell her to snap out of it, tell her to focus, focus, *focus*. But this wasn't the training mat, where it was Eden's job to prepare her for the life of a Rivera. This was Stonecrest, where Calla Thorn called the shots, where Eden could only stand there and watch. She'd made her decision. She'd chosen her side. There was nothing else she could do.

"Dani," Calla prompted. Her voice was disturbingly gentle. "Tell me where the dragon is."

Dani raised her chin, just enough to meet Calla's eyes. Her voice, though weak, betrayed no fear.

"Might I suggest a more classic route? The rack? Jumper cables?"

Far from irritated, Calla actually seemed pleased, as if she'd hoped Dani would refuse. As if she wanted an excuse to keep this going. As if she were enjoying herself.

"Everyone's a critic," Alder said. He looked to Calla, and when she nodded, he lifted his palm again.

The liquid smoke moved more slowly this time along its serpentine path toward Dani. Her breathing quickened, and the vein in her temple throbbed, but she didn't break down. She didn't beg. Eden knew she would rather die than give Calla the satisfaction.

"If you want to play games, then by all means, let's play," said Calla. "Just know that I never lose."

TWENTY-FIVE

Dani couldn't remember all of Dante's circles of hell that she had learned in English class, but she knew now that he was wrong. There was only one circle, as nightmarish as all his imagined tortures combined, and it existed right here in the dungeon of Stonecrest.

It was the kind of pain that obliterated everything outside itself. A black hole of agony that split every atom of her being into a world-ending explosion. She wanted to black out. She wanted to die. She wanted to have never been born at all, if it meant she never had to find herself trapped in this endless wracking torment.

Nox. His name hammered at the inside of her skull, and for a terrible moment she thought that she'd shouted it. But no, her mouth was still closed, her teeth grinding together so hard the pressure reverberated in her eardrums. She wasn't trying to call him back here. She wouldn't let herself do that. But she couldn't stop herself from reaching out, down the dark tunnel of their bond, searching for any modicum of relief. His name had become a prayer. A mantra to keep her anchored. A reminder that it was better to die right here, right now, than be enslaved by the sorcerers for centuries to come. *Nox.*

But no matter how far she reached, she found nothing in the darkness. No whisper of comfort, no hint of strength. She had succeeded, then. She'd pushed him far enough away to save him. And now she was going to die alone.

She was so engulfed by the magic that it took her a while to realize that someone was speaking. The voices were thick and muddled, as if underwater.

"—not going to work. Their soul bond has only been in place a few weeks. They can't hear each other's thoughts yet. She can't sense where he's gone." It was Kieran's voice. The realization gave her a thin edge of clarity.

"In case it has somehow escaped your notice, I have no further use for you," said Calla. "Why are you still here? Are you just addicted to punishment?"

"I'm just telling you the facts. You're wasting your time."

"Besides," came a third voice, one that sent a pang through Dani's heart, more severe than the pain. *Eden.* "Dani has a hero complex. She always has. The more you hurt her, the more determined she'll be to give you nothing. You'll end up killing her before she breaks, and if she dies, the bond will be useless."

The words, delivered in a deadpan that was so unlike the Eden she'd grown up with, whirled around in Dani's addled brain. She couldn't get a grip on them. She forced her eyes open, desperate to get a look at Eden's face. Just one look. Her sister was a blur through the tears Dani hadn't realized were streaming down her face. She couldn't make out an expression, couldn't even tell if Eden was looking at her.

"Eden, I'm beginning to think you may have retained a soft spot for your sister." Calla's tone was casual enough, but there was an undeniable undercurrent of danger.

"That's a strange thing to think," Eden replied coolly. "Especially considering how close I came to killing her myself two days ago."

The two women stared at each other, neither breaking away from the inherent challenge. Then Calla gestured at Alder.

The withdrawal of the pain, draining out of her with the magic, was so nirvanic that Dani sobbed in relief. She didn't even care anymore about Calla seeing her break down. She hadn't given up Nox. He was still safe. Nothing else mattered.

"I must admit," Calla said, turning back to face her, "your sister makes a good point, Dani darling. You do seem to suffer from delusions of heroism."

Dani blinked hard, trying to clear her vision. The high sorcerer's face sharpened into focus, her smooth brow wrinkled in thought.

"I blame feminism," Dani said. Her voice came out raspy and strained.

Calla smiled, but there was nothing pleasant about it.

"The problem with being a hero is that it opens up even more weaknesses to exploit."

Dani nodded gravely.

"Chocolate," she said. "I can't resist it."

"I was thinking something a bit more . . . personal." Calla's gaze swiveled to Kieran. "While I admire your boldness in lying to my face, I can't say I'm particularly impressed. Perhaps it slipped your mind that once upon a time, I had my own soul bond. I know perfectly well that the minds and emotions are linked the moment the bond snaps into place. So now I have to wonder why it might be, when you have every reason to walk out of Stonecrest forever, you are instead standing here, trying to protect her."

Kieran's expression remained inscrutable the whole time Calla was speaking. At the last, his eyes flicked to Dani's for a heartbeat. And she found herself wondering the same thing.

"I propose a new game," Calla said, turning back to Dani.

Before Dani could respond Calla raised a hand, and instantly the ephemeral green noose tightened again around Kieran's neck.

He choked and clawed at it, but his efforts were as useless as before. Calla lifted her hand higher, and Kieran rose with it, his feet kicking against the empty air.

"Stop it," Dani cried, jerking forward so hard that the chair lurched momentarily off its back legs, but the restraints held fast. "Let him go."

"You're not very good at this game," Alder said, tucking his hands into his pockets with a lazy nonchalance that was entirely at odds with the unfolding scene.

Dani realized that the smart thing to do would have been to feign indifference. It could have been believable — he had lured her here to betray her, after all. Too late for that now. Though her mind was determined to never forgive him, apparently her heart had its own loyalties. Calla flicked her wrist to the side, and Kieran slammed into a nearby pillar with a sound that made Dani's own bones ache.

"I'm not as elegant with these things as Alder is," Calla said. Kieran fell to the ground, and the cord loosened just long enough for him to suck in a breath before it yanked tight again. "But I find that the blunt method has its own merits, and is usually just as effective."

Her eyes were those of a predator playing with its meal as she wrenched Kieran aloft once more. Dani struggled harder against her bonds, as if freedom would do her any good. It had been simple before, when it was a choice between her own pain and saving Nox. That choice was clear in her mind. It was a decision that practically made itself after hearing the details of Kieran's and Zephyr's fate. There were worse things than dying.

But now the lines were blurring. Her determination was unraveling with every second that passed. Kieran's lips were turning blue. Whatever lies he had told her, the suffering he'd gone through with Zephyr had been real. The fact that he had stayed, when he had every reason to leave her there alone, was real. This wasn't something that she could just grit her teeth and bear.

"Please, Calla," she begged, beyond pride, beyond dignity. "Please stop."

"You know how to end this," Calla said. "You can stop it whenever you want."

Nox, Nox, Nox. Not a summoning, but a prayer. Another blind reach into the darkness, desperate for anything to shore up her crumbling resolve. Nothing.

"Ready for round two?" asked Calla in response to her silence. She dropped her hand and Kieran crashed to the floor, gasping weakly for air as the noose dissolved. "Kieran darling, is there anything you'd like to say to Dani before we continue? Maybe ask her why she seems to enjoy watching you suffer? Or just some poetic last words she can cling to in the future when she thinks about how she just let you die?"

Kieran was in a limp heap, his forehead pressing into the stone as he sucked in stuttering breaths. Finally, with excruciating effort, he pushed himself up to his hands and knees, and raised his eyes to meet Dani's.

"Only one or two people," he managed, his voice a weak croak, "actually fell for the 'War of the Worlds' broadcast."

Dani tried to breathe, but her lungs and heart were all knotted up inside her chest.

"Skies above, you two are tiring," Calla said. And again she raised her hand. This time the glowing cord twined around Kieran's ankles, binding them together, while a second cord bound his wrists behind his back. A second later he was back in the air, upside down now.

"Goddamn you, Calla," he gasped out, struggling ineffectually.

"That's enough from you, I think." Calla extended her hand palm-up toward Alder, who immediately fished a handkerchief from his pocket and gave it to her. Calla shoved it into Kieran's mouth without ceremony. "There now. Dani, I need you to pay close attention. I know you're out of school for the summer, but one should never take a break from learning. So here's an anatomy lesson for you."

The dagger, which Dani had somehow forgotten about, skittered across the floor and flew into the high sorcerer's waiting grip. With the precision of a surgeon wielding a scalpel, she placed the bright steel tip just below Kieran's collarbone.

"Don't," Dani said, acutely aware of how ineffectual the plea and her struggles were. "Don't, please."

Calla made no indication of having heard her.

"Subclavian artery," she said, and plunged in the dagger almost to the hilt.

Kieran cried out through the gag, his face contorted in pain. Dani tried to scream at Calla to stop, but her throat had closed up and all that came out was a wordless noise of desperation. Calla removed the blade with painstaking slowness, then held it up to the light so that Dani could see the crimson blood coating it. A single drop gathered at the tip and fell. Kieran shuddered, his breath coming in rapid, ragged bursts.

Calla raised an expectant eyebrow at Dani, and when she didn't reply, drove the dagger through the back of his knee.

"Popliteal artery," she said. "That one's a little less popular, but it bleeds just fine." Instead of removing the blade, she turned it deliberately like a screwdriver, which drew another cry from Kieran.

Dani was straining so hard against her bonds that every muscle in her body was burning. Blood was already soaking through

Kieran's shirt at his shoulder and dripping to the stone. The amount of time it took someone to bleed out from multiple severed arteries was not the sort of thing they'd covered in science class. She had a horrible feeling that it would be measured in minutes, not hours. But she wouldn't give up Nox.

Calla yanked the dagger out and didn't hesitate to bury it in his flesh a third time, now in his upper arm.

"Brachial artery," she said. "Are you learning anything yet, Dani?"

Dani tried to speak, tried to beg, but there was no breath left in her body. Kieran's reddening face was a paroxysm of pain. She wouldn't give up Nox to save Kieran. She *couldn't*.

Kieran let out a horrible, wrenching sound as Calla gave the knife in his arm a violent twist.

But how could she not?

Her mind clamored for options. She couldn't give up Nox, and lying would only make things worse, but surely there was something she could give Calla. Something to give Kieran a reprieve.

Something like the nest.

She recoiled from the thought immediately, horrified that it would even occur to her, but now that the idea had seeded, it wouldn't leave her. Nox himself had said the eggs might not even be viable.

"Here's an easy one for you," Calla said, ripping Dani from her internal battle. "Femoral artery."

At the sight of the steel driving into Kieran's thigh, bile rose in her throat. There was so much blood, blood soaking his clothes, pooling on the ground beneath him. How much more could he afford to lose?

"Stop," Dani said, her voice sounding foreign to her own ears. "Stop it. I'll—"

A distant but distinct sound echoed down the passageway and through the chamber. It was a dull, rhythmic pounding.

"What the hell is that?" Calla asked quietly, her glare pivoting to Alder, as if she held him personally responsible for the interruption.

Alder traced a circle in the air, and inside it a blurred image appeared and began to sharpen. The picture that took shape was so entirely removed from the hellhole of blood and misery that she was currently trapped in, it took Dani a few seconds to even register what she was seeing, and then even longer to convince herself she was wasn't hallucinating. There were several people in black full tactical gear with SWAT emblazoned across their chests in white. They were holding what looked like a metal battering ram and charging repeatedly against a door. Not the front door, Dani realized with added shock. The door to the basement. She could make out the eerie red symbol painted on it.

"How did they even get inside?" Calla asked, her voice still dangerously calm.

"We lowered the defense spells to allow Dani and the dragon in." Alder frowned at the image and swiped two fingers across it like it was a touchscreen. The front drive came into view. Blue and red flashing lights obscured all else in the night. "And everyone else is on the hunt. I suppose there was no one to stop them."

Calla cursed, ripped the knife from Kieran's thigh, and tossed it onto the table. A moment later Kieran fell to the floor with a bone-jarring *thump*. He moaned, not even attempting to struggle against the magic restraints that still bound his wrists and ankles.

"Eden," said Calla, and Eden straightened like a soldier waiting for orders. "I am reluctant to leave you with this simple task, considering how spectacularly you failed last time, but keep an eye on them while Alder and I deal with this."

Even in her exhaustion-addled state, Dani could see the resentment that shadowed her sister's features, but Eden said nothing. Only nodded.

Alder and Calla both vanished. Dani had no idea how they planned to deal with the surprise visitors. She knew it would hardly present a challenge for the high sorcerer and her lieutenant, but surely they weren't going to obliterate a full SWAT team and however many cops were waiting out front. That wasn't the sort of thing that just went unnoticed by the outside world. And Stonecrest's security relied on remaining unnoticed.

Dani, are you okay? Nox's voice was a jolt of electric joy through her body. She had to fight to keep her face under control. But the joy was almost instantly drowned out by reality.

You can't be here, she thought. *Get out of here before they sense you.*

You're welcome for the rescue, he replied. *Ungrateful whelp.*

How exactly is this a rescue? she couldn't help but demand. *I'm magically tied to a fucking chair. Eden is watching me like a hawk. Kieran is . . .*

But she couldn't finish that thought. She stared at Kieran's chest and was relieved to see it rise with labored breaths.

I appreciate the faith. Can you at least find a way to get out of the chair?

And then what?

And then it's time to do something stupid.

Dani closed her eyes, struggling to find a few more scraps of strength. She knew by now she couldn't possibly break the bonds, but there were other kinds of strength.

"Eden," she said, and opened her eyes.

Eden turned to her with a blank expression that sent a little chill down Dani's spine. This wasn't the sister she had grown up with—the sister who had made faces at her across the dining table;

who had kept the secret when Dani accidentally spilled sweet tea on one of their dad's first-edition books; who had been there, cheering alongside their parents, the first time Dani made it to the top of the climbing wall.

Dani swallowed hard against the lump in her throat and lowered her gaze slightly. She couldn't bear to look this new Eden in the eye.

"Please, let me check on Kieran."

"No."

"Eden, for the love of god, *please*. He's dying."

"And whose fault is that?" Eden asked coolly.

Dani flinched despite herself.

"Just let me be with him for a few minutes," she begged. "He's already lost Zephyr. He shouldn't have to die alone."

Something flickered in Eden's expression, too fast for Dani to identify.

"Fine," she said, her voice still devoid of any warmth. "If it will shut you up, you can have one minute."

She waved her hand, and the magic strapping Dani to the chair dissipated, though her arms were still tightly bound behind her back. Dani stumbled to Kieran's side and dropped to her knees. His eyes fluttered open when her knees pressed into his side. Blood was trickling along his neck and jaw, mingling with the sweat and tears. His breath came in short, uneven bursts.

Without thinking, Dani lowered her face to his, their lips barely brushing as she took the corner of the handkerchief between her teeth and yanked it out of his mouth. Coughing and sputtering, he tried to sit up, but it wasn't happening.

"Fuck," he managed.

Dani couldn't agree more. She held back the tears and nausea that threatened to overcome her—she could feel warm blood seeping around her knees—and tried to focus. She leaned down again, trying to get a better look at the wound on his thigh, but she couldn't see anything for all the blood.

Even with Nox's presence nudging into her consciousness, she couldn't find any scrap of hope that there was a way out of this. Kieran was bleeding out in front of her, and she wasn't going anywhere with her hands tied behind her back. The SWAT team, wherever they had come from, were only a brief respite from the inevitable.

Then she saw a spark in the crimson wound on Kieran's thigh. She blinked, telling herself it was a trick of the light, but it sparked again. And again. Soon the glimmering magic was unmistakable as it rippled across his leg, arm, and chest.

Carefully, Dani stole a glance in Eden's direction. Her sister was standing at the entrance to the chamber, peering into the dark passage beyond. Dani forced her breathing to slow.

"Kieran, what's happening?" she whispered. The bright red sparks were dancing along the bruising on his neck. The angry blue-violet was fading rapidly.

"I don't know." The rhythm of his breaths had begun to slow. "It feels like . . . Zephyr."

Calla had said that it would be years before the dragon's magic regenerated enough to create another sorcerer, but maybe a small amount had regenerated faster than that. Just enough to pass on to Kieran when Zephyr was gone. A final, parting gift.

"I'm going to get us out of here," Dani murmured, just loud enough for Kieran to hear.

"How?"

"Still figuring that part out."

She stood up and took a step toward her sister. Eden whirled around immediately.

"I hope you're proud of yourself," Dani said, not quite able to keep her voice from shaking. "You're a real sorcerer now. A piece of shit, just like the rest of them."

She really didn't know what her plan was. All she knew was that she had to keep herself out of that chair, and distracting Eden seemed like the way to do it. Fortunately, pissing off her sister was an art form that Dani had perfected long ago. She took another two steps.

"You've always been a sore loser," Eden said, tossing her hair back. Her sleek outfit was unlike anything Dani had ever seen her wear before. There was danger stitched in every tailored line. Even her jewelry looked like a weapon.

"It's not something I have a lot of practice with."

Eden's smug expression shifted into a glare, and she stalked forward.

"I know what you're doing," she said in a low voice. "It's not going to work."

"I'm not doing anything," Dani replied in her best annoying-little-sister voice.

"Listen, you—" A sound from the direction of the corridor snagged Eden's attention, and she looked back.

It was the opening Dani had been waiting for. She braced herself as best she could with her hands tied behind her back and launched into a roundhouse kick. She didn't get the height she needed, and her foot caught Eden in the shoulder. Dani aimed another kick at her stomach, but Eden caught her leg and twisted her to the ground.

Dani hooked her legs around Eden's ankle and rolled, bringing Eden to the ground with her. Dani found her balance first and straddled Eden's hips. She wasn't sure where to go from here—a headbutt seemed like the only option—but in the next second, the restraints melted away from her wrists. She shot Kieran a shocked glance. He'd managed to sit up and was staring back at her, looking equally shocked with himself.

When Dani returned her attention to her sister, Eden was holding a glowing red orb between them. Dani's eyes burned with the nearness of it, and her insides ached with the promise of pain it held. The moment rested on a knife's edge.

Eden hesitated. Dani didn't.

She slammed her fist into Eden's jaw. Her sister's head jerked to the side and she immediately fell limp, the orb disintegrating with her consciousness.

Dani had never been more happy in her life to see Tomás's old Corolla, idling near the end of Stonecrest's long, winding drive. Nox had been waiting at the end of the drainage tunnel for Dani and Kieran. He hadn't been happy to see Eden, even unconscious, but knew better than to suggest Dani leave her behind.

Nox couldn't carry all three of them very far, but he assured them that backup was nearby. When Dani made out the shape of a car, and then Tomás and Sadie, illuminated in the car's interior, she was so consumed by both relief and worry that her stomach hurt. She hadn't wanted to bring her friends into this, hadn't wanted to put them in danger. But at the same time, she couldn't imagine surviving it without them.

She charged Nox with carrying Eden back to the barn and keeping an eye on her until they got there.

And if she wakes up? he asked testily.

Knock her out again, Dani replied. *But, you know, gently.*

Nox looked pleased by this prospect and took flight with Eden's limp body wrapped securely in his tail. Dani's stomachache radiated through her whole body at the sight of her sister, so vulnerable and helpless, but she had no choice. If the only way to save Eden was against her will, then so be it.

"Sorry about the blood on your seats," Dani told Tomás as she and Kieran slid into the back seat.

"Blood?" Tomás twisted around to look at them, his eyes widening slightly at the sight of Kieran (soaked with blood) and Dani (covered in Kieran's blood).

"You should see the other guy," Dani said.

Sadie put a hand on Tomás's cheek and pushed his face back toward the windshield.

"Escape now, freak out later," she told him.

"I can multitask." Tomás threw the car into gear and mashed his foot on the gas pedal. They lurched forward and quickly picked up speed on the downhill drive. He nearly flipped the car swerving onto the main road, but for once Dani didn't complain. She wouldn't mind if he maxed out the speedometer the whole way home. The farther Stonecrest was behind them, the more she relaxed.

"Thank you," she said, once they were far enough away that she could breathe normally again. "So, so much."

"No worries," Sadie said, smiling tightly at her. "We were in the neighborhood."

"How did you find us?" Kieran asked. "Stonecrest isn't exactly on the map."

"Maybe not," said Sadie, "but it has decent cell service." She raised her phone. The Find My Friends app was still open, with Dani's location pinpointed on the screen—or, more accurately, her phone's location.

Kieran looked at Dani in surprise, and she shrugged.

"It seemed like a better idea than breadcrumbs."

"It took us a minute to figure out what Nox was trying to tell us," Tomás said. "Shockingly, charades is not your dragon's strong suit. But once we did, Sadie had the idea to check the app."

"So whose idea was it to SWAT the sorcerers?" Dani asked, even though she already knew.

Tomás grinned.

"We used an old pay phone at the gas station. I gave them the coordinates and told them that they were building bombs in the basement."

"He used an atrocious Russian accent," Sadie said. "It was ridiculous, and I can't believe they actually took the call seriously."

"The timing was perfect," Dani said. The thought of how close she had come to giving up the nest scratched at the back of her mind, but she pushed it away. She *hadn't* given it up, and that was what mattered, right?

She cast a sideways glance at Kieran. Just the sight of him gave her such a rush of confusing, contradictory emotions that she ended up pushing him to the back of her mind too. Right now, she had to put all of her focus into helping Eden. Everything else could wait.

"I do have a question," Sadie said, twisting around to look at Dani again. "If Eden is a sorcerer, isn't that going to be a problem when she wakes up?"

Dani hadn't actually given that much thought. But she couldn't keep knocking out her sister indefinitely.

"I might be able to help." Kieran dug in his pocket and pulled out a crumpled piece of yellowed paper, smeared with blood.

Dani smoothed it out and looked at the collection of symbols and handwritten letters of a language she couldn't understand. A page from Calla's spell book.

"It's the spell she used to keep Zephyr chained and dampen his magic," Kieran said, only the barest discernible quaver in his voice. His features were a tight mask, but she could see the grief like hairline fractures, threatening to break him apart. She couldn't imagine what it cost him to be so aloof right now.

"You can read this?" she asked.

"It's Old Irish—before my time, but I've picked up a good bit over the years from Calla."

She met his gaze for just a moment before looking back to the paper. Despite the haunted look in his eyes that he couldn't quite hide, despite everything, she allowed herself the tiniest bit of hope, just a sliver to carry her through the rest of the night. She was going to reverse what had been done to Eden. She was going to bring her sister home.

TWENTY-SIX

Eden woke to the sensation that she'd just been hit in the head with a sledgehammer. When her eyelids creaked open, and above her was the familiar exposed timber roof of the training barn, her mind went into a tailspin. Had she been dreaming? Was she going to sit up and realize that she'd just fallen off the climbing wall and hit her head, that Calla and Stonecrest and Zephyr and all the rest were just the fevered dreams of an overtired brain?

She wasn't sure which was more disappointing: the thought that none of it had happened, or sitting up and realizing that it had.

The world spun around her in a giddy whirl, and she blinked hard, willing it to stop. Dani was standing in front of her, arms crossed, face set in that ridiculous expression of martyred concern. Eden looked down to find her hands and ankles bound tightly with climbing ropes. Did Dani really expect those to work?

Eden sent a bolt of magic toward the ropes, expecting them to disintegrate. Nothing happened. She tried again. She could still feel the fizz of the magic beneath her skin, could feel it barreling toward the restraints, but then nothing. Like it was being sucked into a void.

"What the hell is this?" she asked.

"Not a good feeling, is it?" It was not Dani but Kieran who replied. Eden jerked her glare in his direction. He was holding a piece of yellowed paper in one hand that had been ripped from a book. Eden didn't need to see the script more closely to know what it was. She'd been trapped by the same spell she'd cast that afternoon with Calla.

Which meant that Kieran had magic that he'd been hiding from the sorcerers all this time. Unless Zephyr had regenerated enough to give him some in death.

She wasn't sure why the thought of the dragon twinged like a spasm in her chest. She didn't want to think about it.

"What exactly is your plan, Dani?" she asked, tucking her legs to the side so that she could sit as gracefully as possible. "Just keep me captive here forever?"

"Why not?" Dani shot back. "You would have done the same to me and Nox."

"You wouldn't have been a prisoner if you had just come to your senses. Dragons are an infestation. If we let them go unchecked, they'll destroy the whole planet."

"And you think sorcerers are going to save us?"

"I think sorcerers are the next step in the evolutionary chain."

"Christ, you can leave off the *X-Men* bullshit. They're just a bunch of bloodthirsty sociopaths."

"I'm one of them now," Eden said, subconsciously pushing more magic outward, only for it to be devoured by the restraining spell. "A slayer and a sorcerer. The first—"

"The first of your kind, blah blah blah," Dani said. "Get over yourself. You want to know what my plan is? I'm going to reverse the process and make you yourself again."

"That's not possible." Eden's mouth was suddenly dry. It wasn't possible, was it? She couldn't go back to who she was before. She would rather die. "Mom and Dad are going to be home soon. How are you going to explain this to them?"

"I have a feeling they'll take my side."

"I have a feeling they'll think you've lost your goddamn mind and tied your sister up in the barn," Eden said, unable to check the smile creeping across her lips. "I'll be crying and confused, and you'll be stuck trying to justify yourself and your filthy dragon. They'll never believe you."

"You're probably right, which is why I figured it would be best for you to do the justifying for me."

"What?" A sinking feeling in the pit of her stomach.

"Eden, baby, what did you do?"

Eden jerked her head in the direction of her mother's voice. Analisa and James were standing just behind her, haggard in their traveling clothes with matching expressions of dismay.

"I didn't do anything wrong." Eden strained against her bonds, feeding magic into them with no result. "Dani is the one in league with a dragon. I've only been trying to help."

"She told us everything."

"She's lying," Eden spat, incensed at the thought of having to justify herself, at the realization that Dani could have told them anything she wanted and they would believe her. She was the gifted one. The one who could talk to dragons. The one who had been handed the world on a silver platter.

"Eden, why didn't you tell me?" Frankie asked. *Frankie*. Eden whipped her head around to find her aunt on her other side, hugging herself, black curls in disarray. "Why didn't you talk to me about this?"

"Like you would have listened," Eden said. "Like any of you would have listened. Frankie, you're the one who told me I should just quit. That I was never going to be good enough anyway."

Frankie shook her head wildly, stricken.

"I never said that, mija. I never meant—"

"Calla saw everything I could be, if I just had the chance. She gave me one."

"I don't understand." Her father knelt down beside her. He

reached up like he wanted to touch her, but his hand fell away. "You never told us—"

"You never *listen*." Her throat burned, and for a horrible second she thought she would cry. She swallowed hard and managed to bring herself back under control. "I did all of this for us. You raised me to be a dragon slayer, and Calla made me a better one."

"Calla kidnapped and tortured your sister," her mother said, almost pleading. "She nearly killed her."

"So?"

"*So?*" both of her parents echoed in shock.

Everyone was staring at her. Eden knew that logically she was in the right, but there was something else she was missing—something besides the cold facts, something complex and fundamental that she'd known once but now couldn't wrap her mind around. It infuriated her.

"Dani turned her back on us," Eden said. "She turned her back on everything our family has ever stood for. She's not a real slayer."

"Hello, I'm standing right here," Dani said.

"It wasn't enough for you to be the child prodigy, was it?" Eden asked her, acid dripping from her voice. "That wasn't special enough for you. So you had to go off and make friends with a dragon."

"It's called a soul bond, and it wasn't my choice."

"Right, I forgot. All you ever wanted was to be normal. How terrible it must be for you, to be the best at everything without trying, to be the fucking Chosen One."

Dani's hands clenched into fists. She took a step forward.

"You're the one who—"

"Girls, that's enough," said Analisa sharply, and for a moment, Eden was a kid again, arguing with her little sister over whose turn it was to hold the remote. Her mother came over to kneel down beside her father. "Eden, please, we're trying to understand. This is hard for us too. We just spent the past several days trying to hunt down a dragon, and then we return to find out that Dani has brought one home. That she's somehow bonded with it."

"It's a lot to process," said James, wiping his glasses on the hem of his shirt.

"It's actually very simple," Eden said. "Dragons are the enemy, same as they always have been. Calla is trying to save the world."

"No, it's not that simple," Dani said. "That's what I've been trying to tell you. Nox—all the dragons—are more than just intelligent. They have a shared history. They have feelings and hopes and heartbreaks. They aren't just savage beasts roaming around the world. I know Nox. He's not evil or vicious. He doesn't deserve to die. Neither did Zephyr."

His name made Eden cringe. She hoped no one had noticed.

"This magic is mine," she said. "It's who I am now. You can't take it away from me."

"This isn't who you are," Frankie said, her dark eyes sorrowful. She bent down and put her hand softly on the top of Eden's head. "Please, let us help you."

For a moment—for just a moment—she was comforted. Frankie's touch was familiar. She was home. Then her mind caught up.

"I don't need your help," she said, jerking her head away. "Don't touch me. And get these fucking ropes off me."

"Not until we figure this out," Analisa said, though the answer clearly pained her.

"Let. Me. Go." Eden pushed her magic outward, not into the ropes but everywhere else. She closed her eyes and imagined bringing the barn down around them. She imagined bringing a stop to all this fury and confusion. Bringing the world to an end.

For a few seconds, nothing happened, and then a tremor rocked the ground. Overhead, the roof beams creaked. Her parents and Frankie scrambled away from her. Eden threw every ounce of strength she possessed behind the magic. She wanted to break the earth and split the sky. She wanted to show them all what she could do.

But the binding spell did its work. The harder she fought, the faster the void consumed her power. Magic sizzled along her nerve endings and shimmered red across her skin, but there was nowhere for it to go. Exhaustion soon overtook her, but still she kept going, until her vision was clouding at the edges and every inch of her body begged for rest. Her magic burned inside her, but it wasn't enough. She wasn't enough.

And finally, when she had nothing left to give, she just gave up.

Seeing her sister like this, helpless and harrowed with aimless fury, gave Dani a profound sense of unease that sank into her bones. Frankie had been at the house waiting for them when they made it back from Stonecrest—apparently her parents, seeing all the missed calls and unable to get in touch with Dani or Eden, had contacted her. Her parents arrived home soon after, having caught an earlier flight. As relieved as she was to see them, and as glad as she was that Tomás and Sadie finally agreed to go home where they would be safe, Dani couldn't help but regret the situation she found herself in. Not only did she have to tell two of the world's best slayers that she was soul-bonded with a dragon, and then convince them not to kill said dragon; she also had to explain why Eden was unconscious and tied up in the barn. And then there was Kieran, whose help she needed, though she could barely bring herself to look at him. And then, of course, the small matter of the high sorcerer wanting to imprison her and her dragon for the next few centuries.

The conversation was the most difficult and awkward one she'd ever had with her family, worse even than her mother's god-awful attempt at the sex talk, which had included The Killers' lyrics and something called a "consent castle". In the end, she'd managed to get the salient points across without anyone losing their cool. Begrudgingly, she had to admit that Kieran had been useful in that respect, his collected calm a much-needed balance to her impassioned ramblings, and he knew so much about dragons and sorcerers alike that her parents couldn't just dismiss him out of hand. Dani wasn't sure how he'd remained so detached through all of this, so soon after Zephyr's death, but she was perversely grateful.

It also lent veracity to their story that they were both covered in blood, Kieran more so than Dani. After the explanations had finished, Analisa had insisted they both go back to the house long enough to wash up. Dani had given Kieran one of her dad's old T-shirts. Somehow it was even more disconcerting to see him in something casual than it had been to see him covered in his own blood.

She'd also wanted to introduce Nox to her family, to finally bridge the gap between the two parts of her life that she'd spent half the summer trying to keep apart, but Nox—though he was nearby to keep an eye on her—absolutely refused. She couldn't blame him, and immediately felt guilty for even broaching the idea. Her parents had killed his friend and mentor. That wasn't something that could be explained away. It was a painful fact that would always exist between them, no matter how much bridging she did.

It was Eden herself who did the best job of convincing their parents of Dani's concerns. To say she had changed was a massive understatement. There was a coldness—a *wrongness*—emanating from her that felt like a nightmare. The words she spoke, equal parts disdainful and uncaring, were barbs in Dani's heart. She just wanted her sister back. And now was her chance.

She grabbed her backpack from the corner where she had stashed it and pulled out the glass-plated pages of the Coombs manuscript. It felt like years ago that she and Kieran had stolen — well, borrowed — them.

"I need your help deciphering these," she told Kieran as she laid them out on the floor.

"What are those?" Her father crouched down to examine them, his curiosity momentarily eclipsing his concern. Dani couldn't help but notice her mother and Frankie exchange a look.

Kieran didn't say anything, and he didn't come closer. Worry curdled in her chest at the expression on his face as he glanced over the pages and then met her eye.

"What?" she asked, though a part of her already knew.

"I took you to the library because Calla wanted to keep you distracted until she was ready to spring the trap," Kieran said softly.

That caught her parents' and Frankie's attention. Dani had strategically left out the part of the story where Kieran had sold her down the river. Not out of any latent loyalty to him; it just seemed counterproductive, when she was counting on his explanations to bring her family to her side.

"Are you telling me these spells won't work?" She struggled to keep her tone even.

"I'm telling you they're useless drivel," Kieran said. "Coombs knew a lot about dragons, but he knew next to nothing about sorcerers. He never came close to creating any working spells."

"Dani, what's going on?" her mother asked.

I told you it couldn't be done, said Nox.

Shut up, she shot back with more ire than she'd intended. She felt a surge of his indignation, but Nox didn't reply.

Eden, who hadn't moved since her last attempt to break free from the spell, laughed. It was a low, eerie sound.

"Only you would be arrogant enough to think you're smarter than the high sorcerer herself," she said, her lips twisted in a sneer. "You can't destroy what she's created."

"Shut *up*," Dani snapped.

"Dani," said Analisa. But Dani couldn't handle more explanations right now. She was being torn in too many directions at once. All she wanted was a moment of quiet. A moment to regroup. A moment to sort through the emotions tangled in her chest. A moment to figure out how she could hate Kieran so very much and still find herself drawn back to the memory of his mouth on hers, his fingers in her hair. It made her hate him even more.

"I just need a minute," she said to her mother, and then to Kieran: "We need to talk."

She grabbed his sleeve and, without waiting for a reply, dragged him out the doors of the barn and into the humid night air. Kieran didn't protest and didn't resist. She marched until she was certain they were out of earshot of her family and then turned to face him. His features were obscured in the darkness.

It was only then, with a flutter of distress, that she realized she didn't know what she wanted to say. A faint breeze stirred around them. The night was fading fast into a murky gray morning, but a few fireflies still drifted lazily across the field, sparking their lazy rhythms. Crickets chittered ceaselessly, underscored occasionally by the grumpy belch of a bullfrog.

"I'm not going to apologize for what I did," Kieran said at last. The way he spoke wasn't arrogant or stubborn. Just honest. "I made a promise to Zephyr. I wasn't going to let him spend the rest of his life in that hell."

"And so you traded me and Nox instead?" she demanded, glad for a hook she could hang her outrage on.

"I did warn you that I was fucked up." His voice was as detached as ever, but Dani couldn't help but think there was a rueful note clinging to the edges. Maybe she was just imagining it. Probably she was.

"No," she said. "You don't get to put this on me. Trusting you doesn't make me a fool. Betraying me makes you a coward."

"Betraying Calla would have meant hurting Zephyr, and he is —" Kieran faltered. The moment of grief was so visceral that Dani could sense it even in the pre-dawn shadows. "He *was* my whole life. The only thing in the world I care about. I never pretended otherwise."

"You kissed me."

"I shouldn't have."

"Well, at least that's one thing you're sorry about," she said, bitterness rising in her throat like bile.

"I didn't say that."

She wanted to slap him. No, she wanted to punch him. She wanted to make him hurt the way she was hurting. But she also wanted to throw her arms around him, to tell him she wished they could have saved Zephyr. She wanted to blame him for everything, but also make him understand that none of it was his fault — Calla had whittled away at his freedom until he couldn't see any choices but the ones she wanted him to make.

She wanted both to kiss him and to never see him again.

He had betrayed her, but then he had nearly died trying to save her. There was no training manual for this. No easy answers. No simple solution.

She took a step back from him, then another, not trusting her own impulses. Silently, she called for Nox. It wasn't long before the breeze tickling past them was fanned into a wind by the dragon's whisper-soft wings. He landed behind Dani, and she felt his antipathy toward Kieran wash over her like a wave. She'd kept Kieran's part in the plot a secret from her family, but it wasn't a secret she could keep from Nox. He was still peeved at her for the way she had driven him away from Stonecrest, but his anger at Kieran was a whole other beast. Dani was suddenly glad that she was standing between them.

"We have to figure out a way to help Eden," she said.

"There isn't one," said Kieran.

He's right, Nox said with an accompanying twitch of irritation, though Dani couldn't tell if it was at her stubbornness or at having to agree with Kieran. Or both.

"It has to be possible," she insisted. "Some angle that we're not thinking of."

Just because you want it to be true, doesn't make it so.

Dani whirled to face him.

Just because you don't know the answer, doesn't mean there isn't one.

She doesn't even want this. She's one of them now. Let her be with her kind. There was no compassion in his words, only a blatant disgust. He might as well have been talking about slugs.

I've told you a hundred times—I'm not giving up on her. If you don't want to be a part of it, then you can fucking leave already.

Nox was gearing up for an equally irate reply, but before he could, Kieran cleared his throat. Dani turned back around. Her eyes had adjusted enough to the dark that she caught a glimpse of the fleeting expression on Kieran's face as he looked between her and Nox. She hadn't considered what it would be like for him to watch her converse with her soul-bonded dragon, when his own bond had been so recently severed for good. There was something fragile about his composure, as if all his grief was straining just beneath the surface. She didn't know how he had managed to keep it repressed for so long—or how much longer he would be able to.

"Calla isn't just the first sorcerer." His tone revealed nothing. "She's the most powerful. And she's been perfecting this ritual for centuries. It's not just some spell that can be undone."

Dani dug the heels of her hands into her forehead, trying to keep her temper in check. She was so sick of everyone telling her how impossible this was, and she was terrified that she was starting to believe them. Maybe Eden had been right. Maybe there was no way to destroy what the high sorcerer had created.

"That's it," she said. A thrill ran down her spine. She dropped her hands. "That's the problem—we've been trying to think of a new process to undo Calla's work. Maybe what we need to do is use *her* process."

What are you talking about? asked Nox.

Kieran said nothing, only waited in silence for her to explain. Dani started to pace, piecing her idea into words that made sense.

"If a human dies before their soul-bonded dragon, the magic from the soul bond just flows back into the dragon, right? Magic doesn't overwhelm the dragon the way it does a human. So what if, while the magic is flowing back to the dragon, it was diverted elsewhere—into a sorcerer. Then wouldn't that create a new soul bond between the sorcerer and the dragon?"

No, Nox said flatly. She had a feeling he was not merely answering her question.

"I don't know," said Kieran. "Theoretically, I suppose."

Dani ignored Nox and plowed on.

"And theoretically, if the sorcerer is no longer bearing the full weight of the magic on their own, wouldn't that help them be human again—a human with a soul bond?"

Dani, no.

"What are you suggesting?" Kieran asked, with enough skepticism that he must have already guessed.

"I'm suggesting that the only way to save Eden is for me to die," Dani said. "Temporarily."

TWENTY-SEVEN

It was a good plan. Dani knew in her bones that it could work. Unfortunately, no one else agreed with her. Nox was adamant that it was a terrible idea—his exact phrasing was "the worst idea ever conceived in the history of the world, and I happen to know that for a fact." Frankie was horrified by the suggestion. Her parents were downright hostile.

And Eden . . . Eden only glared at her with a hatred so intense that it convinced Dani even further that this had to be done.

Kieran, though he hadn't encouraged her in the slightest, did at least admit that it might work, and that he had seen Calla's transference ritual enough to recreate it.

"I won't be in any real danger," she argued, which was perhaps optimistic, but she needed to win her parents over.

"You're saying that you have to die," James said, resting his hands on her shoulders like he was seriously considering shaking some sense into her. "How is that not dangerous?"

"I won't really be dead," Dani said. "If I touch a steady electric current, the electricity will stop my heart long enough for Kieran to perform the ritual. Then you shut off the current and my heartbeat returns to its normal rhythm."

"That won't work," said Analisa, but she wasn't able to hide her hesitation, which Dani seized on.

"You know it will!" She looked between her parents. "You're the ones who insisted we learn exactly how electricity affects the human body, same as with burns and everything else a dragon could possibly do to us. Nox can use his tail. He can control the voltage to prevent internal injuries."

Absolutely not. I'm not going to be a part of this, Dani. There was nothing but iron will behind his words, but Dani ignored him for now. She'd use one of El Toro's electrified whips if she had to, but first she had to get her parents on her side.

"This is ridiculous," said Frankie, speaking up for the first time. "You can't electrocute yourself on the off chance that some gabacho who none of us have ever met before might be able to cure your sister. How do we even know we can trust him?" She shot Kieran a glare that spoke volumes, which he thankfully did not reciprocate. Dani got the feeling he was depending on her family talking her out of this so he wouldn't have to.

"I still don't understand how you can do magic if you're not a sorcerer," Analisa said to him, crossing her arms.

"This isn't about Kieran," Dani said before he could reply. Technically speaking, Kieran *was* a sorcerer now, wasn't he? Albeit one with less magic than most. Dani didn't want to think about that. Eden was her only concern. "You can trust me. I'm telling you, this will work."

"I don't care how sure you are," James said, shaking his head and dropping his hands from her shoulders. "You aren't doing this."

Eden had started to laugh, but there was no mirth in it.

"This is so typical," she said. "No matter what happens, we can't risk Dani getting hurt, can we? God forbid anything happen that might jeopardize her bright, perfect future. I guess that makes me the expendable one, doesn't it."

"No one is saying that." James moved quickly to Eden's side, but she jerked away when he reached out for her. "Eden, we love you. We want to keep you both safe."

"My magic keeps me safe," she spat. "And you're trying to take it away from me."

"It hasn't saved you from anything," Dani said. "It's turned you into a monster."

From the corner of her eye she saw Kieran flinch, but she wouldn't let herself look at him. Eden was her concern. Her only concern. Frankie knelt down beside Eden and started talking to her in soft, earnest tones, interrupted occasionally by Analisa or James with their own attempts at consolation.

Dani was happy to let them hash it out. Nox had been tugging insistently at the edge of her focus, and she couldn't fob him off anymore.

You can't do this, Dani. You'll be breaking our bond forever.

I don't want to do it, but it's the only way. We'll both survive it. We'll be okay.

What about the eggs? Without the soul bond, I might never be able to hatch them.

You'll be bonded with Eden. She's stronger than me anyway. Once she's herself again, she'll be able to help you hatch them.

You don't know that. You don't know what will happen.

Maybe not, but I know what will happen if I do nothing. Eden will go back to Calla, and I'll lose her forever. I can't live with that.

And me? His hurt was a stone in the pit of her stomach. She squeezed her eyes shut, trying to bear it. No simple solution. No easy answers.

It won't be the same, but I won't lose you. And you won't lose me. We have each other now, always. Remember? She wished she could reach out and touch him, to help him better feel the conviction of her words. *I promised to help you hatch the eggs, and I will. However I can. I swear.*

Please, I can't—He broke off. For several seconds, there was only quiet, and then Dani felt a surge of panic. *Something's wrong. I think the sorcerers are here.*

Her stomach sank, and she ran to the door and peered into the gray-blue of the impending dawn. The field appeared empty. In the distance, she thought she could make out a few of the last fireflies. Then she realized the bobbing lights in the distance weren't winking merrily, but were burning steadily and growing larger.

"Sorcerers. They're here."

Analisa went immediately to the gun safe and started typing in the passcode.

"Dani, shut the door," she said. Her brusque tone was not one Dani had ever heard before. She wasn't hearing Analisa the mother or Analisa the trainer. This was Analisa the slayer.

"How many are we dealing with here?" James asked as he accepted a loaded rifle from his wife. Any trace of softness was gone now. He was a Rivera too, after all.

"Maybe six or seven?" Dani said, wishing her own voice could be as composed. "I don't know, there could be more."

"There are at least a dozen regulars at Stonecrest," Kieran said. "Calla probably would have brought them all. She's not going to let you get away again."

"We'll see about that," Analisa said, stone-faced as she loaded a second rifle.

"Mom." Dani tried to breathe, tried to be cool-headed. "You can't fight them. Those might as well be paintball guns for all the damage you'll be able to do."

"Believe it or not," she replied, pulling out a pistol and holster to strap to her hip, "you're not the resident expert on sorcerers, Dani. Your father and I have dealt with them before."

"What."

"Give anyone enough power and they'll start to abuse it," James said. "There have been rogue sorcerers in the past, wreaking havoc. When their own kind won't keep them in check, the responsibility falls to us."

"Apparently it's more systemic a problem than we originally thought," Analisa said grimly. She pulled two tactical vests from the safe and tossed one to James. "Sorcerers are still vulnerable to bullets. The trick is catching them off guard."

So Dick from Kaleidoscope had been right about one thing.

"I'm with Dani on this," Frankie said. "I don't like it. You've never dealt with more than one at a time, and there could be a dozen out there. Maybe more."

"Which is why we'll be drawing them away from here," Analisa said, unruffled, clipping grenades to her vest. "Dani, when the coast is clear, you'll get Frankie and Eden to safety."

"What? No! I'm not staying here," Dani said. "I'm going with you. Nox and I can help."

"And you will," said James, "by keeping your aunt and sister safe."

"If you let me go, I can talk to them," Eden said, in infinitely reasonable tones. "They'll listen to me."

"You'd be more believable if you hadn't spent the past hour crowing about how Calla is going to save the world," Dani said.

"Dani." Her mother cradled her face in both hands and looked her in the eye. "You have to do this for us. Stay here and get them to safety."

"Don't do this." Dani hated how her voice cracked with the plea. "You don't stand a chance without magic."

"I'll go," said Kieran. Dani turned her head to meet his gaze. His dark eyes spoke volumes beyond his words. "I can help them."

"Heroics is rarely a good reason to join a fight," James commented mildly.

"I don't have anything to prove," Kieran said. "Just a score to settle."

"Revenge is almost as bad."

"But an excellent motivator," said Analisa. She grabbed another vest and tossed it to Kieran.

The thought of being bonded for life to a dragon made Eden sick to her stomach. The fact that it was Dani's dragon, being foisted onto Eden out of pity like some kind of consolation prize, was a thousand times worse. She didn't need to be saved.

Did she?

Zephyr was dead. Her family was in danger. Calla had told her that if she wanted to be one of them, she had to accept the cost, but Eden hadn't expected the cost to be one that others would have to pay. Was it still worth it?

While the others were distracted, she'd started picking at the rope around her ankles. The knots were impossibly tight, maybe affected by the same spell that dampened her magic, but she was starting to make some progress by the time Frankie returned to her side.

"What do you want?" Eden asked, but the heat was gone from her voice.

"I want you to stop feeling sorry for yourself," Frankie said, "and tell me what's really wrong."

"What's wrong is that I'm being held against my will by my own family, and they're trying to rob me of my magic because my self-righteous little sister says so, and she's God's gift to humanity so she must be right."

"Eden, I never meant to suggest that you weren't good enough.

The reason I didn't want to be a dragon slayer was because I didn't want to spend my whole life measuring my worth using someone else's rubric. I wanted so much more than that."

"So did I," Eden said, "and that's what Calla gave me."

"But what did she take in return?"

My anxiety. My panic attacks. Everything I hated about myself.

But were those really gone? She'd thought so, but now she wasn't so sure. She couldn't help but feel that those parts of her were still buried deep, lurking beneath the bitterness and rage that had risen to the surface. What if that dark, cold void at the center of herself wasn't a refuge, but a black hole, swallowing the only light she had left?

It had been her decision. She hadn't fully understood the cost, but that didn't matter. The choice was made. There was no going back.

"We have to go," said Analisa, cracking the door open just enough to peer through. "Before they get any closer."

"I don't like this," said Frankie. "I wish you would stay."

"If we stay, then we're all at their mercy," said Analisa, giving her sister a brief hug and leaning over to plant a kiss on Eden's forehead. Eden was too torn to protest. "Once we draw them off, you all get to safety."

Eden risked a glance at Dani, whose face was pinched with uncharacteristic worry as she watched their parents slip out the barn door, followed by Kieran.

They weren't going to survive this.

The thought knocked around inside the void, the accompanying emotions slipping through her fingers every time she tried to catch them. Logically, she knew that she should be upset — more than upset. She should be arguing alongside Dani to go out there with them, to show them what she was worth — no, that wasn't right. She didn't have to prove anything to them. She just had to keep them safe. This was her family. This was her *life*.

Her heart was fragmented into disparate pieces, no longer fitting together. She couldn't figure out what she was supposed to think, what she was supposed to feel. She opened her mouth to tell her parents she loved them, closed it, opened it again. But it was too late; they were already gone, the barn door shut behind them.

Nox, Dani begged, her forehead pressed against the door that had just shut behind her parents and Kieran. *Please. I know you hate them, but they're my parents. You have to help them. Don't let them die. Please.*

There was no answer.

She knew what she was asking of him, to put himself in peril to protect the slayers who had killed Polara. She knew, and she didn't care. She wanted Nox to be safe, but she wanted the same for her parents, and for Kieran. What was the use of all those years of training, if when the chips were down, she couldn't do anything but wait here for them to die? What was the point of being a Rivera, if she couldn't save anyone?

She slammed her hand against the door so hard that her bones rattled. Then she turned on Eden.

"This is your fault," she said, stomping across the training mat. "All you care about is being the best at everything, and now they're going to die."

"Dani," said her aunt warningly.

"My fault?" Eden demanded. "You're the one who teamed up with a fucking dragon, who tried to kill the high sorcerer, who spends every second of every day trying to prove to everyone how much better you are than me."

"I fought Calla to protect Nox," Dani said, "and I didn't even want any of this. I wanted to go to school like a normal person and hang out with my friends and go to my summer job, but you wouldn't let me. Every damn day you're preaching at me to take the family business seriously, to push myself harder and faster, to follow your shining example. Well, I *tried*. And now you're blaming me for it?"

"That's not—" Eden faltered. For the first time since her transformation, she actually looked . . . unsure. "All of it comes so easy to you."

"No, it doesn't," Dani snapped. "You pushed me to be better, so that's what I've always done. And it's never enough for you."

Eden didn't reply, only stared back at Dani, her cold eyes tinged with something like regret.

"I think we should all just try to calm down," said Frankie. "High tempers aren't going to help anything right now."

Outside came the distant thunder of gunfire.

"Mom and Dad won't last five minutes against Calla," said Eden. There was no malice in her tone, only a soft certainty. Her head was bowed.

"They're doing this for you two." Frankie's voice wobbled, but didn't break. "We need to get ready to run, like your mom said."

Dani was quiet, listening for Nox, for an answer or a waver of emotion or *anything*. But there was nothing. It was like he'd purposefully shut her out. Her heart twisted.

"Screw that," she said, standing up. "Frankie, you wait until the coast is clear and get Eden out of here. I can't just wait here for them to die."

"No." Frankie scrambled to her feet. "You aren't going out there. You'll be killed."

"I've faced down Calla twice, and I'm still alive," Dani said.

"You're a fool," said Eden. "You're only alive because she wants you to be."

"Then let's hope that's still the case." Dani stalked to the weapons display, strapped a sheath of three small throwing knives to her thigh, then pulled down a bowie knife. If it was true that a sorcerer could be hurt by physical weapons when they were caught off guard, then a sneak attack seemed like the best option.

"You're impossible," said Frankie, but she didn't try to stop her. Instead, she went to the gun safe and pulled out a black hard case. The Barrett M82 anti-materiel rifle wasn't one that Dani had been allowed to touch yet, much less train with. The art of the sniper rifle was supposed to be a lesson for next year. "Where's the ladder to the loft?"

It took Dani a few seconds to realize what she was planning.

"No," she said. "You and Eden have to—"

"Escúchame," Frankie said, jabbing a finger into her sternum. "I'm the adult here, and I'm not going to turn tail while you run off to get yourself killed. Now tell me where the damn ladder is so I can give you y tus padres locos some cover fire."

Stunned, Dani pointed to the ladder in the corner behind El Toro.

"This is ridiculous," Eden said, struggling against her bonds. "There's nothing either of you can do to help them. Just let me go."

Dani ignored her and opened the door a crack. The sky was lightening quickly, but she couldn't tell if it was because of the dawn or the explosions of magic happening at the far end of the field. Her stomach lurched, and she tightened her grip on the bowie knife. Now or never.

She slipped outside and darted for the line of trees, picking her way through brambles and honeysuckle bushes until she found a deer path that ran parallel to the field. Then she started to run.

The scene ahead loomed larger and brighter, flickering through the gaps in the trees. As she neared, she realized that all the sorcerers were angled toward the trees on the opposite side of the field. She caught a glimpse of her father's golden hair and realized that's where her parents had taken cover. Kieran was between them, a grim expression on his face as he held a glowing red shield steady. It was dimmer than the shields that Dani had seen other sorcerers create, and frayed at the edges, like he couldn't quite round it out, but so far it seemed to be serving its purpose. Her mom and dad peppered the line of sorcerers with bullets, forcing them to keep their own shields up and greatly lessening the number of magic bombs they could fling.

Dani caught her breath at the sight of Calla, moving through her ranks to the no man's land between. She stood bathed in radiant green light like some kind of vision, her hands out in front of her, palms up, in a show of peace. A temporary ceasefire followed from both sides, though Dani couldn't tell if her parents were waiting to hear what she had to say or if they were just reloading.

"This is exactly what I wanted to prevent," Calla said, her voice clear and ringing. "Slayers and sorcerers should be allies, not squabbling amongst ourselves."

"Is that why you waited until we were gone to kidnap both our daughters?" Analisa demanded.

"Eden and Dani both came to me of their own accord," Calla replied with a small shrug. Technically, Dani realized, it was the truth. "Just hear me out. I'm not looking to hurt your girls. Quite the opposite. I want to truly bring them into the fold, to give them a place of honor in the new world we are forging."

"You strapped Dani to a chair and tortured her."

"Dani was being intransigent," Calla said with a flash of irritation. "You've spoiled her, and now she's too stubborn for her own good. We need a soul-bonded pair to create more sorcerers. It's the only hope we have of ridding the world of the dragon menace once and for all."

"And when you're done with them? Do they end up dead in your dungeon too?"

Dani couldn't see Calla's face, but she could hear the smile in her voice as she dropped her arms. Her shield dissipated as well.

"I see Kieran has been spinning you his sob story. Did he neglect to mention that in return for his service I offered him comfort, wealth, and anything his heart could desire?"

"You took everything from me," Kieran shouted.

"I *saved* you from a life of inconsequential drudgery," said Calla, "and instead of thanking me, you threw it back in my face."

"You killed Zephyr."

"No, you did that," was the cool response.

Kieran dropped the shield and lunged forward, but James caught him and pulled him back. Dani bit her lip to stop from crying out as one of the sorcerers summoned a glowing orb. Without turning, Calla lifted a hand. The sorcerer let the orb fade. Kieran raised another shield, but even from a distance Dani could see that he was trembling; whether from exhaustion or rage, she didn't know. Regardless, he wasn't going to be able to hold the line for much longer. She crept forward, dropping into an army crawl once she was out of the safety of the trees. The field grass was at least three feet high, decent enough cover.

"This is your last chance," said Calla, lowering her hand. "The only olive branch I'll be offering. Dani doesn't have to suffer unduly, but she will be coming back to Stonecrest with me. There's no reason for you to die trying to save her from an inevitable fate."

"Clearly, you've never been a mother," said Analisa, as she raised her rifle and fired.

Calla threw up her shield a millisecond before the bullet would have caught her between the eyes. In the same moment, Dani slashed the Achilles tendon of the sorcerer at the rear of the pack. As he cried out in pain and surprise, she hooked her legs around his and took him to the ground. She wouldn't let herself look him in the face, wouldn't let herself hesitate, as she drove the knife into his throat. He made a choking, anguished sound, and then vanished.

She didn't know if he was going somewhere to heal or somewhere to die, but either way, he was gone. One down. Far too many to go.

The others hadn't noticed their fallen comrade, intent as they were on trying to flush her parents and Kieran out of their shelter. She slid a throwing knife free and took aim. The blade buried itself between the shoulder blades of the woman in front of her. She cried out and whirled around, streaking energy in a wide arc that Dani had to flatten onto her stomach to avoid. When the sorcerer's wild eyes locked on Dani, she formed a pulsating orb that Dani had a feeling wouldn't be so easy to dodge. Before the sorcerer could release it, there was a muffled *crack* and her head jerked to the side.

Dani nearly retched as the sorcerer fell to the ground. Barrett M82 rifles were designed to penetrate concrete barriers, and most of her skull was completely obliterated. She wouldn't be healing from that.

They came here to kill us, Dani reminded herself as three other sorcerers turned to face her. Behind them, Calla and the others were back to hurling balls of energy into the trees. Kieran had managed to lob a few of his own, but with nowhere near enough power to penetrate any shields. Dani rolled to her feet and pulled another knife from the sheath at her thigh, but they had already drawn up their shields. It was possible that this hadn't been one of her best ideas.

Before Dani could decide how she was going to maneuver this, a bolt of blue dragonfire rained from the sky and slammed into the sorcerer on the right. His shield protected him from the flame, but not the brunt of the impact, and he dropped to his knees. His shield flickered, and Dani released her knife. It pierced him just below his collarbone—the subclavian artery, Dani noted with vicious satisfaction. From above, Nox blew another stream of fire. Dani squinted against the brilliant light, taking a few unconscious steps backwards from the unbearable heat. By the time the flames had cleared, the wounded man and one of the others had disappeared.

"Cowards," spat the third. He was built like a boxer, with massive hands that looked ready to rip Dani's head off her body. He lowered his shield to fire red magic upward at Nox. Dani stabbed her knife into the dirt and charged him. At Stonecrest, when she'd gone up against Calla, her focus had been split and her goal had been distraction. This time it was different. She had all her wits about her, she was going for the takedown, and she was fucking pissed.

The sorcerer didn't bother raising his shield, no doubt assuming that there was no way a teen girl would be able to tackle him. He swung out an arm. Dani ducked, planted her hands on his shoulders like they were parallel bars, and used her momentum to swing herself up, kicking one leg over his head. She trapped his neck between her thighs and wrenched her entire body weight into a twist that brought them both to the ground. He grunted with the impact. Dani kept her thighs locked as she plucked her knife from the earth and drove it into his chest. He vanished almost immediately.

"Coward," Dani called into the empty air as she climbed to her feet. If Eden had witnessed that, she would have scolded her for showy, ineffective tactics. That particular takedown was a judo move she'd seen Black Widow do in a movie, which she'd immediately looked up on YouTube to teach to herself. No reason fighting couldn't be showy *and* effective.

Nox landed beside her, the razor-sharp scales on his tail extended and electrified, smoke seeping through his nostrils. Dani ran her hand across his flank, taking comfort in the familiar warmth of him.

Thank you, she thought.

I wouldn't leave you here alone, he said simply.

Then they turned to face the onslaught of sorcerers coming their way.

TWENTY-EIGHT

Eden could only hear faint rumbles from the battle outside, along with the louder, periodic shots from Frankie in the loft. Despite knowing that Frankie had received the same training as she had in high school, Eden had never been able to imagine her aunt as a slayer. Now it was hard to think of her as anything else.

"Like riding a bike," she'd heard Frankie mutter to herself after the first shot.

"Frankie, you have to untie me," she called up. She knew it was useless, but she had to try. Out of everyone, Frankie was the most likely to be on her side.

"Little busy right now, mija." Another shot.

"Just listen to me," Eden cried, surprised at her own exasperation. It was the most she'd felt like her old self in days. "They don't stand a chance out there. Let me go. I can talk to Calla. We can work something out."

"I'm not about to let you make *another* deal with the devil."

"Calla's trying to rid the world of dragons—just like our family has for centuries. She's not the bad guy."

"If it walks like a duck and sounds like a duck . . ." Frankie said, and fired another shot. A pause; then her face appeared at the edge of the loft, peering down. "There's no point in ridding the world of dragons if we're just going to replace them with something worse."

"I'm a sorcerer now," Eden said. "If you hate Calla, then you hate me too."

"You're Eden Rivera," said Frankie, unyielding. "You're my favorite eldest niece, and a wonderful sister and daughter. You're talented and smart and thoughtful and loving and damn good on the rock wall. That's what you are. I don't know what Calla did to you, to make you forget that, but whatever it was—it was evil."

"She didn't do anything to me," Eden said, but she choked on her own voice. Heat welled up behind her eyes, and to her horror, she realized she wanted to cry. Frankie's words were a battering ram, slamming against the cold obsidian walls inside her, making cracks for the burning light to seep through once more. "*I* made the choice. I did. There's nothing that I can do to change it now."

"Of course there is," Frankie said, her tone a little softer but no less potent. "Make a different choice."

A distant explosion stole her attention, and her aunt disappeared again. Eden heard her muttering to herself again as she fired another round. Fighting back against the tears that threatened to spill, Eden managed to loosen the rope around her ankles and was working the knot on her wrists loose with her teeth. She just needed to get out of here, to regroup. If she could just have some time to *think,* she could figure everything out. She could center herself, find that perfect calm she'd felt the first time the magic had filled her.

"Well, isn't this amusing." The faintly mocking tone set her on edge immediately, and she raised her head to glare at Alder. He was standing in the center of the training mat, hands in pockets, smirking at her.

"Go away," said Eden, not caring that she sounded like a child. She had no doubt that her eyes were red, but at least they were dry.

Alder just kept smirking and began to survey the barn.

"No need to be ashamed of your humble origins," he said. "I was raised in a shithole too."

Magic burned along Eden's skin, but with the rope still intact, there was nowhere for it to go. Movement above caught her eye, and she looked up to see Frankie at the edge of the loft, silently moving the rifle into position. She immediately dropped her gaze, but it was too late; Alder had seen the shift of her attention.

He waved his hand, and the rifle snapped in half.

"Francisca Rivera," he said, only then turning around to look up at her. "You would shoot a man in the back?"

"Alder De Lange," she said, mimicking his pretentious accent. "I can shoot you in the face if you prefer. Now get the fuck away from my niece."

"You're welcome to come down and make me."

"Leave her alone," Eden said.

"Why should I?" he asked, glancing over his shoulder with a smile that sent a chill down her spine. "Hasn't anyone told you yet that it's a sorcerer's prerogative to toy with humans every once in a while? Keeps them in line."

Before Eden could reply, he waved his hand again. Frankie let out a cry as she fell straight through the loft, landing with a horrible *smack* on the training mat below. Eden didn't bother protesting as Alder crossed the barn at his leisure, while Frankie struggled to drag herself up. She just set to work on the knot again, her magic seething and ready to explode the moment she was free.

There was a bone-shaking *boom* from outside. One of the grenades. Alder looked in that direction, and Frankie seized on the distraction to lurch to her feet and make a run for Eden. Alder's hand barely twitched as he sent her flying back into the wall. Eden winced, but wouldn't let herself be torn from her task.

"You Riveras are all the same." Alder sounded bored now. That wasn't a good sign. "Sickeningly tenacious. Like cockroaches."

Frankie hadn't made it back to her feet, and her breath was coming in short, wheezy gasps. Eden ripped at the knot, but it refused to yield. This wasn't happening. She couldn't let this happen. Frankie wasn't even supposed to be here. She should be at home in her tacky kitchen, singing to her cat and crocheting mythical animals.

But as Alder moved closer and closer to her aunt, a glistering yellow orb taking shape in his palm, Eden realized that there was nothing she could do. She was helpless.

She and her dragon made a good team. It was a thought that ricocheted in the back of Dani's head while she tore her way through the company of sorcerers, always keeping one eye out for Calla. She and Nox had perfected a rhythm. He would wear down the shields so that Dani could go in for the final blow. Sometimes one of her parents would make the shot first. She wondered if they were keeping score—she certainly was. As her father was fond of saying, you were never really done training to be a slayer.

She had to stick close to Nox. He was her only protection against the volley of orbs, either by spitting fire at them or occasionally hitting them with his tail like a baseball. Once he managed to knock one straight back into the sorcerer who had thrown it. Dani gave him double points for that one.

She wasn't having fun, but the weight of doom had lifted from her chest. She was beginning to think they might actually make it through this alive. If they could tear the sorcerers down one by one, then maybe Calla would be vulnerable enough to attack. If Calla was gone, the threat against Nox and her family would be gone too, and she could finally focus on helping Eden.

Nox wrapped his tail around her and yanked her out of the way of a blast of energy. It gave her whiplash, but she managed to keep her feet when he released her.

The barn, he said, apropos of nothing. He was losing momentum. She felt his exhaustion like a creeping, choking vine.

What?

Something's happening at the barn.

Frankie. Eden. She immediately turned to run. Nox tried to follow her, but she gave him a mental push. *My parents need you more.*

She expected him to argue, to tell her that he was willing to protect her but not the slayers who had murdered his mentor. But he didn't. And a few seconds later, Dani heard the gratifying roar of dragonfire behind her. She kept running.

When she reached the barn, she knew she should take her time, assess the situation, come up with a plan. That's what her sister would do.

Dani barreled through the door without slowing down. It only took her the space of a heartbeat to take in the scene. Frankie on the ground. Alder standing over her with a yellow orb in his hand. Dani didn't have any throwing knives left, but she still had the bowie, so she flung that instead.

Alder turned in time to smack it out of the air as if it were a pesky fly. He aimed the orb at Dani instead, but she dove to the side. After the rock-strewn field, the training mat was practically a pillow, and she rolled easily back up to her feet. By now she knew the drill. Avoidance, distraction, then takedown.

She was close enough to the weapons display to grab a tactical knife, careful not to turn her back on Alder. She could have maybe pulled down a sword instead, but she had a feeling Alder would take great joy in bending the blade into a knot, or something equally preposterous. She had better control over a knife, as long as she could get close enough.

"Here is my predicament," Alder said mildly, as if they were picking up in the middle of an everyday conversation. "Calla has been very adamant about taking you alive, but you are an exceptionally obnoxious brat, and I very much want to kill you. I'm accustomed to getting what I want, Dani."

"God, have you always been such a sanctimonious shit?" she asked, tightening her grip on the knife. "It's a miracle you made it into adulthood, because if you had gone to my school you would have gotten your ass kicked every day of the week."

Alder reached out, grasped the empty air, and pulled. Dani was yanked forward as if he had a hold on the front of her shirt. She dug in her heels, but it barely fazed him. She was beginning to realize how he had earned his position as Calla's right-hand man. The other sorcerers were powerful, but they wielded that power like a club, in a brutish and clumsy way. Alder had a finesse that was infinitely trickier to outmaneuver.

He pulled her within arm's reach, and she swiped the blade toward his unprotected neck. He bent her wrist backwards, nearly to the breaking point. She cried out and lost her hold on the knife. It dropped uselessly to the floor. Now Alder had a hand around her throat. Her body shivered with phantom pain at the memory of his magic slithering inside her, eliciting agony from every nerve.

She told herself to move, to break his hold, to do anything but stand there and tremble. Her knees and elbow were locked in place. Her lungs had begun to shrivel. She didn't know if he was using magic to hold her or if her brain had chosen now, of all moments, to switch gears from fight to freeze. If she died here, there was no one to protect Frankie. Eden would go back to Calla's side. Everything would be lost.

But even staring down the barrel of her own shortcomings, Dani still couldn't break herself free.

"Come to think of it . . ." Alder's voice felt far away. "Putting you into a coma would solve all of our problems, now wouldn't it?"

Somewhere in the recesses of her ossified mind, Dani registered a shadow out of the corner of her eye, at the barn door. Instinct—and one last spite-fueled vestige of willpower—drove her into motion. She threw her whole weight into a pivot, so that Alder's back was turned to the door.

A sudden impact juddered through his body, and she saw the strange mix of pain and outrage in his face. His grip on her tightened, then loosened. She ripped away as he staggered forward. There was a gruesome, gaping wound in his back. His expensive suit was charred at the edges.

Dani looked to the doorway; Kieran stood there, his expression unreadable. A second orb was already forming in his hand. Alder whirled around, though he seemed on the verge of collapsing. He opened his mouth, no doubt ready with some patronizing insult. Kieran didn't wait for what he had to say. He flung the orb. Alder threw up a shield, but it was dim and weak, and he fell backwards with the force of the blow.

Dani's knees wobbled and her wrist ached, but she managed to climb to her feet. Tears of relief sprang to her eyes when she saw that Frankie's chest was moving in a steady rhythm. Unconscious but alive. That was something at least.

At the barn's entrance, Kieran was leaning heavily on the doorjamb, his breath coming in heavy rasps. He was paler than she'd ever seen him, with a smear of fresh blood on his jaw and pine needles still clinging to his shirt and hair. He looked barely able to stand, much less summon more magic.

But Alder was already back on his feet, incandescent energy swirling in his palm. His head snapped up, eyes flashing in Dani's direction, practically glowing with their own malevolent gleam. Then he turned toward Frankie instead.

Dani lunged forward, her mind blank with panic. Distantly, she heard Eden shouting her name. She didn't stop, didn't slow down. She slammed into Alder, the impact jarring her bones, but he kept his balance. When she saw that the magic in his hand had dissipated, she allowed herself a split second of relief.

Then came a sharp pain in her chest. She looked down to find the hilt of her own knife sticking out from between her ribs. A sound like rushing water filled her ears, and it occurred to her that once again, Eden's warning about putting herself into a vulnerable position without a plan was dead-on.

"Goodbye, Dani," said Alder, his voice sliding silkily into her consciousness. And before she could gather the strength for a reply—or a knee to his groin—he had vanished.

She dropped to the floor, but it barely registered. Despite how hard it was to breathe, her chest didn't hurt much at all. Maybe the knife hadn't gone in as far as she thought. Maybe it wasn't so bad. Her fingers, slick from sweat, wrapped loosely around the hilt.

"Don't pull it out," came Kieran's voice, jolting her back to her senses. She let her hand drop to the ground at her side.

"I know." It came out as more of a cough than an actual sentence. "I'm not an idiot."

If she removed the knife, she'd bleed out much faster. Not that it really mattered at this point. They couldn't exactly call an ambulance, and she had a feeling that a knife wound wasn't one of the weaker human attributes that she could easily recover from.

Kieran knelt beside her, and she squinted against the bright overhead lights to make out his face through the shadows.

"Fuck," he said, his voice jagged. "I'm sorry. I tried to—"

"It's not that bad," Dani said, displaying what she thought was admirable equanimity. "It doesn't hurt."

"There's a knife sticking out of your chest," he said.

"Thanks, I hadn't noticed." She tried to smile, but it was too much effort. She closed her eyes instead. In the distance, she could make out the electric sizzle of magic and the occasional crack of gunfire. The battle was still raging. Nox and her parents were fighting side by side. Dragon and slayers. She would have given anything to see it, to be a part of it. But she was running out of time.

She was going to die.

The knowledge settled over her like a warm blanket, muting the pain and panic and leaving her only with a sharp, welcome clarity. She was going to die, but it didn't have to be for nothing.

"I need you to do the ritual," she said, opening her eyes.

Kieran stared at her, uncomprehending. Then her words seemed to settle in, and he blinked.

"What? No. Are you serious?"

"Of course I'm serious." She had to pause to catch her breath, which was shortening every second. "You said it yourself: I have a knife sticking out of my chest. If I'm going to die anyway, then I'm going to save my sister."

Maybe Calla had been right. Maybe Dani's fate was inevitable. But if that was the case, then her last act as a free agent would be to make sure Eden would never be under Calla's thumb again.

Kieran was shaking his head.

"I can't, Dani."

"You said you know how to do the ritual."

"That doesn't mean it will work."

"Nothing ventured, nothing . . . fuck, I'm too tired to argue with you, Kieran." She reached up impulsively to touch his cheek, to brush her fingers along the streak of silver over his ear. The simple touch eased some of the chill that was rapidly flooding her veins. "Just try. That's all I'm asking."

"No." He took her hand and squeezed it between both of his. "I don't have much magic left. If I do the ritual, I might not be able to bring you back. I'm going to try to heal you."

"No!" She wrenched her hand away. The sudden movement sent a lancing pain deep through her core, and she gasped. "You have to save Eden."

"I'm not going to just sit here and watch you die."

"What does it matter anyway? You told me yourself you don't care about anyone but Zephyr."

She held his dark gaze like a dare. His mouth was a tight line, his brows furrowed in a faint frown. She didn't know exactly what she was waiting for, but it never came. He said nothing. Dani closed her eyes again. Time was running out; she could feel it in the tightness of her lungs, the labored beating of her heart.

"Do this for me and we're even," she said. The words were whisper-soft, but she sensed Kieran tense up beside her. He still said nothing, but after a few seconds, she felt the gentle pressure of his fingertips just below the knife.

She met his gaze. His expression was inscrutable as he drew his hand away, fingers dripping crimson with her blood. He rose to his feet.

"What are you doing?" Eden demanded as he began tracing the circle around her on the training mat. It didn't take her long to catch on. "You can't do this. Dani, please, untie me. Don't do this to me. Please."

Eden's voice was tight with panic, so different from her previous calm that it almost gave Dani second thoughts. Almost.

"Are you sure about this?" Kieran asked as he dropped down beside her again. He'd finished using her blood to draw both the circle and the line connecting her to Eden. All that remained was for Dani to die.

"As sure as I've ever been about anything," she said, trying for a smile that didn't quite materialize.

Kieran didn't smile either.

"I do care about you," he said softly. "You're the only reason I stayed, when Zephyr was gone."

"I know." She grasped Kieran's hand again, hoping that somehow the connection would ease her descent into darkness. Her pulse thrummed in her skull, a slow march of pain, getting slower every second. "You're not a monster, Kieran. Whatever it is you've become—you're not that."

His eyes on hers were like a universe opening up before her. He held her gaze steadily as he raised her hand to his lips and pressed a gentle kiss to her knuckles. Dani wanted to say more, but the words were a lump in her throat. Her heart ached, and she didn't think she could attribute it solely to the blade. She didn't want to wait any longer. She'd never wanted to be immortal, but neither did she want to succumb meekly to the inevitability of death. With her free hand, she took hold of the hilt.

I'm sorry, Nox, she thought, and pulled the knife free.

TWENTY-NINE

As Dani's fingers wrapped around the knife's hilt, Eden jumped to her feet and ran. Her mind was nothing but blinding white panic. She wouldn't let this happen. She wouldn't let Dani go through with this.

But she wasn't fast enough. Dani's hand, still clutching the knife, fell to her side. Her rasping, uneven breaths filled up Eden's head, drowning out everything else. She dropped to her knees and pressed her bound hands against the wound, trying in vain to stanch the flow, but a part of her knew that it was already too late. There was so much blood. Too much blood. The rise and fall of Dani's chest was almost imperceptible now.

The emptiness inside of Eden screamed with everything she wasn't feeling. The numbness that had felt like a gift now felt like a prison. This wasn't what she wanted. This wasn't a price she was willing to pay. Her magic surged, straining against the ropes that bound her, simmering on her skin. She let it burn, let it fill her up, because anything was better than that emptiness. She pushed outward with a power that felt like rage, like sorrow, like pain and desolation and everything else that she was supposed to feel when she looked down at her sister's lifeblood spilling over her hands. Tremors rippled through the ground, and the walls of the barn began to shudder. And for a second she thought she might break free.

Then the spell in her restraints did its work, swallowing up her power. But not the rest of what she felt.

"Heal her," Eden said, her voice barely a scratch in the new stillness.

Kieran's lips were a tight, unyielding line, but she could read turmoil in every inch of his features. His fingers were intertwined with Dani's, a useless kind of comfort. He looked down at her face, eyes harrowed and dark. He shook his head.

Eden lunged forward and grasped the front of his shirt, jerking him close. The tremors of an aftershock resonated around them.

"I'm not getting back in that circle," she said, dropping each word like a stone. "You're not doing the ritual. So either heal her now, or untie me so I can."

She was locked with him in this moment, this nightmare. She wasn't going to let Dani slip away, let her sacrifice herself in the name of some nebulous greater good, as if it were her responsibility to keep Eden safe and not the other way around. Something shifted in Kieran's gaze, a flash of resignation, and she allowed herself to hope.

Calla's voice was an arrow, lancing straight to her core.

"And here I thought all the action was happening outside."

Kieran flinched at the sound of her voice, but didn't turn. Eden released him and rose to her feet, relieved that her legs supported her. Her hands were still bound in front, but that didn't feel important anymore.

"You have to heal her," Eden said. "You need her alive."

"I'm getting the oddest sense of déjà vu." Calla didn't appear to have been touched by any of the raging battle outside. She was still pristine in every way, down to her perfectly applied lipstick. "Eden darling, I think you probably remember what happened the last time someone tried to give me an order."

She didn't want to be, but Eden was cowed. She couldn't defy the high sorcerer, not now. Not after everything Calla had given her. *But what did she take in return?*

Calla starting walking forward, and Eden moved away from Kieran and Dani. It seemed safer that way—to have Calla talking to her, focused on her.

"This isn't the same," she said carefully. "Dani and Nox's soul bond is brand-new. You can still use it."

"There are other dragons out there, other soul bonds," said Calla. "I'm beginning to think your sister is far more trouble than she's worth. I lost several of my best people today. I'm not happy about that."

Her attention was indeed pinpointed on Eden as she drew closer. Her gliding footsteps were half graceful dance, half predator stalking its prey.

"You shouldn't have come here," Eden said, drawing courage from somewhere deep inside. "Surely you didn't think my parents would just let her go without a fight?"

"All I knew for sure was that you were completely useless to me. A waste of perfectly good magic."

Eden's heart stuttered at the words, but she let them rankle in her chest, let them spark the anger she needed to keep going.

"You lied to me. You manipulated me."

"So now I'm the villain?" Calla asked, her lip curling. She stopped walking. "You're going to pretend you're the innocent victim? That you weren't champing at the bit for your chance to be powerful, to prove to everyone that you're not a sniveling little coward, scared of your own shadow, hyperventilating every time someone looks at you sideways?"

The voice in her head was back, urgently reminding her of everything that was wrong with her and everything that could go wrong and that everything was wrong wrong wrong. Or maybe Calla was the voice now, sliding into place like a puzzle piece, because Eden had been a fool to think she could ever be better than what she was. If Dani was standing here, she would know what to say. She would call bullshit. She wouldn't give Calla an inch. The wrong sister was bleeding out on the floor.

A gleam of amethyst sparked in the corner of Eden's eye, and her heart plummeted. The magic of the soul bond had begun to flow. Dani was dead. Eden kept her gaze forward, locked on Calla's. The world stilled around her in crystalline clarity, and she knew what had to be done.

Make a different choice.

"Bullshit," said Eden. Not for herself, but for Dani.

"Excuse me?" Calla's eyes flashed danger.

"You heard me." A tremor ran through Eden's voice, but she held Calla's glare. "I made a mistake, trusting you, but having anxiety doesn't make me a coward. It doesn't make me weak."

"Are you sure about that?" Calla raised her hand, and it flared green.

Eden's own magic responded, straining to be freed, but with her wrists still bound, she couldn't unleash it. She refused to run, though, and she refused to beg. She wouldn't give Calla the satisfaction. Dani would be proud.

Before Calla could strike, there was a tremendous crash. The barn doors, and a good chunk of the wall around them, splintered inward. Nox was there, tail lashing, blue flame licking through his bared teeth.

What have you done to Dani?

It was the first time Eden had heard his voice: higher and colder than Zephyr's, strained tight with fury.

"I can hardly be blamed for your human's mortality," Calla said.

Nox roared flame, and Calla shot back her own blast of energy. The resulting shock wave jarred Eden's teeth and made her ears pop.

Nox, Eden thought, desperately trying to speak only to him and not Calla. *Hold her in place. Don't let her move.*

Nox must have heard, because his focus snapped to her. But Calla had heard too. She whirled around, then looked down to see the circle of blood she was standing in. Her head jerked toward Kieran, who was murmuring and tracing symbols in the air over Dani's body.

Eden saw the moment Calla understood what was happening, and the cataclysm of fury that engulfed her. That hesitation was only a split second, but it was enough. Nox's tail coiled around the high sorcerer, trapping her arms to her sides. She gave an unholy shriek, radiating magic. Nox bellowed in pain, but he held her tight. He was shimmering now with an amethyst mist that gleamed against his gray scales. He wouldn't be able to hold Calla much longer. She was thrashing and summoning magic around them like a hurricane.

Kieran was still tracing symbols, faster and faster. Dani was coated in the same magical mist, but it was moving away from her in a steady stream. Toward Calla. The soul bond was transferring. If Dani's prediction was right, when Calla was bound to Nox, her magic would be shared between them in a new soul bond, and she would become human again. She would be vulnerable.

Eden tugged at the knot between her teeth as the radiant magic of Dani's bond settled on Calla. The high sorcerer's own poison-green magic began to dim, choked out by the coruscating cloud.

She screamed again and detonated a blast of energy so violent that it blew the dragon away from her. He crashed back through the hole in the wall, rolling in the grass outside. Though the force was focused on Nox, it still knocked Eden backwards into the wall. She gave the knot one final yank, and it came loose. She was free.

Calla was on her hands and knees, gasping, the amethyst magic sloughing off of her. Kieran was finished. The ritual was complete.

Eden moved forward. Slowly. Carefully.

"Calla, it's over," she said. "You're bonded to Nox. You can't use your magic anymore."

Calla's shoulders began to shake. Eden couldn't tell if she was sobbing or laughing. Calla knelt, her face upturned. Though her cheeks were streaked with tears, her features were twisted into the expression of cruel amusement that had become so familiar.

"I should have known," she rasped, "that you could never be one of us. I freed you from emotion, from everything that made you weak, and gave you enough power that you would never have to be weak again. But somehow you still succumb to conscience and sentimentality, to the evolutionary defects of a lesser species."

Calla lifted her hands like an offering, and with what had to be the last, infinitesimal reserve of her own magic, she formed an orb as black as pitch, slick with an oily rainbow sheen.

"Eden darling, you're the type of broken that can't be fixed."

With that she released the orb. It jetted toward Eden, too fast for her to think. She threw up her hands reflexively, and her magic instinctually responded. Eden opened her eyes to find that she now held the orb in her own hands. It pulsated gently like a beating heart, but she could feel in her bones that the only magic it held was death. She raised her eyes to find the high sorcerer watching her, defiant even now.

"Fuck you, Calla," she said. Her magic swelled within her, flowing with her blood, soaring with her thoughts. "I'm not broken. I'm human."

And she flung the orb back.

THIRTY

Dani came back to herself in degrees of pain. First she was aware of her heart, contracting with wretched slowness, every beat a herculean effort. Then her lungs began to burn for air. Her muscles twitched and spasmed. There was a jackhammer in her skull.

Gradually, in the darkness, she was aware of voices above her. The first was a gentle murmur. Kieran. She didn't know how she was so certain, but she was. The second was clearer, stronger. Her sister. Eden.

Their voices were like a call and response, a lulling rhythm that made Dani want to fall back to sleep—if only the pain would lessen. The longer they spoke, the more Dani's thoughts sharpened into focus. They weren't talking to each other, she realized. Kieran was speaking words—a language that Dani didn't recognize—and Eden was repeating them.

The darkness had begun to diminish, until it was no longer her entire world. It was just a simple matter of opening her eyes. She did.

As if waiting for that cue, her lungs expanded so rapidly she thought her chest would explode. She gasped faster and faster in wild succession, trying to calm herself, unable to stop. The light was blinding, bringing tears to her eyes. She was breathing so fast she couldn't get any air.

"Shhh," came a soothing voice at her ear. "You're safe. You're not alone. Squeeze my fingers."

Dani did so, almost mechanically. The voice was a lifeline. She held on with all she had.

"Good. Everything's okay, Dani. Try to focus on your senses. What can you taste? Smell? Hear?"

Blood. The slick, metallic taste of blood filled her mouth. She must have busted her lip or bit her tongue or both.

The barn. She smelled the barn's distinct medley of sweat and rubber and disinfectant.

Her sister. She heard her sister's voice, speaking calmly in her ear, bringing her back to life.

Dani's breathing had slowed to a manageable pace, and the tightness in her chest was loosening. As her eyes adjusted, she could make out the worried faces above her. Kieran. Eden. Her parents. Frankie.

Nox. She reached back into the darkness, groping desperately for the bond between them, searching for a flicker of emotion or sarcasm or *anything*.

For what felt like forever, there was nothing. Nothing at all. And then:

I'm not talking to you right now, you ungrateful whelp. Maybe ever again. That'll teach you to die on me like that.

Dani didn't know if she wanted to laugh or cry. In the end, she did both.

THIRTY-ONE

At her therapist's suggestion, Eden had taken up yoga. In the beginning it had seemed unbearably cliché, but she couldn't deny that the more she got into it, the better it felt. Her therapist's only rule was that she wasn't allowed to push herself. No setting of impossible goals. No torturing herself until she had perfected a position. No drilling herself on technique. All she could do was flow through the movements, focus on her breathing, and let the rest of the world fall away. She did her routine every other morning on the front porch (the barn was still under construction) with nothing but bird calls and the wind chime filling her ears.

It helped. It really did.

What also helped was rolling up her mat and going inside to find Dani sitting on the couch, bleary-eyed and ruffled in her pajamas, staring mournfully into her bowl of cereal. Dani was not a morning person.

"Morning," said Eden.

"Mmm," Dani replied, taking a bite. "How was yoga?"

Eden shrugged and dropped down beside her on the couch.

"Same as always."

"That a good thing?"

"Yeah, I think so."

Dani nodded to herself and finally swallowed her bite.

"Tomás texted me last night. He asked Sadie on a date."

"Took him long enough. What did she say?"

"She texted me right after to tell me she said yes."

Eden smiled and leaned her head back. Things hadn't gone

back to normal, after everything that had happened the month before, but it was starting to look like they might be able to find a new normal. She wasn't the same person she had been before her transformation, but neither was she the person she had become after. Eden wasn't entirely sure what kind of person she was now.

There was still an empty space inside her, a dark, cold center that sometimes threatened to swallow up the light. But she was learning how to live with it, to summon love and compassion and kindness in spite of it, the same way she summoned her magic. She still had panic attacks sometimes. She still found herself spiraling into helplessness or obsessively checking scrapes and bruises for signs that they were really something much worse. Sometimes she still woke up in the dead of night, torn from a nightmare of darkness and dragonfire and Calla's voice twisting around her heart.

Her magic hadn't fixed her, but only because she wasn't broken. She had her demons, just like everyone else. And just like everyone else, she was learning how to live with them. That was the best she could do, and most days it was enough.

"How are Kieran and Frankie getting along?" Eden asked. Once the dust had settled, Kieran had insisted on getting his own place, but Dani had overruled him. She said it wasn't healthy for him to spend all his time brooding alone in the dark. Frankie had offered up her spare room for the time being, and with Dani and Frankie as a united front, Kieran didn't really stand a chance. Eden had the feeling he didn't mind overly much.

"They're fine," Dani said, her tone carefully neutral. "Apparently her cat really likes him and has started sleeping on top of him and stalking him around the house. Frankie has even started cooking on occasion, just to make sure he eats enough. She told me he's too skinny, and then she said she's become her mother and next thing you know she'll be throwing her chancletas at people who piss her off."

"I'd like to see that." Eden chuckled and picked some fuzz off her yoga pants. "Is there anything else you want to talk about?"

"What do you mean?" Dani's attempt at blithe innocence was utterly unconvincing.

"I just mean that you and he seem like—"

Dani shifted abruptly; her bowl, which had been balanced precariously on her knee, toppled to the floor. Milk and cornflakes splattered across Dani, the couch, and the carpet.

"Shit," said Dani, holding her arms out like she was covered in toxic slime and not just her breakfast.

Eden stared at the overturned bowl for a second and flicked her wrist. Red sparks sizzled; a few seconds later, the carpet, couch, and Dani were clean, and the bowl was on the coffee table, its spoon and contents intact.

"I'm not eating that," Dani said, swiping a hand down her shirt as if convinced there was still milk on it. "It's got your magic all over it now."

"You're welcome," Eden said.

The unmistakable sound of The Killers drifted down the stairs, followed a few minutes later by their father's bounding footsteps. He was singing "Somebody Told Me" under his breath, very off-key.

"Morning," he announced as he hit the bottom step. He saluted them both with his cast. His broken right arm hadn't been the only injury accumulated on that day, but it was—thankfully—the worst. Unless, of course, you counted Dani's brief stint of being dead.

"Morning," Eden said, tilting her head back to receive his kiss on her forehead. Dani just gave another wordless grunt. He kissed the top of her head anyway and then mussed her hair.

"Remember, Jaime and Luis are flying in today," he said as he padded into the kitchen. "Your mom wants you to clean your rooms."

"Why?" Dani asked, sounding properly awake for the first time. "It's just Jaime and Luis, and it's not like they're staying in *our* rooms."

Their father's response was to just start singing again.

Eden smiled again and climbed to her feet. She slung her mat over her shoulder and started up the stairs. Her room was already clean—for the most part—but she did have some reading for school she wanted to finish that morning. And later, she was having lunch with Nate. Thinking about it set butterflies loose in her stomach. When she'd reached out to him a few weeks ago, she hadn't even expected him to answer the phone, but he did. He listened to her stumbling apology, which was nowhere near as smooth as she'd practiced, and after a long silence had told her that he needed time to think about it.

And then three days ago he had called her back and asked if she wanted to have lunch and talk. Eden didn't know exactly what that meant, but she wanted to find out. She wasn't sure yet how much she would tell him, if he asked for more details, but she had a feeling it would be as much as it took to convince him to give her a second chance.

As Eden settled onto her bed with her book, there was a knock on her door frame, and her mom popped her head in.

"Please tell me my eyeliner is even," she said. "I have a video call with a client in London in ten minutes."

"Let me see." Eden lowered the book, and her mother came

closer. There was a faint bruise on her cheek that she'd managed to conceal for the most part. "Looks good to me."

"Thank goodness." Analisa sank down on the foot of the bed with all the relief of a runner at the end of a marathon. "Good morning, by the way."

"Good morning."

"Are you going to be here for dinner tonight?"

"If you want me there."

"Of course I do." Her mother sounded surprised. "We need your help with this, Eden. If you're up for it."

She only hesitated for a second.

"I am. I will."

Jaime and Luis weren't the only slayers coming into town. Her parents had summoned everyone they could reach. Eden had no idea how the meeting was going to go. Most slayers had been reluctant to get involved, and with good reason. The sorcerers were quiet for now, but no one expected them to stay that way for long. And Alder De Lange was probably still out there somewhere.

And then there was the problem of how to convince a room full of seasoned dragon slayers that it was time to stop hunting dragons and start helping them instead. Eden had a better idea of how that portion of the meeting was going to go.

But they had to try. Eden wasn't as passionate about it as Dani was—even their parents had embraced the new direction with shocking ardor—but Eden felt she owed it to Nox. And to Zephyr.

Her mother fidgeted like she had something else to say, and Eden waited patiently.

"I don't suppose there's any way to convince you to stick around longer?" Analisa asked.

Eden smiled, but shook her head.

"Sorry—already bought my ticket, and Frankie's friends are expecting me."

Her mother knew all that. Eden's flight to New Zealand was in two weeks. Once she'd finished up her summer courses, she was going to spend a year—maybe more—backpacking her way through the country, meeting new people, trying her hand at eco-farming and whatever else might strike her fancy. Finding herself, her therapist called it. Frankie called it sweet, sweet freedom. After all that had happened, Eden thought she could use a little of both. She wasn't giving up on the Rivera legacy, not by a long shot, but she was putting it on hold for a while. For the first time in her life, she was going to find out what it felt like to just be Eden. The prospect was both terrifying and exhilarating.

"I know," Analisa said with a sigh. "Just thought I'd ask. We're going to miss you. Who's going to lip sync The Killers with me and defend the honor of creamy peanut butter when your father and sister try to buy crunchy instead?"

Warmth expanded in her chest, and Eden smiled.

"I'm going to miss you too."

"Well, I have to get this meeting over with," Analisa said rue-fully. She gave Eden's hand a quick squeeze. "Good luck with your book. It looks awful."

Eden gave a short laugh and mimicked throwing the copy of *Crime and Punishment* at her. Her mother retreated quickly, blowing a kiss over her shoulder as she went. Eden breathed in deeply. She let the familiarities of her home wash over her five senses, not because she needed to, but because she wanted to. Because sometimes she liked to remind herself that she'd made it all the way to this exact moment, safe and alive.

After a minute, she settled back onto her pillows, opened her book, and got to work.

THIRTY-TWO

The basement of the Vasquez house was the same as it had always been, yet somehow Dani couldn't shake the sense that everything was different. She was sitting on the same couch where, a month ago, her fingers had twined with Kieran's in the dark while he told her about the day he and Zephyr had met. Now Tomás and Sadie were beside her, their own hands clasped. The credits of the movie they were watching had begun to roll. It was a terrible low-budget flick about dragons—Dani couldn't even remember the title—that Sadie had insisted they watch. Even after everything, she still wasn't sick of dragons, which Tomás clearly found both endearing and exasperating. Dani found the two of them amusing, even if she still hadn't gotten over the weirdness of her current and former best friends dating. She'd put a moratorium on kissing in front of her, and so far they'd managed to keep the PDA to a minimum.

Nox had begun the movie in her head, with a running commentary that ranged from weary to outraged at the depiction of dragons. About halfway through, he'd given up in disgust and left her in peace, reminding her about their rendezvous later. As if Dani could possibly forget.

"That was truly the worst one yet." Tomás hopped up to turn on the lights.

"I'm getting the feeling that these movies are part of some secret diabolical plan to torture us," said Dani.

"It wasn't that bad!" Sadie tried to maintain an indignant expression, but a grin split her mouth. "Okay, it was pretty bad. Sorry."

"Dani and I get to pick next time." Tomás plopped back down next to Sadie and draped his arm over her shoulders.

"Maybe the next two times," added Dani.

"Fine," Sadie said, throwing her hands up in surrender. "But good luck finding a movie about dragons I haven't seen."

"Maybe Dani has some home videos."

"Very funny." Dani shot Tomás a look, but he just grinned at her.

"Or we could see a real dragon," said Sadie. "I mean, just saying. How's Nox doing?"

"Nox is good," Dani said cautiously. "He's still laying low."

She'd promised not to keep the other half of her life a secret from her friends anymore, but that didn't mean she felt comfortable inviting them on field trips to see her dragon. There was still a very real risk of danger, with many of the sorcerers—including Alder—on the loose. Stonecrest was no more. Dani and Nox had braved a flyover the week before, only to find that the sorcerers had left nothing but scorched earth behind. Not even a stone was left to mark the mansion that had stood there for centuries. Dani was glad it was gone, glad that Zephyr had received a funeral pyre of sorts, but the thought of the sorcerers roaming wild, without a home base or the iron control of Calla, made her more than a little nervous.

Tomás and Sadie had done their own reconnaissance work on the internet, concerned about the fate of the SWAT team and police they'd lured to Stonecrest in order to save Dani. They found a report of the call in the dispatch blotter, along with a brief article in the local news a week after the fact about a terrorism threat that turned out to be a false alarm. The SWAT officer interviewed said that they'd found nothing but an old shack in the woods. No explosives or injuries reported.

As best as Dani could guess, the sorcerers had manipulated the memory of everyone who had responded to the call. A frightening show of power, but better than a massacre. Calla had at least been smart enough not to draw excess attention to herself. Dani could only hope Alder and the other sorcerers would do the same.

"Maybe we could tag along tonight," Sadie said.

"Not tonight," Dani said, too quickly. Her friends exchanged a glance. "Sorry. Tonight is special, though. I can't really explain."

"Of course you can't," Tomás said. Sadie nudged him with her elbow.

"Be nice," she told him, then turned to Dani. "We'd really like to see Nox again, but we can wait."

"Thanks," said Dani. "He wants to see you guys too."

I never said that, protested Nox. She ignored him and stood up to stretch. It was time to get going.

"I'll walk you out." Tomás climbed to his feet. "Then I'm going to come back and kick Sadie's ass at Ping-Pong."

"You wish." Sadie hurled a throw pillow at him. "Bye, Dani."

Dani laughed as she slung her bag over her shoulder and headed for the stairs.

"See you tomorrow."

After the necessary ten-minute farewell ritual to the Vasquezes, which involved Mrs. Vasquez trying to send Dani home with three Tupperware containers of dinner leftovers and Tita trying to catch her up on the latest episode of her telenovela, they finally made it to the front porch.

"You talk to Kieran lately?" Tomás asked, shoving his hands in his pockets. "My dad was asking about him yesterday. Said he found some book about World War II he'd promised to show him."

Dani couldn't help a small smile.

"I'll let him know."

Even after she'd convinced him to live with Frankie for a while, Dani had half expected Kieran to disappear one night without a trace. But so far, he'd stayed. She tried not to let herself speculate about what that may or may not mean, and she tried even harder to convince herself that she didn't care anyway. Even so, she found herself visiting Frankie more often than was strictly necessary, and Frankie had slyly begun making excuses about work she had to do and leaving Dani and Kieran alone at the kitchen table or on the porch swing, sometimes for hours. Zephyr's death hadn't broken him, but it had come close. The more they talked, the more Dani found herself drawn to the raw honesty that existed between them now, a bridge over the betrayal that had come before.

And on those days when Kieran showed up in her driveway, leaning against the sexy black Maserati that he'd somehow managed to liberate from Stonecrest, and invited her to take a spin through the scenic byways . . . if her heart skipped a few beats and her body filled with giddy lightness . . . well, that was a secret only she and Nox knew.

"Guess I'll see you at work then," said Tomás, shifting his weight from one foot to the other. "Keep your phone on, please?"

"Yes, Mother."

Tomás made a face at her, but his heart wasn't in it. There was a glint of true concern in his eye.

"Look," he said abruptly, "I know you always say you don't, but if you ever *do* need to talk about—well, anything—I'm here, okay?"

Dani opened her mouth with the instinctual response that she was fine, but she stopped herself. After five years and countless bags of Skittles and a rescue from certain death at the hands of sorcerers, surely she could give him more than that. She thought about where she was about to go with Nox and what they were about to try. Depending on how the night went, there was a very real possibility she wouldn't be fine at all.

"Can I call you tonight?" she asked. "After this thing with Nox?"

Tomás's brows shot up in surprise, but he nodded.

"Yeah, of course."

"Thanks," she said, pulling him into a hug. For most of her life she'd been convinced that there was no way her family legacy and the normal life she'd built with her friends could ever coexist in harmony; that if she ever let the two sides meet, she would lose everything. Now, for the first time, she let herself believe in a new kind of normal. Difficult, maybe. But worth it.

THIRTY-THREE

The cave felt smaller than it had the last time she'd been here. Maybe Nox was getting bigger.

Dani hugged herself against the damp chill and looked down at the eggs, nestled together in their depthless pool. Their glow seemed fainter as well. Was she imagining things?

The truth was, she was nervous. More nervous than she'd been in a long while, including the time she'd let herself bleed to death on purpose.

Stop it, said Nox suddenly.

"Stop what?"

You're making me nervous now.

"We can always go get pizza instead," she said, but without any conviction. It was time. "You do know what you're doing, right?"

Better than you, he replied in the indignant tone that meant he only had the foggiest idea what he was doing. Which, to be fair, meant he *did* know better.

He sat down next to the pool, tucking in his claws and tail neatly, his wings flat against his back. Dani wasn't sure what she was supposed to do, so she just sat down facing him. He lowered his head so that they were eye to eye.

Are you sure about this?

For the first time she felt a genuine hint of uncertainty in his voice, and could see it reflected in his eyes. She took a slow breath and steeled herself, hoping to give him a measure of her resolve.

Yes, she replied. *I want to do this. I'm ready.*

She lifted her hand and pressed it against the center of his forehead. She closed her eyes, reminding herself to keep breathing. For a few minutes, there was nothing. Only the feel of his smooth scales beneath her fingers and the bluish glow of the eggs against her closed eyelids.

And then: a flicker. A flash. A moment and an eternity.

Her hand began to burn. And burn. And *burn.*

She snapped out of her own consciousness and into a new one, vast and reaching into the impossibly distant past. An entire history of love and heartbreak, hope and hate, victory and defeat. A scattering. A loneliness. An endless aching for a past that felt so near and yet could never be reached.

Nox.

She was immersed in the core of him, in the memory of boundless flight across vast deserts and oceans. In the amber warmth of Polara's eyes. In the terror of separation. The explosive rage at the sight of her skull, held aloft as a trophy in the hands of dragon slayers. The thrumming need for revenge. The long nights stalking the slayers, one by one, learning their movements with the patience and discipline that Polara herself had taught him.

And a newer, fresher emotion, interwoven throughout. Guilt. For all the vicious, murderous thoughts about the slayers, but also for failing to avenge Polara. It was a complex web, impossibly entangled with memories of the past and understanding of the present. There was no easy answer to this kind of torment.

But there was one thread, brighter than the rest, carefully stitched throughout. Hope.

Dani lost herself in the expanse. She gave up trying to parse every memory and instead let the whole of them wash over her. She knew at that moment, Nox was lost in the core of her as well. It was something she had tried not to think about, ever since she first suggested they attempt to share their consciousness. There would be no hiding anymore. Nox would know every lie she'd ever told, every streak of jealousy, every heartbreak she'd ever suffered, and every heart she'd ever broken. He would know all the nights she'd lain awake, hating Sadie and missing her at the same time. He would know the kiss she'd shared with Kieran, and every confusing, contradictory feeling she'd had about him since. He would know that even though she was grateful she wouldn't have to watch her sister grow old and die without her, there was still a tiny part of her that was scared to trust Eden—scared of how much the magic had changed her.

He'd know about that moment in the dungeon of Stonecrest when she had been ready to give up the eggs to save Kieran. The betrayal of Nox in that moment, more than anything, scalded her with shame. And yet. And yet, given the chance, she wasn't sure she would have made a different decision.

No easy answers. And no more secrets. Only trust. That's all they would have left.

When she came back to herself, Dani was so dizzy that all she could do for several minutes was hold her head with one hand and press the other against the stone floor, trying to anchor herself. Nox seemed equally disconcerted, with his chin resting on the ground and tendrils of smoke wisping in and out of his nostrils.

Finally, when Dani felt able to speak, she opened her mouth.

No apologies, Nox said. *We both did what we had to do, to make it this far. All that matters now is that we made it.*

Dani swallowed hard and nodded.

"Did it work?" she asked. Her voice was trembling. She tried to concentrate on their bond. It did feel different—which seemed inevitable, given what they'd both just experienced. But did that mean they were stronger? And if they were, was it enough?

Only one way to find out. Nox sat up. A frisson of nerves and excitement thrilled between them.

Dani knelt at the edge of the pool beside him and watched as he lowered his head straight into the water, almost all the way to the bottom. Then he breathed outward: not air bubbles, but dragonfire. The water refracted the sapphire light all around them. The entire cave dazzled with it.

Dani held her breath as Nox pulled out of the water, his scales gleaming wetly. She stared down at the eggs, willing something to happen, willing them to hatch. Nox shook out his wings and draped one around her shoulders. Together they watched . . . and waited.

Minutes passed at the speed of hours. Dani couldn't tear her eyes away.

It hadn't worked. The thought took root in her mind, no matter how hard she tried to tear it out. It hadn't worked. Their bond wasn't strong enough. Or the eggs weren't alive at all. Sorrow twined through her body, twisting with Nox's. It hadn't worked.

And then one of the eggs cracked.

ACKNOWLEDGMENTS

All my love and gratitude to my family, especially my mom and dad, who have always supported and encouraged me in every aspect of my life and career.

Eternal thanks to my powerhouse agent, Taylor, for making my dream job possible, and to my editor Nicole for all your amazing ideas and insight. Talking dragons and magic with you on professional phone calls has frankly been a dream come true.

Thank you to the HMH team for all your hard work: Mary Claire Cruz, Gabriella Abbate, Emilia Rhodes, Margaret Crocker, Helen Seachrist, Emma Grant, Nadia Almahdi, and John Sellers. You are rock stars!

Puffin and Alli, my dear friends and favorite distraction, I hope movie nights with you will continue for eternity. You are good for my soul.

Much love to Soup, my favorite pharmacist, who has never reported me to the FBI, no matter how many times I text her in the middle of the night to ask about effective ways to poison, maim, and/or kill people. Badger and Laura, thank you for being fantastic friends on the home front and keeping me sane IRL.

Katie Clark, you helped me survive the trials and tribulations of cubicle life, and I'm so glad we found each other. I hope there are many more Margarita Game Nights in our future.

My majaoes—Clare, Emily, Jesi, Kara, Katie, Nöel—you are the most wonderful found family, and I'm grateful for you every single day. Emily, I can't begin to express how grateful I am for all the time and genius you give me during our marathon brainstorming sessions. Writing magic wouldn't be the same without you. Clare, you are an incandescent soul and the best backup thesaurus a girl could ask for.

Kara, you are my best friend, my biggest cheerleader, my most honest critic, and truly a goddess among gods. I would never have reached this point without you, and I'll always be grateful for everything you do and everything you are.

In loving memory of Sophie, my very own cat-dragon, who inspired Nox's persnickety personality. Rest in peace and snuggles.

WANT MORE?

If you enjoyed this and would like to find out about similar books we publish, we'd love you to join our online Sci-Fi, Fantasy and Horror community, Hodderscape.

Visit hodderscape.co.uk for exclusive content form our authors, news, competitions and general musings, and feel free to comment, contribute or just keep an eye on what we are up to.

See you there!

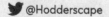